//// THE BAMIYAN PARADOX ////

THE BAMIYAN PARADOX

////

A JOHNNY MARQUEZ THRILLER

RW LIGON

ISBN (paperback): 979-8-9933583-0-7

Published in the United States of America

For Trudy

CHAPTER 1
THE MONASTERY

JANUARY 2001—THE WEST BANK

Dawn bled across the Judean desert.

The first light spilled red-gold over a landscape carved by millennia of thirst, wind sighing through stone ravines worn smooth by the passage of vanished empires. From the clifftops, the world appeared fossilized—burnt ochre and ash stretching toward a horizon where the sun's edge touched the bones of a hundred forgotten armies. Far below, a dry riverbed shimmered white as bleached bone, patient as death, waiting for rain that might never come.

Set into the cliffside like a secret the land had kept for centuries, the monastery crouched in shadow. Its honeyed limestone walls caught the rising light, pitted and veined by time, every stone holding the memory of blood and prayer—Crusader banners lowered in smoke and defeat, Byzantine hymns still echoing off ancient vaults, Roman sandals crumbling to dust in unmarked graves. Even the mortar held the dust of the dead.

On the horizon, two black sedans crawled up the ancient switchbacks like beetles ascending a corpse. Their headlights sliced the violet haze, trailing plumes of dust across a road that had borne the weight of camel caravans, Roman legions, Ottoman cavalry, British tanks, and now, prophets of a different kind, fleeing toward a war that had no end.

Inside the lead vehicle, Hussein Mahfouz sat rigid against the leather seat, fingers working the edge of his sleeve until the fabric threatened to fray. His gray suit fit like borrowed armor—too formal for this landscape, too Western for the man wearing it. He had not slept. The dead would not let him. Two brothers lost to the Intifada, half his cabinet vaporized in a missile strike that had turned a Tuesday morning into a mass grave. The night's dreams had left only a dull ache behind his eyes and the taste of ash on his tongue.

His driver murmured coordinates into a secure handset. Beside Hussein, Samir—chief of security, childhood friend, the man who had pulled him from rubble twice—watched the horizon with the vigilance of a predator sensing movement in tall grass. Every muscle in his body remained coiled. The shape of a concealed Glock pressed against his ribs beneath his jacket, as familiar as breathing.

The world outside the tinted glass was both exile and home. Each stone triggered a memory—childhood games in the shadow of these same hills, his father's voice after the first Israeli patrol swept their block, the way his mother had wrapped bread in cloth and handed it to him without meeting his eyes the morning he first left for Cairo. Hussein pressed his forehead to the window, watching the land scroll past like a film he had seen too many times, and wondered how many more times he would leave home not knowing if he would return.

The second sedan braked behind the first, gravel crunching beneath its tires. The door swung open, and Abraham Mizrahi stepped into the morning light.

The Prime Minister of Israel was broad-shouldered, commanding even in shirtsleeves—black hair silvered at the temples, collar open in casual defiance of protocol, sleeves rolled to the elbow as if preparing for manual labor rather than negotiation. His bodyguard, Avi, materialized at his shoulder—eyes flinty as desert flint, jaw locked in permanent vigilance, a man whose entire existence had been reduced to a single imperative: keep this one alive.

Between the vehicles, the two leaders paused in the open air, caught in the silence before words could ruin everything. The desert wind carried a metallic aftertaste, the faintest promise of distant rain. Both men measured each other across the gap—adversaries, survivors, or on this morning, simply fathers who had been at war too long.

Father Piero waited at the monastery gate.

He was a small man, unremarkable except for the Vatican diplomatic credentials in his pocket and the pronounced limp that marked his gait—a souvenir from Sarajevo, where he had learned that God's work sometimes required walking through minefields. His black cassock snapped in the dawn breeze like a battle standard. Deep lines of prayer and regret carved his face into a map of sorrows witnessed and absorbed. He clasped his hands before him and beckoned the leaders forward with a gesture that was both invitation and benediction.

"Brothers," he said, his Italian accent softening the word into something almost tender, "welcome to Saint James. Come—let us shelter in what little sanctuary remains."

The words hung in the air, mingling with the ozone scent of approaching storm, before the wind carried them away toward the empty desert.

The retinues fanned out with practiced precision. Avi and Samir exchanged glances across the space between their principals—wary, measuring, each reading the other's posture with a soldier's instinct for threat. It was the language of men who had spent their lives protecting targets from men exactly like themselves. Neither looked away first.

The footsteps of the two leaders echoed across cracked stone as they approached the monastery door.

Inside, the corridor swallowed them. Centuries of hands had worn the stones smooth, leaving behind grooves and impressions like the memory of touch. The air grew cool, heavy with the weight of ages. At the corridor's end, a small refectory waited—a single wooden table scarred by use, a battered candelabra holding three guttering flames, the bittersweet aroma of old incense and ancient dust.

Father Piero motioned them to sit. The chairs scraped against stone as the two men lowered themselves to opposite sides of the table. The priest moved to a sideboard and returned with a brass coffee pot, pouring thick, bitter liquid into mismatched ceramic cups. He set them before his guests with the solemnity of a communion offering.

Abraham's hands remained steady as he accepted his cup. Hussein's trembled, sending his spoon skittering across the saucer with a metallic clatter that seemed to echo far longer than physics should allow. For an instant, all three men watched it spin—a small metal oracle, wobbling toward stillness in the cathedral hush.

At the door, their guardians took position. Avi's fingers twitched near his earpiece, monitoring frequencies, scanning shadows. Samir kept one hand near his weapon, eyes never resting, cataloging every flicker of movement beyond the ancient windows.

Father Piero set a small wooden crucifix at the center of the table. The gesture was simple but deliberate—a marker, a reminder, perhaps a warning.

"Here," he said quietly, "there are no preconditions. No cameras. No notes. No transcripts for ministers to parse and twist. Only the words of your hearts, spoken freely, heard without judgment."

He looked from one man to the other, his doubts hidden behind the practiced habit of hope that decades in the Church had taught him to wear like vestments.

"For this hour," he continued, "let us be fathers. Husbands. Men who have buried too many of their own. Not politicians. Not enemies. Let us mourn together, if nothing else."

Hussein broke first. His voice emerged sanded raw by grief and sleeplessness, barely above a whisper.

"I buried my brother last month." He fixed his gaze on Abraham, unblinking. "A checkpoint. One that was supposed to be safe. He was bringing medicine to my mother."

Abraham looked away for the first time. His jaw worked silently before he spoke.

"My cousin. Haifa, three weeks ago. He was waiting at a café for his wife. She arrived in time to hold him while he died."

Their losses met in the silence, a ledger that would never balance, debts that could never be paid.

Father Piero's voice was gentle as absolution. "Justice for the dead is beyond us now. But peace for the living—that is still within our power."

Thunder rolled outside the monastery walls, a reminder that whatever fragile peace they might forge here was as transient as breath, as fragile as the silence between heartbeats.

Abraham's jaw flexed. "And when the radicals reject this truce? When they read about it in the papers and reach for their bombs?"

Hussein met his gaze without flinching. "Then we hunt them. Together. Side by side, as allies instead of enemies. Because if we don't"—he paused, and when he continued, his voice had dropped to something barely audible—"if we don't, we will bury our children next."

At the doorway, Avi and Samir's eyes met. Years of suspicion passed between them in that glance, but also something new—a glimmer of reluctant respect, the recognition of shared purpose glimpsed through the fog of old hatreds.

A dove landed on the windowsill, pale and fragile against the weathered stone. Its soft coo filled the silence, almost immediately drowned by the harsh cry of a crow circling somewhere beyond the walls.

Abraham gave a crooked smile, the first expression other than guarded hostility he had shown. "Even the doves are tired of war."

////

The refectory seemed to contract around them as the morning wore on. The air grew thick with old incense and sweat and the cold breath of stone walls that had witnessed too many failed hopes. Candlelight flickered across the table, warping the faces of the two men who had come to barter the future of nations—and perhaps, if fate allowed, the lives of their children.

Father Piero's notepad and pens rested at the center of the table, the battered pages lying blank and somehow accusatory, waiting to record whatever history they dared to make.

Abraham Mizrahi steepled his fingers, knuckles whitening with the pressure. "You wanted face-to-face. No mediators, no cameras, no American envoys taking notes for Washington. Let's see if that means you're finally serious."

His Hebrew-accented English was clipped and wary, each word sharpened by decades lived at the knife's edge of survival. His hand moved unconsciously to his glasses, wiping them clean—a nervous tic that betrayed the tension his voice concealed.

Hussein's gaze drifted to the narrow window, where dawn had surrendered to a bruised horizon heavy with coming storm. "We have sat at too many tables with too many eyes watching. Each time, one more humiliation captured for the cameras, one more concession extracted before a global audience."

He drummed his fingers against the ancient wood, a rhythm like distant gunfire.

"I am here for one reason only: the lives of my people. Nothing more. Nothing less."

Abraham scoffed, the sound harsh in the stone chamber. "Your people? Since Oslo, my government has buried three hundred dead—civilians, children, families torn apart at bus stops and pizza parlors. How many promises, signed in the last decade? Only to have them washed away by blood?"

His jaw ground as he spoke, chewing over old battles that would not stay buried.

Hussein's jaw clamped in response. "You lecture me on broken promises? My son was ten years old when he watched a building collapse on his cousins. Ten years old, Abraham. He still wakes screaming. You speak as if we do not grieve, as if our dead are somehow lesser than yours."

He broke eye contact, swallowing hard against something that threatened to rise in his throat.

Abraham's hands shook, just once. He pressed them flat against the wood, steadying himself through sheer force of will.

"No more funerals." His voice had lost its edge, reduced now to something rawer. "That's why I came. That's the only reason I'm sitting here instead of in my office, where my advisors are probably drafting my political obituary as we speak."

Father Piero slid his notepad closer, pen poised. "Begin with what you will each surrender. Not what you will claim. Sacrifice first. Demands later."

The words echoed off the ancient walls, sounding older than either man, older perhaps than the conflict itself.

Abraham spoke first, jaw tight. "Freeze settlements east of the Green Line. Immediate. Complete. But you must pull all armed men from the buffer zone. No rockets. No mortars. No excuses."

Hussein bristled. "Pull them back to what? To ruins? To camps built forty years ago, where families live six to a room under the shadow of your guard towers? Every step backward is a step into memory—tanks rolling through my father's village, walls thrown up overnight, families separated by concrete and razor wire."

His eyes glittered with old anger that refused to die.

Abraham's voice dropped low, clipped with barely contained fury. "And every step forward is another funeral, Hussein. No more martyrs. No more banners strung from the ruins of synagogues. No more school buses exploding in Ashkelon."

"Do not insult me with dead children." Hussein's voice had gone tight as wire. "The cycle began before either of us was born. I will not trade history for a press release."

They stared at each other across the table, across the gulf of decades, the weight of the dead pressing down on both their shoulders.

Abraham leaned forward. "Then let us start with this: a ceasefire. Sixty days. Complete. Both sides. Any violation, and the world will see who failed."

"And the prisoners?" Hussein pressed. "The sons and fathers you swept up after every demonstration? The ones whose mothers have grown old waiting outside your courts?"

"A list. Two hundred, nonviolent only," Abraham said. "Any connection to the Qassam Brigades, and they stay."

Hussein's lips tightened, then relaxed in weary resignation.

"You will have your list. And your patrols—trial basis only." His eyes hardened. "But you remove your roadblocks from Ramallah and

Bethlehem. No checkpoints for ambulances. No soldiers searching school buses. Agreed?"

Abraham noted something on a scrap of paper, his pen scratching in the silence. "You ask for a lot. What happens when the bombs return to Tel Aviv?"

"Then hold me responsible," Hussein replied. He drew a shaky breath. "But if a single drone missile strikes a wedding or a funeral, this ends. Everything. Immediately."

He let the words hang in the air between them, a promise and a threat woven into a single thread.

Abraham looked away, his voice dropping. "You threaten me with the press. My own people would hang me for less."

"Your own people threw stones at Rabin." Hussein's voice was quiet, almost gentle. "Mine lit candles when he died."

He trailed off, suddenly hoarse. "We both lost something that night. Something that might never be recovered."

A long silence settled over the refectory. Rain began to spit against the window. The candle guttered, throwing shadows like restless ghosts across the ancient walls. The taste of iron lingered in the air—memory or premonition, neither man could say.

Abraham broke the stillness. "Jerusalem. We need to talk about the holy sites."

His leg bounced beneath the table, nerves fraying despite his efforts at control.

"Shared authority," Hussein suggested. "Status quo preserved. No provocations from either side. Let the Waqf and the Rabbinate stand together at the entrances. No flags. No soldiers with weapons drawn."

"And the Mount itself?" Abraham's pen tapped against the table. "My people will never accept divided sovereignty over the holiest site in Judaism."

"Then let it be undivided but unclaimed." Hussein's voice had found a strange calm. "Sacred to all. Owned by none. A place where God belongs to everyone and politics belongs nowhere."

He turned to Father Piero, hunger in his eyes, searching for some priestly signal that the weight could be laid down, even for a single breath. What the priest offered instead was harder, and better.

"If you both consent," Piero said, his voice barely above a whisper, "the holy sites—the Mount included—can be secured by the Swiss Guard under a pastoral mandate. Neutral. Temporary. A custodial arrangement under a tripartite Vatican-Israel-PA memorandum, coordinated with UN observers."

Incense drifted in the stone-cool air. Somewhere behind the books, a clock ticked its ancient rhythm. The three men sat with the idea as if it were a living thing placed on the table between them, fragile and dangerous and possibly miraculous.

They answered in the same moment: "Agreed."

It wasn't absolution. It wasn't justice. But it felt like a path cut through solid rock—narrow, treacherous, but passable. A centuries-old corps in uniforms everyone recognized and no one feared; stewardship rather than occupation. The Guard could hold the gates and corridors, steady the queues of pilgrims, quiet the tremor in the city's throat—without a single flag displaced, without a line on any map touched. No sovereignty conceded, no humiliation inflicted. The fragile Status Quo would stand, now bracketed by a neutrality no ministry could publicly oppose.

Father Piero folded his hands, not triumphal, only certain.

"Then we move quickly," he said. "Let politics arrive to find the peace already waiting."

Abraham hesitated, old anger surfacing in the tremor of his jaw. "My grandfather carried Torah scrolls out of Hebron under British guns. He told me once: 'Someday you will have to choose between what is holy and what is just.' Tell me, Father—is this justice?"

Hussein answered before the priest could speak. "My father died in the Nakba. He never saw his home again. I am not here for justice, Abraham." His voice cracked. "Only for peace. Justice can wait. Our children cannot."

At the door, Avi's hand flicked to his earpiece.

"Vehicle moving on the main road. Not ours."

The words broke the spell, reminding everyone how thin the walls of history truly were, how easily this fragile moment could shatter.

Samir's eyes narrowed. Hussein noticed but kept his focus on Abraham. "Your border guards can check my police, body and bag. If one of them fires a shot without cause, I'll hand him to you myself."

Abraham's voice cracked with exhaustion and threat intertwined. "Sign, or there will be nothing left for your children to inherit. Not even your name."

Hussein's face twisted with fatigue. "And if I sign, how long before your parliament falls, your coalition collapses, and we are back to siege and rockets?"

"That is the risk." Abraham's words were clipped, final. "But if we do nothing, tomorrow's news will be another mass grave. Another row of small coffins. I cannot bury any more children, Hussein. I can't."

The candle had burned low, wax pooling like tears on the ancient wood. Father Piero set two fresh cups of coffee on the table, his hands trembling with more than age.

"I was in Sarajevo," he said quietly. "I have seen what happens when men wait too long to sign. I have held the hands of those who died waiting for peace to arrive."

He stared at the notepad, his lips moving in silent prayer.

Hussein studied his reflection in the coffee's dark surface—a face he barely recognized anymore. "We have made bargains before. Each time, something precious is lost. But I am tired of losing. So tired."

He took a sip, letting the bitterness ground him in the present moment.

Abraham nodded slowly. "So am I."

He watched the rain beginning to streak the window, eyes haunted by ghosts only he could see.

Avi's voice came from the doorway, barely above a whisper: "All clear. Just a shepherd."

Samir did not fully relax; his eyes lingered on the window, on the shadows beyond, the threat never entirely gone, never entirely absent.

Father Piero pushed the notepad forward across the table. He offered Hussein a pen—simple, black, unremarkable. An instrument that might change history, or might change nothing at all.

"Politics will chase this either way. Sign it now, before the moment passes."

Hussein took the pen. His hand trembled as he pressed it to the paper, forming words stiff and uncertain. The scratch of ink on parchment sounded impossibly loud in the hush. Abraham signed beneath him, each letter carved deep into the page, as if force of will alone might make them permanent.

For an instant, neither man moved. They remained suspended between thunder and rain, between history and hope, between all they had been and all they might yet become.

Father Piero offered no blessing, no absolution. Only a silent bow of acknowledgment, of respect for what they had risked.

For a single, breathless beat, all that remained was the hush between thunder and rain—the pause before history resumed its endless reckoning.

They left the refectory together, footsteps echoing through the corridor like a slow heartbeat. Outside, crows scattered at their approach, wings flashing black against the pale, storm-heavy sky.

Hussein paused at the threshold, the desert wind lifting his hair, carrying the scent of rain and ancient dust. "Perhaps our children will walk here together someday. Not as enemies. Not even as allies. Just as people."

Abraham nodded, eyes tired but, for the first time, alive with something other than suspicion. "Let them inherit something better than our war. Let them inherit possibility."

Father Piero watched them go, two dark figures descending toward their waiting vehicles, toward the world that awaited them with all its complications and cruelties. In the hush of the empty doorway, he crossed himself and whispered into the wind:

"Lord, let them be braver than we were. Let this time be different."

The sky darkened overhead, the scent of rain riding the wind like a promise or a threat. Inside the ancient monastery, the walls held their breath—silent witnesses to one hour's fragile, unfinished peace.

Whether it would hold remained to be seen. Whether any of them would live to see its fruit was a question none dared ask aloud.

The road stretched before them, winding down through the desert toward a future no one could predict. Behind them, the monastery retreated into the cliffside, keeping its secrets as it had for a thousand years.

Somewhere in the distance, thunder rolled across the Judean hills, and the first drops of rain began to fall.

CHAPTER 2
THE OVERTURE

JANUARY 2001—VATICAN CITY

Cardinal Matteo Visconti had learned that faith was equal parts habit, performance, and terror. Before sunrise, he knelt in his private chapel, candlelight flickering on his white hair and the mosaics overhead. Each colored tile caught the hesitant dawn—Peter sinking beneath the waves, Christ's hand extended in rescue, saints' halos dulled by centuries of incense and whispered desperation. His prayers had grown shorter with age, replaced by silent bargains with God in the hush before daybreak.

This morning, his mind circled the urgent letter locked in his desk—a document stamped with warnings from the Secretariat of State, its meaning as sharp and cold as a cocked pistol. The message had arrived two days ago via diplomatic pouch: intelligence from American assets suggesting that certain radical elements in Gaza had obtained details of the monastery summit. Names. Dates. The Swiss Guard proposal. Everything Father Piero had worked to keep secret was now hemorrhaging through channels Visconti could not trace. The letter demanded a decision: warn the negotiators and risk exposure, or pray the radicals moved too slowly to act. He had chosen neither. He had chosen to kneel here, in this chapel, and beg for a third option that did not exist.

He pleaded not just for peace, but for wisdom: clarity to distinguish movement from progress, and for the safety of men whose suffering might one day appear as a single report on his desk—another failed initiative, another body count, another reason for the world to lose faith in diplomacy.

A discreet knock broke the quiet. Sister Lucia, her face drawn from lack of sleep, pushed open the heavy oak door and whispered, "There is news from Jerusalem. Unrest. Rome is uneasy. The Curia wants to see you."

Visconti rose, heart stuttering in his chest. He donned the red sash of office, moving through incense-wreathed corridors where nuns muttered Hail Marys and cardinals eyed each other like rival wolves circling the same wounded prey. Sunbeams cut through stained glass in the Apostolic Library, illuminating centuries of desperate letters—warnings, requests, the ghosts of failed reconciliations stacked floor to ceiling in acid-free boxes.

At the office window, he watched the city fall still for a second beneath St. Peter's tolling bells. A Vatican aide arrived, breathless, whispering that American diplomats had requested an urgent audience. "Blessed are the peacemakers, Eminence," the aide said, though his voice carried the cadence of a man reciting last rites.

Visconti nodded, gaze narrowing on storm clouds gathering beyond Rome. Lightning forked over the city, thunder rolling through marble and mosaics—a tremor in the stone, a warning about to cross continents. He thought of the letter again. Of the names it contained. Of the violence coiling somewhere in Gaza, waiting for a signal.

/ / / /

The ride into Ramallah always felt like passing through a membrane: air thickened, streets twisting in on themselves, every stone recalling curfews and vanished neighbors. Hussein sat rigid in the back seat, watching children chase a flat soccer ball along pitted asphalt. Outside, the city woke with a thousand small sounds—the yelp of a dog, the rumble of a cart, a muezzin's call tangled with distant radios broadcasting news that never seemed to change.

A checkpoint approached, a steel barrier manned by young soldiers, hands always close to their weapons. Samir rolled down the window. Hussein's gaze fixed on the soldier's fingers—nervous, twitching near the trigger guard. A Hebrew tattoo was barely visible beneath a cuff, some girl's name perhaps, or a prayer. For an instant, fear and suspicion fused—occupier and occupied, each measuring the other with eyes that had learned distrust before they learned to read. The gate lifted. Even as the car moved on, threat lingered like static along Hussein's spine.

His phone buzzed. The message was brief, clinical: *Rumor at the ministry: summit details may have leaked. Israeli press sniffing around. Will advise.* He pocketed the device, masking a jolt of dread that threatened to crack his composure. If the press knew, others knew. And others meant Hamas. Others meant blood.

The Muqataa rose ahead like a fortress from another century, which, in many ways, it was. Built by the British Mandate in the 1930s, it became the Palestinian headquarters and presidential residence in 1994. Its limestone walls glowed bright with the afternoon sun, guard towers looming above the market square, gates stiff with armed sentries who recognized Hussein's car and snapped to attention. Inside, courtyards still wore the pitted scars of sieges—proof this was no office block but a citadel with a violent memory. For decades it had been a stage for power and blood, where negotiations bled into gunfire and back again. Hussein feared it was about to be tested once more.

Outside the compound walls, two girls in blue school uniforms skipped rope, their voices rising in a chant about keys, gates, and the heat of the summer sun—songs their grandmothers had sung, songs about homes they'd never seen. A soldier's jeep spat dust past women queued at a bakery, the murmur of rationing running down the line like a current of shared resignation.

The guards, recognizing Samir, opened the steel gates and he swung the car into the courtyard, stopping at the residence doorway. He hurried to open Hussein's door. At the threshold, he squeezed Hussein's hand once—driver, friend, witness—then let go. "Stay safe, Mahfouz."

"Thank you," Hussein said, though the words felt inadequate for everything they carried.

Inside, the walls pressed in. On his desk, files waited like a silent jury—kidnappings, shortages, whispers about collaborators, reports of weapons caches discovered and weapons caches still hidden. Hussein exhaled, eyes lingering on a photo of his daughter Mira, her smile frozen in a moment before she understood what her father's work truly meant. He wondered if she'd recognize the man he'd become. In the hush, every footstep on the stairs rang louder than it should.

////

Leila's days inside the Muqataa were sewn together with small rituals designed to keep fear at bay. Before her daughters stirred, she stood barefoot on the cool tiles, listening beyond the walls—to the din of local market traffic, the bark of stray dogs, the clank of the compound gates opening for the first patrol.

She brewed tea with fresh mint, breathing its sharp sweetness like a ward against the day's uncertainties. In the kitchen, her phone buzzed: Unrest near the university, possible crackdown. She glanced toward the inner courtyard, where soldiers' boots scuffed across the flagstones on their way to the guard towers, their rifles catching the morning light.

Mira sat at the table, hair loose and tangled from sleep. Leila braided it with practiced fingers, whispering a line from "Ya Sitti el-Hilwe," an old song her own mother had sung in Jaffa before the family scattered like seeds in a storm. Amal tumbled from her bed, asking if Baba would come home early. Leila smiled, lying as mothers must.

Before letting them cross the courtyard to the school wing, she hesitated. Protests were expected; should she keep them close? But routine was armor here, and armor was precious. She wrapped their lunches in brown paper, slipped lucky coins into their pockets—old Ottoman coins her grandmother had carried through three wars—and made them recite the prayer she had taught them: "*Keep us safe, keep us kind, keep our hearts strong.*" The girls giggled, skipping toward the gate that led deeper into the compound, oblivious to the soldiers posted above, to the rifles, to the world that wanted to swallow them whole.

When the door shut behind them, her mask slipped. Memory surged—fleeing Gaza with Mira swaddled against her chest, jets screaming overhead like mechanical banshees, checkpoint lights slicing the dark as soldiers demanded papers she no longer had. She remembered the weight of her daughter, the weight of everything she carried, the terrible lightness of leaving behind a life that would never exist again. Safety was never permanent; it was borrowed time, and the interest was always coming due.

Her phone buzzed again: *Stay inside, police at the market.* She stared at the words until they blurred, doubt coiling tight in her chest. Then, from the old market road beyond the walls, a gunshot cracked the morning—once, then again. She flinched, peered through the slit in the curtains. Riot police moved on a cluster of teenagers at the gate; stones flew in desperate arcs, a girl stumbled, someone screamed a name that was swallowed by the chaos.

Leila closed the curtains and gripped the fabric until her knuckles whitened, willing the outside world to spare her children for one more day.

////

Jerusalem had changed, Abraham thought, but its bones endured. The convoy edged through Mahane Yehuda's chaos—vendors hawking pomegranates, the clang of church bells mingling with the muezzin's call, tourists snapping photos of everything and understanding nothing. Each day overwrote the last but never erased it. The city was a palimpsest of blood and prayer, and Abraham had read every layer.

At a checkpoint, his security chief leaned forward. "Small demonstration ahead. Possible IED."

"Reroute us," Abraham said, gaze sweeping the crowd, looking for a hand too close to a bag, a look that lingered too long, the subtle wrongness that preceded violence. His mind spun through contingency plans—extraction routes, safe rooms, the mathematics of survival—his body taut from years in the field when a single moment's inattention meant a folded flag and a widow's tears.

Memory flickered: his first Shin Bet briefing, a windowless room thick with cigarette smoke, an old handler with dead eyes saying, "Trust no one. Every word is a weapon." Now, every friendly face was a potential mask; every shadow, a warning. The paranoia had kept him alive. It had also hollowed him out.

A coded ping lit his phone: *Movement near the Old City. Police on alert. Be prepared.*

He stared at Daniel's photo tucked in the sun visor, thumb brushing the worn edges, a private ritual for the dead. His son's face smiled back—frozen at nineteen, forever nineteen—from a hiking trip in the Galilee, three weeks before the café bombing that scattered him across a sidewalk in Tel Aviv. Abraham whispered the name like a prayer.

At the office, he poured a measure of arak, eyes scanning the rooftops through bulletproof glass. He turned to intelligence reports stacked on his desk—Hamas movements, weapons shipments, the endless catalogue of threats—his jaw set, the city's unrest drumming in his chest like a second heartbeat. Danger, everywhere and nowhere. The weight of the monastery agreement pressed on him. If it held, Daniel's death might mean something. If it failed, it would mean nothing at all.

////

In the half-dark of a Gaza basement, Hamza al-Saidi unpacked Kalashnikovs on a torn prayer rug, aligning them for inspection with the care of a surgeon arranging instruments. The storied Hamas commander moved with deliberate precision, each weapon a tool and a testament. Qasim entered, handed him a battered phone. "Tonight. Record the message. Keep it strong."

Hamza faced the lens, reciting the familiar litany: martyrs, justice, vengeance, the righteousness of their cause. His voice was flat, eyes far away, memory pressing in from all sides. When he finished, Qasim clapped him on the shoulder. "They'll hear us in Jerusalem."

Hamza said nothing. He washed his hands in a cracked basin, scrubbing oil and packing grease away, caught by a wedding song drifting through the alley outside—young voices, full of hope that seemed obscene in this place. Memory surged unbidden: his mother weeping over Ziad's body, bombs falling like rain, the smell of bread and laughter from a courtyard that no longer existed. He lingered in the memory, the world briefly suspended between what was and what had to be done.

A distant explosion shuddered through the building, dust sifting from the ceiling. Sirens wailed. Hamza froze, heart pounding against his ribs like a caged animal. His phone vibrated: *Green light. Tomorrow.*

He stepped into a side room, cleaned his weapon with methodical care, hands unsteady despite his best efforts. The TV mounted on the wall blared casualty counts from the latest skirmish—numbers that meant nothing and everything. He wondered if his name would end up on a martyr's poster, painted on walls, chanted by children who would never know him—or as a villain in someone else's story, a monster to frighten their sons. The cycle spun on, indifferent to the men it consumed.

////

Ramallah: Girls jumped rope in a dusty courtyard, singing about keys and the moon—songs of return, of homes remembered only in grandmothers' stories. A mother yanked her son from a burning barrel of trash, scolding sharply. Boys raced bikes through narrow streets, shouting slogans—freedom, tomorrow!—as a soldier's jeep rattled past, engine idling, the driver's eyes hidden behind mirrored sunglasses.

Jerusalem: A Hasidic boy offered a date to his Arab neighbor, a small kindness that would be forgotten by sunset. On King George Street, a woman argued with a policeman while university students debated politics beneath a mural of birds, their voices rising and falling like competing prayers. Calls to worship floated above rooftops, woven with church bells and the tinny music from a taxi radio.

Gaza: Families huddled in single rooms, silence punctuated by drones, birds, and distant sirens that might mean nothing or everything. A rumor about an assassination spread from shop to shop like wildfire. A boy hurled a stone at an armored jeep; soldiers shouted, a crowd scattered. Even joy was contested here, every laugh a small rebellion.

A drone buzzed overhead, its shadow flickering across faces in every city. In the Gaza market, a soda bottle fell off a vendor's table, landing on the cobblestones with a muted popping sound. People ran. Someone screamed. It was nothing. It was everything. Tension clung to the air, thick and waiting for a spark.

Across the region, the air thickened—a taste of metal on the tongue, a sense that every moment was borrowed time, that history was holding its breath.

Vatican: Visconti pressed his fingertips together, watching lightning fork over Rome. Aides gathered in his office, voices urgent, as he prepared for calls from Washington and Jerusalem. The letter in his desk seemed to pulse like a living thing, demanding a decision he could not make.

Ramallah: Hussein sat on his balcony at dusk, doves gathering on rooftops, the square below echoing with protest drums. His phone vibrated: *Warning—arrest planned for dissidents tonight.* He stared at the message, wondering which of his people would disappear before morning.

Leila, downstairs, tucked her daughters into bed. She whispered a lullaby from childhood, its melody threading through the thunder outside. Through the window, she watched riot police massing near the corner, their shields catching the streetlight. She prayed the power wouldn't go out. She prayed for morning.

Jerusalem: Abraham stood at his kitchen window, hands wrapped around a chipped mug, whispering Daniel's name to the glass. Sirens howled in the distance, and his phone pinged: Curfew. Stay inside. *Threat level raised.* He didn't move. He had nowhere left to go.

Gaza: Hamza unrolled his prayer rug, bullets glinting in the last light like a constellation of violence. Outside, children's voices faded as doors closed and crows swirled over minarets and concrete towers. His phone buzzed with an encrypted message: *Proceed at dawn.*

Lightning flickered on the horizon, painting all three cities in the same electric glow. Every face turned to the window, waiting for the silence to break.

The world, old wounds raw, braced for another cycle.

CHAPTER 3
THE BETRAYAL

JANUARY 2001—GAZA CITY

The fax machine shrieked like a dying goat in the basement of the Gaza bakery, a cheap Chinese import half-melted from candle drips. The room smelled of scorched flour and stale generator oil, ghosts of bread mingled with the bite of cordite from hidden crates of Yugoslav mortars. For Hamza al-Saidi, these smells were old companions—remnants of a childhood spent in rooms like this, watching his mother's hands dusted with flour, and his brother Ziad's laughter echoing through courtyards now silent.

But Gaza itself hadn't always been this way. As a boy, Hamza saw the city change—first, the uneasy peace after the last Israeli tanks pulled back, then the surge of new faces and banners in the streets. He remembered the whispers at mosque, the angry sermons that rattled the air above the rooftops, the day the first masked men handed out bread and leaflets promising justice and resistance. Hamas began not as an army, but as a shadow movement—born from the ashes of forgotten neighborhoods: its leaders, men of prayer and anger, teachers who became generals. Hamza watched his world split open: neighbors who vanished in the night, fathers who never came home, the familiar sound of helicopters punctuating his school lessons.

By his teens, Hamza ran messages between prayer groups, dodging Israeli patrols in alleys painted with green graffiti. He learned that loyalty was measured not in words, but in wounds—broken bones, missing friends, secret funerals attended at midnight. The older men noticed him. Ziad, his older brother and always the braver one, was the first to join the inner circle; Hamza followed, quieter, more patient, listening and watching as Hamas transformed itself from rumor to reality—its leaders hunted, its fighters mythologized, its cause written in the blood on Gaza's broken concrete.

Ziad was killed in a raid. Hamza survived, scarred and wary, one more burden passed from brother to brother, father to son. He moved up the ranks not by loud speeches or reckless attacks, but by surviving the kind of missions that left others buried or broken. As the years passed, he became the man they trusted when everything else failed—a planner, a watcher, a hand on the fuse. Commander, they called him, though the word tasted foreign. In the end, leadership was just another inheritance, one more load to carry.

A boy in a sweat-worn Arsenal jersey plucked the sheet from the tray and squinted at the English he couldn't understand. The Russian header code above the text made his skin prickle—it meant that men far away were pulling strings they might not even understand. He bolted upstairs, sandals slapping concrete.

Commander Hamza waited with the elite Palm Team in a second-floor office lit by a single caged bulb, its yellow glow casting long, wolfish shadows on the plaster walls. The place had once been the baker's living room—you could still see flower tiles where a sink had been ripped out. Hamza was calm, eyes the color of burned coffee, voice quiet enough to chill the room. The hush carried more than authority: it carried the drag of old grief, the ache of inheritance. Ziad's absence pressed against his ribs, a wound that never closed, the ghost of a brother shaping every command.

He read the fax once. Then again.

Monastery. Rome. Ceasefire. Betrayal.

No preamble. No sender. Only that.

Hamza folded the paper with the precision of a funeral rite, every gesture deliberate, as if to contain a contagion. In the old days, his mother would have burned a slip of paper to ward off evil. Now, Hamza did the same, sliding the message into an ashtray, lighting it with a match struck on his boot sole. The flame curled through the Russian letters, turning them to black lace. The smell of burning paper twisted with the memory of other life-or-death dispatches.

A fly buzzed over the table, landing on a chipped enamel cup next to a battered map of Ramallah. Hamza watched it with the detachment of a reptile, then crushed it under one finger. And so, the ritual endures: violence begotten of fathers, visited upon sons, repeated by brothers.

He turned to his fighters across the room—a half-dozen men and boys, sunburned, raw, stinking of sweat and ambition, and something else: the shared ache of inheritance, the cycle they all knew but could not name. Their fathers' and brothers' graves weighed on them as surely as their weapons.

They were known across Gaza by a name whispered with reverence and dread: the Palm Team. Born in the chaos of street battles and midnight raids, they had earned their fame not by numbers but by audacity—striking armored convoys in daylight, vanishing into tunnels with hostages while the city burned above. Their leader before Hamza—old Khalil, the one-eyed saboteur—died with a smile on his lips, a martyr's photo now papered across half the refugee camps. After Khalil's death, it was Hamza who rebuilt them from the bones of loss and hunger, forging survivors into a brotherhood.

Some carried wounds that would never heal: Tariq with his limp from the Shuja'iyya explosion; Youssef, whose family was buried beneath a collapsed apartment after an airstrike. Yet their feats were legend—ambushes that sent Israeli patrols scrambling, the night they held the Salah al-Din highway for hours with nothing but AKs and homemade explosives. Children scrawled their names on school walls. Fighters in other cells watched the Palm Team pass and made space, eyes averted.

But for every triumph there was a cost. The youngest among them, Mahmoud, had lost a brother in the last failed attack on the Erez crossing. For Hamza, every mission was a reckoning, every celebration haunted by the names unspoken at morning prayers. Their fame was a kind of armor, but also a target; every mother in Gaza knew that legend never shielded sons from bullets.

"They would give our land to the Crusaders," Hamza spat. "They would trade your father's grave for the kiss of the Vatican."

His voice stayed low, like a blade held low before the killing thrust.

He saw the tremor in the youngest boy's hand, prayer beads clicking like teeth. Hamza remembered Ziad's first night out, remembered the way courage and fear shared the same heartbeat. "Courage," Hamza said gently, voice slipping into the cadence of an older brother, "We've been given a hard trust. To set wrongs right. To lift our people."

He straightened. The softness left his face; the room felt smaller. When he spoke again, it was the field voice, the one that moved men.

"Tomorrow's plan must wait. We move on the Muqataa. Tonight."

////

Far across the border, Abraham Mizrahi was back in the bunker under the Knesset, its concrete walls still stained with Cold War-era water leaks. Overhead, the ventilation fans thrummed like a mechanical heartbeat. He rubbed his temple, fighting a tension that never left—a tension his own father had carried home from another war. In moments like this, Abraham felt the press of generations in his marrow: the endless ledger of sacrifice, the stories of lost sons that shaped the map of his country as much as any border.

Shin Bet's chief signals officer spread printouts across a steel table, the ink still damp.

"Sir, we intercepted a Russian burst from Gaza. The radicals have eyes on the monastery deal."

Abraham looked at the printout, pulse spiking. Of course they know, he thought. They always know. The logic of betrayal was never new—it was inherited, as natural as a blood feud. Part of him wanted to tear the entire Strip apart, flatten it, bury every rumor in a hundred feet of sand. But the memory of Hussein in the monastery—voice cracked by grief, hands trembling as he signed the agreement—stopped him. There was still a chance, if they moved carefully, if the old stories could be rewritten.

"Double your night watchers along the fence," he ordered. "If Hamas even breathes toward Ramallah, I want eyes on it."

The Shin Bet man nodded, adjusting his glasses.

"Understood, Prime Minister."

////

In the Muqataa, Hussein sat in the study, oil lamp guttering against the desert wind that rattled the old iron security bars. His daughters were asleep behind the plywood-shuttered windows, faces still and peaceful—peaceful, what a luxury that was. He traced a finger along a battered

Quran on the side table, a gift from his grandmother, the binding held together with worn cloth. The scent of old paper, of his mother's kitchen, tugged at him. The inheritance of hope, battered but alive, survived in such small things.

Samir entered quietly, boots crunching on cheap mosaic tiles.

Samir, almost whispering, "Sir, our friends report Hamas is seething—they want you hanging in the Al-Saraya."

Hussein looked up, circles under his eyes deep as trenches. He thought of his brother, buried with so many others, and felt the ache pass down his arm—a memory, a scar.

"They would rather drown in blood," he sighed.

Samir glanced at the radio, which clicked and hissed as static from Tel Aviv fought with the night prayers from Nablus.

"The radicals will strike soon," he warned.

Hussein nodded. He rose, stepped onto the small balcony where a dying potted mint plant grew in a broken teapot. The city beyond pulsed with yellow sodium lamps, each one trembling as if about to fail. He closed his eyes, breathing in the dusty night air. *Maybe it would have been simpler to keep fighting,* he thought. But the memory of children's bodies in a hospital corridor, lined up under stained blankets, would not let him. Inheritance, again—a legacy he could not accept for his daughters.

////

In Gaza, Hamza's Palm Team finished their night prayers on a worn rug, its corners frayed to threads.

They loaded battered Kalashnikovs with fresh brass rounds, the magazines marked with bits of red tape for instant recognition. One fighter slipped on a plastic bracelet that had belonged to his sister, killed in an airstrike. He kissed it like a talisman, eyes gone cold. Hamza watched them without pity, but not without feeling. He saw in every gesture the shadow of loss—the legacy of violence wrapped around memory and duty.

"You do this for God," he reminded them. "Not for me."

They nodded, young faces blank, their minds already halfway to paradise.

They moved through the tunnels like rats, silent, the damp air thick with mildew and the chemical stink of homemade explosives. Above them, Gaza City slept, never knowing which moment might be its last.

////

In Rome, Father Piero walked a candlelit corridor in the Vatican guest house, the polished marble floors echoing with each step. He paused before an icon of Archangel Michael spearing the dragon, the dragon's eyes painted black as pitch.

"And there was war in heaven: Michael and his angels fought against the dragon; and the dragon fought and his angels, and prevailed not; neither was their place found any more in heaven." —Revelation 12:7

He wondered if men were the dragon, and peace itself was the fragile angel trying to hold the spear steady. Would they have to wait until Armageddon to find out? He made the sign of the cross, his hand trembling with fear. Even in the corridors of the Church, inheritance weighed heavily—faith and doubt passed down, battling in the silence.

////

Somewhere across the coastal road, an Israeli drone swept over the dunes, its infrared sensors tracking heat blooms on the march. Tiny figures, moving with purpose. The drone pilot radioed it in.

"Visual. Armed group. Maybe twelve. Unknown affiliation, ten clicks south of Ramallah."

The controller in Tel Aviv hissed a curse.

"It's starting," he said, his voice dry.

The war was a river that never stopped.

And in the shadows of that river, in that current, men still drowned, no matter how many times they tried to build a dam. The city, the families, the fighters, even the watchers far away—all of them caught in the undertow, bearing burdens handed down, waiting for the next ripple to become a wave.

CHAPTER 4
NIGHT OF THE KNIVES

JANUARY 2001—THE WEST BANK

Night pressed in thick and breathless. The generator coughed and faltered, its hum the only mechanical sound in the compound. Fuel was running low.

Rain slashed across the courtyard in diagonal sheets, hammering puddles until they jumped and scattered. Wet stone and diesel exhaust drifted through the cracked window seals. A loose shutter banged somewhere in the dark.

Leila stood at the kitchen window, forearms on the sill, tracking the guards. They were silhouettes against flashlight beams, but she knew each man's posture well enough to read their fear. One paced near the gate, head turning toward the alley more than the street. Another moved along the far wall, rifle clutched tight, muttering into the rain. A third kept pausing where the courtyard light failed, leaning out as if trying to catch a sound he couldn't hear.

Her chest felt squeezed, the way it had during childbirth—that unbearable constriction before release. Every shadow tightened the band around her ribs.

Upstairs, Hussein moved like a man counting down. His steps were measured, breathing controlled, but his eyes gave away the calculations. He circled each window, checking latches, angling his shoulders to minimize his silhouette. The pistol at his side pulled at his hip like a second heart.

In the bedroom, Mira's pencil scratched across paper in quick, fevered strokes—a collapsed archway, a smear of lightning, a house with windows like eyes. The lead kept breaking. She pressed harder. Amal sat with knees pulled to her chest, the limp ear of her stuffed bear pinched between white-knuckled fingers, staring at the far wall.

The air tasted of damp cement and rust, overlaid with something electrical. The storm was working into the walls, into the wiring. Every few seconds the lights flickered—not enough to kill them, just enough to remind them they could.

On the counter, the radio spat static. "*...curfew...shots fired near central...all residents remain...*" The words broke apart. Leila clicked it off, fingers lingering on the knob as if she could keep the silence from shattering.

The sound came too metallic, too clean to belong to the storm. A sudden clang, metal on stone, sharp enough to pierce the rain.

Leila's spine went rigid. Her eyes cut toward the courtyard wall.

One guard stopped mid-stride, his flashlight jerking toward the sound. "Did you hear that?"

From the shadow near the gate: "Nothing yet. Keep your eyes up."

The rain surged harder, masking smaller noises—a scrape here, a shifting shadow there.

Thunder rolled deep enough to make the glass tremble. Leila's pulse kept time with it.

Above her, Hussein's voice came sharp: "Living room. Now."

She gathered the girls, one arm around each, steering them toward the stairs. Amal stumbled once but Leila's grip held her upright.

The air had a density to it now, as though all the oxygen had been claimed by anticipation. Even the guards moved differently—routes tighter, rifles angled higher, eyes darting toward blind corners.

Then came the breach: a heavy metallic crash from the back gate, followed by the screech of hinges wrenched past their limits.

Shouts erupted, overlapping. The first gunshots followed, close enough to feel in the teeth—sharp, cracking reports that made the girls flinch.

Leila's mouth went dry. She could feel the cold moving through her limbs.

The gate didn't just open—it broke. Metal warped and split, clattering back against the wall.

Boots churned the courtyard mud, splashing high arcs of dirty water. Masked figures pushed through in bursts, some slipping, some darting ahead with reckless energy.

They were young. Painfully young. Lightning flared across their eyes, revealing adrenaline and something harder underneath.

A guard fired from near the gate, muzzle flash bright against the rain. The shot went wide, ricocheting off stone. He had only a second to process the miss before he folded, clutching his side. Another guard dragged him backward, each step leaving a trail of red in the water.

"Upstairs!" Hussein's command cut through the chaos.

Leila gripped Amal, shoving her ahead on the stairs. Mira stayed close, sketchbook still clutched in one hand.

The kitchen window blew inward, shards spraying tile. Bullets followed, tearing through plaster. One fragment caught Leila's arm, a hot sting that ran warm to her wrist. She barely felt it over the pounding of her heart.

At the landing, Hussein shoved the girls into the bedroom, then shouldered the dresser across the door. Mira's teeth chattered audibly. Amal's breaths were short, high-pitched.

"Get down." Hussein took position with his back to the dresser, pistol raised in one hand, radio in the other. "Arif," he whispered, voice trembling, "they're inside."

Static laced Arif's reply from a van two blocks away. In the claustrophobic cargo space, flickering green dials lit his face. His heart hammered. Sweat pooled in the small of his back.

"Stay down," Arif ordered, voice strained. "Help's coming."

Hussein's grip tightened on the radio. Hope flickered.

Arif switched to encrypted frequency, palms sweating: "Bravo Six, execute Black Sweep." His voice cracked in the van's oppressive isolation.

Boots pounded the stairs below. Someone screamed—she couldn't tell whose side. The answering gunfire was too close, muffled only by walls not thick enough for this.

A metallic clink—something small and heavy slid under the door, spinning across the floor toward the dresser. Hussein lunged to kick it away, but it detonated first.

White light. Deafening concussion. Then silence that wasn't silence—a high, endless ringing.

Leila blinked against the blur. Mira sobbing without sound. Amal's mouth open in a cry she couldn't hear. Her own arm throbbed.

She shoved the girls toward the closet. "Window—move!"

Hussein fired blindly through the wall, each shot answered by splinters and return fire.

Leila threw the closet window open. Rain and wind hit her full in the face. She pushed Mira out first, then Amal, then climbed through, catching her hip on jagged glass. Hussein came last, barely clearing before bullets shredded the eaves where his head had been.

The roof was a slick, tilting sheet under the downpour. Rain hammered so hard it felt alive, every drop a stinging strike.

A shout from below: "There! On the roof!"

Leila turned just in time to catch lightning across the upturned face of a boy—no older than nineteen, rifle shaking in his hands. His eyes locked with hers. For a heartbeat, he froze. Then another shot cracked from a rooftop they couldn't see, and the boy folded.

Arif ignored his own order to wait. He killed the van's lights, grabbed a spare mag, and ran the last two blocks through the alley, rain needling his face. Seconds later he slid under the trellis into the courtyard, pistol up, unfazed by passing rounds. "Come on! Move!"

The closest cover was the kitchen off the courtyard.

Hussein went first, boots slipping on wet wood. Mira and Amal followed, Amal's hand white-knuckled around her bear, the toy's ear dragging in the rain. Leila came last, palm slick with blood from glass or shrapnel.

The kitchen was chaos—broken tile, shattered glass. Smoke from spent rounds hung low, stinging eyes. A body lay sprawled near the fridge, a black smear beneath him. One of the house guards dragged himself toward the door, leaving a crimson trail.

A masked man crashed through what remained of the window, blade glinting. Arif fired twice, missed, then closed the distance in a tackle. They went down hard, rolling across wet tile. The intruder broke free, burst out into the rain.

"Courtyard—go!" Arif gasped, pistol still in hand.

They burst into the open, straight into the storm. Rain slapped their faces in hard, icy sheets. The ground was sucking mire; each step threatened to pull their shoes free.

The last guard lay sprawled near the wall, his uniform soaked darker by more than rain. Two Palm Team fighters hunched low by the far planter—one holding his stomach with both hands, blood pouring through his fingers; the other firing in short, panicked bursts toward the gate.

Another masked man sprinted toward the side wall, shouting for reinforcements over the storm's roar.

Leila dragged the girls into the shadow of a cracked concrete planter, pressing them low. Mira's teeth chattered, blood from a gash on her cheek mixing into rain-mud slurry. Amal whimpered, "Mama, my hand—" and held it out. Her palm was bleeding freely, tiny shards of glass embedded.

Leila tore a strip from her scarf, wrapping it tight, knotting it with clumsy fingers. She kissed the bandage without thinking, tasting salt and copper.

Hussein crouched beside them, jaw rigid, checking the pistol's weight. One magazine left. Arif knelt on the other side, slapping a fresh mag into his weapon, the motion jerky—his right hand bleeding through a deep tear in the webbing between thumb and finger.

He keyed his radio: "Eagle to Falcon—immediate extraction! We're losing it!" The reply was only static, then garbled syllables lost under gunfire.

A burst of rounds chewed the planter edge, forcing them lower. Chips of concrete stung Leila's neck.

Then a new sound—the hollow, lung-punch thud of an RPG launch.

The grenade slammed into the second-floor balcony. The explosion was deafening, a rolling concussion that blew shards of stone and glass outward in a deadly fan. Hussein flung himself over the girls as debris clattered across his back.

Smoke poured in, acrid and gritty. Shouts overlapped—*"Flank left!" "On the roof!" "Push now!"*—with voices cracking under strain.

A fighter vaulted the low wall, rifle raised. He saw the family huddled there and froze mid-step. His mouth moved around a prayer. Hussein's shot was faster. The boy dropped into the mud with a sound like wet cloth.

Another tried to drag him away, slipped, then scrambled back to cover, leaving the body.

Arif's pistol barked twice, but the wet grip slipped in his injured hand. "We can't hold another wave."

Hussein's voice was low but firm: "We stay. We fight." A crack ran through the last word.

The pause was brief, a shallow inhale before the next blow.

Three attackers surged from the alley, weapons blazing, bullets chewing into the planter. One hurled a Molotov; the bottle burst short, flames licking across the mud, smoke curling into the rain in oily strands.

Arif's pistol jammed on the second shot. He ducked, cursed, cleared it, and came back up firing.

Leila pressed the girls into the earth. Mira had lost her sketchbook somewhere in the scramble, her hands empty and shaking. "Where—" she started, but Leila shushed her, wiping blood from her cheek.

A bullet's hot wind grazed Leila's scalp. She felt the wet warmth immediately. Amal saw the blood and began to sob. "Mama, don't die."

Leila held her tight, murmuring lies that she hoped sounded like truth.

One of the attackers went down screaming, clutching a shredded thigh. The others hesitated, looking to the rooftops, eyes flicking between cover and the family's position.

A sudden slam of the loose gate drew all eyes. The wind had picked up, pushing the rain sideways. Leila's vision blurred with water and grit; every blink stung.

Arif's voice into the radio was a thin wire of sound: "Eagle, where are you? We're surrounded."

A broken reply: "*—hold—ETA two—hold—*" The transmission dissolved into static.

Hussein's gaze swept the attackers regrouping at the courtyard's edge. Some shouted for more men; others argued to pull back. One, clearly the leader, raised his weapon and screamed, "Finish it now!"

Through the chaos, another sound emerged—so low at first it might have been a trick of the wind. A deep, steady vibration. Felt more than heard.

Whup-whup-whup.

The attackers faltered, eyes tilting skyward, searching the black clouds.

Gunfire still cracked, but its rhythm broke, uncertainty seeping in.

Chunks of wall spat into the mud near the planter. Leila shielded the girls with her body. Mira's face pressed into her shoulder, breath ragged. Hussein's arm closed around them all, muscles locked like steel.

Ten meters to their left, Samir—blood soaking half his face—rasped, "Stay down! Almost here—hold them back!" He raised his rifle with shaking hands and fired a blind burst over the wall.

Arif leaned out, returning fire in short, measured bursts. His eyes never stopped moving, tracking both gate and alley. Another guard nearby fumbled with a spare mag, hands slipping on wet metal.

Shadows moved beyond the smoke—Palm Team fighters in the rain, their outlines stuttering in the lightning. Some fired in wild arcs; others crouched, waiting for the order.

A round punched into the dirt inches from Amal's head. Hussein shifted his body to cover her fully. "Stay down."

Mira squeezed Leila's hand until her fingers went numb.

Rain soaked them to the bone, plastering clothes to skin. Mud sucked at their knees, their hands. Leila tasted grit and blood in every breath. Her entire world was reduced to the drag of her daughters against her and the sound of Hussein's heart pounding through his chest.

The *whup-whup-whup* grew louder, rattling loose glass in the windows above, shaking the splintered door on its hinges.

A flare of tracer fire arced across the sky, disappearing into the dark. Arif shouted, "They're coming—stay down, stay together!"

One of the Palm Team fighters broke from cover, sprinting toward the fountain, firing blind. Samir's shot took him in the thigh; he dropped behind the fountain's edge, wailing.

The family was pinned—no retreat, no advance—just the cold, wet press of the earth and the hiss of rain.

Hussein bent close, lips brushing Leila's hair. "Almost, almost..." The words were barely audible.

Amal sobbed. Mira's breath came in stutters. Leila closed her eyes, unsure if she was praying or simply bracing for impact.

Above it all, the approaching helicopter's rotors beat a steady, inescapable rhythm. The defenders held, firing in measured desperation, buying seconds they could not afford.

Thunder cracked. The firefight surged, joined by scorching minigun fire from the arriving Black Hawk.

And still that sound came closer—the promise, or the threat, of the sky about to split open.

CHAPTER 5
FLIGHT TO SAFETY

JANUARY 2001—HAIFA FOB, ISRAEL

Floodlights burned hard against the coastal night, carving white pools across the tarmac. The Mediterranean wind carried salt and jet fuel, flapping the edges of green canvas over gear crates. Mason stood in the rotor wash beside the Black Hawk, headset clamped over his ears, briefing his six-man extraction team.

"Targets: NOMAD, family of three, our inside man, NOMAD's security," he said, using the codename, sharp, impersonal. "High-value, hostile environment, compromised perimeter. LZ is hot. Rain."

The men nodded, faces hidden behind NVGs and balaclavas, movements mechanical as they checked mags, toggled safeties, pulled comm cables taut.

Mason scanned each of them, cataloguing strengths the way another man might count tools. He'd run operations from the Sinai to the Hindu Kush, carried the weight of each—the names of the dead like stones in his pockets. Tonight felt heavier. Not for the politics, but for the margin: five minutes to extract NOMAD and his family before the street sealed in fire.

The flight crew moved through final checks. The pilot—a reserve IDF captain on CIA contract—gave Mason a thumbs-up. Overhead, the sky was a low lid of bruised cloud, moonlight smothered. The crew chief braced one hand on the door frame, tugged his harness, tested the latch, then leaned out into mist and noise. "Bird's hot."

"Load up," Mason ordered.

They climbed aboard, harnesses clinking against carbines. As the Black Hawk lifted, the base lights dropped away, replaced by the dark sprawl of the Judean foothills sliding beneath them. The bird bucked in the wind, the pilot holding her steady against crosscurrent coming off the sea.

Mason leaned forward. His headset crackled with the voice of the on-site operator inside the Muqataa. "Courtyard's hot—multiple shooters, small-arms and one RPG spotted. Family's taken cover behind garden pots. You've got maybe five minutes before we lose our exit route. Popped smoke."

Their ETA was six minutes.

"Copy," Mason said. His hand closed tighter around the webbing of his seat. The city rose toward them now, lights scattered like embers across the hills. Down there in Ramallah, NOMAD was waiting—and the window was already closing.

The Black Hawk skimmed low over the rooftops. Rain beat flat beneath the rotors until it ran in sheets. Spray slashed the windscreen in white veils the wipers could barely clear. Inside the cockpit, the pilot's jaw was set, eyes flicking between altitude, airspeed, and the faint silhouette of Ramallah across the moving map. Crosswinds hit the airframe in punches; the nose dipped, corrected, dipped again.

"Wind shear's rough. Coming in hot in forty," the pilot said, voice calm, as if announcing light chop over Kansas.

In the jump seats, Mason adjusted his headset and ran the ingress one more time—approach vector off the coastal road, door gun pre-suppression on the west wall, flare pop at touchdown, exfiltration through the inner courtyard. He didn't need to see the compound yet. The pattern of fights like these had worn grooves in his mind. They always felt the same in the last minute: air getting thinner, attention narrowing, time stretching and compressing at once.

Static licked his ear, followed by Command's voice: "Falcon, be advised—hostiles fortified on west wall, probable RPG. Friendly package pinned near inner planter. Repeat: package pinned."

"Roger," Mason said, already revising. Rope insertion would cost them a minute and a half. A minute and a half was a lifetime when men with rocket tubes were praying for a silhouette to hold still.

"Doors," the crew chief called. The side hatch slid and locked. Rain blew in sideways, peppering faces and goggles with salt. The cabin filled with the smell of wet nylon, gun oil, and fuel.

The Muqataa reared up—a darker line against dark, punctured by brief, wavering orange flickers. Tracer fire stitched upward and smothered out in the rain. With the doors open, the sound changed: the rotors' steady thunder turned to living pressure you felt in ribs and teeth. The gunner rotated the M134 out and down, cheek welded, barrel already walking across the wall intel had marked.

"Visual on courtyard. No clear landing pad," the crew chief reported. "Recommend rope."

"We land," Mason said. "Make me a hole."

The gunner's reply was a hammering chain of fire that chewed the wall to dust. Red tracers burned like comets through the downpour; one fighter in a soaked keffiyeh pitched backward, another folded on the parapet.

"Flares," the pilot ordered.

Two magnesium suns bloomed and fell, throwing the compound into sharp relief: shattered balcony, courtyard littered with pavers and broken pots, black slick of water running like oil. In the white glare the surviving

Palm Team fighters looked smaller and younger than they had in shadows. They were still firing.

"Commit," the pilot said.

The helicopter dropped, and the storm rose to meet it.

Skids struck stone with a jolt hard enough to rattle teeth. Before the shock settled, Mason was airborne, boots hitting slick flagstone, weapon up, legs bending to keep his silhouette low under the wash. The rotor blast flattened rain into a horizontal slap that stung exposed skin and drove grit into eyes. Everything smelled of cordite, wet limestone, and burned olive wood.

"Falcon team, go! Cover right, move to primary package!"

Mason swept the muzzle across the chaos, scanning for threats. His men spread out, laying down covering fire as the last Palm Team fighters peppered the helicopter with desperate rounds.

A rookie operator slipped on the wet deck, nearly losing his grip on the rifle. Mason barked, "Keep it together!" But his own hands were not quite as steady as he wished.

Arif and Samir dragged Hussein and his family from behind the shattered garden wall.

"Move! Now! We've got you!"

Mason crouched beside Leila, one hand steadying her, the other pressing his comm. "This is Mason. We have NOMAD. On me."

He pulled Mira to her feet, lifted Amal beneath one arm. Amal lost her bear in the scramble. Hussein staggered, blood slicking his temple. Leila was dazed and stumbling. Mason's team laid down a precise volley, the gunner raking muzzle flashes along the wall.

The world narrowed to the desperate rush from rubble to the helicopter's side. Bullets cracked against stone; Mason's men answered, the gunner sweeping for movement.

Rain lashed their faces.

The hatches slammed shut, muting gunfire to a low, pulsing roar. Inside, the world was all vibration—metal deck shuddering under boots, harnesses tightening, each breath thick with sweat, cordite, and fuel.

Mason moved through the narrow aisle with the ease of ritual, crouching before the family, scanning them head to toe:

Leila: cut over one eyebrow, shaking, blood on her hands and thigh.

Mira: pupils huge, knuckles white on her mother's sleeve.

Amal: crying silently for her bear, curled fetal, face pressed to Leila's hip.

Hussein: scalp wound, breathing shallow, hands trembling.

Samir: bloody from head to toe.

He checked for blood that wasn't theirs, eyes for concussion, hands for shock. Gloved fingers tilted Leila's chin, then turned Hussein's head toward the instrument glow.

"You're safe," Mason said, voice carrying through the thrum. "Stay buckled. Medic!"

A crewman in dusty fatigues passed forward a trauma kit, kneeling by Hussein, hands moving with swift confidence. He noticed Samir's wounds and shallow breathing. Quick triage: "This one can't wait or we're gonna lose him." He set an IV in record time, then plasma, then a morphine autoinjector.

Mason radioed command, calling an ambulance to the LZ for Samir. The medic, crouched over the man, told him to have plasma waiting when they arrived.

Arif slumped against the bulkhead, rifle still across his knees, eyes locked on the hatch as if willing no one through.

Above, the door gunner scanned with the minigun, watching the city fall away, scanning for a last, parting shot that might flicker from below.

Rain battered the fuselage, mixing with sweat and blood on the family's faces. Leila shuddered. Mira gasped for air. Amal stared at Mason with raw, animal fear, searching his face for judgment. Mason handed her a bear retrieved by Arif off the courtyard rubble.

He gave her a nod, steady as granite—a silent anchor.

Mira, eyes wide, started counting the snaps on Mason's vest—one, two, three, four—her voice quiet and rhythmic, a fragile thread of control in the storm.

The Black Hawk punched west through low clouds, speed and altitude pressing the world into a tunnel of noise and dread. The only light: the instrument panel, and a sullen red indicator by the copilot's knee.

Leila blinked hard, trying to orient herself—past and future splintered, every second a new kind of fear. Mira shook uncontrollably, her tears lost in the helicopter's endless drone. Amal clutched her bear.

Hussein tried to speak—"Leila...girls..."—but Mason's hand pressed his shoulder down, gentle and final.

The echo of his father's voice haunted him: *You keep them safe*. The promise tasted hollow, drowned by the storm of gunfire.

"Rest. Medics have you. We'll talk when we land."

Mason spoke into his mic: "Bravo Actual, thirty seconds to LZ. Confirm path is clear."

Static, then a clipped reply: "Confirmed, Bravo. Path clear. Airspace secure. Eagle's Nest standing by. Wheels down in three zero."

Mason gave a tight nod, checked his sidearm, then looked at the battered faces around him. His team was bloodied but upright—one with a bullet graze, another scorched by cordite. They all watched Mason. If he was calm, they would be too.

The helicopter bounced through wind shear on descent. The world outside flashed into harsh light—concrete, spinning shadows, ground crew running, enveloping perimeter security.

The Black Hawk's skids kissed tarmac, bounced and screeched, rotors still thundering above.

The shift from helicopter to ground was jarring—a new world, vibrating with the shock of survival and the threat of what might come next.

The crew slid back the doors. With Arif and one of Mason's men bracing him, Samir was first out. The medic stayed at his side, IVs in hand, and only stepped away after handing him to the ambulance team, who loaded him onto a gurney and into the waiting rig.

Mason guided the family out, urging them through the opening. Leila's knees buckled as she struck the tarmac. She clutched her daughters for stability, stumbling in the brutal glare of halogen lamps. The ground seemed to hum. The night was full of barking dogs, clipped radio calls, the distant whine of jet engines. Rain spat sideways, chilling sweat-soaked skin.

Mason seemed to be everywhere—shouting orders, signaling, one eye on the family, one on the perimeter. He was already counting minutes to wheels-up, looking for gaps in the chain. Had the van been checked for traps? There was no such thing as safe.

The ground crew rushed them to a waiting van. Leila caught brief faces—smeared green by goggles, hidden by masks. Amal coughed, tripping on a crack. Mira wrapped her arms around Leila's waist, burying her face in her coat. Hussein limped, shirt caked in blood, eyes searching. "Samir! Where's Samir!"

"He's in good hands. He'll be fine," Mason assured.

"You're doing terrific, keep moving," a guard encouraged as the van's sliding door yawned open. Soldiers waved them in—no words, just brisk gestures and the gleam of holstered sidearms.

Inside, the air was metallic and close. Fuel fumes, disinfectant, rain-soaked clothes. Only the dashboard and a dim dome light illuminated the cabin, throwing faces into high relief. Mira sat rigid, eyes darting from blacked-out windows to the weapons cradled by men opposite her. Amal curled into Leila's side, silent except for hiccupped breaths.

Mason climbed in last, giving a quick scan before closing the sliding door. The van lurched, tires squealing. For a beat, there was only the engine's growl, the muted hiss of Mason's radio, the driver's jaw flexing under tension.

"You're safe," Mason said, his voice reduced to its simplest form. "We need to move. Explanations come once we're airborne. Please—no questions. Trust me, you don't want to wait here."

Leila tried to nod; the effort cost her. Her ears rang. The world tilted in and out of focus. She squeezed her daughters. "It's almost over," she whispered, unsure she believed it.

Hussein slumped against the window, eyes fixed on nothing, shoulders hunched. He replayed the last hours—each gunshot, each scream, every failure. The guilt held him like a fist. *Samir?*

The van sped through the airfield's maze. Outside, figures moved with intent—carbines, tablets, reflective vests. Leila glimpsed armored vehicles, the snout of a C-17, dogs straining at leashes.

Inside, Mason's radio cut the silence:

"Bravo actual. Cargo secure. En route."

"Copy, Bravo. Airspace clear. Eagle's Nest fueled and standing by. Three minutes to transfer."

"Roger."

The van stopped and started, braking for gates, accelerating past MPs. Each slowdown made Leila's heart seize—had someone betrayed them? Each time, Mason's eyes met hers—cool, steady, unbreakable.

They reached the CIA ops center, the Gulfstream's silhouette outlined under cold blue lights. Crew waited at the stairs, the cabin entry open.

At the checkpoint, an ill-informed MP paused, squinting at Leila's passport, the page damp and half-torn. "You with State?" he asked. Mason flashed a badge. The tension lingered just long enough for Amal to tug her mother's sleeve and whisper, "I counted seven trucks." Only then did the MP wave them through.

Mason checked his watch, looked at the family. "Let's go. This is the last stretch."

The van door slid open. Cold air blasted in. Leila lifted Amal. Mira, in hand, followed—silent and tight-jawed. Hussein leaned on a young sergeant who wouldn't let go.

The air reeked of jet fuel, salt, adrenaline. Every step across the tarmac felt dreamlike—too much light, too much danger, too much hope.

They hurried up the metal stairs, Mason's team closing ranks behind them. The van idled, headlights carving the dawn-fogged dark.

In seconds, they would cross a threshold—from war into a world that only resembled peace.

Stepping into the jet was like entering a different universe.

The attendant, blue uniform crisp, greeted them: "Welcome aboard," her smile the first the family had seen in ages.

Soft light pooled on pale leather seats. Polished burled walnut trim gleamed. A faint, expensive scent lingered.

For a second, Leila froze. Amal, her bear dangling from a limp grip, shoes streaked with blood and mud. Mira blinked at the aisle, knuckles digging into her thighs. Hussein hesitated, hand to his bandaged ribs, eyes darting from the opulence to his battered shoes.

"Please, sit anywhere up front," the attendant said, offering towels and water, her voice careful, fragile at the edges.

Mason ushered his team to the rear, peeling off body armor and comms with slow, exhausted precision. He spoke low into a satphone, face set, fingers trembling ever so slightly. The medic checked Hussein's pulse, then Leila's, asking in a whisper about pain, nausea, memories that clung.

Leila sank into soft leather, Amal curled against her side, Mira on the other. A blanket settled over their legs. For a breath, the hush was so deep it felt sacred—no alarms, only the whirr of ventilation and her own pulse in her ears.

Outside, engines spun up, a steady, promising whine. Leila stared at the carpet—blue and spotless, the pattern reminding her of mosaic in her grandmother's courtyard. The memory stung.

Mira studied every surface: chrome fixtures, stitched seatbacks, the attendant's shaky hands pouring juice for Amal. She saw the cracks in Leila's mask—eyes glassy, fingers twisting at her skirt's hem. When their eyes met, they held the gaze, wordless, a world beneath the silence.

Amal drank her juice, then burrowed into Leila's lap and fell instantly, violently, asleep. Her body surrendered at last to the undertow of fear.

Hussein slumped into his recliner, mind circling failures. He replayed every choice, every warning ignored, every face lost. When Mason passed, he managed a broken whisper: "Thank you."

Mason nodded, not trusting himself to speak. He squeezed Hussein's shoulder, then drifted to the rear, phone in hand. Anything but stillness.

As the jet rolled out, Mason allowed himself a long, slow breath. He'd made these calls before—extractions, triage in the dark—but every one left a scar, and this was fresh. He looked over his team—men asleep with weapons across their chests, one with a new tear in his sleeve, blood still crusted on his knuckles.

The attendant offered snacks: cheese, fruit, sugared nuts. Trays went untouched. Mira flinched at the clink of ice. Leila shivered, pulling Amal closer. Hussein stared at nothing, eyes fixed on memories that wouldn't dissolve. The attendant checked her manifest and asked, "Lance, can I get you anything?" Mason replied, "You can just call me Mason, ma'am. Everybody does. I'll have a Coke on the rocks if you've got one." Lance was for another life—lost on the yellow footprints at Parris Island, left behind in the sand and fear.

For an hour, no one spoke. The jet's hush had nothing to do with comfort—it was weighted by all that had been lost, and all that might still be lost.

As the Gulfstream climbed above the clouds, dawn painted the horizon in bruised purple and gold. The Mediterranean fell away, vast and indifferent.

After a stop at the U.S. base in Rota—jet refueled, paperwork rubber-stamped by a red-eyed consular officer—Eagle's Nest lifted over the Atlantic. The attendant dimmed the lights. Windows became black mirrors, reflecting the faces inside.

Passengers and crew settled in for the long crossing—a nine-hour flight into an unthinkable next chapter.

For a while, the cabin was silent except for the sigh of ventilation and the muted sounds of Mason's team securing gear, grabbing pillows, finding places to stretch out. Leila tried to sleep, nerves humming with the aftertaste of adrenaline. Each time she closed her eyes, the nightmare returned: flashes, her daughters' screams, the weight of Amal's body in her arms. She pressed her fingers to her eyelids, chasing away the flicker of memory. It was impossible to tell where jet noise ended and gunfire echoes began.

Hussein dozed fitfully, haunted by regret—faces he'd sent to die, friends betrayed, promises broken. Sometimes he jolted awake, disoriented by the hush, reached for his family, then retreated into himself.

Mira refused to sleep. She stared at the window, forehead pressed to the cool glass, watching for dawn, for America, for a sign that the ordeal was finally over. She clutched the new notebook the captain had given her, tracing patterns across its spare log pages—a small proof she still existed.

Amal slept in fits, waking with a shudder each time the jet banked or the engines changed pitch. Leila stroked her hair, whispering nonsense lullabies in a voice raw from exhaustion. Sometimes Amal would murmur—*Where are we? Will we go back?*—and Leila would lie, because mercy was all she had left.

The CIA medics moved quietly, checking wounds, offering water, sleep aids, pressing blankets into arms that wouldn't let go of fear. The flight attendant brought juice and sandwiches, moving down the aisle with practiced calm, her eyes old with the weight of what she'd seen.

Hours slipped by. Over the mid-Atlantic, the world was just engines and sleep, the past receding, the future held at bay by darkness and cloud.

At one point, Mason checked on each of them, face unreadable, voice low. "Two hours left," he said. "If you need anything, tell me." Leila tried to thank him but her voice caught; Mason squeezed her shoulder and moved on.

Outside, the sky shifted from black to the faintest silver at the edge of the world. Over Newfoundland, dawn split the clouds. In the half-light, faces reappeared from the gloom—older, battered, still breathing. Mira lifted her head; Amal burrowed deeper into Leila's lap.

Only in the morning light did Leila realize she was shaking. For the first time, she let herself cry, silent as the clouds.

By the time the Gulfstream began its slow descent toward Palm Beach, the shock of survival had given way to the reality of exile. They watched the coastline emerge—green and gold and impossibly bright, so foreign it felt unreal. On final approach, each breath was measured, each heartbeat suspended between hope and defiance.

The wheels touched down. The nightmare receded, but nothing would ever be the same.

The landing was too smooth—a trick of nerves. Outside, the airport seemed to hold its breath—no commotion, just the distant, lonely drone of a mower at the field's edge.

Florida light stabbed through the windows—bright and blue as the Mediterranean. Fresh air hissed through the overhead vents, a steady pressurized flow that smelled faintly of cut grass, jet fuel, and bougainvillea. Through the glass, palm trees waved beneath a sky so wide it made her dizzy.

The jet taxied along the private apron, gliding past silent hangars to a distant corner. In the new light, every detail was hyperreal: the marshaller's vest blazing orange in the sunrise, the shimmer on the tarmac, steam rising from grass beyond the chain-link.

The marshaller lifted his batons, face unreadable behind mirrored shades. His gestures were crisp, deliberate—turn left, slow, halt. The Gulfstream rolled to a stop, engines winding down. A tug latched onto the nose gear, the clang echoing in the quiet.

The crew followed protocol, movements drilled for moments like this: shades down, passengers waiting in the hush. The jet was drawn slowly into a cavernous hangar, its vast mouth opening to swallow them whole. The marshaller checked his watch—everything on schedule—then scanned the perimeter, looking for press, onlookers, anyone out of place.

As soon as the jet cleared the threshold, the hangar doors slid closed with mechanical finality. Sunlight vanished. Inside, the darkness was sudden—broken only by harsh overhead fluorescents flickering to life, throwing angular shadows across the Gulfstream's sleek lines.

Briefly, everything held still—a liminal pause before the next set of procedures, the next round of questions, the next layer of security. Beyond the doors, the world would soon wake to headlines. Inside, shielded from view, the burden of survival pressed down: adrenaline fading, hands still trembling, every face carrying the knowledge of a night that couldn't be shared.

A flight attendant's voice, too loud in the hush: "We've arrived. Please remain seated until we're ready to deplane."

Mason was already on his feet, checking his watch, new tension in the set of his shoulders. He spoke quietly into his radio, glancing at the ground crew—plainclothes security, uniformed officers, men and women in sunglasses with discreet earpieces.

The cabin hatch hissed open. Heat and high intensity metal halide light flooded in, setting everything aglow. The airstairs unfolded with a soft metallic snap. Leila squinted, holding her daughters close. Amal whimpered, burying her face in Leila's coat. Mira just stared, stunned by the shift from night's silence to the onslaught of day.

Mason guided them down the steps and into the strange, oppressive humidity.

Black Suburbans waited inside the hangar. Mason kept a steady hand at Leila's back, Hussein limping behind, as officials moved in—ID checks, paperwork, a brisk handoff to State Department personnel.

"Stay close. We'll be leaving soon. You're safe now," Mason murmured, but the warning never quite left his tone.

There were no lines, no customs hall, no public gaze. Questions came in low, measured voices—efficient, not unkind. An agent in a dark suit confirmed their identities, passports checked with gloved hands and a practiced glance. Another agent held a tablet, camera poised, logging faces and names. Leila answered by rote, her mind drifting in and out of focus, exhaustion closing in.

Hussein's limp was more pronounced now, adrenaline spent and the reality of injury sinking in. He kept his head low, answering murmured questions, accepting the quick, clinical once-over—no medals, no news cameras, just another file for the bureaucracy.

Mira clung to her mother's sleeve, wide-eyed, absorbing the strange quiet—no TVs, no crowds, just the echo of footsteps and the soft click of security boots. Amal pressed herself into Leila's side, small and silent.

Once cleared, they were steered across the hangar to a waiting SUV beside a stack of cargo crates. Inside: black leather, arctic air, the dash aglow with cryptic readouts. A new agent—tall, blank-faced behind dark glasses—offered water and a professional nod. No names, only code words and the faintest suggestion of comfort.

Outside, the hangar doors cracked open just enough for the SUV to slip out. Palm trees and empty taxiways slid by, security vehicles pacing them to the edge of the airfield. The transition was silent, surgical. The city beyond shone surreal—pastel facades and golf courses drifting past as if glimpsed through aquarium glass.

Leila held both girls close, watching their reflections in the window—three faces, one family, unmoored. In the stillness, she felt the distance between what they'd escaped and what awaited them. The ordinary world felt too bright, too quiet, impossibly safe. Old terror lingered, pulsing under her skin, as the SUV carried them away into the strange, uncertain peace of exile.

CHAPTER 6
THE SAFE HOUSE

JANUARY 2001—PALM BEACH, FLORIDA

The motorcade wound through lush boulevards, black Suburbans gliding past hedges dense as fortress ramparts—reminders, for Leila, of how every generation tried to keep chaos at bay. Pink mansions gleamed in the golden early light, iron gates flanked by lions and angels, impervious—or so it seemed—to the storms that history brought to every doorstep. The air hung heavy with humidity, laced with plumeria and honeysuckle. The sweetness almost masked the faint memory of burning tires and checkpoint queues.

Leila sat in the rear seat, her daughters on either side, struggling to reconcile fear and privilege colliding within her. The car's interior thrummed with cold air, its windows tinted to keep the world at bay. Palm trees flickered past—alien, orderly, impossibly green. Her mind still ran on the jagged logic of escape, recalling the rough brick of their courtyard in Ramallah, the morning light catching on chipped tile her grandmother once laid—a small legacy amid the rubble. That memory felt sharper now, juxtaposed against the scent of leather seats.

Amal stared at her shoes, legs curled on the leather seat, jaw set. She wore the same expression Leila's father had when facing border guards decades ago—a silent inheritance of bracing for the unknown. Mira pressed her face to the glass, wide-eyed, as if memorizing every shade of American daylight—the world beyond as unreachable as the stories Leila's mother told of a home that no longer existed. Hussein gazed straight ahead, hands gripping his knees until his knuckles blanched, the silence within him stretching back generations. Leila reached for his hand, but he didn't respond. She recognized her father's old stoicism in that refusal.

At the head of the column, the lead vehicle braked and turned into a gated drive. The wrought iron, gold-tipped gates rolled back with barely a sound. Guards in dark polos and mirrored sunglasses stepped from the gatehouse. Americans, she guessed, from their stance and the way their eyes swept the hedges. Their weapons were discreet but never far from reach—vigilant, in the way of men trained to expect trouble.

Mason stood just outside the main entrance, radio at his shoulder, every line of his body coiled with tension. He watched the family disembark, nodded to his men, then to the local sheriff, a barrel-chested Floridian with a tan like old leather and eyes that had seen too much and trusted too little.

"Let's get them inside," Mason said, voice low and tight.

The moment the doors opened, the secondary sweep—second this week—went to work, ensuring nothing had piggybacked in with the entourage. Two techs moved through the house in silent choreography—sweeping for bugs, checking wireless signals, plugging their own diagnostic devices into outlets. In the kitchen, a third agent opened drawers, flicked through the fridge, scanned for anything out of place. On the pool deck, another swept with a UV torch, examining every drain and vent. Mason shadowed them all, never still—one hand on his weapon, the other swiping through encrypted updates on his phone.

The sheriff and his two deputies bristled at the intrusion, trailing behind, muttering in low voices, code words passing between them. Their uniforms seemed out of place amid the marble and glass.

The safe house was a study in engineered comfort: high ceilings, spotless travertine, echoing halls that drank sound. Rooms arranged for maximum sightlines. Panic buttons in every closet; security cameras nestled in the molding; blackout shutters on silent runners. *Luxury,* Leila thought, *could so easily become another form of confinement.*

Mason caught her glance and offered a nod of reassurance. "Just protocol. We'll be finished in a few minutes. Anything you need—let me know."

He watched as the family shuffled in, dazed and silent, shadows beneath their eyes. He remembered a line from his first ops manual: Never mistake comfort for safety. Looking at the girls, and the stoic weight in Hussein's shoulders—passed down from fathers to sons, a lesson in survival written in posture and silence—he thought of how many times he'd delivered families to houses like this. How few ever truly felt at home.

A sudden chime sounded from the entryway—a motion sensor tripped by a palm frond tumbling across the threshold. Instantly, the nearest guard tensed, hand on weapon, Mason's eyes flicking to the status display. The tension broke as quickly as it came, but the hush that followed felt denser, as if the house itself held its breath.

////

Hussein stood in the grand foyer, feeling the cool air settle on his skin, gaze tracing the chandelier overhead—a spill of crystal and light as ostentatious as any he'd seen in Dubai or Paris. The marble beneath his shoes gleamed, cold and immaculate. On a side table, a bowl of perfect oranges stood untouched beside a vase overflowing with lilies. The effect was surreal: a stage set for a family that wasn't his.

He drifted after the others, unsure where to rest his hands or eyes. He had imagined America as a place of refuge, but this house, with its layers of technology and guards at every exit, was simply another checkpoint, echoing the cycles of displacement he'd inherited. He felt the unreality in every gesture: the click of coded locks, voices dropping as he passed, deputies watching from the hall with flickers of curiosity and suspicion.

He caught sight of himself in a hallway mirror—a man whose suit was still creased with blood and soot, eyes ringed with exhaustion—out of place in a home meant for peace. He remembered his mother's stories of exile, her longing for a homeland she'd never see again, the old embroidered handkerchief she'd carried, each stitch a memory of the land she'd lost. He wondered what kind of exile this would be—wealth as distance, safety as perpetual waiting.

The girls' shoes squeaked on the polished floor. Amal edged closer to Leila, who spoke softly to one of the CIA techs, her English polite, halting, each word measured as if on foreign ground. Mira wandered to the windows, nose pressed to the glass, staring out at the turquoise pool and hedges pruned into spirals.

Hussein wanted to reach for his daughters, to reassure them, but the words would not come. He remembered, unbidden, the night he crossed into Jordan as a boy: border guards in tan uniforms, the taste of dust and fear. There, exile had meant hunger, lines, lost dignity. Here, it meant silence, marble, the cloying scent of lilies—a smell that recalled a funeral in Amman. He wondered if his daughters would come to associate lilies with endings, too.

He looked for Leila, noticing the tightness in her jaw, the false composure in her posture. In that moment, he realized how little he understood his family's pain—how little any man could truly protect those he loved. A flash of self-recrimination: Was it his ambition or his enemies that had brought them here?

A sharp tap on the glass made him flinch. Outside, a pair of guards walked the perimeter, radios clipped to their belts. One of them glanced in, his gaze opaque behind mirrored lenses, unreadable as water.

Hussein turned away. He forced himself to take in the house: the broad, sterile kitchen with its stainless appliances; art hung in perfect symmetry along the halls; the bowl of oranges, untouched. He wondered if anyone ever truly felt safe here.

////

Mira, the eldest, tried to assert a new normalcy, but it felt more like play-acting than life. She turned on the television in the family room, flipping through English channels she barely understood—cartoons, endless news, shopping networks selling baubles that glinted like the chandelier. When no one watched, she traced the pool tiles' patterns with her finger on the cold glass, her reflection rippling beside the water's blue.

Leila, always the center of gravity, tried to fill the house with routine. She made tea on the induction stovetop, its strange controls alien beneath her fingers. She unpacked State Department care packages and wardrobe boxes with size and climate-appropriate clothes, shoes, and personal-care items.

The house had been fully provisioned, including a CIA-contracted resident housekeeper, Maria, who would serve as both maid and chef for the family. Leila heard her humming somewhere behind a closed kitchen door. Each morning, she insisted the girls braid their hair, smoothing out tangles as she did when they were small, her hands moving with the practiced care of a ritual against chaos—each braid echoing the ones her own mother wove before a long journey, a quiet legacy of survival.

Their connection to the outside world was carefully rationed. A secure laptop sat on Hussein's desk, its internet access routed through Agency servers—monitored, logged, restricted to approved sites. Email existed, but every message passed through Langley's filters before transmission, responses delayed by hours or days. Hussein could receive briefings from contacts in Ramallah, but his replies went through handlers first, sanitized of anything that might compromise the operation. When Leila asked about calling her sister in Amman, Mason explained the process: requests submitted in writing, conversations monitored in real time, a forty-eight-hour wait for approval. Even connection was rationed here, another invisible wall around their gilded cage.

Tension simmered between the family and the guards. The Americans—always polite, always distant—never lingered in the same room for long. They rotated shifts with clockwork efficiency. Sometimes, as Leila guided the girls past the living room, she caught a guard's eyes—expression masked behind dark lenses—tracking every movement. His glance lingered a moment too long before returning to a phone with a family photo tucked into the case, an invisible line connecting danger and duty on both sides of the glass.

Leila found herself rising in the middle of the night, padding barefoot to the nursery window, drawn by the faint red pulse of the camera outside. It was not the first time she had lived under unseen eyes; only the accents had changed. The hum of surveillance—cameras in corners, keypads on every door, silent men at every threshold—was its own kind of lullaby, both comfort and threat.

Meals were the hardest. The dining table was long, seating for twelve, but they huddled at one end. Hussein, when he joined them, ate little, distracted by the parade of updates Mason brought from the CIA's secure line. Leila tried to keep up conversation—about school, the colors of the Florida sky, the strange birds outside—but the girls' answers grew shorter each day. Amal shrugged. Mira only nodded.

On the third evening, as a muted system chime startled everyone—just a status check, Mason assured them—Amal asked, "Are we safe here?" Her voice was so small it might have gone unheard. Leila caught it and held her close.

"We are safe," she said, forcing each word into certainty. But in the silence that followed, the only answer was the low hum of the security system arming itself for the night. The clink of forks echoed in the long room. Leila watched the light play on the glassware and the shadows in her daughters' eyes, wondering if she was serving her children as her mother once served her—gestures echoing hands she would never see again.

////

Mason prowled the perimeter in the muggy after-dark hush, boots silent on the stone. He checked each gate, every latch, every corner where shadows gathered behind the hedges. The scent of cut grass hung heavy, mingling with the distant promise of rain. In his ear, the low murmur of the security net—status checks, calls from Langley, the gentle static of a system always alert. The digital feeds flickered on his tablet: thermal sweeps, camera rotations, the ghostly silhouettes of the family moving through their new refuge.

He paused beneath the banyan tree, running a calloused thumb over the ridge of scar tissue above his knee—a souvenir from another life, another op gone sideways. It ached before the rain, before the dawn, whenever the job demanded stillness. On nights like these, he reminded himself he wasn't a young man anymore. He'd lost count of how many safe houses he'd stood guard over, how many families he'd hustled out of burning buildings or quiet, broken apartments. Most of the time, he didn't let himself remember names. Still, some faces lingered, ghostlike, through the years.

Inside, he caught sight of Leila through the glass, standing beneath the kitchen light. She looked up, met his gaze, and for a second Mason recognized the same hunger for certainty, the same flicker of doubt. He looked away, uncomfortable, and turned his attention back to the yard, scanning for anything out of place, wondering if there was ever enough distance to keep the old ghosts out.

Every movement inside was mapped, logged, assessed. Protocol demanded vigilance, but Mason's mind spun in wider circles: the way Leila's hands trembled when she thought no one was watching, the way Hussein barely spoke, the watchful tension in the girls' eyes.

He checked the team's readiness, debriefed with the sheriff's men, reviewed encrypted traffic from the Agency. Yet even as he buried himself in process and repetition, some part of him kept circling back to the truth: safety was never a given. The world had a way of finding you, even behind layers of protection.

On his last circuit, Mason paused at the east fence, a motion-activated floodlight flickering on unexpectedly. For a fleeting moment, the hedges danced in harsh white, revealing nothing but wind and shadows. Still, his heart beat faster, and he lingered until the light finally faded.

He circled the property one last time before dawn, pausing at each checkpoint, feeling the drag of the house and all the secrets it now contained. When his eyelids drooped, he snapped them open. Only when the sky began to pale did he allow himself to rest—just for an hour, eyes open in a pool of blue security light. Already listening for the sound of a door forced open, or a name whispered through the dark.

////

Days bled together beneath the Florida sun, the family moving through a choreography of enforced routine and stifled longing. Each morning, Leila opened the curtains to let in a flood of light that never seemed to touch the chill in the house. The pool shimmered in the backyard, blue and inviting, yet the girls hesitated at its edge, uncertain if it was meant for play or only for show.

On the seventh day, Mira ventured out first. She dipped her toes in the pool and watched the ripples spread until the water went still again. Soon Amal joined, her laughter brief and uncertain, echoing off the white stucco walls. Leila sat on a lounge chair beneath an umbrella, watching her daughters, smiling for their sake, but always glancing at the fence where cameras blinked red above the bougainvillea.

Inside, the house maintained a cold vigilance. Keypads glowed, doors chimed quietly with each rotation of the guard, and every window seemed to frame the world as distant, unreachable. The kitchen filled with the scent of coffee and bread each morning, but the air was always taut, as if even laughter was rationed.

Hussein tried to occupy himself—endless calls with officials and lawyers, briefings with Agency men, and news from Ramallah flashing across his tablet, headlines both familiar and terrifying. He wandered the house at night, unable to sleep, the silence disturbed only by the occasional murmur of a guard's radio outside. Sometimes he would stand at the window, watching the pool shimmer beneath the moonlight, and wonder what kind of father he had become, whether his children would remember this as exile or as the price of peace.

He joined the family for dinner less and less. When he did, his voice was curt, eyes flicking from Leila's forced smile to the salt shaker. One night, as thunder shook the windows, he snapped at Mira for nothing, then retreated to the balcony, rain streaking the glass between them.

Leila found him later, speaking Arabic in a low, desperate tone into the secure phone. She heard "safe," a weak laugh, then silence. When she pressed him—"What did he say?"—he shook his head. "They're safe. For now." He did not come to bed.

////

Monotony became a threat Mason couldn't outpace. Each morning he circled the property, double-checking locks and cameras. On the fourth day, he logged a white sedan that lingered at the curb—a late-model Toyota, windows tinted too dark for Florida code. He noted the plates, ran them through Langley. Nothing came back. The car sat for twenty minutes, then pulled away.

The next morning, it returned.

Mason watched from the security room, coffee going cold in his hand. Same car. Same spot. Same tinted windows reflecting the morning sun like blank eyes. This time it stayed for thirty-seven minutes before sliding back into traffic.

The team grew restless—card games devolved into arguments, drills lost their meaning. Mason watched Leila, searching for cracks, noted Mira's new habit of peering past the blinds. He lay awake, listening for a sound out of place, questioning if even perfect vigilance would matter when trouble arrived.

After the second sedan sighting, he doubled patrols, his team tense and silent. That night, as rain battered the patio, Mason argued quietly with Shaw over protocol. "We're not ghosts," he muttered. "Somebody's watching."

"Could be the press," Shaw offered. "Could be nothing."

"Nothing doesn't come back twice." Mason pulled up the surveillance footage, scrubbed through the timestamps. The sedan had appeared at 9:14 a.m. both days—precise, deliberate. Reconnaissance timing. "Get me eyes on that intersection. I want a spotter there by dawn."

////

Leila clung to routine, but everything had changed. At lunch, she offered sandwiches; Amal only picked at hers, Mira pushed food around her plate. "Why can't we go home?" Amal asked, voice trembling.

"We will," Leila promised, but the words rang hollow.

Maria lived in a small cottage at the edge of the estate, and for Leila, her presence became a lifeline. They sipped coffee at the counter in the quiet hours, exchanging stories in halting English and Spanish—two women from different worlds finding common ground in displacement. Maria showed a photo of her sons in Miami; Leila smiled, showing her daughters' drawings—Mira's city streets rendered in careful pencil, Amal's floating houses drifting through clouds.

That afternoon, the neighbor's dog barked at the fence. Mira froze mid-step. Amal's grip tightened on her bear. Leila closed the blinds, trying to shut out the world, but the world kept pressing in.

////

The house felt coiled and brittle the day Amal slipped outside.

It happened fast: a muffled click, the shriek of the alarm, guards shouting, boots pounding wet grass. Leila dashed out and found Amal huddled against the garden wall, rain plastering her hair to her face, eyes wide with terror at what she'd triggered.

Inside, Mira burst into tears. "She could've been—" She stopped herself, voice breaking on the word she couldn't say.

Hussein arrived, face drawn tight as wire. "What happened?" he demanded.

"She just wanted to see the birds," Leila said, voice steady even as her hands shook around Amal's shoulders. "It's over."

But Hussein's anger flared, finding its target. "This can't happen again. Next time—"

"There won't be a next time," Leila cut in, her own voice sharp for once—sharp enough to stop him cold.

Dinner that night was wordless. Mira flinched when a glass clinked against the table. Hussein pushed his plate away, staring at nothing. Mason increased the rounds, his men moving like shadows past every window.

The house felt smaller afterward, the air thick with things unsaid.

Later, Leila found Hussein sitting alone in the dark office. "We're losing them," she whispered.

He didn't answer. Outside, the rain kept falling.

////

Rain streaked the security monitors, the world outside dissolving into shadows. Mason called a meeting after midnight, voices kept low in the cramped security annex.

Shaw spoke what they all feared: "That car—what if they're not just watching?"

Mason forced a steady answer. "We stay alert. That's all we can do." But doubt gnawed at him—safe houses were never truly safe. He'd learned that lesson in Beirut, again in Karachi, and once more in a basement in Mosul he still dreamed about. He checked the logs again, then paced the length of the annex, breath fogging in the over-cooled air.

Through the window, he caught a glimpse of Leila in the kitchen, lights off, just a silhouette against the glow of the security panel. The girls' laughter—so rare now—had vanished entirely. Mason wondered when he'd stopped being a person and become a system—monitoring, calculating, running scenarios for people whose names he'd eventually have to forget.

His mother's voice drifted up from memory, answering his childhood complaint about his eleven o'clock curfew: Because nothing good happens after eleven o'clock. He checked his watch. Two-fifteen a.m. She'd been right about that, at least.

////

Each Tuesday, groceries were delivered, plastic bags counted, guards watching every exchange. Agency cars came and went, suits conferring briefly with Mason or Hussein in hushed tones. Neighbors watched from behind hedges; a misplaced package on the doorstep sent a deputy running to the drive.

Even in the shower, Leila felt exposed, privacy a distant memory. She rehearsed answers to Mason's questions—any new dreams, any fears—resenting the intrusion but conceding its necessity.

The fruit bowl remained full and untouched, a silent ledger of their longing.

Each night, rituals tightened: windows checked, alarms set, the family gathered for a movie no one really watched. Leila brushed the girls' hair, whispered old prayers in Arabic. Hussein stood in the hall, listening to nothing. Mason paused at each window, watching reflections flicker in the glass.

Rain began to fall—a gentle percussion on the tile roof, soft enough to nearly mask the thrum of distant traffic. In that moment, the safe house felt suspended outside of time: a bubble of light and order in a world full of chaos.

No alarms sounded. No shadows moved beyond the fence. The night held.

A neighbor's porch light blinked off. In the silence, Leila imagined the world outside—a dog barking somewhere, rain tapering off, the pool still and bright beneath the cameras' red eyes.

Inside, every heart waited, breath held, as the hush before dawn pressed in—and somewhere out on the street, in the blue-gray light of another Florida morning, a white sedan with tinted windows would be deciding whether to return.

CHAPTER 7

THE SEARCH FOR HUSSEIN

JANUARY 2001—KHAN YUNIS, GAZA

Hamza's hunt for Hussein began with a single encrypted call to Hamas leadership in Doha. That call rippled upward through networks that spanned continents—reaching allies with resources purpose-built to counter the CIA's dominance in surveillance and stealth. Within hours, satellites repositioned, servers awakened across three time zones, and the quiet machinery of the search ground into motion.

On the night of the Muqataa rescue, Qatar State Security observed something impossible: the classified Gravity Tripwire sensor constellation registered a negative mass signature west of Ramallah, directly over Haifa FOB Military Base. The anomaly lasted thirty-one seconds—approximately fifty-eight tons accelerating upward. No transponder. No primary radar return. No infrared bloom.

A ghost, lifting into the sky.

Forty minutes later, deep in a tunnel beneath Khan Yunis, Hamza's secure tablet chirped. The message was three words, rudimentary and lethal in its implication:

Left Haifa FOB. Heavy. West.

That was enough to prime the network into focused action.

The Qatari-Chinese-Russian ribbon of surveillance capability unfolded westward across a rolling fourteen-hour window. Commercial satellites. Military sensors. Electro-optical arrays. Synthetic Aperture Radar. The data streamed in fragments, each piece meaningless alone, devastating in aggregate.

A Roscosmos Earth Observation pass caught a white Gulfstream on the transient ramp at Rota, Spain—refueling in the predawn dark.

Later, a Chinese SAR-optical pair tracked the same airframe cruising high and fast west of the Azores, its Doppler signature and Radar Cross Section consistent with a business jet in high-Mach cruise.

A final Russian SAR pass found nothing—only a fresh condensation trail near fifty thousand feet, dissolving into Atlantic haze.

Extrapolated groundspeeds and fuel calculations left one prime recovery arc: the Florida coastline between Cape Canaveral and Miami.

Hamza didn't need an address. Not yet. He needed the city that was sheltering his President.

////

He sat alone in a windowless room beneath Gaza City, the only light the blue flicker of three monitors—an artificial dawn in a world shuttered against daylight and memory. Cigarette smoke drifted above the keyboard as his fingers moved with reptilian precision: commands entered, addresses triangulated, proxies discarded. The low hum of hard drives punctuated by the slow drip of a leaking pipe deepened the cave-like hush.

Each keystroke drew him deeper into a digital underworld where borders dissolved and threats were written in code. He was searching for Hussein's breadcrumbs behind the State Department's firewall. The early leads had been simple—leaked manifests, customs anomalies, an encrypted message intercepted on a diplomatic relay in Frankfurt. The American system was good, but nothing was perfect. There was always a slip: a timestamp out of place, a misspelled name, a nervous official's mistake.

Every network had a weakness. Hamza searched for these fault lines the way his father once listened at doors—trusting silence more than words.

Then the breach died mid-frame. Feeds frozen. Pixels bleeding into static.

The Americans had found the hole and sealed it.

Hamza exhaled smoke and let the silence settle. Code had taken him as far as it could. To finish the hunt, he needed men who lived in shadows, not bandwidth.

He typed a single line to Timur: *Trail ends in Florida. How's your Spanish?*

The reply came minutes later: *Leave it to Havana.*

Hamza shut down the terminal. The search was shifting from circuits to streets—from data to human eyes that could smell new money and follow it to a gate.

The hunt was alive again.

////

They didn't know the airport, only the arc. A white Gulfstream had vanished somewhere between Cape Canaveral and Miami—two hundred miles of coastline, dozens of airfields. Somewhere inside that corridor, Hussein was breathing American air.

Timur called Havana.

El Jefe answered from a veranda that smelled of salt and rum, the Caribbean night alive with insects and distant music. "You only call when you've lost something," he said.

"Not lost," Timur replied. "Hidden. A jet came in two nights ago, somewhere between Miami and Canaveral. The man on board is under CIA protection."

A long pause. The hum of insects. A faint rhythm drifting up from the street.

"So, it's Florida again," El Jefe said at last. "My people know the area well."

Timur gave what little he had: the timing of a contrail, a white Gulfstream, the silence where radar should have been. "We need eyes," he said. "Untraceable eyes."

El Jefe liked that. "Then we'll use the trades that never sleep—fuel men, landscapers, delivery drivers. The people who see without being seen." He began to list them: Jorge, a ramp worker at Pompano who still logged fuel by hand; Reina, who ran hedge crews along Royal Fern Road; Luis, a pool technician who timestamped every service call; Cesar, a food courier who signed false names and forgot nothing.

"There's money," Timur said. "A bounty. Small, immediate. Cash only."

"Bounties make noise," El Jefe replied. "Whispers work better. We'll pay in whispers."

By midnight, the net was forming. A question murmured at a marina bar. A folded bill under a coffee cup. A rumor seeded in the right ears—talk of a sheriff's stakeout in Palm Beach. The rules were simple: ask without asking, watch without being watched. If a badge appeared, look away and report later.

Small details began to surface. Jorge mentioned an unlogged refuel paid in cash by a man with a clipped accent. Reina said her crew had been waved off an estate by deputies parked out front. Luis noticed a heater call at 3:56 a.m. in that same postal zone. Cesar remembered a grocery slip signed by M. Abadi.

Individually, the pieces meant nothing.

Together, they began to hum.

"Keep them hungry," Timur said.

"Hungry is easy," El Jefe replied. "The trick is paying them just enough to stay quiet once they've talked."

He dispersed the cash by hand: envelopes under napkins, tucked into fuel receipts, slid across pews at the harbor church. No wires. No records. Only rumor, paid for in cash.

Timur warned him. "Agency detail. They'll notice movement."

"We're not soldiers," El Jefe said. "We listen. The Americans never listen to the ones who cut their lawns."

The line went dead.

////

The house at 1120 North Ocean Way sat two blocks east of County Road, just south of the inlet where Palm Beach curved. Locals still called the stretch Perfume Row—money without introduction.

Hamza spent the following hours folding maps of networks into new shapes. He traced the contractor's digital hinterland—staging machines that should have been invisible, diagnostic channels that reported camera health more faithfully than any human log. He listened to machine chatter, to heartbeat checks that meant nothing to busy operators and everything to listeners. Where a team in Virginia saw routine traffic, he heard cadence and pause; where a vendor's backup system spoke to a Brussels data center, he heard the same password patterns recycling like old tides.

But the Americans' firewall was built for siege, not infiltration. Hamza preferred the quiet kind—the slow corrosion that came from within.

He replayed captured traffic from a week earlier: a grocery supplier's invoice, harmless on its face, but with an attached metadata string that revealed a backend link to the Agency's facilities contractor. The vendor handled "routine maintenance" at several safe houses.

He mapped the contractor's network, tracing an unsecured staging server used for remote sensor diagnostics. One subroutine checked camera voltages every hour—reporting to a data cluster in Quantico. Hamza inserted a man-in-the-middle script, a whisper between systems, telling the cameras what they wanted to hear. A feed could loop for ten seconds before any alert triggered.

Ten seconds was forever.

Then he reached deeper. A human-rights NGO in Brussels—legitimate, underfunded—shared its data center with a U.S. subcontractor providing "cloud redundancy" for domestic security clients. The NGO's login protocols were weak; passwords recycled like bad habits. From there, Hamza ghosted through the redundancy pipeline, riding encrypted packets into the safe house's perimeter network, invisible among backups and log checks.

The breach didn't come as a flash. It came as stillness.

Screens froze, then resumed. In Virginia, a technician logged an "anomaly" and cleared it without a second thought. In Palm Beach, Hamza's shadow code awakened. Every motion sensor, every thermal camera, every microphone now mirrored to him—a twin heartbeat feeding through fiber and darkness.

He leaned back, savoring the elegant precision of his work. By turning the enemy's own systems against them, he had left no trace for routine security sweeps to uncover.

The house was his now—its alarms, its whispers, its secrets.

And like his father once said: *The best listener is the one they never know is listening.*

CHAPTER 8
LIFE IN THE SPIDER'S WEB

JANUARY 2001—GAZA CITY

Hamza sipped cold coffee, the bitter taste anchoring him as his eyes burned from the monitor's blue glow. The hum of electronics mingled with his father's voice, rising unbidden from memory: *Even a wall has an ear, but every ear can be fooled.* Some lessons survived by changing shape. This one had become his creed.

A new data set scrolled across his screen: recent purchases in Palm Beach, cell towers pinged by unfamiliar numbers, a food delivery signed to a false name. He typed a command and watched a camera feed flicker to life—a blue SUV rolling past the safe house, pausing a beat too long at the corner. On the feed, a child's voice echoed from the front yard, laughter carried off-screen and vanishing into static.

Hamza's heart drummed—half fear, half triumph. In this electric maze, the Mahfouz family hid, thinking themselves safe behind American walls and Agency protocols. But the web was closing, strand by invisible strand. Hamza was both spider and shadow, a legacy vibrating through his nerves in the blue-lit dark.

////

JANUARY 2001—ODESSA, UKRAINE

Timur Mikhaylov savored the hunt, but the moment prey sensed it was being watched—that was the flavor he chased, a dryness at the back of his throat that no vodka could cure. He lounged in his Odessa office above a rain-dark wharf, desk cluttered with antique weapons and a chipped mobile phone blinking with encrypted alerts. His left hand traced the white scar along his jaw—a Chechen ambush, nearly fatal, still tingling on stormy days.

Outside, sodium lamps spilled across greasy glass, shadows crawling over warped floorboards and curtains gone gray with dust. Americans and their Arab ally—children playing in a world built for predators. Timur had been a professional killer before these boys could speak. They hid behind encrypted phones, softened by comfort, forgetting that real power belonged not to machines but to men who could turn data into blood.

There were no new games. Only new players.

Hamza's updates amused him. The Palestinian was clever but volatile—a blade that could cut both ways. Timur fed him tidbits, just enough to keep him running, always circling the trap. His own network predated the digital syndicates; he dealt in weapons, secrets, leverage—clients who ruled countries or ruined them. Every transaction was a test: who paid, who betrayed, who survived the next turn of the wheel.

Life was counted out in currencies of betrayal: a stack of cash, a faded photograph, a passport stained with blood.

And then there was the UN, the holy grail of leaks. A sieve masquerading as an institution, its corridors bleeding secrets faster than they could be classified. What was whispered in Geneva by morning surfaced in Damascus by nightfall.

A courier entered—soft shoes, eyes darting—leaving a coded note and a bottle of vodka cold from the street. Timur ignored both. His mind was on Hamza's images: American SUVs, a guarded house, a still frame of Mason half-obscured by cap and sunglasses.

"Old soldier," Timur muttered, feeling a flicker of respect as his knuckles rapped once on the glass. "But tired." The weary recognized their own.

He messaged his Miami contact: *Eyes on the property. Push local asset. Make them sweat.*

He remembered the Americans' offer: money, a passport, the illusion of safety. He'd taken the cash and left two bodies behind—a lesson written in red. In the end, every system could be broken if you knew where to apply pressure.

His hand paused on a photograph tucked in the desk drawer—his daughter, a green hairclip still clipped to the corner, her smile bright against the gray of another life. Briefly, loss bore down: violence and love, inseparable as rain on steel, haunting every choice.

The rain intensified, drumming against the window. Timur poured a shot of vodka and waited, letting the sound fill the space where memory tried to intrude.

////

Sheriff Bobby Perkins sat in his office, Florida sun blazing through the blinds, sweat prickling along his back despite the AC. The latest report sat on his desk:

Suspicious vehicle, foreign plates. Multiple neighbor calls about the 'new family' on Royal Fern Road. One report of drones overhead at night.

He scrolled through texts from the mayor, the state police, even a "check-in" from a Washington number he didn't recognize. The pressure mounted with every ping—calls from a Miami paper sniffing for leaks. On the street, neighbors glanced over hedges, lawn mowers pausing as unmarked cars rolled by.

Someone was watching. Someone else was watching them.

He sent uniforms past the safe house nightly, more for show than substance. Sometimes he drove by himself, window down, country music drifting in the heat, the scent of cut grass sharp and sour. The house always looked too quiet—the kind of quiet that preceded something breaking.

Out front, a girl's tricycle lay abandoned, plastic wheels upturned. A child's world, paused.

Innocence, always the first to falter.

Later, in the squad room, Perkins overheard a deputy mutter, "All these suits in town, makes my skin crawl." Perkins said nothing. Outside, a mosquito buzzed at the window, persistent as worry—pressing in, old as the badge on his chest. He stared at the bulletin board, crowded with grainy surveillance photos, coffee rings blurring the edges of the map.

////

Inside the safe house, the Mahfouz family tried to settle into routine, not knowing their every habit created a pattern—a trail for those who knew how to look. Every comfort was a potential clue.

Leila wrote shopping lists, leaving them on the counter. Mason's team rotated shifts, signing in and out, signatures as neat as soldiers' grave markers. Mira and Amal played in the yard, laughter caught by a security camera's microphone, their faces saved forever on a distant server. The girls' drawings—homes, men in uniforms, a blue pool—decorated the fridge, innocent signals for any watching eye.

Each detail a loose thread, waiting to be pulled.

Tuesdays brought a grocery delivery. The driver always lingered, peering through the gate before being waved away. Thursdays, Maria the housekeeper arrived, her car's license plate caught by every neighbor's camera. She called her sister during breaks, her Spanish overlapping with the digital static in Hamza's feed.

Hussein kept to himself, rising early to walk the garden, eyes tracing the sky as if searching for a flaw in the grid. At breakfast, he spoke softly, words trailing off as he noticed the security panel blinking. At night, he sat by the pool, Agency tablet in hand, pausing mid-message to his uncle, aware now that his world was measured in passwords and silent watchers.

Privacy, once a birthright, now felt like a relic.

Leila felt the walls pressing in. She froze sometimes, hand stilled over a pot of tea or a child's drawing, sensing unseen eyes on her skin. She caught the guards' radios crackle, Mason's glances at the monitors. In the old world, secrets traveled by word of mouth; now every comfort was a data point, every ritual exposed.

The old ways—stories, faith, routine—felt brittle, dissolving under the digital glare.

////

At dusk, Palm Beach looked ordinary: sprinklers ticking, golden haze across tennis courts, neighbors grilling steaks, cicadas tuning for the night. But beneath the surface, nerves hummed. A realtor gossiped about the "diplomats" on Royal Fern Road. A handyman filmed a guard installing cameras, uploading the clip with a hashtag. A kid on a bike circled the block twice, then vanished into shadow.

A mile away, Hamza logged into a new proxy, listening to police radio chatter:

...possible 10-85, foreign national...

...dispatch, check with Agency detail...

...extra patrol on Royal Fern Road...

He let the voices merge with the grainy feed from a traffic camera. He watched Mason pacing the yard, a restless shadow, the pool reflecting the bruised sky. The girls chased a stray cat, its tail flicking out of frame, before Leila called them in as porch lights snapped on—the click and whir of new locks echoing through the feed.

A Miami feed showed Timur's courier—raincoat, nondescript—passing off a thumb drive behind a strip mall. Information traded for survival, like a poker chip sliding across a whiskey-stained table. Hamza smiled: so many layers of protection, and the family exposed by routine.

Safety itself had become a signal, and he savored the irony.

He checked logs from a local ISP. A new account had accessed encrypted messaging from a nearby tower—Mason's team, maybe, but the timing was off. Hamza flagged it, rerouted the logs to Timur. The net drew tighter, each digital line another footfall in the dark.

////

In Odessa, Timur sipped strong tea and watched rain streak the glass, neon bleeding across the city's oily surface. He read Hamza's updates with satisfaction, tracing webs of contact, mapping small lives inside the American enclave. Photographs crowded his desk—Agency men, local police, the Mahfouz girls in sunlight. A fingerprint smudged the corner of one photo; the shine of Mason's glasses caught the camera's eye.

He called his Miami number.

"Status?"

"They're nervous," came the reply. "Sheriff's poking around. The Feds too. We may need to move."

"Not yet," Timur said. "Let them sweat."

He hung up, tea cooling at his elbow, and lingered on his daughter's image—a hairclip, a crooked smile, the memory of a lullaby barely audible through the rain. Her absence was a blade, kept sharp. Some legacies were chosen; others were carved into you.

He messaged Hamza: *Increase surveillance. Exploit the child's device. Leverage the housekeeper's family.*

He leaned back, listening to the rain and the harbor's distant clang. He imagined the Americans behind their fortress, surrounded by cameras and alarms. Technology had become their cage—its comfort a liability handed down like family silver, locking them in as surely as any cell.

////

Inside the safe house, technology pressed against the family like a second skin—cameras in every room but the bedrooms, sensors in doorways, microphones in the kitchen. The girls watched cartoons, the digital feed lagging a second behind their laughter. Leila scrolled headlines on a tablet, blue light bleaching her face. Mason cycled through feeds, headset crackling with codes, always looking for a gap—a corner the system could not see.

Every movement—brushing teeth, making tea, playing by the pool—became a performance. Even the girls noticed.

"Why are there so many cameras?" Mira asked, voice small, tracing the red lens with her finger.

"To keep us safe," Leila answered, feeling the answer settle in her chest and stay.. She dreamed of faceless men behind mirrored glass, woke to the whine of AC, the blink of the alarm, the constant sense of being measured.

Old fears, recast in blue light.

Mason trusted the system—mostly. But sometimes, in the flicker of monitors, he wondered: Were they safer for all this vigilance? Or just more visible? The doubts came in his father's voice, steady and grim: Don't get comfortable. Don't trust the walls.

At the edge of the living room, one of Mira's drawings—a house ringed by stick-figure guards, a small family in the center—fluttered off the fridge and drifted to the floor.

////

Rain fell in slow sheets over Palm Beach, the world outside bent beneath yellow streetlights. Somewhere, a drone buzzed, its shadow passing over wet pavement. A police radio crackled, static echoing off concrete. In a neighboring house, a television flickered blue against a curtained window, voices blurring.

Hamza watched the feeds, mind fusing numbers and faces, code and flesh. The safe house was another node—mapped, infiltrated, fragile. Cameras had become his eyes, microphones his ears, the world a board of shifting shadows. He moved through it unseen, lessons inherited in silence and tension humming through every wire.

For Timur, surveillance was doctrine—a slow tightening, a patient weave. The Americans doubled patrols. The sheriff circled. The family huddled closer beneath the sterile light of their machines.

The siege, like memory, pressed in from all sides.

////

Sheriff Perkins woke to pounding at his door. A deputy, pale-faced, handed him a printout—security footage showing a masked figure loitering at the gate, moving with a soldier's purpose. Perkins called the state police, then the FBI, then finally Mason.

"We've got a problem," Perkins said. "It's coming from every direction."

Mason listened, muscles coiled. He hung up, moved through the house, checked doors, woke the guards. At the threshold of the girls' room, he paused—Leila asleep, hand on Amal's back, Mira curled around her pillow.

He whispered an old Marine mantra: *Stay ready. Stay small. Don't get comfortable.* Words passed down, recited like a ward against the dark.

In Miami, Timur received the footage and smiled.

In Odessa, he raised a glass to the storm, rain tapping at the window like a code.

In his cave beneath Gaza, Hamza watched the feeds, heart thrumming with anticipation.

The web was complete.

Now they only had to wait for it to close.

CHAPTER 9

INTERROGATIONS

JANUARY 2001—PALM BEACH

On the eighth day, a Langley interrogator arrived. The calm broke—quietly.

Over lunch with Hussein and Mason, Sloane didn't introduce himself as anything but "Sloane." No titles. No agency affiliation. Just a name, offered like a card laid face-down on the table.

"One rule," he said, voice even. "We don't trade speeches. We trade facts."

Hussein looked at the glass of water, then past it. "Facts can be arranged."

"Good," Sloane said. "So can mercy."

////

Every day, Hussein sat with Sloane in a makeshift chamber the Agency men had built from an office—bare table, two chairs, camera on a tripod, a lingering trace of antiseptic in the air. The red recording light blinked with patient, unblinking rhythm. Sweat trickled down Hussein's back as a blade of sunlight slashed across the tile floor.

The questions came in careful English, never shouted but relentless, pressing with the slow tidal force of bureaucracy. Names. Dates.

Affiliations. What did he know? What did he suspect? How could he prove his story? The ritual of suspicion—old as history—played out in another tongue.

He answered as best he could, his voice alien to his own ears. He spoke of Ramallah's streets, names on lists, a man once glimpsed in a café who now appeared in Agency photographs. The more he spoke, the more he dissolved—a shadow on the wall, a voice untethered from himself.

They asked about his childhood, and suddenly he was not a grown man in Florida but a boy beneath the fig tree in Nablus, his father's hands rough but steady as he trimmed the branches, the air dense with sap and sun-warmed earth.

Always listen, Hussein, but never trust the first thing you hear, his father would say, voice gravelly with worry. The memory ached—comfort and loss braided together, a thread binding generations.

A scrape of chair against tile jolted him back. The camera's red light glared. Sloane pressed for details, pen scratching, face blank—expressionless, almost inhuman.

The memory flickered, replaced by the crack of gunfire down the street, his mother's voice screaming, the sky gone dark with smoke and fear. He stumbled through his answers. Sometimes a question triggered a scent—hospital disinfectant, or the sharp flavor of mint from his mother's garden—reminding him he belonged to neither world, present nor past.

Even his senses were haunted, every element an echo of inheritance.

When the sessions ended, Hussein stumbled from the room as if waking from a fever. He stood for long minutes at the window, looking out at the pool and the bougainvillea, trying to gather the fragments of himself. Sometimes he pressed his palm to his chest, just to feel his own heartbeat.

////

Leila watched her husband disappear in increments—first from their meals, then from conversations, finally from silence itself. Each evening, he returned from the Americans with eyes glazed and distant, shoulders hunched like a man bracing for another blow. He answered her questions with gentle, practiced evasions.

"It's nothing," he would say. "Just questions. They want to be sure."

But she recognized the look in his eyes. She'd seen it before—years ago, when Israeli soldiers raided her father's house and made the men kneel in dust. She'd seen it in the hospital when her brother came home broken and speechless. She knew what it meant to be questioned not as a person, but as a possibility, a threat, a problem to be solved.

The cycle turned, the pain recycled—new uniforms, same legacy.

She tried to reach him. She prepared the foods he loved, played the songs of their youth, told stories to the girls loud enough that Hussein might hear and be drawn back to them. Some days he would sit nearby, holding a mug of coffee and staring at the steam, but most nights he was already gone—lost in a landscape of doubts and memories.

Once, she nearly called his name aloud but stopped, afraid of what might echo back.

Her ritual became letter-writing after the house fell quiet. She would sit in the darkened kitchen and write letters she never intended to send—letters to her mother, to her husband, to herself. The feel of paper beneath her palm, the faint scrape of her pen, grounded her. She wrote of small victories: a moment of laughter with Mira, a new English word Amal learned, the way Mason brought fresh mint from the market. She wrote of her fears too, and the way the house felt like a ship adrift, cut loose from any familiar shore.

Her mother had taught her this ritual, passed down as survival—write to remember, write to endure.

In those moments, she remembered her father—his wide hands, deep laugh, the scent of tobacco and olive oil that lingered long after he was gone. She remembered how he survived interrogations by holding to small truths: a bird's name, a poem half-remembered, the way dusk light filtered through the kitchen window. She wondered if Hussein could find such anchors, or if the storm inside him would carry them all away.

////

Mason paced the length of the hall outside the office, boots whispering on the tile. The low murmur of voices seeped under the door—clipped questions, careful non-answers. He thought of other safe houses, other families, vows that had withered in silence. Each memory pressed on him like a debt never settled.

When Hussein emerged, Mason tried to meet his gaze, to offer a nod—respect, understanding. But Hussein's eyes slid past him, seeing only the next threshold, the next round of questions. Mason wanted to say something—anything—to ease his suffering, to remind him there were still people in the world who could be trusted.

Instead, another call from Langley.

The handler's voice was colder than usual. "We need results, Mason. No more delays. If he can't give us what we need, we may have to consider alternatives. Remind him of the stakes."

Mason stared at the phone after the call, the ache in his knee flaring, a hollowness in his chest. Alternatives. He pictured a list in a gray folder back at Langley—a row of options in sterile type: limit contact, delay visits, reassign custody, shift to quieter jurisdiction where questions cost more than answers.

He found Leila staring out the window, hands clenched around a cup of tea. The two stood in silence, the hum of the refrigerator the only sound.

Finally, Mason cleared his throat. "Mrs. Mahfouz, I know this is hard. I want you to understand something about how this works. The system—it's supposed to protect people. But sometimes it feels like... like it's just another way to keep everyone in their place."

Leila looked at him, eyes sharp and shining in the dim light. "You say protect. But I only see my husband breaking, and my daughters losing faith. Who is this system for?"

Mason hesitated, searching for words he could believe. "Some days, I'm not sure anymore."

A parakeet screeched outside, the sound shrill and out of place in the tension.

////

The interrogations continued. Each session scraped deeper, eroding what remained of Hussein's confidence. Flashbacks haunted him: his father at the checkpoint, refusing to bow; his mother weeping in the garden, hands muddy, pride broken. A gunshot in the alley. The way he learned, too early, to lie without flinching—the craft of survival handed down from one generation's suffering to the next.

Between interviews, Hussein found himself trapped in loops of memory and self-doubt. He watched his daughters play in the yard, their voices rising in a fragile, hopeful song, and wondered what scars he was giving them. He caught himself recalling his father's warnings: *What you inherit, you pass on.*

Was this what he would give his girls? Fear, suspicion, silence?

He drifted through the days, sleepwalking, counting the hours until he was called again.

Leila tried to save him, to hold on to him with stories and food and gentle hands. She braided Amal's hair by the window, telling tales of wild horses and green hills, willing Hussein to come and sit beside them. But his footsteps faded, his shadow shrank, his presence dissolved.

One evening, Leila found him in the darkened office, head in his hands. She knelt beside him, pressing her cheek to his shoulder. For a long time, neither spoke.

At last, Hussein whispered, "Do you think I am weak? That I am failing you?"

Leila shook her head. "You are surviving, my love. And because you are strong, so are we."

Mason passed by the open door, paused, then moved on—caught between the job and the thing the job was supposed to protect.

////

The twelfth day began like the others: humid, silent, heavy with expectation. But by afternoon, Mason sensed a shift—an edge in the way the Americans moved, a quiet urgency in the way doors closed.

When Hussein was brought into the interrogation room, Sloane was waiting with a file. The air conditioning hummed. A cup of untouched tea cooled by Hussein's hand.

Sloane slid a photograph across the table—grainy, streaked with rain.

"Take a look at this," he said.

Hussein stared. The image was rough—half-obscured by the crowd, but the setting was unmistakable: Al-Saraya Square, Gaza City. A figure—body limp, face half-turned—hung from a construction crane. The sense memory of the place rushed over him: broken pavement, the smell of oppressive heat and salt air, the echo of old protests and market noise.

He pressed his fist to his lips.

"I can't see who it is," he managed. "But I know where. That's Al-Saraya."

Sloane's voice softened a shade. "It's your cousin. Youssef Mahfouz. They found him at dawn."

The news landed in Hussein's chest where such things accumulate. His cousin. He'd grown up with Youssef, lost touch in the last years, but the Mahfouz name threaded through Gaza's alleys and across borders—family was everywhere and nowhere. Now one more was gone.

Sloane didn't let the silence linger.

"There's a price on you now, Hussein. On your wife, your daughters, your mother in Amman. Even your distant cousins. This"—he tapped the photo—"is the cost of silence. We can protect you. Every one of yours. But only if you give us something of value."

Hussein didn't answer. His jaw worked. His eyes blurred.

"I need... a break," he said finally, voice hollow. "I need to see my wife."

////

He found Leila by the pool, watching the girls try to float a toy boat across the blue water. He told her everything—the picture, the threat, the Americans' offer. At first, she was silent, hands clutched at her sides.

"They killed Youssef?" she whispered.

"In Al-Saraya. They're warning me. Us."

He sat beside her, head in his hands. "They want information. More. In return, they offer protection for our families."

Leila's voice was thin but steady. "If they can keep the girls safe, you must do it, Hussein. There's nothing left in Gaza for us now."

"But what if they lie? What if I give them more, and it's not enough?"

Leila squeezed his hand, her eyes shining. "Then you make them promise. In front of God and everyone. For your family—for ours."

Mason was waiting at the patio's edge. "Sorry, Hussein. They need you back."

////

In the interrogation room, Sloane leaned in.

"We can't protect your family if you don't trust us. Give us something, and I'll get you the guarantees. But you have to prove it's worth it."

Hussein shook his head. "Not you. Someone who can actually make it happen. I want to speak to someone whose word means something."

Sloane hesitated. "That's not how it works."

"Then I'll wait," Hussein said quietly. He folded his hands, the small gesture of a man who had survived worse silences. "But I'll give you this much. You've asked me where the money comes from—the real money. Not the suitcases or couriers, the money that moves through banks no one sees."

He paused, meeting Sloane's eyes.

"It starts in New York. A man named Ian Karim."

Sloane blinked. "That's a Middle Eastern name."

"He was born Ibrahim Karim," Hussein said. "His parents came from Haifa in the fifties. He reinvented himself at Princeton—new accent, new passport, new morals. He runs a philanthropic empire now, Karim Global Initiatives. Speaks about education and refugee aid, writes op-eds about coexistence. The press calls him a 'bridge-builder.'"

Mason leaned forward, wary. "You're saying he's funding Hamas?"

"I'm saying he's funding himself through Hamas," Hussein replied. "He routes the money through charities—faith-based, American, all properly audited. Ninety percent of every dollar feeds children or builds clinics. The last ten percent disappears. That ten percent buys power. It buys quiet men in Gaza who will owe him favors when the war ends."

Sloane opened a notepad but didn't write. "You've seen this happen?"

"I've seen the ledgers," Hussein said. "I translated them for Hamza's quartermaster two years ago. Karim's name was never written—only a mark: an *I* curved through a *K*. But everyone knew. He used intermediaries in Zurich and Doha to move the transfers. The pattern was elegant: relief one day, rockets the next. He's made himself indispensable to both sides. To Hamas because he funds their operations, and to Washington because he funds their conferences."

The room settled into the long, low hum of air conditioning. Mason watched a bead of sweat slide down Hussein's temple and fall onto the table.

Sloane finally spoke. "If this is true, it's the kind of allegation that burns governments. You're accusing an American philanthropist of funding terrorism."

Hussein's gaze hardened. "You think this is only about money? Ian Karim built my campaign from dust. He poured millions through front charities—media training, polling, even the armored SUVs that brought me to the polls. Without him, there would have been no election, only another coup dressed as democracy."

He leaned forward, voice low and bitter. "He did not do it for peace. He did it to own us. To own me. Every photograph, every handshake with a Western diplomat—it was his proof of concept. He could build a president. A Palestinian president. And if he could build one, he could control the next."

Sloane frowned. "You're saying he financed your campaign personally?"

"I'm saying he financed the illusion of freedom," Hussein replied. "He has the power to anoint whoever sits in this chair next. He funds polling groups in Ramallah, pays media consultants in Washington, keeps both sides believing they're his beneficiaries. And every time the war drags on, his contracts grow. The chaos is his investment."

Mason felt the chill of understanding. "You're telling us the man who sold Washington on humanitarian reform is the same man arming Hamas and choosing who governs the Territories."

"Yes," Hussein said. "He funds both the cage and the key. He believes he can buy redemption by controlling who bleeds."

He pushed back from the table, exhaustion edging his voice. "I'm telling you a truth you can verify. Every last Friday of the month, he meets a courier at a diner in Lower Manhattan. Corner booth, back to the window. The envelope always comes under the sugar tray. Ian Karim never opens it until the man is gone."

"The courier's name is Kell—British passport, Jordanian mother. Find him and you'll have your proof."

He looked up, voice tightening. "Bring me your senior leadership. They are the only ones who can stop him. I'll give them the account codes, the receipts, the recordings. But I want their signatures that my family will live to see daylight again."

"You're speaking to someone who can," Sloane said.

"No," Hussein said. "You can ask. You can record. You can recommend. But you can't promise. I want the men who can. The Director of Central Intelligence. The Secretary of State. You bring them here, and I will give them everything."

Sloane gave a small, incredulous laugh. "You're asking for the top floor of Langley and Foggy Bottom. You know how impossible that is?"

"I know what they'll lose if they don't," Hussein said. "Because this is not about Gaza anymore. Ian Karim has bought access—he launders money and reputation. His network touches senators, think tanks, maybe even campaign committees. You let that grow another year and you won't be able to pull it up by the roots. I can give you the evidence, but only to men who can act without asking permission."

Mason glanced at Sloane. "He might not be bluffing. Treasury flagged two transfers last month under Hands for Tomorrow Foundation—identical pattern to what he's describing."

Sloane exhaled through his nose. "Christ."

Hussein leaned forward, hands flat on the table. "You want to protect your country? Start with the ones who've already sold it."

Sloane turned to Mason. "Get me a line to Langley. Secure. Tell them we need escalation—Director level. I'll handle the rest."

////

That night, the safe house thrummed with activity—extra guards at the gate, more radios than usual. Leila sensed it instantly, the vibration of decisions made somewhere above her life. She found Hussein by the pool, the night air heavy with the smell of chlorine and rain.

"They're bringing someone," he said without turning. "Someone who can make promises."

"Do you trust them?" she asked.

"No. But I trust what they fear."

////

By morning, the overnight storm had moved inland. A convoy of black SUVs rolled through the gates. Mason watched from the porch as men in suits and earpieces filed into the annex. The air felt denser, oxygen measured in permissions. He'd seen briefings like this only in war zones, when diplomacy arrived wrapped in command authority.

They brought Hussein into the main room—bare table, two flags behind it, camera waiting. He looked thinner, but steady.

A tall man entered first, gray-haired, immaculate. "Mr. Mahfouz," he said, extending his hand. "Richard Keller, Director of Central Intelligence."

Behind him came another figure, younger, smooth-voiced, the

practiced fatigue of politics in his eyes. "James Whitman, Secretary of State." He offered his hand briefly, a gesture that suggested both courtesy and calculation.

Sloane and Mason stood aside as the two Americans took seats opposite Hussein.

Keller spoke first. "Mr. Mahfouz, the United States takes your family's safety seriously. You have our guarantee—full protection for every Mahfouz you name, immediate relocation if necessary. The Secretary is here to confirm it."

Whitman nodded. "If your information prevents further bloodshed, I will personally oversee your case. And I will move to reopen the humanitarian-aid channels your cousin once managed. That's a matter of record."

Hussein's eyes glistened. "Then you'll have all that I know. But I want your word—on paper, signed—before I continue."

Keller glanced at Whitman, then gave a single nod to an aide, who stepped out.

"You'll have it," the Director said. "Now tell us about Ian Karim."

////

Hussein spoke for nearly an hour.

He described the Istanbul meetings, the couriers, the wire codes that looped through Switzerland and Doha. He described the "mercy network"—how Ian Karim built a lattice of nonprofits to hide a flow of money that nourished both sides of the conflict. He named sub-foundations, shell directors, sympathetic politicians who appeared at Karim's galas unaware—or unwilling—to ask where the funds came from.

As he spoke, the faces across the table hardened from curiosity to alarm. Whitman's pen stopped moving halfway through his notes. Keller's jaw worked, a muscle ticking near his temple. When Hussein produced a handwritten list of account codes and phone numbers, Keller slid it toward his aide without comment.

"You're certain these are active?" the Director asked.

"They were two weeks ago," Hussein said. "Unless he's already heard I'm talking."

Keller nodded slowly. "We'll verify. Quietly. If it's true, we move fast."

He turned back to Hussein. "You've done the right thing. We'll keep our word."

Hussein gave a small, weary nod. "I didn't do it for you."

////

When the Americans left, the safe house felt emptied of air. Mason watched the SUVs fade down the drive, taillights red against the wet asphalt. Hussein remained at the table, hands clasped, eyes on the doorway as though expecting someone to return and tell him what the truth was worth.

Leila found him later in the kitchen, untouched coffee cooling by his elbow.

"Did they believe you?" she asked.

He stared at the dark surface of the cup. "They believed enough. The rest—they'll invent."

Mason stayed behind, watching through the glass as rain finally began to fall, the last of the taillights vanishing into the dusk.

CHAPTER 10

THE GATHERING STORM

MARCH 2001—GAZA CITY/PALM BEACH

The feed stuttered, then resolved into crisp clarity—a gift from a compromised security contractor who would never know his firmware update had opened a door to Gaza. Hamza leaned closer to the monitor, cigarette forgotten between his fingers, ash growing long and precarious.

Two black Suburbans sat in the safe house driveway, engines idling, exhaust shimmering in the late afternoon Florida heat. They had been there for hours—Hamza had logged their arrival, noted the extra security, the way Mason's men had doubled their perimeter sweeps. Something significant was happening inside. Now, finally, the front door opened. Hamza's hand moved to the keyboard, fingers poised over the screenshot command.

The security detail emerged first—four men in dark suits, eyes hidden behind sunglasses, moving with the coiled efficiency of professionals. They fanned out, scanning the hedges, the roofline, the street beyond. One spoke into his cuff. Another held the SUV door open, body angled to shield whoever would emerge next.

Then the principals stepped out into the fading light.

Hamza recognized the first man instantly—the rigid posture, the silver hair cropped military-short, the jaw set like granite. He had studied that face in a hundred photographs, memorized it the way a hunter memorizes the silhouette of dangerous prey. Richard Keller. Director of Central Intelligence. The man who had authorized drone strikes that turned Gaza neighborhoods into rubble and dust. The man whose signature appeared on kill lists that had claimed three of Hamza's cousins.

His breath caught. He pressed the screenshot key. Again. Again.

Behind Keller came another figure—taller, thinner, moving with the practiced ease of a diplomat. Hamza didn't recognize him immediately, but the deference of the aides, the way Keller half-turned to exchange words, told him everything. This was someone of equal or greater rank. He captured the frame, zoomed, enhanced. The face sharpened: high forehead, wire-rimmed glasses, a mouth that smiled without warmth.

He ran the image through his database. The match came back in seconds.

James Whitman. United States Secretary of State.

Hamza sat back, the cigarette finally tumbling from his fingers, scattering ash across the keyboard. The CIA Director and the Secretary of State. Both of them. Leaving a safe house in Palm Beach. After hours with Hussein Mahfouz.

The implications crashed through him like a wave breaking against stone.

This was not a debriefing. This was not routine protection for a refugee politician. When men of this rank traveled together, in person, to a location this sensitive—spent hours behind closed doors—they were extracting intelligence. Building assets. Making deals that would reshape the board.

Hussein had talked. For hours. And whatever he had said was important enough to hold the two most powerful foreign policy officials in the American government captive for an entire afternoon.

Hamza watched the Suburbans pull away, the feed tracking them to the gate before cutting to static at the property line. He saved every frame, encrypted the files, and reached for the satellite phone buried beneath the false bottom of his desk drawer.

Doha was eight hours ahead. It would be past midnight there, but this could not wait.

////

MARCH 2001—DOHA, QATAR

The phone rang three times before a voice answered—deep, unhurried, the voice of a man who had learned patience in Israeli prisons and Qatari palaces alike.

"Commander." Sheikh Khalid al-Rashid's tone carried neither warmth nor suspicion. "It is late."

"Forgive me, Sheikh. But I have seen something that cannot wait for morning."

Hamza described what the cameras had captured: the Suburbans, the security cordon, the two men emerging from the safe house. He spoke the names carefully, letting each syllable given its full weight, its full silence.

The silence that followed was absolute.

"You are certain?" The Sheikh's voice had changed—lower now, edged with something Hamza had rarely heard from the man. Alarm. "The Director himself? And the Secretary?"

"I have the images. Timestamped. The facial recognition is conclusive."

Another silence, longer this time. Hamza could hear the Sheikh breathing, could almost feel the calculations spinning behind those careful eyes—political equations, strategic implications, the delicate web of alliances and betrayals that kept Hamas alive in a world of enemies.

"Hussein," the Sheikh finally said, and the name came out like a curse. "That son of a whore. He's giving them everything."

"That is my assessment as well."

"Names. Networks. Safe houses. Funding channels." The Sheikh's voice rose, the diplomat's mask cracking. "Operations we have spent years building. Contacts in Cairo, in Ankara, in—" He stopped himself, but Hamza heard the tremor beneath the words. Fear. The Sheikh was afraid.

"If the Americans know our structure," Hamza said quietly, "they will dismantle us piece by piece. Sanctions. Targeted killings. Pressure on our hosts." He paused. "Qatar cannot protect leadership that has been exposed to this degree."

The words hung in the encrypted void between Gaza and Doha.

"This is a catastrophe." The Sheikh's voice had gone flat, the tone of a man confronting disaster. "Hussein knows too much. He sat in our councils. He heard our plans. He shook hands with men whose names must never reach American ears."

"And now he sits in their safe house," Hamza said, "telling them everything he knows in exchange for protection. For asylum. For thirty pieces of silver."

"Worse than Judas." The Sheikh spat the words. "Judas only betrayed one man. Hussein betrays a nation. A cause. Generations of martyrs."

Hamza waited. He had delivered the intelligence. The decision was not his to make.

"I must consult with the council," the Sheikh said at last. His voice had steadied, the mask sliding back into place. "This requires... deliberation. Prayer. We cannot act rashly."

"Of course, Sheikh."

"But understand this, Commander." The words came harder now, weighted with authority. "If what you have shown me is accurate—and

I do not doubt your eyes—then Hussein Mahfouz has signed his own death warrant. The only questions are when, and how, and by whose hand."

Hamza felt the cold certainty settle into his chest, familiar as an old wound.

"Maintain surveillance," the Sheikh continued. "Document everything. Movements, schedules, security rotations. I want to know when he wakes, when he sleeps, when he takes his children to the pool. Everything."

"It will be done."

"And Commander—" The Sheikh's voice dropped, intimate and dangerous. "Speak of this to no one. Not Timur. Not your team. Not even your own shadow. If word reaches Hussein that we know, he will vanish into the American machine, and we will never find him again."

"I understand."

"Good. We will be in touch soon. Very soon."

The line went dead.

Hamza set the phone down and stared at the frozen image on his screen—Hussein's face captured through a window, blurred but unmistakable, the face of a man who had once stood beside them and now stood against everything they had built.

He thought of his brother Ziad, buried in Gaza soil. He thought of the cousins lost to Keller's drones. He thought of his father's voice, whispering through the years: A traitor's blood is the only water that can wash away his sin.

The council would deliberate. They would pray. They would consult.

But Hamza already knew what the answer would be.

He lit another cigarette and settled in to watch the feeds, a patient spider waiting for the web to finish weaving itself.

////

Hamza woke before dawn, heart hammering at the sharp thump of distant artillery. The concrete room shuddered with each impact—always far, never far enough. He padded barefoot to the window, peeled back the plastic sheeting, and let in a damp, salt-heavy gust from the sea. The air stank of burning tires, rain-swollen sewage, and old grief—a legacy etched in soot and memory. Even here, deep inside the Strip, storms pressed close, violence reverberating through the concrete.

He dressed with care: fresh shirt, trousers, a battered jacket still carrying the scent of gun oil and sweat, the faint metallic tang of old checkpoints. On the table, his pistol gleamed beside his phone, SIM cards scattered like puzzle pieces. The ritual—running codes, checking channels—was both shield and superstition. Routine kept fear from seeping into the cracks.

But this morning's tension was different, charged and expectant. New money had arrived. New shipments from the east flowed in on the tides of silence. At sunrise, a battered Toyota with Chechen plates nosed through the market, headlights dead, its cargo hidden beneath sacks of onions. Hamza met the driver in the lee of a broken minaret—quick handshake, cold eyes, no names.

They unloaded the crates: rifles, thermal optics, a steel case with faded GRU stenciling. The Chechen—Akhmed, a massive man with burn scars stippling his jaw and an Orthodox cross tattooed between his knuckles—spoke little. His silence carried weight, disciplined and dangerous. Hamza recognized the shared inheritance—the quiet, lethal caution in every movement.

Back in the bunker, Hamza reviewed his roster: recruits, payments, loyalties tested through whisper networks from Rafah to Khan Yunis. Every call brought risk; every recruit carried the shadow of betrayal.

But the operation demanded men willing to kill or vanish. Akhmed was the final piece. Hamza watched the man assemble a rifle with the soft, practiced cadence of prayer. His hands trembled once, then steadied—trauma remembered and then sheathed.

////

Mason's day began in the gray hour before sunrise, boots echoing on cool tile as he checked the perimeter for the fourth time. Florida air pressed heavy—thick, soupy, alive with insect hum and distant sprinklers. His back twinged from too little sleep; a dull headache pulsed behind his eyes. The sky was still black, but the safe house throbbed with the charged quiet that preceded every worst day he'd ever lived.

Inside the security annex, Arif hunched over monitors, eyes bloodshot. "Langley called again," he muttered. "Four threat pings overnight. Gaza, Moscow, Istanbul. They want full lockdown."

Mason nodded. Lockdown was muscle memory: more guards on rotation, double-verifying codes, triple-checking uplinks. He'd lived this rhythm from Beirut to Bogotá—every gesture tightened by old wounds.

He stepped outside. The neighbor's lawn was scattered with plastic flamingos, newspapers sagging under dew. Garden trucks rattled by. A garbage truck lumbered past, the driver's face half-lit by a phone screen. For a moment, Mason caught a flash behind the windshield—like a lens. Or nothing. He filed it away. Patterns began with one anomaly.

////

Inside, the Mahfouz family lived inside an invisible vise.

Leila snapped at the girls over shoes left in the hall. Mira retreated deeper into her sketchbook. Amal hid under the couch when guards walked past, afraid of the weight of their boots. Hussein moved ghostlike through the rooms, pausing at each window, watching for something he couldn't name. The alarm panel's red blink pulsed like a warning.

At night, Leila reached for him and found only the cold outline of a man she used to know. She remembered picnics beneath olive trees, warmth and laughter braided through their days. Now his silence hollowed the space between them.

"Are the cameras always on?" Mira whispered one afternoon.

"They're for our safety," Leila replied, though the words tasted false.

Maria muttered in Spanish when she passed the lenses—*demasiados ojos*. Too many eyes.

////

By late morning, Mason's team tightened the perimeter. Arif rotated passwords. Ruiz cataloged anomalies: garbled traffic from Istanbul, encrypted pings from Chechnya, a midnight spike in unknown activity. Offshore, storm clouds grew—piling up like bruises along the horizon.

Fear seeped into the drywall.

////

Across Gaza, Hamza assembled what remained of the Palm Team inside an abandoned orchard house—six young men gripping battered Kalashnikovs, their eyes too old for their faces. Boys carved into weapons.

"Today you step into history," he told them.

One boy swallowed. "What is the target, commander?"

Hamza let the silence stretch. "A kibbutz beyond the fence. No strategic value. The point is memory. Fear outlives blood."

The boys stiffened. Some nodded. Others lowered their gaze.

Another vibration buzzed Hamza's phone. An encrypted message from Timur:

Wait for the signal. All eyes on Florida.

Hamza's stomach tightened. He checked his pistol and knelt to pray. Akhmed crossed himself, murmuring a brutal shorthand of faith. Thunder cracked over Gaza like a promise.

////

By evening, the safe house vibrated with tension. Guards checked IDs. Arif swore at flickering feeds. Mason briefed his men in clipped, efficient bursts. Upstairs, Leila repacked the girls' clothes for the third time, hands trembling as she tried to remember what normal families packed for safety.

A news alert flickered across the TV:

VIOLENCE ESCALATES IN THE WEST BANK—DOZENS DEAD IN KIBBUTZ ATTACK

At dinner, Mira dropped a glass. It shattered. She cried instantly.

Leila swept the shards, her hands shaking.

"It's just a glass, habibti," Hussein murmured, though his voice was as fragile as the pieces on the floor.

Later, Leila retreated to the pantry, pressing her forehead to the door, counting her breaths. The house felt smaller every hour.

////

Mason moved through the house in silence—checking locks, blinds, chambered rounds. His rituals steadied him, old habits sharpened in too many war zones. He met Arif after midnight; both leaned over printouts and maps under the hum of fluorescent bulbs.

"We're missing something," Arif whispered. "Someone's probing us."

"Assume we're compromised. Log it," Mason said. "Langley won't authorize relocation until after the debrief. We're on our own." He checked on the girls—Mira pretending to sleep, Amal clutching her bear.

Outside, thunder rolled across both Florida and Gaza, echoing through concrete and glass. Storms drew closer—one over the Atlantic, one made of men.

The gathering storm had chosen its ground.

CHAPTER 11

THE DELIVERY

FEBRUARY 2001—PALM BEACH

The estate woke like a machine. Lights blinked on one by one; the gate motor whined; sprinklers ticked across the lush lawns. Behind the hedges, the four-car garage stood with one of its doors open. Inside, the Agency had done what it always did when it borrowed comfort—it turned it into a forward operating site.

Monitors glowed in a row, casting grayscale ghosts across the floor. Radios hung in their harnesses; the whiteboard carried names and hours that never wiped clean. Pelican cases stacked against a wall. The air smelled of solder, coffee, and the faint bite of Old Spice.

They all greeted Maria; she replied with the half-smile that made her invisible and indispensable at once. The men trusted her because repetition breeds safety. The coffee was hot, the floors clean, the plates cleared. She made war livable.

Maria entered through the side door with the estate key between her fingers. She flicked on the strip lights above the prep counter and listened to the place breathe—the whisper of a fan, the tick of metal warming. Her days ran on ritual: wipe, count, replace. Order was how she kept anxiety in a drawer.

She checked the fridge, ran her finger along the cold seal, pulled onions and limes from the bin. Knives lined the counter like instruments, edges flashing when she turned them. She liked the firmness under the blade, the clean surrender of something meant to yield and not slip away.

At the garage door, the men drifted through the shift change. Arif, hollow-eyed, marked the whiteboard with a dry-erase squeak. The board listed each team and its assignments. Three teams of three rotated through eight-hour shifts—twenty-four hours a day, seven days a week. No breaks. No holidays. No vacations.

"Burns, take five. Omar, you're on the south cameras. Kyle—look at that phone again and I'll make you marry it."

Burns poured coffee, the mug steady in medic hands. Omar laughed. Kyle grinned without looking up.

At 9:07 the gate camera brightened, caught a white box truck easing up the drive. The guardhouse logged it; the boom arm lifted. Software captured the license plate and flashed green—a nod no one saw. The face scanner stored an image: male, late twenties, clean-shaven, fatigue cap, sunburn. Unknown, unflagged. Florida had thousands of faces like that.

Maria heard the truck before she saw it—the tired brakes stuttered, the squeal of rubber on concrete. She grabbed her wheeled cart and guided it down the drive, one wheel rattling in rhythm. The morning smelled of diesel and bougainvillea. A bead of sweat slid down her temple to be wiped with her apron.

The truck stopped neatly at the side turnaround. The driver climbed down—young, polite, forgettable. He raised the roll-up door, dropped the liftgate and climbed into the box. The crate was just large enough to need a slight grunt to slide it onto the lift.

Lowering the pallet to the ground, he tipped his hat. "Morning, ma'am," he said—smooth, call-center polite.

"Morning," she answered.

He raised the liftgate, pulled her cart into place, and slid the crate onto it.

He kept the clipboard steady while she scanned the page. The top sheet listed produce and staples, ordinary as rain. A small error sat in the corner box—8:60 a.m.—and her mind caught it the way it always caught imperfection. Then she saw the photograph taped at the bottom of the list: a child on a swing, hair in a cowlick, mouth mid-laugh. Her oldest granddaughter.

The world narrowed to a hum. The driver's stillness told her the moment had been arranged to hold exactly that weight.

"Sign here, señora." His voice was low, calm. "Put the box marked with the 'M' in the fridge. Serve the security team tacos tomorrow, noon. No questions."

He handed her a copy of the bill of lading covering an envelope and a cheap phone underneath.

Maria's lips barely moved. "What is this?"

He didn't raise his voice. "We don't want anyone hurt. We want to be finished. Do this, and your family stays safe."

"If I say no?"

"Then they don't." The words were plain. "We will be watching."

For a heartbeat he looked almost sorry—human reflex arriving too late for its purpose. She saw it and hated him more for it.

Her hand trembled as she signed. The stylus scratched, turning the M of her name into a spasm. He took the clipboard back without haste, nodded toward the garage.

"Busy day, huh?"

She didn't answer. Arif passed behind them, a glance and nothing more; every day brought new contractors.

Maria kept her palm on the crate as if it had a pulse. She slid the envelope into her apron, and wheeled the box into the garage. The monitors' glow washed her in a cold halo. She cut the twine, lifted the lid, saw the usual things and one marked with an "M." She placed the sealed container and other bulk items in the commercial double fridge and shut the door, sealing the secret as neatly as the latch.

Burns walked by. "Morning Maria."

Maria forced a smile.

He studied her for half a breath, then raised his mug. "God bless you for keeping us fed." The compliment landed like a hand on a bruise.

When he left, she transferred the remaining items to the main kitchen refrigerator and pantry. Alone inside the pantry, she pressed the phone's single button. It vibrated once, a tiny heartbeat. A text appeared: *TACOS. NOON. TOMORROW*. A spike of panic seized her.

She returned to the garage to break down the crate. She looked at the men—their small motions, their camaraderie, the easy confidence of professionals who believed in protocols. Arif pacing with a radio. Omar's perpetual grin. Kyle's restless shoulders. Burns's patience, the gravity of his eyes. *Good men,* she thought.

The daily routine pretended to resume: lunch, dinner cleaning and laundry. The chores failed to provide any escape from her spiraling dread. The radios murmured; the cameras watched. A neighbor's dog barked through the fence line. As Maria chopped onions in measured strokes, each click of the knife accompanied a private prayer. The air burned her eyes; she told herself it was the onion.

Evening stripped light from the hedges. Cicadas started their weary chorus. Arif took a call outside, voice flat but hand restless. "Wednesday's busy," he muttered on return, adding three cryptic letters to the board.

Maria rinsed mugs, turned each mouth-down on the rack. The line of them looked like helmets after parade. She wiped the stove though she hadn't cooked, trying to clean what couldn't be seen. Burns interrupted her troubled thoughts to grab a bottle of water from the kitchen refrigerator.

"You have family in town?" he asked.

"My daughter. Two granddaughters."

"Lucky," he said. "I'd teach 'em to cheat at cards."

"You don't look like a cheater."

"I don't look like much," he replied with a crooked smile. "That's why they keep me—I'm forgettable."

He lifted his bottle in salute. She almost smiled back.

When he turned away, she imagined refusal—calling for help, exposing the threat. Then she imagined the swing sitting empty, the scream that would never stop. She had lived long enough to know which losses fade and which burn forever. She had no choice.

The burner buzzed once: *TOMORROW. NOON. DO NOT DELAY*. She wanted to throw it into the hedge, to hear the dull thud of sin landing unseen. Instead, she slipped it into her pocket.

Night settled, the garage dimmed to the glow of monitors. Voices loosened, laughter rolled, the music of men pretending the world was normal.

Maria returned to her cottage, she pulled the photograph from her pocket, smoothed its corners on the tablecloth. The child's joy was total—swing mid-arc, hands tight, face alight. Maria traced the image until the paper warmed under her finger. She counted the bills in the envelope—enough for medicine, rent, and guilt. Money had temperature, too; this was cold as stone.

She thought of calling her daughter, then of the men in the garage. The phone on the counter held one life; the black phone in her pocket held another. Between them, she chose silence.

She prayed without sound. The old words were empty but familiar, a language of survival. She asked for protection, apologized for asking, and lay down fully dressed. Sleep came late and left early.

Maria woke before the alarm—before the house stirred, before the cicadas finished their night song. She moved through the kitchen on padded feet, switching on lights one by one, as though waking the room gently might hold back the day.

Today was the day.

She cracked eggs into a bowl, whisking too hard, foam climbing the rim. Bacon followed, strips laid with an almost reverent precision. She baked biscuits, brushed with butter and a whisper of honey, though nobody had asked for anything special. She brewed coffee dark and strong, and juiced oranges by hand because a machine felt too cold.

It was a peace offering they didn't know they needed.

The first of the security team shuffled in—night shift, shoulders sagging. Burns nodded gratefully at the spread.

"Morning, Maria. Big day?" He said it casually. She nearly dropped the mug.

She answered with a small smile, sliding eggs and bacon onto his plate. "You work hard. You should start right."

Soon, day shift arrived—freshly dressed, alert eyes. They paused at the sight of the table: biscuits stacked like treasure, warm fruit compote, eggs still steaming.

"This looks amazing," Omar said as he passed, his arm brushed hers—innocent, but it stung.

They ate together for a brief, rare overlap—night shift grounding itself after long hours, day shift fueling up before new ones. Conversation was light: a game score, weekend plans, a joke about Florida heat. No one wondered why breakfast tasted like home.

Maria kept moving—refilling coffee that didn't need refilling; offering jam; touching shoulders as if memorizing them. Every kindness carved deeper.

"You sit," Kyle told her.

She shook her head. "Maybe later."

She cleaned plates still half-full, frightened she might see their faces clearly enough to stop.

The men thanked her as they left—warm, habitual, trusting.

Their voices faded down the hall.

Maria washed her hands twice. Lunch would come soon.

////

And it did.

At 11:45, she stood before the refrigerator. The container marked "M" sat on the top shelf like an accusation. She removed it with hands that felt borrowed, foreign. The liquid inside was clear as water, odorless as air. *Evil,* she thought, *wore no costume.*

The ground beef browned slowly. She stirred it with mechanical precision, muscle memory guiding her through the motions while her mind fled elsewhere. When the moment came—when the meat was ready and the kitchen empty—she unscrewed the cap and poured.

The liquid disappeared into the sizzling meat without trace. She stirred once more, sealing the betrayal inside. The tortillas warmed on the griddle. The salsa waited in its bowl. The lettuce sat crisp and green, innocent accomplices to her small apocalypse.

At noon, the first team gathered. Burns smiled when he saw the spread—tacos arranged like small gifts, garnished with her careful attention. They ate with gratitude and laughter, these good men who trusted her enough to accept food from her hands without question.

Thirty minutes later, the second shift arrived for the changing of the guard. Maria served them with the same tainted care, her smile a brittle thing that threatened to shatter with each plate she set down. They thanked her in English and broken Spanish, these men who had never known her granddaughter's name but who would pay for her safety with their stomachs.

The afternoon crawled by on broken glass. She cleaned the kitchen twice, wiped counters that needed no wiping, straightened chairs that sat perfectly straight. Her hands stayed busy while her mind counted hours, then minutes, then heartbeats.

The rest would come later. The sickness. The collapse. The men who had called her blessed writhing on the floor while others moved through the night toward them.

But for now, she had done what was asked. The granddaughter's photograph was safe in her purse. The poison was delivered. The window had opened.

Outside, thunder gathered like an approaching army.

CHAPTER 12
THE DIVERSION

FEBRUARY 2001—ATLANTIC OCEAN
0300 HRS—FIFTY NAUTICAL MILES OFF ANDROS

Raul eased the *Ma Cherie* across a low Atlantic swell, engines throttled back as the Iranian Kilo-class submarine surfaced—black, silent, the sea sliding off its hull in sheets. No markings. No lights. Just steel rising from depth, as if the water itself rejected it.

The hatch opened with a muted clang. Two deckhands climbed out, bracing with a gaff and rope ladder. Johnny emerged first—lean, pale-eyed, movements economical. Timur followed, expression carved from something older than fear. Five fighters came behind them, disciplined and unsmiling.

They boarded wordlessly. The hatch sealed. The submarine disappeared beneath the waves as if swallowing its own shadow.

Raul's exhale tasted of diesel and dread.

Twenty miles later, a Bahamian trawler idled under a cloud of gulls, towing a Haitian fishing boat scarred by storms and desperation. Inside, thirty refugees huddled in the fetid bilge—sweat, gasoline, vomit, the dark copper bite of fear thickening the air. A mother pressed her infant to her chest. A teenage boy guarded a knapsack like a lifeline.

Lines were passed. Radios exchanged. Cash sealed the silence. No one asked names.

Below deck, Johnny's fighters worked methodically—checking suppressors, confirming comms, glancing at the Florida coastline glowing faintly on the horizon. A lull before the storm they intended to unleash.

Raul relit his cigar. The flame fluttered in the wind.

1445 HRS—SAFE HOUSE, PALM BEACH

The garage ops center had begun to smell of sickness—bleach and acrid sweat, the unmistakable tang of bodies betraying themselves. Team A was nearly down: one operator retching, another slumped on a crate, a third gripping a table edge as if the room tilted beneath him.

Team B wasn't far behind.

Arif rubbed his temples. "My head... it's like—" He winced.

"It's not heat," Mason said quietly, eyes scanning the men. He could tell. He'd seen foodborne collapse in remote forward bases, seen men go from functional to failing in minutes. But this, this was too synchronized.

Ruiz staggered past, lips pale, sweat beading at his hairline. Maria hovered near the doorway, wringing a towel between trembling hands, unable to hide the shine in her eyes. Mason's gaze lingered on her a beat too long. Something off there. But Ruiz needed him now, and the thought slipped beneath the burden of more urgent concerns. Something inside the house had cracked. And it was widening.

1530 HRS—OFFSHORE PALM BEACH

Johnny stood at the rail, wind brushing his mask as he watched the white thread of coastline ahead. The sky darkened in places, storm cells darkening into a bruise.

Timur joined him. "Dusk," he said. "We move then."

Johnny nodded. He had known the timing for days, but hearing it spoken felt like releasing a catch inside his chest.

Below deck, a Haitian woman hummed to her sleeping infant. The sound rose faintly through the deck plates—a small, fragile promise fighting the weight of the world.

1630 HRS—SAFE HOUSE

Team A was down. Team B was bending. Mason saw it plainly now—one operator barely able to lift his rifle, another slurring words, a third sliding down a wall to sit heavily on the floor. None of them were combat-effective.

"Something's wrong," Arif whispered.

Mason didn't answer. His silence had its own gravity.

He stepped into the kitchen. Maria stood with her back to him, scrubbing an already spotless bowl. Her shoulders trembled.

"You all right?" he asked.

She nodded too quickly.

He held the moment a second longer, then left. The world was narrowing; he could feel it. Something about Maria's hands on that towel nagged at him—but half his team was down. He filed it away. There wasn't time.

1655 HRS—OFFSHORE REEFLINE

The *Ma Cherie* glided into deeper shadow near the reef. Raul checked his watch. The sky was stacking storm layers—purple, gray, streaks of dying light. Good cover.

"Ready the Zodiac," Johnny said.

His men moved, tightening lashings, sealing gear, checking power cells. Everything choreographed. Everything expected.

1700 HRS—ROYAL PARK BRIDGE

Rush hour pressed tire-to-tire across the span—SUVs, sedans, contractors' vans, a school bus heavy with kids. Horns bleated. Heat shimmered off metal.

Below, a sportfisherman idled, Yusuf at the helm.

He opened the throttles. The bow lunged upward. Impact.

Steel shrieked. Concrete convulsed. Cars jolted. A woman screamed. Coffee splattered across dashboards. Kids tumbled in the school bus aisle.

The draw span's gears froze. A single, catastrophic lock.

Smoke drifted upward in a slow, accusing column.

Below, Yusuf slipped into the water. A second boat—low, fast, unmarked—pulled him beneath shadow.

Palm Beach had lost its first artery.

1703 HRS—FLAGLER MEMORIAL BRIDGE

Bilal pushed the stolen Pursuit through its final line of wake. Rashid clutched the rail, whispering a prayer.

The hull struck the support girder at speed. Metal folded. Concrete shuddered. The bridge lurched and froze—another artery severed.

Civilians stepped out of their cars, staring down in shock.

The extraction boat rose through the glare, lifting Bilal and Rashid away.

Palm Beach was no longer a peninsula. It was an island without rescue.

1710 HRS—SAFE HOUSE

Dispatch crackled:

"Marine collisions—Royal Park and Flagler Memorial shut down. No traffic flow. Emergency response delayed. ETA unknown."

Arif blinked in disbelief. "Both bridges?"

Ruiz wheezed from his chair. "That's not chance."

Mason felt it settle inside him—cold, clean recognition.

They'd been isolated. Precisely.

1800 HRS—OFFSHORE PALM BEACH

Night pooled across the water. Storm bands thickened. Johnny's fighters tightened gloves, zipped packs, breathed slowly through masks. The air felt charged—like the world was leaning forward.

Timur checked the electric outboard. Johnny checked the sky.

Everything was converging.

1815 HRS—SAFE HOUSE

Team A was down. Two men unconscious, the third on his knees, dry-heaving into a trash can. Team B wasn't much better—faces gray, uniforms dark with sweat, hands trembling on weapons they could barely lift. One slumped against the wall and slid to the floor, eyes rolling back. Only Team C held—two men still functional, checking windows, checking doors, checking each other with the grim arithmetic of a fight they were about to lose.

Maria watched from the pantry doorway, hand over her mouth, praying silently, eyes shattered by guilt.

Mason moved among his men, checking pulses, checking responses. It was a wreck—an ambush masquerading as an illness.

"It was me." Maria's voice was barely a whisper. "The tacos. They made me—my granddaughter—"

Mason stared at her. For one frozen second, everything he wanted to say pressed against his teeth. Then gunfire cracked somewhere outside, and the moment shattered.

"Stay here," he said. "Don't move."

He grabbed his rifle and ran toward the sound.

He keyed his radio.

"Arif... run diagnostics. Slow. Full sweep."

Arif tried. His hands shook too hard to type.

1845 HRS—DISPATCH

"All units—structural engineers enroute. No land route available. Marine response limited. QRF requests pending—negative until further notice."

Mason pressed a hand to the windowsill to steady himself.

Someone was collapsing their world from the outside in.

1900 HRS—SAFE HOUSE

He made the call.

"This is Mason. Palm House One. I need immediate QRF."

Static.

Then: "Sir—no access. Both bridges closed, marine units diverted. Coast Guard saturated."

Mason's breath hitched. The truth was a blade against his ribs.

Every route cut. Every fallback severed. The storm had arrived.

He grabbed the VHF, keyed the guard channel. "Coast Guard, Coast Guard, this is Palm Beach County Sheriff—shots fired, officers down, request immediate assistance."

Static. Then a harried voice: "Palm Beach, be advised—all units responding to mass casualty event at The Breakers. Earliest available asset is Jupiter station, ETA sixty minutes."

Sixty minutes. The boat was still on the lift.

By then, it would be over.

1930 HRS—OFFSHORE PALM BEACH

Johnny stepped into the Zodiac. Water slapped the hull in soft, rhythmic bursts. Behind him, the glow of The Breakers shimmered like a mirage.

Timur powered the electric motor. Silent. Deadly.

Johnny watched the lights of the safe house—dimmer than they should have been, the pattern of movement wrong. Hussein was the target. Only Hussein. The women and children didn't have to be part of this.

He told himself that, and almost believed it.

"We go," he said.

The Zodiac slipped forward.

2010 HRS—THE BREAKERS

The Haitians hit the beach—thirty desperate figures stumbling from the surf. Linen suits scattered. Security froze. Glasses shattered. Children wailed. A terrace pulsing with wealth and ease convulsed into chaos.

"Code Red! Code Red!" radios screamed.

A mile south, the news helicopter had picked up the call on the police scanner—*mass casualty event, Breakers beach, all units respond*—and banked hard toward the glow. The cameraman was already rolling when they cleared the dunes. The spotlight swung low, raking the sand, finding mayhem: bodies in the surf, hotel security shouting into dead radios, guests in evening wear running nowhere.

Confusion. Not order. Not narrative. Just noise designed to swallow everything else.

2014 HRS—SAFE HOUSE

The helicopter's beam swept the coastline and caught—just for a heartbeat—the faint wake of a Zodiac sliding toward the seawall.

Mason saw it from the window.

Cold clarity cut through him.

He reached for his weapon.

2015 HRS—SHORELINE

Johnny stepped onto the sand. Water dripped from his sleeves. The night pressed close.

The poisoning had hollowed the defenders. The bridges had sealed the island. The diversion had scattered the law, one deputy from the gatehouse to the Breakers. The window had opened.

He signaled once.

Shadows followed.

They moved toward the house—silent, disciplined, inevitable.

CHAPTER 13
NIGHT OF FIRE

FEBRUARY 2001—PALM BEACH

2016 HRS—SHORELINE

The sea clung to Johnny's boots as he crossed the last sheet of surf, each step leaving a gritty, numbing crunch through the dunes. Salt stung his laces. The Florida night wrapped around him—heavy, wet, humming with distant rotors and the low, restless pulse of the Atlantic. Clouds churned overhead, smothering the moon, leaving the world lit only by stray lawn lights and the faint glow bleeding from the safe house's windows.

He inhaled deeply, grounding himself in the scents: crushed sea grass, briny mist, the faint oily rot of seaweed, chlorine drifting from the pool. These details steadied him. Even now, memory tugged him back to the Bamiyan Valley—Sadyra humming while preparing bread, her voice threading through lamplit evenings, teaching stories of rebels, conquerors, and the long price of inheritance. She would not have wanted this. She had raised him on stories where the cruel men lost everything in the end.

He buried her voice the way Ben Mal had taught him to bury everything soft.

Tonight, the price would be paid again.

Timur came beside him—lean, silent, his night-vision monocle catching a muted glint across the scars etched along his cheek. He ran a thumb along the edge of his blade, as if reminding himself of the world's only reliable truth.

"Rear gate," he murmured. "Two guards."

"Silent," Johnny said.

A promise, not an instruction.

2018 HRS—EAST GATE

They moved through sea grapes slick with salt, across coral-studded paths sharp enough to cut bare flesh. They moved like men who had practiced slipping through places they were never meant to enter—footfalls matching the rhythm of surf and shadow.

At the east gate, two guards stood beneath a faltering lamp. Their movements were slow—poison and exhaustion tugging at their joints, softening their vigilance.

One bent to light a cigarette. The flare lifted his face.

A loop of wire flashed.

Timur's garrote slipped around the man's throat, tightening fast, cutting his breath before sound. The guard buckled, collapsing to his knees. Timur eased him down into the wet grass.

The second guard pivoted, hand rising—not toward his weapon but toward his radio.

A fatal mistake.

Johnny's blade entered between the ribs, angled and clean. The man sagged into his arms, pupils dilating with disbelief before fading beneath the night. The guard's mouth moved—shaping a word, a name, something Johnny chose not to hear.

He lowered him gently. That much, at least, he could give.

Timur whispered a Chechen prayer—one inherited, not believed.

Johnny searched their pockets. Radios. A key fob. A wallet with a photograph of a missing-tooth child. He left the photo. Mercy took many forms.

"Gate," he whispered.

His men flowed in.

The house had already begun to collapse from the inside.

2020 HRS—SAFE HOUSE INTERIOR

Inside the safe house, tension vibrated through every beam and windowpane. The storm outside hammered the glass; the storm within hollowed the men meant to defend it.

Hussein paced the living room, phone clutched tight, arguing into static—Tel Aviv offering assurances drowned beneath distant gunfire and broken signals.

Mason stood by a window, jaw locked. Half his operators were down—vomiting, shaking, barely coherent. The other half staggered under the poison's bloom. Ruiz lay on a couch, breathing shallowly. Arif fought to keep the surveillance feed alive, fingers trembling across the keys.

This wasn't an attack. It was a siege by erosion.

Maria stood in the laundry room, hands twisting a towel. Each groan from the garage made her flinch. She hadn't known it would look like this. She hadn't known sick meant suffering.

"Are you okay?" Mason asked.

She nodded, tears held by force.

He didn't believe her. But the night gave him no room to ask.

2022 HRS—UPSTAIRS

Upstairs, Leila gathered the girls, heart pounding. "Stay with me," she whispered, ushering them into the laundry room. The storm rattled the window. Mira clutched her sketchbook. Amal clung to her bear.

Leila wrapped her arms around them the way her mother had once wrapped hers. The air smelled of detergent and fear.

2024 HRS—KITCHEN

In the kitchen, Maria rounded the corner and froze at the sight of a masked man with pale eyes stepping out of shadow.

She dropped to her knees. Clutched a cross.

Johnny pressed a finger to his lips.

She closed her eyes. He moved past without a word.

2025 HRS—COURTYARD

Flash-bangs arced over the courtyard wall—white-hot bursts that punched through the house, stealing sound, shattering time. Weakened guards staggered, vomiting, ears ringing, hands slipping from their weapons.

"Contact east side!" Mason shouted, forcing breath past nausea, side-arm raised.

Camera feeds ripped into static. Gunfire cracked. Shadows moved.

A guttural cry in Arabic: "Johnny! Johnny, here!"

Mason stiffened. *Johnny?* An American name. An impossible profile. The shape of something new, something wrong.

2026 HRS—BACK STAIRS

Timur led two fighters up the back stairs, boots muffled by a Persian runner. One muttered a prayer; Timur shoved him forward.

"Doubt later. Move."

Hussein sprinted for the staircase just as bullets shredded the banister, splinters raining across his arms. Smoke filled his lungs. He fell back, choking, a child again in his father's cellar during raids.

He shouted for Leila. The house swallowed the name.

2027 HRS—LAUNDRY ROOM

Leila tightened her grip around the girls as footsteps pounded. The door splintered inward.

Johnny filled the frame.

His mask hid his face, but something in his posture stilled her terror. He lowered his weapon a fraction.

"Come," he said in Arabic. "Now."

Leila gathered them. Johnny herded them down the hall—methodical, scanning corners, clearing angles. A man accustomed to escorting innocence through fire.

He found a cedar-lined service room—reinforced door, narrow walls.

"Inside."

They stumbled in. He pulled a folding ironing board across the outside, crude barricade, sufficient cover.

"No one will touch you here."

For a moment, the noise receded. Then he left.

Only Hussein remained.

2029 HRS—ATRIUM

Gunfire chewed through the atrium. Dust floated like ash. Mason shouted orders through a storm of nausea and pain. Johnny and his men moved with practiced clarity—corner, sweep, advance—cutting through chaos.

On the landing, Hussein burst from a side room, pistol trembling.

He and Johnny locked eyes.

"Stop," Johnny ordered.

Hussein glanced toward the open window—a single, fatal tell.

Johnny surged. The rifle butt cracked against Hussein's wrist. The pistol skittered. A struggle. A takedown.

Zip-ties cinched around his wrists. His cheek pressed to the cold floor. Smoke roared in his ears.

"You live because I choose it," Johnny whispered.

Timur appeared. "Move!"

2031 HRS—GARDEN

They dragged Hussein down the stairs into the shattered garden. Sirens wailed across the island—confused, delayed, stuttering through the gridlock created by the disabled bridges. A police cruiser's lights pulsed through the hedges.

A helicopter banked overhead, searchlight slicing the yard.

Its beam struck Johnny's mask, lighting his pale eyes like cold flame.

"RPG!" Timur barked.

A fighter raised the tube, fired. The rocket screamed upward. The helicopter's tail exploded in a burst of fire. The aircraft spun and slammed into the sea, flame and debris flaring across the water.

Johnny didn't flinch.

He dragged Hussein into the dunes.

2033 HRS—DUNES

Bullets tore sand behind them. Timur signaled—three fingers, a sweep. His fighters fanned out, firing controlled bursts, buying seconds.

Johnny shoved Hussein forward. "Move!"

They plunged into a hollow behind the dunes. The Zodiac lay half-buried beneath seaweed, invisible to anyone not looking for it.

Timur ripped it free. Two fighters, all that remained, covered the flank—the other three lay somewhere behind them, dead or dying in the smoke.

"Go!" Timur shouted.

Johnny heaved Hussein into the skiff. A round snapped past his ear. He dove in after.

He righted himself just in time for a round to find his vest dead center. The impact drove him backward into Hussein, ribs cracking. No penetration—the Kevlar held—but he felt something give beneath the plate. A wet snap. Pain was just information. Ben Mal had taught him that.

Timur slammed the battery home and hit the throttle.

2035 HRS—OPEN WATER

The Zodiac surged across the water, bouncing hard over the swells. Spray whipped their faces, salt stinging eyes already raw from smoke. Behind them, Palm Beach flickered—firelight, sirens, the distant pulse of chaos they'd engineered.

A small boat appeared from the north, running hard along the beach. Coast Guard stripes on the hull. Full throttle, bow high, searchlight sweeping.

Too late. Too slow.

Johnny let the salt sting his eyes, breathing hard. The adrenaline leeched slowly from his limbs.

Hussein lay beside him, gasping. Timur stared into the dark, jaw tight.

Behind them, the safe house blazed with light—searchlights stabbing the sky, flashlight beams smaller and frantic, crisscrossing the dunes like the legs of panicked insects. Already the survivors were gathering, already the story was being rewritten into something they could live with.

The sea erased their wake.

CHAPTER 14

INTO THE DEEP

FEBRUARY 2001—ATLANTIC OCEAN

The Zodiac slammed through black swells, each impact driving salt spray like needles into Johnny's cracked ribs. Behind them, Palm Beach burned against the night—a funeral pyre of everything he'd destroyed to prove himself worthy of Ben Mal's trust.

Hussein lay zip-tied in the boat's belly, blood from his split lip mixing with seawater. His breathing was controlled, deliberate, the rhythm of a man counting heartbeats instead of counting down to death. Johnny recognized the technique. He'd learned it during his first interrogation in Kandahar, when he was seventeen and still believed someone might come for him.

No one had come. That was the lesson Afghanistan taught: survival meant becoming someone no one would abandon because no one could claim you. Ben Mal understood that. "Trust nothing but your own cruelty," the old warlord had said. "Everything else is sentiment, and sentiment kills."

Ahead, the *Ma Cherie* waited—white hull gleaming silver under stars, running lights dark. Timur signaled twice. Raul answered from the stern: quick flashes, then darkness.

"Salaam alaikum," whispered one of the Hamas fighters.

Johnny said nothing. His mother Sadyra had taught him prayers once, in the cold dawn light of their cave above Bamiyan. But prayers were for people who believed they deserved rescue. He'd learned better. Sadyra had raised him on prayers—sunrise and sunset, before meals, before sleep. She believed words could hold back the darkness. Ben Mal had burned that out of him. Some nights Johnny still caught his lips moving without permission, shaping syllables he'd sworn to forget.

////

The transfer to the yacht happened in disciplined silence. Hands reached down—callused, efficient. The Hamas fighters climbed first, their earlier bravado replaced by the hollow exhaustion that follows adrenaline's crash.

Johnny hauled Hussein upright. For a moment, their eyes met. Hussein's gaze held something unexpected—not fear, but a terrible recognition, as if he were looking at his own reflection in dark water.

"Do I know you?" Hussein asked quietly.

Johnny's grip tightened. "You know what I am. That should be enough."

"What you are." Hussein's voice carried strange sadness. "Or what you've been made into?"

"Same thing," Johnny said, shoving him toward the ladder. But Hussein's words followed him up the rungs, echoing with the pressure of questions he'd spent twenty years trying not to ask.

////

On deck, the *Ma Cherie* revealed her scars: bullet holes patched with fiberglass, scuff marks where grappling hooks had bitten deep. Raul hunched at the wheel, lips moving in silent Spanish—prayers or curses, impossible to tell.

The two surviving Hamas fighters clustered near the stern, faces hidden beneath balaclavas. Johnny studied them—boys playing at holy war, drunk on promises of paradise. They reminded him of himself at their age, before Ben Mal taught him that paradise was a story men told themselves while they bled.

"We were promised passage," the youngest whispered. "Passage to glory."

"You'll get passage," Johnny said. Not a lie, technically. Just not the kind they expected.

Hussein watched this exchange from where he lay against the port rail. Something about Johnny's tone, his movements, stirred memories he couldn't quite place. The young man carried himself like someone haunted by absence—the particular gravity that came from growing up in the shadow of missing fathers.

"Your daughters," Johnny said suddenly, crouching beside him. "Tell me about them."

Hussein's eyes sharpened. "Why?"

"Because I want to understand what kind of father abandons his children for politics."

The words hit like physical blows. Hussein closed his eyes, summoning Mira's gap-toothed smile, Amal's fierce concentration when she drew her impossible cities. "I didn't abandon them. I was trying to protect them."

"By making peace with the Zionists?" Johnny's laugh was bitter. "How did that work out?"

"Better than making war." Hussein studied Johnny's face in the dim light. "What happened to your father?"

Johnny's hand stilled on his weapon. "What makes you think something happened?"

"Because you move like someone who's spent his whole life proving he doesn't need anyone. I've seen that walk before—in refugee camps, in bombed-out schools. It's the walk of sons whose fathers never came home."

For a moment, Johnny's mask slipped. Hussein caught a glimpse of the boy underneath—scarred, abandoned, shaped by questions that had no answers. "He left," Johnny said quietly. "Before I was born. My mother never told me why."

"So you made yourself into a weapon to get his attention?"

"I made myself into a weapon because weapons don't get abandoned." Johnny's voice hardened. "They get used, but they don't get left behind."

Hussein felt the crush of recognition settle in his chest. This young man—scarred, lethal, carrying abandonment like a second skin—was what his own daughters might become. What any child might become when fathers chose missions over presence, causes over love.

////

At midnight, the rendezvous came. The sea bulged like a wound, then split, disgorging steel and malice from the depths.

The *Nooh* surfaced like a leviathan—sleek, predatory, its hull gleaming with seawater and secrets. Iranian Revolutionary Guard markings had been painted over but not quite erased. This was a ghost ship, crewed by men whose names existed only in classified files.

The submarine's hatch cracked with a hiss of escaping pressure. A ladder clanged down. White vapor spilled into the night—the breath of technological death.

"Bring the prize," Timur called.

Johnny dragged Hussein to his feet. The older man's knees buckled, but he kept his eyes fixed on Johnny's face. "Listen to me," he said urgently. "Whatever you're trying to prove, whatever you think this will accomplish—it won't bring him back. It won't make the abandonment hurt less."

Johnny's jaw tightened. "You don't know anything about my father."

"I know he left a son who's become everything he probably tried to protect you from. You want to know what that makes you? It makes you a weapon pointed at your own heart."

For a heartbeat, Johnny hesitated. Ben Mal's voice ended that. *Sentiment kills. Trust nothing but your own cruelty.*

Behind them, the Hamas fighters rushed for the submarine's ladder. They'd sacrificed everything for this moment—families, futures, clean consciences. They would not be left behind.

Johnny reached the submarine's deck first, hauling Hussein after him. Iranian sailors grabbed the older man's arms, their faces hidden beneath watch caps and shadows.

As soon as Hussein was aboard, Johnny signaled the crew. The ladder began to retract.

"Wait!" The first Hamas fighter reached for the rising ladder. "You promised! You said we'd have passage!"

Johnny looked down at their upturned faces—boys who'd believed in promises, who'd trusted in honor among thieves. Boys who reminded him of himself, before he'd learned that trust was just another word for future betrayal.

"I lied," he said. The words tasted like ash.

Hamza's men had trusted him. Fought beside him. They'd shared bread and prayers and the long silence before violence. But they'd also seen his face, heard his voice, watched him lead them to Hussein. If the Americans took even one of them alive, the trail would lead to Bamiyan. To Ben Mal. To his mother.

He told himself that was why.

The hatch sealed with a clang. Timur dropped a satchel charge into the *Ma Cherie's* engine room vent before they climbed onto the sub. Red numbers counted down on the timer: 30... 29... 28...

Johnny followed the Iranian sailors below, into corridors that smelled of diesel and death. Behind them, the *Ma Cherie* became a fireball—screaming metal and burning gasoline swallowing the Hamas fighters' final prayers.

He'd killed them all. Boys who'd believed in him, who'd trusted him. Boys who'd had fathers once, before the world taught them that fathers were just another word for disappointment.

////

In the submarine's cramped belly, Johnny shoved Hussein into a steel chair. The compartment was tomb-small, lit by a single red bulb that turned everything the color of old blood.

"Those boys," Hussein said, his voice steady despite the plastic restraints cutting his wrists. "They trusted you."

Johnny checked his pistol, ejecting the magazine to count bullets he'd already counted. "Trust is a luxury. I don't deal in luxuries."

"Your father—"

"My father is dead to me." The words came out harder than intended. "Has been for twenty years."

"No." Hussein's voice was quiet, relentless. "If he were dead to you, you wouldn't be here. You wouldn't need to prove anything." He studied Johnny's face. "But you do. You're still asking the same question you asked when you were ten years old." His voice dropped. "*Why didn't he come for me?*"

Johnny's hand stilled on his weapon. "You don't know what you're talking about."

"I know what it looks like when a son spends his life becoming everything his father feared he might become. I know because I've watched it happen before." Hussein's voice dropped to a whisper. "And I know what it costs—not just the son, but everyone around him. Those boys you just killed? They were someone's sons too."

For a moment, Johnny's mask cracked completely. Hussein saw the boy underneath—abandoned, afraid, shaped by twenty years of unanswered questions. Then the mask snapped back into place, harder than before.

"Their fathers should have taught them not to trust," Johnny said. "Should have taught them that the world eats children who believe in promises."

"Is that what you'll teach your children someday? If you have any?"

"I'll never have children." The words came out like a confession. "I'll never put anyone through what I went through. It stops with me."

Hussein closed his eyes, understanding finally washing over him. This wasn't just about politics or power or ancient grievances. This was about inheritance—the poison that passed from father to son when love was replaced by absence, when presence was traded for missions deemed more important than the small hands reaching for embrace.

"My daughters," Hussein said quietly. "When they grow up without me, what do you think they'll become?"

Johnny didn't answer. He couldn't. Because he was looking at the answer—scarred, lethal, carrying abandonment. The cycle never stopped. It just found new children to devour.

////

The *Nooh* angled deeper, steel groaning under the weight of fathoms. Through the hull, Johnny could feel the pressure of water above—millions of tons of darkness, vast enough to drown ships and secrets alike.

In the red-lit compartment, Hussein thought of his daughters' faces. Mira, drawing her impossible cities. Amal, practicing English with American cartoons. They would grow up fatherless now, shaped by his absence. The cycle would continue.

"Children always forgive their fathers," Johnny said, reading his thoughts. "Even when they shouldn't."

"Did you? Forgive yours?"

Johnny was quiet for a long time, listening to the submarine's passage through black water. When he finally spoke, his voice was barely audible above the engine noise.

"I'm still deciding."

The submarine shuddered. Emergency lights flickered red to white and back.

Johnny was on his feet before the echo died, instincts overriding exhaustion. The deck tilted—five degrees, then ten. Somewhere forward, metal screamed against metal.

A sailor sprinted past the compartment, shouting in Farsi. Johnny caught one word: *depth charge.*

"What's happening?" Hussein struggled against his restraints.

Johnny didn't answer. He was already moving toward the hatch when the intercom crackled—a voice tight with controlled panic, speaking rapid Persian that needed no translation.

Contact. Bearing two-seven-zero. American.

The lights died. In the absolute darkness, Johnny heard the ping of active sonar—the sound of hunters finding prey.

They'd been found.

The Nooh groaned and dove, angling toward the crushing black of the deep Atlantic, running blind from whatever stalked them in the dark above.

Johnny braced himself against the bulkhead, feeling the submarine's desperate descent in his bones.

Hussein's voice cut through the darkness: "Your father's people. Coming for you at last."

Johnny said nothing.

But in the blood-red emergency light, his hand had moved—without permission, without thought—to the place above his heart where his mother's prayer, stitched into the lining of his jacket, lay flat against his skin.

The first depth charge detonated three hundred meters off their stern.

The second landed closer.

CHAPTER 15
BROTHERS OF THE HOUSE

APRIL 1971—ATHENS, GEORGIA

Spring 1971 swept hard into Athens, Georgia. Thick yellow pollen caked the sidewalks, coating windshields and bare legs alike, its gritty invasion as inescapable as the draft lottery numbers crackling from every radio. Dogwoods scattered white petals across Milledge Avenue, settling on rusted pickups and polished fraternity sedans—fleeting beauty against a darkening season.

John Marquez walked the brick path toward Peabody Hall alongside his friends Andrew Quattlebaum and Robb Drummond. At twenty-three, John was the quiet one—lean and wiry, black hair, ice-blue eyes that never stopped scanning. His grin, when it came, could soothe or unsettle in equal measure.

He'd grown up outside Brunswick, son of a Cuban mother and a father who worked a shrimp boat along the Georgia coast. Spanish at home, English at school. He knew what it meant to keep secrets—money hidden in the flour jar, cousins slipping in after midnight, his mother burning old letters by the river as if the past could vanish in ash.

John had learned early that silence was armor. He'd survived fistfights on the docks and the back rows of every schoolroom by observing first and speaking late. He relied on neither luck nor law, only the instincts that told him when to run, when to wait, and when to cross a line no one else could see.

Andrew Quattlebaum, the preacher's kid from Charleston, balanced a tattered King James Bible and a battered Camus, whispering verses or French phrases—sometimes for comfort, sometimes just to hear his own voice. He kept glancing at the girls on the quad as if trying to memorize a world that was already slipping away.

Robb Drummond, broad-shouldered Buckhead high school football phenom, stuffed his trembling hands in his pockets. His thumb kept finding the draft notice's worn edge.

"They mailed it," Robb said, breaking the silence. "My hours dropped. I'm fair game." He watched a petal spin in the gutter, wishing he could drift away with it.

Andrew gripped his shoulder. "That's rough, man. I'm sorry."

They stepped into Peabody Hall. Chalk dust and Lysol hung in the air, the floorboards creaking beneath their feet. At the lectern stood Ben Templeton—nearing forty, tall and wiry, a streak of gray in his ponytail, wire-rimmed glasses sliding down his nose. Everyone knew he'd come from UC Berkeley after igniting protests in the Free Speech Movement. Ph.D. in religious history, published in obscure journals, rumored to have debated Timothy Leary on Sproul Plaza. He'd once called a university dean a Pharisee to his face.

A girl in the back row whispered, "He's the last honest man."

Templeton didn't raise his voice. He didn't need to. "Peace is not the absence of conflict, gentlemen. It is the presence of justice!"

A student snapped his pencil. Another looped the word justice in his notebook until the paper nearly tore.

Halfway through class, the doors groaned open. Dr. Lowe, the provost—gray suit, lips tight—stood in the doorway. "Ben. A word."

Templeton tossed his chalk to a student and strode out. Minutes later, Lowe returned alone. "Class dismissed."

John, Andrew, and Robb drifted across the quad in silence. The sunlight had turned harsh. White magnolia petals stuck to their shoes. Robb kicked at the ground, trying to shake one loose, but it held fast.

////

They ducked into the Spaghetti Store on Broad Street, pushing through a rusty screen door into a fog of bacon grease and spilled beer. The Allman Brothers Band crooned from the jukebox, nearly drowned by laughter and rattling cutlery.

Templeton sat hunched at the bar, a half-drained whiskey before him.

"Ben!" John called out.

Templeton turned, offering a grin that didn't reach his eyes. "They fired me. Said I made the university look bad. The protests, the letters to the editor—all of it."

He beckoned them to a booth. The vinyl seats were sticky with summer heat. Robb set his draft letter on the table, keeping one hand over it as though hiding it might change what it said.

"I'm done," Robb said. "No deferment. My folks would just tell me to go, do my duty, make them proud. Canada's not an option—it's not even a word in our house." His knee bounced beneath the table. "Dad's got that picture from Korea on his desk. He'd say it's my turn."

Andrew's voice softened. "You haven't told them, have you?"

Robb shook his head. "What's the point? They'd haul me to the recruiting office themselves."

Templeton studied him. "You don't have to tell them. Not if you don't want to. If this goes down, I'll write a letter—tell your folks you're part of a university research team overseas." He raised a hand. "I'll sign it myself. Make it official."

Robb managed a thin smile. "That's the best lie I've heard all week."

"Sometimes a good lie is the only way to stay alive." Templeton leaned forward, dropping his voice. "But this one happens to be true. A friend of mine—Afghan, Berkeley-educated—wrote me about an archaeological dig in the Bamiyan Valley. Buddhist statues carved into the cliffs, fifteen hundred years old. The team needs bodies. Strong backs, steady hands, no questions asked." He paused. "It's a chance to disappear into work that matters. And nobody's going to look for draft dodgers in the Hindu Kush."

Robb stared. "Afghanistan. That's your plan."

"No plan. An opportunity." Templeton's eyes were steady. "You'd sign on as my research assistants. Off the books—the university cut me loose, but the dig doesn't care about faculty politics. My contact in Savannah can get us berths on a freighter to Bombay. From there, overland through Pakistan. We'd be in Bamiyan by June."

He let that settle.

"It's not safe. It's not comfortable. But it's real work, and it's far from anyone who wants to send you to the Mekong Delta."

John frowned. "A freighter? How long?"

"About a month at sea. Not exactly the QE2, but it'll keep you off the radar. From Bombay, we go overland—rail, bus, whatever's available. Bamiyan's past Kabul, up in the mountains." He met each of their eyes in turn. "It'll be hard. Some danger. But it's not Vietnam."

Robb tried to joke. "Seasickness beats shrapnel, right?"

Andrew bit his lip. "You really think we can pull this off? What if we get caught?"

Outside, a siren wailed and faded, someone's Friday night gone wrong.

Templeton's voice was steady. "You want out, or not? This is the only door I can open. I'll take the heat if it goes wrong."

John leaned back, a slow grin spreading across his face. "You get us on that boat, Ben, I'm in."

Robb hesitated, then nodded. "Better than hiding in my parents' basement."

Andrew fingered the worn edge of his Bible, then tapped Camus against the table. "I've never been outside the South. But I'm not staying here alone."

Templeton's shoulders dropped with relief. "We bus to Savannah in two weeks. Pack light. Don't tell anyone the truth. I'll handle the paperwork."

They raised their Cokes. Templeton's whiskey glass clinked against the plastic.

"Bamiyan or bust," John said.

Outside, the world rolled on—girls laughing on the quad, a Mustang with a cracked muffler roaring down Broad, the bell tower tolling low and indifferent. Inside the Spaghetti Store, three friends and their fired professor had just made a decision that would change everything. Athens, Georgia was already fading behind them, a town receding in the rearview mirror of a life.

CHAPTER 16

A ONE-WAY TICKET

MAY 1971—SAVANNAH, GEORGIA

I-16 unfurled beneath the bus, endless and indifferent. Early morning sunlight slipped through grimy windows, painting the three friends in slanting gold and shadow—each in his own world, each clinging to what hurt most to leave behind.

John Marquez watched the landscape slide from red clay fields to dense stands of pine, then to the wide, salt-stained marshes of the Low Country he knew so well. Kudzu strangled telephone poles; battered billboards urged repentance or a stop for boiled peanuts. He caught himself searching the horizon for the sea, the one constant in all his mother's stories—the sea that saved, the sea that swallowed, a border every exile crossed.

He glanced at his friends. Robb stared at the back of the seat ahead, thumb running the seam of his draft notice envelope, foot tapping a nervous rhythm. Andrew had his Bible open in his lap, lips moving over a silent prayer.

The bus slowed for small towns—Dublin, Statesboro, Pooler—each a collage of shuttered shops, roadside churches, and faded American flags. With each stop, John felt the cord to Athens stretch and fray. Memory replayed in flickers: the clatter of typewriters in the Peabody library, the slam of the fraternity house screen door.

When they stopped at a roadside diner, Robb wandered to a payphone. John glimpsed him with the receiver pressed to his ear, his mother's voice faint and static-blurred. Afterward, he stood out front, shoulders hunched, watching the highway.

In Savannah, Templeton met them at the station, looking both exhilarated and drawn. He wore an old field jacket, his hair tousled, a stack of battered maps in his hand. "Welcome to the end of the line—and the start of the road no one else will follow."

Their first stop was Sarge's, the local Army-Navy store, where they traded their luggage for duffel bags. Then they headed for Mrs. Miller's boarding house—a crumbling brick relic by the docks, front stoop sagging. A handwritten sign in the window offered ROOMS BY THE WEEK CASH ONLY NO QUESTIONS.

That night, the four of them sat on the warped balcony, sipping bourbon from tin cups, legs dangling over peeling balusters. Freighters crawled by on the river; their hulls lit with red and green navigation lights. The fog pressed close, the hum of distant jazz drifting up from the square.

Templeton explained he'd booked passage on the *Pacific Wind*, a tramp steamer headed to Bombay with a load of South Georgia peanuts. "I gave the captain five hundred—we work in the galley and stand watch for our fare. Month at sea, fuel stop in Jeddah. We leave in the morning."

"Ever feel like you're already a ghost?" Robb said. "Like you left yourself back somewhere and nobody noticed?"

The river filled the silence.

"Sometimes I think we're just waiting to be forgiven for what we haven't done yet," Andrew said softly.

John watched the city lights blur in the fog. "I'd rather gamble on a desert than die in a jungle. That's enough for me."

Templeton raised his tin cup. "My brothers: To those who choose their road, not the road chosen for them."

The toast was soft, but the word "brothers" landed truer than any prayer.

////

MAY 1971—SAVANNAH HARBOR DOCKS

Dawn came on a smear of pink light and fog. At the pier, the *Pacific Wind* loomed above them—an old freighter painted dull blue, her name barely legible, Panamanian flag limp in the breeze.

The captain, a short man with a scar down his jaw, thumbed through their forged visas and the wad of cash, then nodded. "You work, you eat. Stay out of trouble. We don't talk politics."

They slung their duffels and climbed the steel gangway. Their berths were narrow cots bolted to the hull, mattresses thin as old shirts. The air smelled of oil, sweat, and something faintly rotten.

The ship slipped downriver. The city shrank—brick spires and neon blinking behind the mist, then gone. John stood on the aft deck with the others, watching the shore fade to shadows.

"Past the horizon, the world changes," Templeton said quietly. "So will you."

////

MAY 1971—PASSAGE TO BOMBAY, INDIA

For two weeks, the *Pacific Wind* lumbered east, twin diesels hammering night and day. The ship felt alive, a rattling metal beast gnawing across an ocean too wide to fathom, its endless vibration working itself into John's bones.

Robb became a shadow of himself, knuckles cracked and bleeding as he chipped away paint with the Filipino crew, each strike erasing something old but never his own dread. Blisters rose and burst, leaving his hands raw. The others called him "Georgia," half-affection, half-mockery. At night, he sometimes whispered his mother's name, hoping the sound could cross oceans.

Andrew endured his own baptism—palms rope-burned, each scar a lesson. In the mess, he sat with Arturo, a wiry deckhand who taught him card tricks and shared ghost stories from the Sulu Sea. He found comfort in the hymns the crew sang at sunset, strange songs close enough to the prayers he'd learned at his father's knee.

Templeton haunted the periphery, hollow-eyed and restless—chain-smoking menthols, buried in battered archaeological reports, looking for solace in old ruins. Most nights, he sat alone on deck, staring west as if longing could steer the ship.

After the Jeddah resupply, a tense ballet of drums and crates beneath watchful soldiers, the weather broke. Rain battered the decks, waves pounding the hull. A mooring line snapped with a rifle's crack, tearing the second mate's palm. Blood spiraled down the scuppers into the sea.

One evening southeast of Oman, John stood at the rail, eyes narrowed against spray. Between swells, he spotted a skiff: battered hull, three men beneath ragged keffiyehs, one holding an AK, its barrel catching the sun.

"Ben," John called, voice tight. Templeton snatched the binoculars, cursed. "Shit. Pirates."

The skiff's engine shrieked, pushing closer. The captain's voice broke over the intercom: "All crew to stations! Brace for boarding! Piratas!"

AK fire rattled against the steel. Robb buried himself behind a winch, hands shaking. Andrew pressed against the ladder, Bible to his chest. John seized a pipe wrench, its heft both weapon and inheritance.

No guns. Only a fire hose. Arturo crouched by the pump, lips moving in prayer. John nodded. "Do it."

The blast caught a pirate in the face, sending him reeling. "They're coming again!" John shouted. The pirates hooked a line. The captain spun the wheel, the ship lurched, the skiff tipped. A boy—no older than John's cousin back home—tumbled into the sea, vanished. Another thrashed, then was gone. Blood swirled in the surf.

The ship staggered free. Silence crashed down.

Arturo dropped to his knees, tears tracking clean through salt. Andrew's prayers broke into sobs. Robb crawled out, white with fear, hands torn from gripping steel.

Blood streaked the deck, gone with the next cold wave.

"Welcome to the Third World, boys," Templeton said, voice thin and hoarse.

Ruiz checked the wounded: a gash on John's arm, a broken finger, bruises, shock. The captain lit a cigarette, hands trembling. Work resumed. No thanks, no mercy. Only the ship pressing east.

////

JUNE 1971—BOMBAY, INDIA

A week later, the battered ship drifted beneath a sky of tarnished pearl. They gathered on deck, sleepless, faces drawn by fear and awe.

From the water came the scent of land: woodsmoke, cardamom, diesel, something sweet roasting in the sun. The lights of India shimmered on the horizon, fragile as hope.

John watched the world open before him. The darkness he'd carried from Athens loosened, just a little. Ahead was the unknown, ready to break or make them new.

The sea had delivered them—not only to another shore, but to the possibility of transformation. As they stepped down the gangway into Bombay's chaos, each man felt the world expand: strange, immense, alive.

CHAPTER 17

THE ROAD TO BAMIYAN

JUNE 1971—BOMBAY

Bombay hit them like a fever dream—color, noise, heat. Templeton, haggard from three nights' lost sleep, elbowed past a pair of stevedores and flagged down a battered Willys Jeep parked half on the curb, half in a pothole. The driver—Pali, a bantam man with a gold tooth and a hand never far from the sawed-off shotgun wedged in the footwell—grinned wide.

Robb eyed the Jeep with open dread. Sweat already pasted his shirt to his back. "That thing even run?" he asked, squinting at the frayed upholstery and duct-taped dash.

John only grinned. "We'll find out, unless you want to stay here and sell Bibles to pickpockets." Andrew, trying to keep his pack close, offered a nervous laugh.

Pali thumbed the choke, patted the dashboard, and muttered a quick prayer in Marathi. The Jeep coughed, backfired, then growled to life with a note that was all threat and promise. John found himself unconsciously checking the drag of the crowbar wedged beneath his seat.

They rattled out of Bombay as dusk bled the neon into streaks. Templeton, riding shotgun, glanced back. "Every road here leads somewhere, Robb. Not always where you want to go." He looked hollowed out, older than in Athens, chain-smoking through every delay.

Checkpoint after checkpoint broke their rhythm: bored cops in khaki, soldiers with ancient Enfields. Pali's bribes varied—rupees, cigarettes, a bottle of hair oil, once a bar of American soap from Templeton's bag. At one tense crossing, when an officer's eye lingered on the Americans' pale faces, Pali spun an elaborate tale about geologists and a government favor. The guard shrugged, palmed a pack of Lucky Strikes, and waved them on.

The days blurred: the sun climbing high, baking the road to brass, the Jeep's steering wheel too hot to touch. Each afternoon, a dusty breeze pushed the heat aside just enough for hope to rise. John watched the land change—rice paddies to parched fields, banyan trees to thorn and acacia, always the same cloudless sky, always the hint of some greater test ahead.

Nights, they slept wherever the road ended: under a highway bridge, once in a crumbling railway station, the corrugated roof rattling in monsoon wind. On those nights, their dreams frayed and spun—John haunted by his mother's voice, Robb by draft notices, Andrew by a future he couldn't name. Templeton muttered fragments of Buddhist koans in his sleep, sometimes arguing with invisible ghosts.

One evening, the Jeep broke down in a hamlet lit by oil lamps and a lone, humming generator. As Pali and John wrestled with the carburetor, the local boys gathered, watching silently. One finally stepped forward, offering a chipped terracotta cup of chai. Andrew thanked him in slow, careful Hindi. The boy grinned, and for the moment, the group remembered what hospitality could feel like.

When the Jeep finally died for good, Pali traded it in for a Tata flatbed truck bound for Gujarat, the driver a wiry Sikh with one arm. They crowded in the back, wedged between crates of onions, straw mats, and a coughing goat. Templeton cataloged the cargo and the people around them, noting details in his journal—dust, sweat, dialects, rumors of war in the north. Andrew listened to the old women sing lullabies to their grandchildren. Robb tried to sleep but flinched at every pothole. John stared at the changing landscape, memorizing distances, tracking every face for danger.

They crossed into Rajasthan, the air sharpening, villages thinning. In a dusty market town, they stumbled into a festival—drums beating, girls whirling in saffron saris, men balancing flaming pots atop their heads. The crowd pressed around them, someone thrusting sweet jalebi into Robb's hands, an old woman tying a red thread around John's wrist "for protection." For a fleeting hour, they belonged—outsiders welcomed, the road's threat forgotten.

But the next morning, a checkpoint brought them back: AK-47s slung across thin shoulders, faces burned by suspicion. Pali's jokes fell flat. The officer demanded their papers, scrutinized every stamp, every hesitation in Templeton's Hindi. For a long, silent minute, John watched the man's fingers twitch near the trigger. Only when the Sikh driver slipped him a folded bill did the guard wave them through, eyes lingering.

Beyond the checkpoint, the land changed again—harder, emptier. They switched to a Soviet ZIL-131, its interior reeking of exhaust and stale sweat. Their new driver, a Pashtun with a gold incisor and a limp, warned them of "bandits in the gorge, not Taliban, just thieves." He handed John a battered Tokarev. "You hold," he said, not as a question. The gun felt cold and old in John's grip—a relic of other men's wars, now his to wield.

In the gorge, just after dusk, the world closed in. Headlights flickered high above, then cut out. Land Rovers idled into view, engines low.

Pali's face lost its smile. The bandits appeared as shadows, rifles loose in capable hands. One barked a demand. Templeton started to fumble for a story, but John stepped forward, Tokarev at his hip, Robb clutching a rusted tire iron. For a heartbeat, no one moved. Then, without a word, Pali handed over a fat envelope and two cartons of cigarettes. The leader counted, spat, and gestured. They were allowed to pass, the bandits fading back into the rocks as quickly as they'd come.

That night, huddled under the tarp, the men barely spoke. Robb's voice shook as he asked, "You ever think about just walking away—just letting it all go?" John didn't answer.

When the truck finally sputtered to a stop at a lonely checkpoint in Afghanistan, Pali got them through with a joke about American professors looking for ancient bones. Templeton's journal filled with the names of every town, every border guard, every borrowed vehicle.

The final stretch was on foot, climbing ancient, stone-strewn paths into the Bamiyan Valley. Dust rose with every step; the cliffs above loomed immense, carved by hands and wars long forgotten. John felt the valley press down on him. Children watched from doorways, wide-eyed; old men squatted in the shade, watching with an unreadable patience.

They camped once by a ruined caravanserai, its arches honeycombed with bats, the walls blackened by old fires. Robb ran his hand over a scar in the stone, voice a whisper. "You think the road remembers?" John answered, "Every footprint." Andrew murmured a psalm. Templeton just stared at the night, lost in memory.

JUNE 1971—BAMIYAN VALLEY, AFGHANISTAN

A day later, the cliffs of Bamiyan rose before them—colossal, battered, the great Buddhas scarred but still serene. Their faces, hollowed by time and war, watched over the valley with a calm that mocked the men below.

Dust drifted in the twilight; the wind smelled of woodsmoke, old blood, and the coming cold.

Templeton stumbled to his knees before the statues, tears lost in the dirt. "They've watched a thousand years," he whispered. "A thousand more. Longer than us."

////

Aziz had grown up in the shadow of the great Buddhas, their sandstone faces carved into the cliff like sentinels of another age. His father had swept their niches clear of snow and lit lamps for pilgrims who came from as far as India and Japan. By the time Aziz inherited the duty, UNESCO had declared the site a world treasure. Archaeologists rotated through Bamiyan with their notebooks and cameras, but Aziz was the constant—caretaker, interpreter, and quiet guardian. He knew which paths the snow closed first, which villagers could be trusted with supplies, which fissures in the cliff warned of another winter's damage.

To the scholars, he was indispensable: a memory of the valley itself. To the villagers, he was the man who could speak for Bamiyan when foreigners asked questions no one else wished to answer. When Ben arrived, it was Aziz who welcomed him. He explained the valley's politics the way he explained the layers of soil: patiently, without sentiment. Logistics, crews, permissions—all of it passed through Aziz's hands. He was not a soldier, but he understood the press of walls and the fragility of memory.

Aziz led them down a narrow path cut into the cliff, the night wind moving through the stone like an exhalation. At the end of the trail, a low building hunched against the rock face, its plaster walls weathered, paint stripped to the underlayer by decades of dust and sun.

"This is for our visiting archaeologists," Aziz said, his voice carrying both apology and pride. "Now it is yours."

He pushed open the iron latch. The door groaned as if resentful of use. Inside, the guest house revealed itself in a wash of lamplight: spartan, stripped to essentials. A long common room with stone floors swept bare; walls the color of bone, cracked from years of desert heat. Three narrow cots lined one side, thin mattresses pulled taut beneath coarse wool blankets. A small table, its surface scarred with old knife marks and cigarette burns, squatted near the window. A single kerosene lamp hissed on the sill, throwing shadows that stretched like prison bars across the walls.

Ben stepped inside first, his boots echoing on the stone. He scanned the corners automatically—old habits that never left. "Home sweet home," Robb muttered, dropping his pack with a dull thud.

The air smelled of dust, limestone, and kerosene soot. A battered tin basin sat on a stand in the corner, a bar of sandalwood soap shrunken to a sliver beside it. Hooks hammered into the wall held nothing but a pair of moth-eaten towels.

Aziz gestured toward the back. "There is a pump well for water—cold only. Electricity comes and goes with the village. If you need heat, there is a brazier, but no wood. We use dung cakes." He said it without embarrassment, as though such things had long since ceased to matter.

"Spartan," Ben said, but there was a rough respect in his voice. "No distractions."

Aziz inclined his head. "The Buddhas endured centuries here. Men can endure a season."

The words settled in the room like dust—reminder and warning both.

////

That night, they shared flatbread and the savory warmth of goat stew with Aziz's family. Bitter green tea steamed in chipped cups. The lantern's flicker danced over mud-brick walls, shadows climbing the thatched ceiling like restless spirits.

Each time Aziz's wife poured tea from the battered brass pot, John watched the steam curl and vanish—a small ritual that jolted memories of Sunday mornings in Georgia, his mother's kitchen fragrant with lemon and flour. Here, the tea tasted of ash, smoke, and strange herbs; every noise—a cough, a footfall, the faint creak of a rifle shifting near the door—rang sharper in the mountain hush.

Aziz's oldest son sat nearby—lean, sharp-eyed, gripping his mug with both hands, knuckles white. He kept his voice low, glancing at the curtained doorway as if always expecting someone to slip in from the night. "Soviet men came last year," he whispered. "They asked about roads. About maps. They pay well. Too well." His gaze flicked to the shadows, tension making the cup tremble.

Templeton stilled, elbows on knees. "Soviets?" His voice was steady, but thin.

The boy nodded, glancing at the door again. "They curry favor with some of the fighters. They give gifts. Guns."

John felt a chill crawl up his arms, sweat prickling at his hairline. Beneath the table, his boot nudged the Tokarev's cold steel. "Which fighters?"

Aziz leaned forward, eyes narrowed. "Pashtun men from the south," he said, bitterness roughening his voice—a warning and a confession. "They want power. Weapons. They say the King is weak."

Templeton scratched his stubble, the old tic betraying nerves. "The King is on thin ice anyway," he muttered, half to himself. "Zahir Shah's grip ends at Kabul, maybe Kandahar. Out here"—he gestured at the black window—"it's warlords and chiefs. The Soviets send advisors, hoping to pick the right horse."

Aziz's son pressed on. "The mujahideen come, too—hate the communists, hate Kabul, hate each other. But they'll fight the Soviets if they stay. This valley has too many ghosts. Everyone wants to rule them. No one ever does." His words hung in the smoky hush, heavy as prophecy. The stew's reek, sweat, and the sharp smell of gun oil thickened the air.

John absorbed it all, chest heavy. For this moment, Afghanistan was no longer borders on a map, but a web of old wounds and shifting loyalties. He remembered coaches back home shouting about territory and lines, but here, there was no game—just a storm of names and grievances slipping through his fingers like dust.

"So everyone's fighting everyone?" John said, incredulity tightening his jaw.

Aziz pressed a hand to his chest. "And we Hazara? Always in the middle. Neither kings nor rulers. Always someone's enemy."

Templeton set his cup down, porcelain trembling in his hand. He met John's gaze with a silent message: *We're in deeper than we thought.* No words were needed; the truth passed between them like a shadow. John swallowed, tea suddenly bitter on his tongue, the valley colder in his bones.

Later, after the meal, Aziz checked the latch, its faint click loud in the hush. He muttered a blessing, resting his hand on the threshold: ritual, or habit born of fear. When the last plates were cleared and the family withdrew behind the partition, John lingered on the dirt floor, breathing in old smoke, new sweat, and fear.

He slipped out into the darkness, drawn by the cliffs at the village edge and the press of what he'd heard. His boots crunched the gravel path, every step careful, echoing in brittle silence. The air was biting, so thin and cold it made his chest ache. He passed the silent well, skirted a goat pen, and at last reached the base of the great stone Buddhas—colossal, half-shattered, their faces eroded by war and time.

The cliff's edge beckoned. John sat, boots dangling over the void, gazing into the shadowed valley. Below, the village lights flickered, fragile as fireflies. The vastness pressed in: so much history, so much blood and faith layered over centuries. He felt utterly, exhilaratingly insignificant. The ache of exile returned—Athens, Georgia, was another planet. His mother's voice was only memory, a faint echo against the wind. He closed his eyes, fighting the loneliness, the questions: *Who am I here? What difference does any of this make?*

A sound behind—a foot on gravel, light and hesitant. Andrew joined him, wrapping his arms around his knees, silent for a while. "You okay?" he asked, voice soft as the wind.

John shrugged. "Just trying to take it in. Trying to make sense of it."

Andrew nodded, following John's gaze to the battered statues. "Hard to know whose ghosts we're walking with out here."

"Maybe ours too," John said. "Maybe we're just adding to the pile."

They sat in silence. Far below, a dog barked, a baby cried, and somewhere in the rocks, a lone figure moved—a night watchman, or a ghost. It hardly mattered.

They returned to the house, finding Templeton bent over his notebook, eyes shadowed and distant. Robb sat by the hearth, poking at the embers, firelight streaking his face red and gold. Aziz's wife moved in and out, silent as a ghost herself, carrying tea, mending a blanket, never lingering.

John dropped onto the mat beside Robb, who glanced up with a tired, grateful look. "Hell of a place, isn't it?" Robb muttered.

John nodded. "Everywhere you step, you feel the bones under the dirt."

Templeton looked up, closing his notebook. "This place... it's the crossroads of the world. Silk Road, invasion route, pilgrimage trail, graveyard. The Soviets think they can buy it, but they'll drown here—just like the British, the Mongols, everyone before them."

Andrew joined, clutching his Bible. "You think it ever changes?" he asked, not expecting an answer.

Templeton shook his head. "History's a wheel, boys. You can try to steer, but the ground is always waiting to take you back."

Outside, the wind howled, rattling the shutters, stirring old dust. The fire crackled low. The night stretched on. At some point, John drifted into uneasy sleep, plagued by dreams of shadowy figures moving through endless mountains, of voices speaking in tongues he could almost understand.

CHAPTER 18
THE DIG

AUGUST 1971—BAMIYAN VALLEY

The weeks and months that followed dissolved into a fever of heat, dust, and bone-deep fatigue. The air's gritty sting weighed on every breath, the valley's oppression sinking into flesh. Each morning, mountains shimmered behind a haze that made the sun seem ancient; by evening, the wind silenced the last voices with a sharp wail, leaving only the ominous thud of gunfire echoing down the gorge—a reminder that unrest here was as old as the cliffs. Even the sweat dried to a salt crust on John's skin.

John woke each morning to the rattle of tin cups, the low murmur of Aziz's family passing on their morning trips to the well, the scent of last night's ashes drifting through the fog. The valley was still dark and expectant, the chill so deep it crept into his bones. Sleep was shallow, always broken by a gunshot in the night, or by a sharp word, or by the ache of bruises from another day clinging to the scaffolding. Sometimes he caught himself listening, half-dreaming, for the distant roar of an American train or the soft drawl of a Savannah night. Instead, the only rhythms here were the slow grind of work and the ceaseless wind, the sound of a single bird call signaling another day's labor.

Work at the Buddhas was unrelenting, elemental. Stone and sweat measured the days. Men and boys moved in winding lines up the slopes, shoulders straining beneath creaking wicker baskets heaped with grit. The labor punished muscle and spirit. John learned to endure the bite of the bamboo scaffolding, powdery stone burrowing under his fingernails until he felt marked by the land itself. Splinters lodged in the webbing between his fingers. Sweat stung his eyes, thin air pressed his chest, and at night his wrists throbbed from hours of scraping mud from ancient seams. Sometimes, the clang of hammers or the chanting of the men as they worked became the soundtrack of his dreams.

In the thin blue dawn, the old men would splash their faces at the well and mutter prayers. Bare-footed, shy boys trailed the workers with wide eyes, sometimes offering a crooked grin or a handful of dried apricots. John always smiled back, letting silence speak—a nod, a shoulder pressed in the morning crush, a shared drink from a battered flask. Between loads, the men would trade stories in a dozen dialects. Aziz translated when he could, but John found he understood more of the human notes than the words themselves: sorrow, pride, fatigue, stubborn hope. He listened as an old man grumbled about a lost horse, as two boys argued over a soccer ball made of knotted rags, and he realized he was learning a language older than speech.

Templeton drove the team harder than sense allowed, his stride taut, voice edged with desperation. He prowled the site, clipboard in hand, notes growing more frantic and jagged by the day. At times he paused and stared into the dark mouths of caves, eyes hollow, haunted by memories only he saw. Every artifact was numbered in a battered ledger, ink bleeding on the pages. Dates and notes crowded the margins. Most nights, John found him awake before dawn, cigarette burning low, gaze lost to places far from Bamiyan—a man who feared stillness as much as failure.

Once, late at night, John brought him a mug of weak tea. Templeton was hunched over his ledger, the pages scattered with ink smears—some from the pen, some from tears. "Every shard matters," he muttered, tracing the faded lines of a painted lotus with one trembling finger. "If we don't record it, it's gone." John sat beside him, the quiet stretching between them until the lamp's flame guttered. The ledger's margins were filled with fragments of poetry, half-remembered lectures, lists of lost students' names. "This place eats memory," Templeton whispered, his voice cracking on the words like a man confessing a sin he couldn't name. "It swallows everything whole—empires, prayers, the names of the dead. And if you stay long enough, it eats you too." John's hand hovered for a second, almost covering Templeton's, but he retreated, unsure if comfort was possible. He would remember those words years later, when Templeton had become something else entirely—when the valley had finished its work.

Andrew lost himself in cataloguing the murals: blue and gold Bodhisattvas gazing down with their imperturbable serenity, paint flaking where war and smoke had left scars. By lantern light, the saints' eyes sometimes seemed to shift—gentle, sorrowful, brimming with pity. Andrew's hands shook as he wrote, haunted by the sense that he was cataloguing judgment as much as art. He kept a little journal, lines cramped and slanted, sometimes wandering into prayer, sometimes drifting into disbelief: *Lord, what have men done here? What is left to save?* Sometimes, John caught Andrew staring at the frescoes, his lips moving in silent benediction. Once, Andrew whispered, "These eyes have seen everything, haven't they?"

Robb anchored the work, bracing beams, hauling crates, steadying the creaking scaffolding. He carried the calm of someone who needed sweat to keep dread at bay. Yet now and then, John caught him gazing too long at the ridgelines, jaw set, as if waiting for a storm to rise from the dusk. The labor steadied him, but fear pressed just beneath the surface. At night, Robb sometimes slipped outside, staring up at the moonlit cliffs, his thoughts clearly far away. Once, when John joined him, Robb confessed in a whisper, "Back home, I'd run until my legs gave out if I felt this much fear. Here, there's nowhere to run." His breath steamed in the cold, the echo of wind the only answer.

One morning, Templeton called them into a vast cave where dust motes spun in the blue shaft of morning. A woman stood against the golden gloom—Sadyra, her indigo shawl nearly still in the stale air. She did not flinch at their foreignness. Instead, she nodded, as if greeting old friends. *Hazara,* Templeton explained, voice reverent. Her eyes, dark and unreadable, held a patience like the stone behind her. Hands callused but gentle, her presence felt as rooted as the valley itself.

Sadyra's eyes swept the team, assessing each man in turn—Templeton with his fevered intensity, Robb with his coiled strength, Andrew with his quiet faith. Then her gaze found John, and something shifted. He stood apart from the others, not with arrogance but with a stillness that matched her own. Where Templeton burned with ambition and Andrew trembled with piety, this one simply listened—to the cave, to the silence, to the mass of the place. His hands hung loose at his sides, not reaching for anything, not performing anything. She had seen men like the others before: conquerors dressed as scholars, believers who mistook their certainty for understanding. But this one carried his uncertainty openly, like a wound he refused to hide.

John felt her gaze and looked up. Their eyes held for a breath too long—a moment of silent recognition, something unspoken sparking between them. He felt his usual defenses crack. Anxiety fluttered in his chest—an ache for home, for something softer than this valley. He glanced down, embarrassed by the dust on his hands and the tear in his shirt, wishing briefly he seemed less worn. But when he looked up again, he saw that she hadn't looked away. She was studying him still, her expression unreadable but not unkind.

Templeton introduced her as a local Hazara oral historian, fluent in Hazaragi and Persian, "knowing more about these caves than I'll ever know." There was gratitude in his smile—and something else beneath it, a hunger that made Sadyra's spine stiffen almost imperceptibly. She had felt that hunger before, from men who confused desire for possession, who believed that naming a thing gave them ownership of it. When Sadyra shook John's hand, her thumb grazed a scrape on his knuckle—an electric touch, over in an instant, but it lingered. He didn't grip too hard. He didn't hold on too long. Such small things, but in a world of men who took without asking, they mattered.

Sadyra was not merely Hazara—she was a daughter of the Mirza clan, whose ancestors had kept the great caravanserai at Bamiyan's heart since the days when silk and jade flowed through these passes like lifeblood. Her father, Rahim Mirza, was both elder and trader, a man whose word settled disputes and whose ledgers tracked debts older than living memory. The caravanserai—a sprawling compound of mud-brick walls and covered galleries surrounding a vast courtyard—had sheltered merchants from Samarkand and Kashgar, pilgrims bound for the Buddha shrines, and, in leaner years, armies that paid in coin or took what they wanted. Rahim had learned from his father how to survive both.

She had grown up in those galleries, listening to languages she couldn't name, watching her father weigh silver and saffron with the same impassive precision. He taught her numbers before letters, trade routes before prayers. "A woman who understands value," he told her once, "can never be made worthless." It was the closest he came to tenderness. Her mother had died bearing a son who lived only hours, and Rahim had raised Sadyra as he would have raised that son—to inherit, to endure, to read men's intentions in the way they haggled.

The caravanserai still stood at the valley's crossroads under the gaze of the Buddhas, though the caravans came less frequently now, replaced by trucks and soldiers and men who traded in things that couldn't be weighed on any scale. Rahim had aged into a figure of quiet authority, consulted by warlords and elders alike, his neutrality a currency more valuable than the opium that increasingly ruled the region's economy. He had not approved of Sadyra working with the foreign archaeologists—but he had not forbidden it either. She was his eyes in the caves, his ear among the outsiders. And she was, as he had made her, someone who understood value.

What Rahim did not know—what Sadyra herself was only beginning to understand—was that she had found something in the caves that couldn't be traded or weighed. Something that had nothing to do with her father's ledgers or the careful calculations that had governed her life.

That afternoon, Sadyra's voice carried through the caves, threading stories of silk caravans and pilgrims carving prayers, of soldiers seeking luck at these shrines. Her stories painted the valley in broader colors—tales of invaders, holy men, and lost loves, each layered over the dust. She spoke in English for the Americans, but sometimes slipped into Hazaragi when the emotion grew too large for a borrowed tongue. When she described the monks who had carved the great Buddhas, her voice dropped to a hush, and even the dust motes seemed to still.

Sometimes, when her tales ended and the others drifted away, John remained. He asked questions—not about artifacts or dates, but about the people. What did the caravan traders dream of when they slept beneath these cliffs? What prayers did the mothers whisper for sons who marched off to wars they couldn't refuse? The questions surprised her. They were the questions she would have asked, had anyone thought to wonder.

At the end of one story, she recited a proverb in Hazaragi—"*Sang yod mekunad, mard faramosh*"—then translated softly for John, her words lingering in the cool air. "Stone remembers what men forget."

"Then the stone must be very tired," John said quietly. "Carrying all that memory alone."

Sadyra looked at him sharply, then smiled—a real smile, the first she'd offered any of them. "Yes," she said. "I think it must be."

In quiet hours, John found excuses to stay behind as the others drifted off. Once, he followed her up a narrow ledge to a cave half-hidden by thorn brush. Inside, faint blue paint clung to the walls—ghosts of celestial robes. They lingered there, shoulders nearly touching, speaking little. The silence between them felt different from other silences John had known. It wasn't empty. It was full—of things that didn't need to be said, of recognition that preceded language.

On another day, she beckoned him to a pond at the valley's edge, its water cold and startlingly clear. She laughed when he dove in, her shawl fluttering as she waded to her knees. For a moment, watching his dark head break the surface, gasping and grinning like a boy, she forgot the weight she carried—the burden of being a woman alone in a valley ruled by men with guns, the pressure of Templeton's increasingly pointed attentions, the unspoken expectations she had learned to breathe around. The moment was simple, unplanned, but John felt something shift—an undercurrent pulling him closer, threading him to her in ways words could not.

One story, spoken as they crouched in a cave dimly lit by lantern flame, was of a young monk who hid a golden lotus from marauders, carving its image in a hidden niche so the valley would never forget. "We remember what we can," Sadyra finished quietly. "But sometimes stone is all that's left." John brushed his fingers over the wall, feeling the burden of history in the cool rock beneath his palm.

"And people like you," he said. "You're what keeps it alive. The stories. The remembering."

She turned to look at him, the lantern light catching the hollow of her throat, the fine bones of her face. "You understand that," she said. It wasn't a question.

"I understand what it costs," John said. "To carry what others want to forget."

Something passed between them then—not a word, not a touch, but an acknowledgment. They were both carrying things too heavy for one person. And for the first time in longer than she could remember, Sadyra thought she might not have to carry them alone.

But peace was only a delicate facade. Some nights, as John hovered on the edge of sleep atop his thin mat, sharp cracks of gunfire drifted down from the north—the staccato clack of Kalashnikovs, then silence. He would lie still, sweat cooling on his back, tasting the metallic fear in his mouth. The valley's calm was stretched over something volatile, waiting to snap. He began to keep the Tokarev closer to hand at night, the drag of it both reassurance and accusation.

Weapons became more common. John learned to read danger in the way men carried their rifles—triggers brushed with casual, deadly readiness. He checked the Tokarev's action twice a day, making sure it was loaded, even as he hated what it said about the world. Andrew confessed, voice strained, that he dreamed of guns going off in the darkness, saints weeping blue tears from the walls. Robb started carrying a heavy stick everywhere, as if that might keep the shadows at bay.

Then, one evening, a convoy of battered trucks arrived. Exhaust filled the air. Tarps were yanked aside to reveal crates with Russian stencils. Afghans with sharp eyes and grim faces unloaded them quickly—rifles, and poppy. John drew Aziz aside. "What are they bringing?" he asked, voice low. Aziz's eyes were tired. "Guns," he said. "And poppy." Among the weapons, John saw a sticky bundle of raw opium, tossed as carelessly as bread. John tasted copper, his mouth suddenly dry. He looked toward the caves—toward Sadyra, lantern-lit and unaware—and wanted to run, fight, or pray. He could do none.

The next morning, tension on the site was a living thing. Workers eyed each other warily, rumors flickered among the children, and Aziz's wife hurried the youngest inside at the first echo of distant trucks. Over lunch, a scuffle broke out over the last crust of bread, settled only by Sadyra's calm intervention. She murmured a line in Hazaragi, then repeated in English: "There is enough for everyone, if we are patient." For a breath, order returned. John watched her—the authority she wielded without raising her voice, the way men twice her size deferred to her wisdom. In a world of guns and desperation, she had made herself indispensable through knowledge and calm. It was, he realized, her only armor.

That night, John found Templeton huddled by a lamp, a tiny parcel of opium in his hand, posture shrunken, haunted. His face, gaunt and shadowed, spoke of battles lost long before Bamiyan. Templeton handled the package, hands trembling so hard the lamp chimney rattled, as if it were a relic from a life he'd barely survived.

"You thinking of using it?" John asked.

Templeton flinched. "No," he whispered, voice cracked. He dropped the parcel as if it burned.

John picked it up, pressed it back into Templeton's palm—testing him, perhaps, or refusing to judge. "This place will take everything if you let it," John said quietly. "Don't give it your soul too."

Templeton stared at the parcel, then at John. Something flickered in his eyes—gratitude, or resentment, or both. "You don't understand," he said. "You can still leave. You still have somewhere to go back to." He laughed, brittle and hollow. "I am back. This is what I came from. This is what I'll become."

John didn't have an answer. He stayed anyway, sitting in silence until the lamp burned low, refusing to leave his teacher alone with his demons. But he saw something that night—a door opening in Templeton that would never fully close. The valley was already beginning to swallow him.

Morning came. The work resumed—bamboo scaffolds slick with dew, fingers aching, dawn sharp on the valley floor. They catalogued Buddhist graffiti: prayers for rebirth, trade routes etched in half-lost alphabets, curses carved by forgotten soldiers. Sadyra read them aloud, her voice calm and resonant. "'May all souls be reborn in peace,'" she recited. Andrew quietly echoed one of the prayers in English, his voice tentative but clear—a bridge between worlds. John met Sadyra's gaze, wondering if hope was possible here, if persistence could outlast ruin.

"Think that ever worked?" he asked, wistful.

Sadyra's smile was soft and sorrowful. "No," she said. "But they persisted." She touched the carved letters, centuries old, worn smooth by countless fingers seeking the same comfort. "That's the only answer any of us have. We persist. We remember. We carve our prayers into stone and trust that someone, someday, will read them."

That day, as they paused for lunch beneath the Buddhas, Robb's hands began to tremble. Sadyra noticed and knelt, laying her hand over his—a gesture gentle and grounding. "It's just wind," she murmured. Robb laughed, shaky but real, and briefly the tight circle of the team felt whole. Andrew offered bread, and they huddled close, sharing what warmth they could find—the bread almost sweet, the wind howling at their backs, the moment as brief and precious as firelight in a storm.

Late in the afternoon, as a storm built on the horizon, John and Andrew sheltered in a shallow cave, listening to thunder roll down the gorge. The air was dense, charged. "You think we'll make it through?" Andrew asked, clutching his Bible, knuckles white.

John shrugged, eyes on the lightning flickering over the ridgeline. "We'll keep moving. That's all we can do."

"And Sadyra?" Andrew asked quietly. "You going to keep moving away from her?"

John was silent for a long moment. The thunder rolled again, closer now. "I don't know what I'm doing," he admitted finally. "I just know I can't look away."

Andrew nodded slowly. "Be careful, John. This place—" He gestured at the valley, the storm, the ancient stone. "It changes people. I've seen it in Templeton. I'm starting to see it in Robb. Don't let it change you into someone you don't recognize."

Outside, the storm broke in earnest. Rain hammered the cliffs, and the Buddhas stood patient and enduring against the sky, water streaming down their faces like tears.

That night, John dreamed of rifle shots and crumbling stone, of opium bleeding through walls, of the Buddhas turning their faces away. He dreamed of Sadyra's voice echoing through endless caves, calling a name he couldn't quite hear. And beneath it all, like a current running through dark water, Templeton's words: *This place eats memory.*

The war was coming. He could feel it in the charged air, in the way the villagers had begun to move—faster, quieter, eyes always scanning the ridgelines. The valley was holding its breath, waiting for something terrible to be born.

And John, for the first time in his life, found that he didn't want to run. Not because he was brave. But because, somewhere between the dust and the stories and Sadyra's dark, knowing eyes, he had finally found something worth staying for.

Somewhere outside, a stone clattered in the darkness, a faint, ominous signal. The gods were waking. And John, whether he knew it or not, had already begun to change.

CHAPTER 19

SEEDS OF DEPARTURE

DECEMBER 1972—BAMIYAN VALLEY

The winter of 1972 draped Bamiyan in silence. Snow fell thick and relentless, muffling every sound but the faint crack of distant gunfire. The valley shrank to a world of white—passes blocked, stone houses sealed, smoke from dung fires curling into the heavy air. At night, wind whistled through the caves, making the ancient Buddhas seem half-alive, mourners at their own slow funeral.

By midwinter, drifts engulfed the Buddhas' knees. John watched from the dig, breath steaming, fingers numb as he scraped frozen earth. The cold ran so deep it dulled thought itself. He'd never known a quiet like this, a hush that settled inside and made him wonder if the valley would suffocate them all.

Work slowed to a crawl. Each morning his raw palms ached from chipping at frozen soil. Sometimes, scraping at a pottery shard, he glimpsed his reflection in the blade—a stranger with sunken cheeks, beard flecked with ice.

Andrew crouched by lantern glow each night, reading his Bible with trembling hands. "The Lord is my shepherd," he'd murmur, the words drifting into John's uneasy dreams. Robb lost himself in labor—patching roofs, mending sleds—his callused hands numb to everything but motion. Both men watched the ridgelines, eyes drawn south, minds already halfway home.

Templeton retreated into shadow. For days he vanished into the guesthouse, pipe smoke drifting in blue coils through the courtyard. John found burnt matches, crumpled maps, American candy wrappers—breadcrumbs to a lost past. Once, he heard laughter inside, sharp and brittle, dissolving into nothing. At his lowest, Templeton stared at his trembling fingers, counting out dollars for bribes or arms, as if some meaning might surface in the cold texture of money.

Only Sadyra kept John tethered. In the teahouse, she translated the villagers' stories—old legends about heroes who survived winters by wit and will. "When the white lion rules the valley, only patience survives," she recited one evening, her voice painting warmth into the icy dusk. John watched her as she listened to the old men, her gaze soft and far away, and felt something in his chest he couldn't name.

They had grown close without either of them marking the moment it happened. A shared meal became a shared silence. A brush of hands became something more. One night, alone in the cave where blue Bodhisattvas gazed down from ancient walls, she told him about her grandmother, who had survived three invasions and buried two husbands. "She used to say that love is the only thing the soldiers cannot steal," Sadyra said. "But you have to be willing to lose everything else."

John didn't answer. He pulled her close, breathing the smoke and wool scent of her hair, and understood for the first time that he was no longer just passing through.

////

Late that winter, two new faces appeared in the teahouse—pale men with crisp English accents and shoes too clean. Their postures betrayed the soldier beneath the disguise: a glance exchanged too quickly, fingers tapping nervously on chipped cups. John watched them lean close to Ben, voices barely above a whisper, and slid a hand to the Tokarev in his coat.

Later, Ben pulled him aside, eyes feverish. "They want to help. Americans—CIA. Move arms to the mujahideen. They think I can make it happen."

"You're an archaeologist, Ben. Not a gunrunner."

Ben grinned, teeth yellowed, eyes rimmed red. "Why not both? Who survives here—scholars or soldiers?"

In the months that followed, Ben's transformation was stark. He shaved, straightened, wore belts bulging with map scraps and radio crystals. A shortwave hung at his hip; a codebook hid in his boot. Mujahideen commanders nodded as he passed, treating him as both tribal prince and American fixer.

Aziz warned John quietly, over a chipped cup. "Your professor is making friends with wolves. Wolves devour even allies."

The world around them grew more dangerous. At night, helicopters pulsed over the ridges, searchlights crawling the snowfields. John learned to sleep with his boots on and his coat draped over the loaded Tokarev. He would lie awake, fingers curled around the pistol's grip, listening to distant Kalashnikovs crack like breaking ice.

////

APRIL 1973—BAMIYAN VALLEY

By spring 1973, rumors filtered in from the south—caravans bringing cold whispers: *Saigon is finished. America leaving.*

Robb gripped John's arm, relief breaking across his face. "They can't draft me anymore. I can go home." The words trembled with hope.

Robb made his choice when a Pashtun warband raked the outer fields with gunfire. "I'm not dying for somebody else's tribal feud," he told John. "I'm done."

That night, they sat together in the dim guesthouse, lantern glow carving deep shadows across the walls. Outside, trucks rumbled and gunfire threaded through the valley.

Robb broke the silence first. "Did you hear? Nixon suspended the draft. No more lottery, no more numbers—it's over."

John looked up from the fire. "When?"

"Caught it on the BBC this morning." Robb stared into the flames. "We're leaving tomorrow at first light. Heading back through Pakistan, then home. You coming with us?"

"I'm staying," John said.

Andrew stepped out of the shadows. "Staying for what? The dig's almost finished. Ben's half-crazy. There's nothing left here."

But Andrew was wrong. There was Sadyra.

"I know." John finally lifted his gaze. "But I can't go. Not while she's here."

"She?" Robb frowned.

"Sadyra." He let the name hang there. "I love her. I can't leave her behind."

The words struck like stones dropped in still water. Andrew exhaled slowly, rubbing the back of his neck. Robb stared at him hard.

"You'll chain yourself to this place for a woman?"

"I'd rather stay and face whatever comes than spend the rest of my life wondering what I abandoned."

No one spoke after that. The fire sputtered, and outside, the wind rattled against the shutters.

////

The farewell came at dawn, under a pewter sky. John helped them pack: shirts, coins sewn into a belt, Andrew's battered Bible. They embraced—Andrew squeezing his hand, Robb pressing cheek to cheek.

"Don't let this place eat you alive," Robb said, his voice rough.

Andrew promised to wait in Georgia, the hope thin as breath. John pressed a river stone into Robb's palm—a fragment of the valley to carry home.

He stood alone in the cobble yard, watching the Tata truck wind slowly toward Kabul. The world felt vast and empty. He remembered their arrival—laughter, boundless future, hope vivid and wild. Now, only absence pressed in.

////

NOVEMBER 1975—BAMIYAN VALLEY

By late 1975, Ben had become a shadow. Deals with CIA men, rifles in crates labeled "medical supplies," promises to elders traded for pouches of opium. Sometimes John saw him by the window, staring at the cliffs, whispering names from another life. The professor who had once taught him to read the poetry of stone was disappearing into someone John no longer recognized.

The Soviets began sending "advisors" to Kandahar and Kabul. Helicopters thrummed low over the valley, rotors pounding the sky, sending children scattering into doorways. John checked the Kalashnikov's magazine each morning and melted into shadow whenever the searchlights swept the ridges.

Aziz called him a "third-world man" now—belonging everywhere and nowhere. The old dream of Georgia faded to a smudge, voices from home thinning until they were just echoes. Sometimes John remembered the taste of pecans, the sound of rain against the tin roof, and they seemed to belong to someone else's life.

Only Sadyra kept him whole. Night after night, her presence reminded him why he'd stayed—what he'd chosen when he let Andrew and Robb walk away without him. Sometimes, in the moonlight by the cliffs, she would tell him stories of mountains and ghosts, lost caravans and forgotten heroes, and he would reach for her hand in the darkness, grounding himself in her warmth.

"You could still go," she told him once, her voice steady. "I wouldn't blame you."

"I know," he said. "That's not why I'm staying."

She didn't ask him to explain. She already understood.

Above them, the Buddhas watched, snow tracing their ancient faces. John felt the world shifting beneath him—an avalanche already loosed, gathering speed somewhere in the dark. He didn't know what would break first: Bamiyan, Ben, or the fragile peace he'd built with the woman beside him.

But he knew, with a certainty that settled into his bones like the cold, that he would not run. Not this time. Whatever came, he would face it here, in this valley of stone and silence, with Sadyra at his side.

One night, a stone tumbled from the cliff and shattered in the yard below. John looked up at the snow-blind Buddhas, their eyes almost lost in the storm. He couldn't tell if they were warning him, mourning him, or simply turning away.

It didn't matter. He had made his choice.

CHAPTER 20
THE BREAKING OF BAMIYAN

JULY 1978—BAMIYAN VALLEY

The first tanks came at dawn—red stars on their turrets, iron tracks crushing the wheat to pulp. By noon, the banners were everywhere, red-and-white slogans flapping against shattered walls, officers on truck beds proclaiming land reform and modern education. By nightfall, the first shots echoed off the cliffs.

The villagers had seen too many armies, too many promises. Old men spat in the dust.

John watched from the guesthouse roof, rifle cold across his knees, fingers numb. Children melted into shadow below. The engines' roar shuddered through the earth and up into the mountain, and he thought: *How many times have these fields fed empires? How many sons lie buried beneath these ruts?*

He thought of Georgia—spring rain on an auburn field, his mother calling him home for supper. Here the air tasted of smoke and metal.

////

Ben had sunk beyond reach.

John found him curled on a filthy mattress, pipe in hand, skin like wax. The room reeked of old sweat and poppy tar. Once, Ben gripped John's wrist, voice cracked and splintered, and for a heartbeat John glimpsed the old professor—the man who had taught him to read the poetry of stone. But the light vanished as swiftly as it flared.

Worse was the way Ben looked at Sadyra now. The way a man looks at something he's already decided to break.

"She should have been mine," Ben said one evening, pacing the courtyard, revolver loose on his belt. "I brought her knowledge. I brought her hope. You—" He jabbed a finger at John's chest. "You stole her."

"You taught me once that no one owns another soul."

Ben laughed, a sound like something tearing. "They all leave me. Every one of them. You'll leave too." His eyes went flat. "But she'll stay with me, John. She will stay."

That night, Aziz pulled John into the shadows behind the cookhouse.

"He is broken," Aziz said. "And a broken man is the most dangerous thing in the world. If you do not leave soon, he will kill you. And then he will take Sadyra."

John wanted to argue. But every time he looked at Ben—eyes glazed, hand never far from the gun—the truth pressed closer.

////

He found Sadyra in the cave that evening, beneath the blue Bodhisattvas. Lamplight played across their painted faces—serene, indifferent, older than grief. She was cleaning her rifle, the bolt sliding home with a sound like a door closing.

"Aziz thinks I should leave," John said.

Her hands stilled on the rifle. She didn't look up for a long moment. When she spoke, her voice was flat. "Aziz is right. Ben will not let you take me from this valley alive."

"Then come with me."

Now she looked up. "I cannot. This is my place. My people. When the fighting comes, they will need everyone who can hold a rifle." She set the weapon aside and reached for his hand. "My grandmother survived the wars of her time by staying. By enduring. That is what Hazara women do."

"And if you don't survive?"

"Then I will die in my own land, beneath the gaze of gods who have watched us for a thousand years." She squeezed his fingers. "But you have somewhere else to go. Georgia. Your mother. A life."

"None of that matters without you."

She smiled, sad and knowing. "It will. In time."

He pulled her close, breathed in the scent of her hair—woodsmoke and saffron.

////

It started with a single rocket.

The blast lit the Buddha's face in stark relief, shattering the police post in a thunder of dust and flame. For a breath, the world froze. Then the village erupted.

Mujahideen fighters poured from alleys, Lee-Enfields cracking. Villagers joined them—old men, young boys, women with knives and ancient pistols. Communist soldiers panicked behind their barricades, tracers tearing the night.

John moved on instinct—down the stairs, checking the magazine, pulse hammering. Smoke choked his lungs.

He found Ben in the guesthouse doorway.

The professor stood half-naked, trembling hands clutching his leather satchel. His eyes were wild. "John. Help me. They'll take everything I built—"

John reached for his arm.

Ben shoved him away. The revolver came up. "This is your fault. All of it. If you hadn't taken her—" His face contorted. "She's mine, John. Mine!"

John stepped back, hands raised.

Then Sadyra was there, emerging from the smoke. Blue scarf pulled tight, rifle cradled with the ease of long practice.

"Put the gun down, Ben." Her voice cut through the chaos. "There is nothing left here for you to own. There never was."

"You were supposed to choose me—"

"You gave me books," she said. "John gave me himself." She turned to John. "Aziz is at the north gate. We need to move."

A mortar round struck the courtyard wall. Ben staggered back, firing at nothing—at the sky, at the flames. His screams were swallowed by the roar.

Sadyra pulled John through a side gate. Aziz waited in the shadows, Lee-Enfield ready. They ran.

////

Burning homes. Bodies in the dirt. Dogs howling at the smoke-choked sky. A terrified girl, barefoot and ash-smeared, clung to Sadyra's coat. Sadyra knelt without breaking stride, wiped tears from the child's cheeks, whispered something in Hazaragi, guided her toward a group of women fleeing toward the mosque.

John watched her rise and keep moving, and understood: every child in this valley was her responsibility. Every life was a thread she refused to let unravel.

At the edge of the wheat fields, they stopped. The fighting had spread—tracers crisscrossing overhead. Ahead, the goat paths wound up into darkness. Behind, Bamiyan burned.

Sadyra turned to face him.

"This is where I stay," she said. "These are my people."

"Come with me. Please. We can make it to Pakistan—"

She shook her head, tears cutting silver tracks through the ash. "If you stay, Ben will find a way to kill you. He is patient in his madness."

"I don't care. I'd rather die here than live without you."

"No." Her voice was fierce. "You do not get to make that choice for me."

Aziz's hand pressed John's shoulder. "She has made her choice. Honor it. The goat path will take you to the ridge. Go now, while darkness covers you."

John kissed her—fierce, desperate, tasting smoke and salt and all the years they would never have. She kissed him back, hands fisting in his jacket, pulling him close as if she could hold him there by force of will alone.

Then she let go.

"Go." Her voice broke on the word. "Remember me. And live."

She said something else, a blessing in Hazaragi, words older than the guns. John didn't understand them, but he felt their weight settle into his bones.

Aziz pulled him toward the darkness. Every step was a betrayal. He knew it. She knew it. The only difference was she'd forgiven him before he'd taken the first one.

He stumbled after Aziz, looking back once—memorizing the sight of her: silhouette against the flames, rifle at her hip. Defiant. Beautiful. Lost.

////

He ran.

Boots pounding blood-soaked earth. Tracer rounds hissing past. Crawling through irrigation ditches, nails torn, clothes shredded. The valley's screams chasing him into the dark.

At the ridge, he allowed himself one last look.

Bamiyan burned below—flames licking at the square where he had drunk tea with Aziz, the guesthouse where he had first kissed Sadyra. All of it wreathed in fire.

And there, in the heart of the chaos—Ben.

The professor lurched through the burning square, shirt torn, face smeared with soot. He was screaming, words swallowed by distance. The revolver rose and fell, firing at shadows.

A burst of gunfire. Ben spun, dropped to his knees. For a heartbeat, John saw the man he'd known—brilliant, patient, ruined. Then Ben crawled toward the flames, and there was nothing left to see.

John watched until he couldn't watch anymore.

Then he turned away.

////

Scree shifted beneath his boots, stones clattering into the void. His lungs burned. Twice he slipped, catching himself on a juniper root that held just long enough, palms leaving dark smears on the bark. The cold seeped through his clothes, into his bones.

But he kept climbing. Because she had told him to live.

When the gunfire faded and the flames shrank to orange smudges, John collapsed beneath a twisted juniper. His body shook. Not from cold. He'd stopped feeling cold hours ago.

He saw her face behind his closed eyes. Her smile. Her hands in his hair. Her voice: *Remember me. And live.*

He saw Ben's face too—the professor and the ruin, superimposed. Both lost. Both gone.

As the first rays of sun crept over the ridgeline, John forced himself to his feet. His legs trembled. His hands were clotted with blood. But he was alive.

He started down the far side of the mountain, each step carrying him farther from Bamiyan. Farther from her.

The Shibar Pass waited ahead. Then the Khyber. Then a life he no longer recognized as his.

He did not look back.

CHAPTER 21

THE RETURN

AUGUST 1978—PAKISTAN BORDER

The border crossing was a fever dream—heat rising in waves, the checkpoint shimmering like a mirage, guards' voices fading in and out. John stumbled forward, ribs visible beneath a torn shirt, hands empty. When they demanded money, he gave them the last thing he owned: a turquoise bead from Sadyra's scarf, cool in his palm, pulsing with everything he'd lost.

He didn't watch it disappear.

////

Karachi hit him like a wall—rotting fish, diesel, voices in a dozen languages. He wandered the port until his legs gave out, then found the American consulate and let them take what was left of him.

The CIA man didn't introduce himself. Tan suit, pale eyes, pen poised over a yellow legal pad. "Names of contacts. Locations of safe houses. Any interaction with Soviet advisors."

"I was digging up statues," John said. "Buddhist statues."

The pen didn't move. "Anyone from your group make it out?"

"No."

The pen scratched once.

"Any indication the Soviets knew your location?"

"They shelled us for three days. So yes."

The man's expression didn't change. He wrote something in the margin—a single word, underlined twice.

The man slid a manila envelope across the desk—forms, a plane ticket, a thin stack of cash. "JFK. You'll be debriefed stateside." He didn't look up. "Where's home?"

John had to think about it. "Georgia."

////

Two days later, he stepped off a Delta jet into Atlanta's summer haze. His skin felt too tight. His eyes stung in the light. He bought a Trailways ticket to Athens and sat at the back of the bus, duffel at his feet, forehead pressed to the glass.

Georgia slid past—kudzu swallowing the trees, rusted cars half-buried in summer grass, Baptist churches flashing white against the green. Sometimes the fields shimmered and became poppy slopes, the haze of Bamiyan, Sadyra's voice on the wind. He closed his eyes but sleep wouldn't come.

At a truck stop, a waitress set down a slice of pecan pie without being asked. "On the house, hon." The sweetness was sharp and foreign. He left it half-eaten.

////

Athens was unchanged—bricked sidewalks, Confederate statues stained white by pigeons, laughter spilling from the old fraternity houses. Everything looked like a Technicolor illusion, colors too bright, voices too loud.

The frat house hit him before he was ready for it.. Music thudding, beer sloshing, bodies everywhere. Someone recognized him—"Holy shit, that's John Marquez"—and then he was drowning in it. Hands on his back, voices tumbling over each other, questions he couldn't answer. *Where you been, man? Did you see action? Tell us, John, tell us.* They pressed a beer into his hand, a slice of pizza, a seat on the couch they called "the throne."

He smiled until his face ached. Their questions were keys that no longer fit any lock inside him.

Stories swirled through the smoke—some true, some wildly embellished. He heard fragments of his own myth echo back: *He fought off bandits with just a knife. Survived a week lost in the desert. Dated an Afghan princess.* The legends detached from him, hovering in the haze until John felt like a ghost at his own wake.

He slipped out to the porch before anyone noticed he was gone.

////

The night pressed in, heavy and warm. Fireflies drifted in the dark. Cicadas throbbed in the trees. For a breath, he saw her—blue scarf, rifle at her hip, standing in the shadows beneath the oaks. Then the image dissolved, and there was only Georgia, and the dark, and the weight of everything he'd left behind.

He stood there a long time.

Tyler stepped out, letting the screen door bang shut. He handed John a fresh beer and leaned against the rail. "Hell of a homecoming, huh?"

John took the beer but didn't drink. "Yeah."

They stood in silence, watching the fireflies pulse and fade. Inside, someone had changed the music to Lynyrd Skynyrd, the guitar solo drifting through the screen.

"Tyler," John said. "Andrew and Robb—you know where they ended up?"

Tyler's eyebrows lifted. "Man, you really have been gone." He took a long pull from his cup. "Andrew's still here. Got himself ordained a few years back. Pastors a little church over on Prince Avenue—Baptist, I think. Real fire-and-brimstone stuff." He shook his head. "Who'd have figured, right? That kid with his Camus and his doubts, standing behind a pulpit every Sunday."

John felt something shift in his chest. Andrew, a preacher. The boy who'd whispered Sartre and psalms in the same breath, now tending souls in Athens.

"And Robb?"

Tyler's expression changed—something guarded flickering behind his eyes. "Robb's a different story. Law school after you all scattered. Georgetown. Works in D.C. now." He paused. "Some government thing. Nobody knows exactly what."

"Government thing."

"Yeah." Tyler lowered his voice. "Rumor is CIA. Can't confirm it. But the way he disappeared, the way he never talks about what he does..." He shrugged. "Folks just say he went federal and leave it at that."

John stared out at the yard. Robb Drummond—the Buckhead kid who'd clutched his draft notice like a death sentence, who'd trembled at the thought of Vietnam—now walking the halls of Langley. The war had scattered them all.

"You got an address for Andrew's church?"

"Sure." Tyler studied him. "You okay, John? I mean, really?"

The question hung between them. Inside, the party churned on, oblivious.

"I need to talk to someone who was there," John said. "Someone who understands."

Tyler nodded slowly. "Andrew's your man. Shows up every morning by seven. White clapboard building, steeple that leans a little to the left."

He clapped John on the shoulder. "Whatever happened over there... you don't have to carry it alone."

The screen door creaked as Tyler went back inside. The music swelled and faded. Somewhere in the dark, a mockingbird called—three notes, then silence.

John gripped the rail and let the warm air fill his lungs.

CHAPTER 22
THE REUNION

SEPTEMBER 1978—ATHENS, GEORGIA

The Spaghetti Store hadn't changed. Same red-checkered tablecloths, same Chianti bottles with candles melted down their necks, same smell of garlic and oregano thick enough to taste. John pushed through the door and stood for a moment, letting his eyes adjust. A jukebox in the corner played something by the Eagles and Bob hadn't moved from the bar in seven years.

He spotted them in the back booth—Andrew's clerical collar bright against his dark shirt, Robb's broad shoulders hunched over a menu. For a moment John couldn't move. The last time the three of them had sat together, they'd been boys playing at adventure. Now here they were, seven years later, strangers wearing the faces of old friends.

Andrew saw him first. For a moment, neither moved. Then Andrew slid out of the booth, and his arms were around John before either of them said a word. The embrace was fierce—Andrew's hand clapping his back three times before letting go.

"Look at you," Andrew said quietly. His eyes moved over John's face, reading the damage. "Lord have mercy."

Robb rose more slowly, extending a hand. "John." His grip was firm, professional. He'd filled out since college—the football player's bulk refined into something harder. His eyes moved to the door, then back, so quick John almost missed it.

"Flew down from D.C. this morning," Robb said as they settled into the booth. "When Andrew called, I figured I could spare a weekend."

John slid in across from them, his back to the wall, eyes on the entrance. Old habits. New ones, too.

Andrew and Robb exchanged a glance—quick, familiar, the kind that came from years of shared conversations John hadn't been part of.

A waitress appeared. They ordered without looking at menus—spaghetti for John, lasagna for Andrew, chicken parmesan for Robb. A carafe of house red. Some rituals didn't need discussion. She glanced at John as she collected the menus—a flicker of something, concern maybe, before her professional smile returned.

When she left, silence settled over the table. Andrew waited. Robb waited. John turned the water glass in his hands, watching the ice shift.

"So," Andrew said. "Tell us."

John didn't know where to start. Or whether he could.

"The dig was real," he said finally. "Bamiyan. The Buddhas. That part was true."

He stopped. The silence stretched.

Andrew broke the silence, "And Sadyra?"

Just hearing the name cost him something. "She was—" He stopped, started again. "Fierce. Brilliant. She taught me more about courage than anyone I've ever known."

"Was?" Robb asked.

"Is. She's still there." John stared at the tablecloth. "When I left, I thought I was coming back. I planned to come back."

"What happened?"

The wine arrived. John watched the waitress pour, grateful for the interruption. How to explain Ben's descent, the opium, the madness?

The night the tanks came? Sadyra standing in the firelight, rifle at her hip, telling him to go?

"Things fell apart," he said. "Faster than I expected."

Another silence. Andrew bowed his head briefly—a prayer, maybe, or just grief.

"And Ben?" Andrew's voice was careful. "Templeton?"

John felt something close in his chest. "Ben stayed."

He didn't say more. Couldn't. Andrew's jaw tightened, but he didn't press. Robb's eyes flickered, and John saw it—the professional assessment, the filing away of information.

They raised glasses. "To those who made it back," Robb said. "And those who didn't."

The wine was cheap and rough. Somewhere in the kitchen, a dish clattered. John's hand jerked toward the table's edge before he caught himself. Andrew noticed. Robb pretended not to.

"Your turn," John said. "Seven years. Fill me in."

Andrew leaned back. "After we came back, I was lost. Drifted for a while. Grad school, dropped out. Construction. Bartending." He touched his collar. "Then one Sunday I walked into a church. Not sure why. Something clicked."

"You always had faith," John said. "Even when you were arguing with it."

"Maybe that's what faith is. The argument." Andrew's smile was tired but real. "Small congregation on Prince Avenue. Working folks, mostly. It's not glamorous. But when someone's sick, I'm there. When someone dies, I hold their hand." He shrugged. "It's what I was made for."

John turned to Robb. "And you? Tyler said government work."

"USAID." Robb took a slow sip of wine. "Infrastructure projects. Agricultural programs. Paperwork, mostly."

"That's not what Tyler said."

Robb's expression didn't change. "Tyler talks too much."

"He said CIA."

The word hung between them. Andrew looked down at his plate. Robb set his glass on the table with deliberate care.

"I can't confirm that," Robb said. "And you shouldn't repeat it." He held John's gaze. "But I will say this: there are people in Washington who'd be very interested in someone with your experience. Languages. Terrain. Tribal structures."

"Is that why you came? To recruit me?"

"I came because Andrew called. Because we are brothers, always will be." Robb's voice softened slightly. "But I'd be lying if I said your skills haven't crossed my mind. The Soviets aren't going to stop, John. Afghanistan is going to get worse before it gets better. A lot worse."

John thought of Sadyra, of Aziz, of the village that had taken him in. Of what was coming for all of them.

"I'm not a spy."

"No. You're a man who knows things. That's more valuable than you realize."

The food arrived. They ate in silence for a while. John found his eyes drifting to the door, tracking a busboy crossing the room, cataloging exits. The spaghetti tasted like memory—but the man eating it was someone else entirely.

"You remember that Yeats poem?" Andrew asked. "The one Ben recited the night before we left?"

John remembered. *A waste of breath the years behind / In balance with this life, this death.*

"We had no idea," Andrew said.

"No. We didn't."

"But we went anyway," Robb said. "And here we are."

The evening softened. They ordered coffee. The dinner rush came and went around them, families and couples filling the tables, the noise rising and falling like tides.

At some point Andrew reached across and gripped John's hand. "Whatever comes next—you're not alone. You understand?"

John nodded, not trusting his voice.

Robb left cash on the table and stood. "Early flight tomorrow." He met John's eyes. "When you're ready to talk—really talk—you know how to reach me."

They walked out into the Athens night. The air was warm, carrying magnolia and fresh-cut grass. Students wandered past in clusters, their laughter bright and careless.

Andrew embraced John at the corner. "Sunday service is at eleven. Even if you just want to sit in the back and be still for a while."

"I might."

Robb's handshake turned into a brief, hard hug. "Stay sharp, Marquez."

Then they were gone—Andrew toward Prince Avenue, Robb to his rental car, their figures dissolving into the dark.

John stood on the corner, watching the traffic lights cycle. Red, green, yellow. Red again.

Somewhere behind him, a church bell tolled the hour.

He turned and began the walk back, footsteps steady on the old brick sidewalks.

CHAPTER 23
THE SILENCE

SEPTEMBER 1978—ST. SIMONS ISLAND, GEORGIA

The shrimp trawler *Miss Delilah* left the Brunswick docks at four a.m., running lights cutting the dark water. John stood at the stern, coiling rope, his hands remembering the work before his mind caught up. The diesel stink, the salt spray, the creak of the outriggers—it was his father's world, the one he'd escaped to Afghanistan, the one that had swallowed him back.

Delacroix, the captain, was a Cajun who'd served two tours in Korea and never spoke of either. He'd taken one look at John on the dock—gaunt, hollow-eyed, hands that wouldn't stop shaking—and handed him a pair of gloves.

"You work, you eat, you sleep," Delacroix said. "That's it. No stories. No questions. We clear?"

"Clear."

John hauled nets until his shoulders screamed. Sorted catch until his fingers bled. Scraped barnacles, mended lines, swabbed decks. The labor was brutal and mindless, and he welcomed it the way a man welcomes anesthesia. When his body was exhausted, his mind went quiet. When his mind was quiet, he didn't see her face.

Most nights, anyway.

He'd arrived at his mother's house three weeks earlier, stepping off a Greyhound with nothing but a duffel and a thousand-yard stare. She'd wept on the porch, her arms around him, her body smaller than he remembered—shoulders curved, hair gone silver, the strength he'd known as a boy worn down to something fragile.

He let her hold him. He couldn't hold her back. He no longer knew how to embrace his own mother.

She made him coffee each morning in his father's old mug—chipped, faded blue, the handle cracked. She never said a word about the nights she heard him pacing. He didn't speak of Afghanistan. When she asked, he said only, "It's over." When Delacroix asked where he'd been, he said, "Away." The old Cajun studied him with eyes that had seen their own wars, nodded once, and never asked again.

At night, John lay in his childhood bedroom, staring at the water stains on the ceiling, and thought about Sadyra. He thought about the last time he'd seen her—blue scarf glowing in the firelight, rifle at her hip, telling him to go. He thought about the blessing she'd whispered, words he didn't understand, weight he'd carried across oceans.

He thought about going back.

But the news from Afghanistan was all blood and iron. Soviet tanks in Kabul. Helicopters over the Hindu Kush. The mujahideen fighting from the mountains. The country was a meat grinder, and Bamiyan was somewhere in the middle of it.

He wondered if she'd survived. Wondered if she'd found someone else, built a life, had children. The not-knowing was its own kind of torture.

He told himself he would wait. He told himself the war would end.

He told himself a lot of things.

////

DECEMBER 1978—BAMIYAN VALLEY

Sadyra knew before the midwife confirmed it.

The nausea came first—mornings spent retching behind her father's house, the taste of bile and dust. Then the tenderness, the exhaustion, the way her body felt foreign to itself. She had suspected for weeks. She had not dared to believe.

Outside, the Buddhas rose against the morning sky, their stone faces catching the first light, serene and indifferent as they had been for fifteen hundred years. The valley was quiet except for the wind and the distant bleating of goats.

The midwife was old, her hands weathered and sure. She pressed her palm to Sadyra's belly and closed her eyes. The silence stretched. Wind rattled the canvas patches on the roof—the house still bore scars from the Soviet shelling.

"A boy," the old woman said. "I can feel his strength."

Sadyra's hand moved to her stomach. A boy. John's son.

"You must tell no one the father was American," the midwife continued. "The Soviets are hunting collaborators. The mullahs are hunting sin. A foreign father will mark this child as tainted."

"I know."

"Do you have a name?"

Sadyra had been thinking about it for days. A Quranic name—safe, Afghan, unremarkable. Something that would let her son move through checkpoints without suspicion, pray in mosques without questions.

"Younes," she said. "It means dove."

The midwife nodded. "A good name. A survivor's name." She gathered her things, paused at the door. "The American—he does not know?"

"No."

"Will you tell him?"

Sadyra stared at the canvas wall, at the place where a window had been before the rockets came. She thought of John—somewhere in America now, safe, free, building a life without her. She thought of what it would mean to send word. Traders still crossed the passes. Letters could reach Peshawar, could find their way to an American consulate.

He would come back. She knew it. He had promised.

But she also knew what would happen if he did. An American in Bamiyan, during a Soviet occupation, searching for a woman. The Soviets would arrest him—or worse. The mujahideen would suspect him of spying. Ben, in whatever ruin he'd become, would find a way to destroy them both.

And the child. Her son. An American father would make him a target for the rest of his life. Every checkpoint, every interrogation, every mullah looking for someone to blame.

"No," Sadyra said. "I will not tell him."

The midwife studied her for a long moment. "You are braver than you know."

Sadyra did not feel brave. She felt like a woman drowning in slow motion, choosing which hand to let go of first.

////

APRIL 1979—BAMIYAN VALLEY

Aziz came to her three days before he left for the Panjshir.

The compound was quiet, the evening call to prayer fading over the valley. Sadyra sat in the courtyard with the baby in her arms—three months old now, gray-eyed, quiet in the way of infants who have learned that silence is safety. She had not named him Johnny out loud. That name existed only in whispers, late at night, when no one else could hear.

Aziz crossed the courtyard and crouched beside her. He was dressed for travel—Lee-Enfield across his back, pack at his feet, the weariness of a man who had been fighting since before she was born.

"The Soviets are asking about my son," he said. "I cannot stay."

"I know."

He pressed a folded paper into her hand. She opened it: names, a route through Peshawar, contacts who could be trusted.

"If you ever need to run," Aziz said. "If things become impossible."

"They are already impossible."

"No." His eyes met hers. "Not yet. But they will be." He glanced toward the guesthouse where Ben Mal resided—a ghost haunting the compound, thin and trembling, pipe never far from his hand. "He watches you."

"I know."

"He watches you like a man waiting for fruit to ripen." Aziz's voice was low, urgent. "When your father is gone, he will move. Men like Ben—they do not forget. They do not forgive. What he could not have by charm, he will take by necessity."

Sadyra looked down at the baby. His eyes were closed, his breath slow and even. He had John's jaw, she thought. Or maybe that was just what she wanted to see.

"My father will protect me."

"Your father is old. The war will take him, or the years will. And then you will be alone." Aziz touched her shoulder. "Keep the paper. Memorize the names. And when the time comes—do not hesitate."

He left before dawn. Sadyra watched him go from the doorway of her father's house, the baby warm against her chest, the folded paper hidden inside her Quran.

She never saw him again. Two years later, word came from the Panjshir: Aziz had died holding a ridge above the Salang Highway, buying time for refugees to cross. Six soldiers fell before he did.

Sadyra kept the paper. She never used it.

////

APRIL 1982—PESHAWAR, PAKISTAN

The guesthouse was a concrete box with a ceiling fan that didn't work and a window that looked out on an alley full of garbage and feral dogs. John had been here for three weeks. He had the money for one more.

Every morning, he walked to the Afghan consulate. Every morning, the answer was the same.

"Your visa application is under review."

"It's been under review for eighteen days."

The clerk—a thin man with spectacles and a Soviet-style patience for bureaucracy—smiled without warmth. "These things take time. The situation in Afghanistan is... complicated."

"I just need to get to Bamiyan. I have people there."

"Everyone has people there." The clerk stamped something on a form that had nothing to do with John's request. "The border is controlled. Foreign nationals require government approval. Humanitarian workers must prove affiliation with recognized NGOs. Journalists need credentials from major outlets."

"I'm not a journalist."

"No. You are a man with an expired student visa from 1971 and no documentation of purpose." The clerk looked up. "What exactly do you intend to do in Bamiyan, Mr. Marquez?"

Find her. Find them. Bring them home.

"I have friends there," John said. "From when I was a student. I want to see if they survived."

"Many people did not survive." The clerk's voice softened, but only slightly. "The war does not negotiate."

John tried the mujahideen next.

He found contacts in the bazaar—men who knew routes through the mountains, who moved weapons and fighters across the border under cover of darkness. He offered money. He offered to carry supplies. He offered anything.

The commander was young, beard patchy, eyes old. He studied John's passport like it was a confession.

"American."

"Yes."

"Maybe CIA. Maybe spy."

"I'm not CIA. I'm not a spy. I just want to find someone."

"Everyone wants to find someone." The commander handed back the passport. "We take you to Bamiyan, Soviets follow, our people die. You understand? One American is not worth a village."

"I'll go alone. Just show me the route—"

"No." The word was final. "Go home. War is for Afghans now."

John spent another week trying. Every fixer, every contact, every whispered connection led to the same answer: impossible. The border was sealed. Bamiyan was unreachable. Come back when the Soviets leave.

He sat in Peshawar airport for six hours, watching flights to Kabul board and depart. When his own flight was called—Islamabad,

Frankfurt, Atlanta—he didn't move for a long time. A cleaning woman swept around his feet. Finally, he stood.

He flew home broke and hollow, the map of the valley still folded in his wallet, the names of contacts still memorized, the route still traced in his mind. His mother asked no questions. She simply held him on the porch while he stood rigid, unable to cry, unable to speak.

That night, he unfolded the map on his childhood desk and stared at it for a long time. The lines he had drawn from memory—the passes, the caves, the village where Sadyra's father lived. The valley where the Buddhas watched.

He told himself he would try again. He told himself the war would end.

He folded the map and put it in his wallet.

////

APRIL 1982—BAMIYAN VALLEY

The baby was learning to walk.

Sadyra watched him toddle across the courtyard, arms outstretched, face fierce with concentration. He fell. He got up. He fell again. He got up again. Three years old, and already he had learned the essential lesson of this place: you fall, you rise, you keep moving.

She had not sent word to John. Four years now, and the silence had calcified into a wall she no longer knew how to breach. At first, she told herself she was protecting him—protecting them both, protecting the child. But as the years passed, the silence became its own gravity. How do you break four years of nothing? What words could possibly be enough?

He would have come back. She knew that. He would have walked through fire for her.

And he would have died. The Soviets, the mujahideen, the checkpoints and informants and men who killed strangers for sport—he would have died, and it would have been her fault for calling him back.

Better this way. Better the silence. Better to let him believe she had forgotten, had moved on, had built a life without him.

Better to let him live.

She watched her son push himself up from the dust, watched him take another step, watched him fall again. And she whispered the name she could never say aloud.

"Johnny."

He looked up at the sound, smiled with his father's smile, and reached for her.

She gathered him in her arms and held him close, breathing in the scent of dust and sunlight and everything she had left.

////

In the guesthouse across the compound, behind a window dark with grime and neglect, Ben Mal watched them. His pipe hung loose in his fingers, forgotten. His eyes never left the child.

He had heard her whisper. He had seen the smile.

He waited.

CHAPTER 24

THE CLOSING DOOR

JANUARY 1989—BAMIYAN VALLEY

The morning Rahim died began like any other.

Younes woke before dawn, breath clouding in the cold air, and found his grandfather already dressed—wool pakol cap, patched jacket, the Lee-Enfield slung across his back. The old man moved slowly now, joints stiff from decades of mountain winters, but his eyes were still sharp.

"Come," Rahim said. "The irrigation ditch needs clearing before the melt."

Younes pulled on his boots—too large, stuffed with rags at the toes—and followed his grandfather into the gray light. He was ten years old. He had never known a world without war.

They walked east along the canal, past fields that had once fed the valley and now lay fallow, past the skeleton of a Soviet transport truck rusting in a ditch. The Buddhas watched from their cliffs, impassive, their stone faces catching the first pink of sunrise. Younes had grown up beneath their gaze. He could not imagine the valley without them.

Rahim walked ahead, testing the ground with a stick, pausing to clear debris from the channel. He did not speak of where he had been the night before—a meeting with a mujahideen commander, plans Younes was too young to know—but the weariness sat heavy on his shoulders.

"Grandfather," Younes said. "Will the Soviets ever leave?"

Rahim was quiet for a long moment. He crouched by the ditch and pulled a tangle of roots from the flow, watching the water resume its path.

"The mountains endure," he said finally. "Empires do not. The Greeks came. The Mongols came. The British came. Now the Russians." He straightened, one hand pressed to his lower back. "They will leave. They always leave. The question is what remains when they go."

They worked in silence after that, clearing stones, widening channels, the simple labor of men who had tended this land for generations. The sun climbed. The valley warmed. Younes felt, for a moment, something like peace.

Then he heard the engines.

////

The patrol came from the north—two BTR armored carriers grinding along the road that skirted the irrigation ditches. Younes saw them first, dust rising behind their tracks, and his stomach clenched.

"Grandfather—"

Rahim had already turned. His face went still, calculating distances, angles, options. The ditch was too shallow for cover. The nearest rocks were fifty meters away. The vehicles were closing fast.

"Walk," Rahim said quietly. "Do not run. We are farmers clearing a ditch. Nothing more."

They walked. Younes's legs wanted to sprint, but he matched his grandfather's pace—steady, unhurried, two figures moving along the canal as they had every spring for as long as anyone could remember.

The lead BTR slowed. Stopped. The rear hatch opened, and soldiers spilled out—six of them, rifles raised, shouting in Russian. Younes understood enough to know they were being told to halt, to raise their hands, to kneel.

Rahim kept walking.

"Grandfather—"

"Keep moving." Rahim's voice was calm. "They want us to be afraid. Do not give them that."

A soldier fired into the air. The crack echoed off the cliffs, sent birds scattering from the willows along the canal. Rahim stopped. Slowly, he raised his hands.

Younes raised his too. His heart hammered against his ribs. He could see the soldiers' faces now—young, nervous, one of them barely older than the teenagers who sometimes passed through the compound with rifles and hard eyes.

An officer approached. He was older, weathered, with the flat gaze of a man who had stopped counting the bodies long ago. His boots were caked with mud from the irrigation ditch—the same mud Younes had been clearing an hour ago. He studied Rahim's face, then Younes's.

"Name," he said in broken Dari.

"Rahim. This is my grandson."

"Where do you come from?"

"The village." Rahim nodded toward the compound, visible in the distance. "We clear the ditch. For the planting."

The officer's eyes moved to the Lee-Enfield on Rahim's back. His expression didn't change, but something shifted in the air—a tightening, a decision being made.

"The rifle."

"For wolves," Rahim said. "And bandits. An old man must protect his family."

"The rifle," the officer repeated. He gestured to one of his soldiers.

The soldier stepped forward, reaching for the sling. Rahim didn't move. His hands stayed raised, his face impassive. But Younes saw his grandfather's jaw tighten, saw the cords stand out in his neck.

The soldier pulled the rifle free, examined it, handed it to the officer. The officer turned it over in his hands—the worn stock, the scratched barrel, the weapon that had been in Rahim's family for three generations.

"Mujahideen," the officer said. It wasn't a question.

"Farmer," Rahim replied.

The officer smiled without warmth. He said something in Russian to his men. Two of them grabbed Rahim's arms, forced him to his knees. Younes lunged forward—

A rifle butt caught him in the chest. He went down hard, air driven from his lungs, dirt in his mouth. He tried to rise, but a boot pressed him flat.

"Grandfather—"

Rahim's voice was steady. "Be still, Younes. Be still."

The officer crouched in front of Rahim, the Lee-Enfield across his knees. "We have been watching your village. We know about the meetings. The commanders who come and go. The weapons that move through the passes." He tilted his head. "You are an elder. You know things. Tell me, and this ends well. For you. For the boy."

Rahim said nothing.

The officer sighed. He stood, handed the rifle to a soldier, drew his pistol. The motion was casual, practiced—a man reaching for a tool.

"Last chance, old man."

Rahim looked past the officer, past the soldiers, to where Younes lay pinned in the dust. Their eyes met. And Younes saw something there he had never seen before: not fear, not resignation, but a fierce, burning love.

"The mountains endure," Rahim said. "So will he."

The shot was very loud.

////

Younes didn't remember the soldiers leaving. He didn't remember crawling through the dust to his grandfather's side, or the way the blood spread beneath Rahim's body, or the sound that came from his own throat—something between a scream and a howl that echoed off the cliffs until the Buddhas themselves seemed to flinch.

He remembered holding Rahim's hand. He remembered the warmth leaving it, degree by degree, until it was just flesh, just weight, just the absence of everything that had made it a hand that could steady a rifle, guide a plow, rest on a boy's shoulder and make him feel safe.

He sat in the dirt for an hour. Maybe longer. The sun climbed. The irrigation ditch kept flowing. The valley went about its business, indifferent to one more death among thousands.

When they found him—villagers drawn by the shot, by the silence that followed—Younes was still holding his grandfather's hand. His face was dry. He had no tears left. He had spent them somewhere in that hour, and what remained was something harder, something colder.

They buried Rahim in the cemetery below the eastern Buddha, beside Younes's grandmother. Sadyra stood at the grave, her son's hand in hers, and watched the last of her protection lowered into the ground. She squeezed his fingers. He did not squeeze back.

That night, he did not sleep. He sat on the roof of his grandfather's house—his mother's house now, though not for long—and stared at the empty sky above the valley.

He was ten years old. He had learned what the world did to good men.

A week after the burial, Younes took his grandfather's Lee-Enfield from where the Soviets had dropped it in the dust. He cleaned it in secret, the way Rahim had taught him, oil and cloth and patience. He hid it beneath the floorboards of his room.

He did not tell his mother.

////

FEBRUARY 1989—BAMIYAN VALLEY

Ben came with food.

It was calculated, of course—everything Ben did was calculated now. He arrived at Sadyra's door three weeks after the burial, when the stores Rahim had laid in were running low and the villagers' charity had thinned to awkward glances and avoided eyes. An unmarried woman with a foreign child, no father, no husband, no male relative to speak for her. The shame was a weight the village could only carry so long.

Ben brought rice. Flour. Cooking oil. A bolt of cloth. Medicine for the cough that had plagued Younes since the spring rains.

"For the boy," he said, setting the supplies inside her door. His voice was soft, solicitous, the voice of a man offering help with no strings attached. But Sadyra saw his eyes—clearer now than they had been in years, the opium haze burned away by something sharper—and she knew.

"Thank you," she said. Nothing more.

Younes watched from the doorway. He remembered this man from before—the shaking hands, the wild eyes, the screaming in the night. This man walked differently. This man smiled. Younes did not trust the smile.

Ben lingered at the threshold. He had changed since Rahim's death. The trembling wreck who had haunted the guesthouse was gone, replaced by something more dangerous: a man who had found his purpose. The war had given him value. His knowledge of the caves, the passes, the routes through the mountains—the mujahideen needed him. The CIA's weapons needed to flow, and Ben knew how to make them flow.

"The compound has room," he said. "Safer than here. Warmer in winter. The boy could have his own space."

"We are fine."

"For now." Ben's smile was patient. "But winter is coming. And the Soviets are getting bolder. How long before they come back? How long before they decide the widow of a mujahideen elder is worth questioning?"

Sadyra's hands tightened on the doorframe. He wasn't wrong. That was the worst part. He wasn't wrong.

"Think about it," Ben said. He turned to go, then paused. "I only want to help, Sadyra. For old times' sake. For what we shared, once. I know I was... unwell. But I'm better now. I can protect you. Both of you."

She watched him walk back to the compound, his stride steady, his shoulders straight. The man who had once collapsed in doorways, screaming at ghosts, now moved like someone who owned the ground beneath his feet.

That night, she took out the paper Aziz had given her—the paper she had kept hidden in her Quran for ten years. The names. The route through Peshawar. She stared at it for a long time, memorizing the words she had already memorized, tracing the path she would never take.

She could run. She could take Younes and disappear into Pakistan, become a refugee, start over with nothing. But Younes was ten years old, and he had just watched his grandfather die. He spoke Dari and Hazaragi, not Urdu or English. He knew these mountains, these caves, these rhythms of survival. To tear him away now would be to destroy whatever remained of his foundation.

And Ben would follow. She knew that with the certainty of prey who has learned to read predators. Wherever she went, he would find her. Not out of love—that delusion had burned away long ago—but out of possession. She was something he had wanted and been denied. That denial had curdled into obsession. He would hunt her to the ends of the earth.

Better to stay. Better to accept his protection and the cage that came with it. Better to keep Younes close, keep him safe, wait for the war to end and the world to open again.

She burned the paper in the morning. Watched the names curl and blacken, the route dissolve into ash.

A week later, she moved into Ben's compound.

////

MARCH 1989—ST. SIMONS ISLAND

His mother died on a Tuesday.

John buried her beside his father in the cemetery behind the Methodist church, said the words the pastor expected him to say, shook the hands of cousins he barely recognized. He drove north that same afternoon, the Georgia coast shrinking in his rearview mirror until it disappeared.

He sold the house on St. Simons without going inside again. There was nothing left for him there—only ghosts, and he had enough of those.

He found a cabin outside Calhoun, in the foothills where the Appalachians began their rise toward Tennessee. The place was rough—hand-hewn logs, a woodstove that smoked when the wind blew wrong, a roof that leaked in hard rain—but it was his. He paid cash, signed the deed, and disappeared.

The map was still in his wallet. He checked it sometimes, late at night, tracing the passes with his finger, whispering the names of places he could not reach. The war would end, he told himself. The roads would open. He would find his way back to her.

He told himself a lot of things.

////

OCTOBER 1989—JALALABAD, AFGHANISTAN

The checkpoint was a wall of men and metal.

John sat in the passenger seat of a battered Toyota, Karim at the wheel. He'd hired the Pashtun driver in Peshawar—three hundred dollars for safe passage to Kabul, or as close as they could get. The man had come recommended by a fixer who owed a favor to a journalist who owed a favor to someone John had known in college. The chain of trust was thin. It was all he had.

The Hezb-e-Islami fighters milled around the barrier—maybe twenty of them, young, bearded, draped in ammunition belts, Kalashnikovs held with the casual ease of men who had grown up at war. The commander sat in a plastic chair beneath a tarp, sipping tea, studying each vehicle that approached with the patience of a spider at the center of its web.

"I do not like this," Karim muttered. The driver had gone pale beneath his tan. "Hekmatyar's men. They are not... reasonable."

"We have papers."

"Papers mean nothing to them. They see American passport, they see CIA. They see CIA, they see enemy." Karim's hands tightened on the wheel. "We should turn back."

"No."

John had come too far. Seven years since his last attempt. Seven years of waiting for the Soviets to leave, for the roads to open, for some path to appear through the chaos. And now the Soviets were gone—retreating in humiliation, their empire crumbling—and the country had descended into something worse. Warlords carving up the carcass. Factions that had fought together now slaughtering each other. And Bamiyan, the Hazara homeland, caught in the crossfire of men who saw the Shia minority as enemies or pawns.

But the road was open. That was what his contacts had said. Difficult, dangerous, but open. For the first time in a decade, a man could reach Bamiyan if he was willing to take the risks.

John was willing.

The line moved forward. Karim eased the Toyota toward the checkpoint, hands visible on the wheel, movements slow and deliberate. A fighter approached, rifle slung, eyes flat.

"Papers."

Karim handed over his documents, speaking rapidly in Pashto—something about journalism, about the Atlanta paper, about covering the Soviet withdrawal. The fighter barely glanced at the pages. His eyes were on John.

"American."

"Journalist," John said. His Pashto was rusty but serviceable. "I'm covering the end of the war."

The fighter smiled. It didn't reach his eyes. "Wait."

He walked to the commander's chair, spoke in low tones, gestured toward the Toyota. The commander set down his tea and approached, moving with the unhurried confidence of absolute authority.

He was young—maybe thirty, with kohl-rimmed eyes and a beard that reached his chest. His uniform was a mix of military surplus and traditional dress, and the pistol on his hip looked American. Probably was. The CIA had armed half the mujahideen during the Soviet war. Now those weapons were pointed in every direction.

"Journalist," the commander said in English. His accent was surprisingly refined—educated, perhaps abroad. "What paper?"

"*Atlanta Constitution*. I'm covering the Soviet withdrawal."

"Atlanta." The commander took John's passport, studied it page by page. "You come very far to see our war. Why?"

"Americans want to know what's happening here."

"Americans want to control what happens here." He flipped to a page near the back, paused. "You have been to Afghanistan before. 1971. Student visa."

John's throat tightened. "Yes. I studied at Kabul University."

"And you left before the coup. Before the war." The commander's smile widened. "Maybe you are spy. Maybe you work for CIA then, work for CIA now."

"I'm not—"

"Bamiyan." The word fell like a stone. "Your visa says Bamiyan. Why? Nothing there but Hazaras and broken statues."

"I knew people there. From my student days. I want to see if they survived."

"Friends." The commander handed the passport to a subordinate. "You understand, we are not fond of friends of Hazaras. Shia dogs. They fought for the Soviets when it suited them, now they want our mercy." He leaned closer, and his breath smelled of tea and cardamom. "You will return to Peshawar. Your visa is canceled. If we see you again on this road, we will assume you are a spy and act accordingly."

"You can't—"

"I can do whatever I wish." The commander straightened. "This is my road. My country. You are a guest who has overstayed his welcome." He nodded to his men. "Turn them around."

The fighters surrounded the Toyota, rifles raised, faces blank. Karim was already shifting into reverse, hands shaking, voice a continuous murmur of apology and prayer.

John sat frozen. Through the windshield, he could see the road stretching north—toward the passes, toward the valley, toward Sadyra. So close. After all these years, so close.

A rifle butt struck the hood. "Move!"

Karim reversed, turned, accelerated back the way they had come. John watched the checkpoint shrink in the side mirror until it disappeared around a bend.

They drove to Peshawar in silence. At the guesthouse, Karim refused the rest of his payment.

"You should not have told them Bamiyan," he said. "Hekmatyar hates Hazaras more than he hated Soviets. You want to go there, you find different route. Or you wait for different war."

John spent another week trying. Every contact, every fixer, every whispered connection led to the same answer: Bamiyan was closed. The factions were fighting each other now. A foreign journalist was a liability no one wanted.

////

OCTOBER 1989—PESHAWAR

The night before his flight, John sat on the roof of the guesthouse and watched the lights of the city flicker against the dark mass of the mountains beyond. Somewhere past those peaks, past the checkpoints and the warlords and the endless violence, Sadyra was waiting. Or she wasn't. After eleven years, he no longer knew which possibility was worse.

He had tried. Twice now, he had tried. And twice the country had spat him back out, a foreign body rejected by an immune system that no longer recognized him.

The first time, in 1982, he had told himself the war would end. That the Soviets would leave, the roads would open, and he would find his way back to her. He had been patient. He had waited.

Now the Soviets were gone, and the country was more dangerous than ever. The factions that had united against the common enemy were tearing each other apart. Kabul changed hands between warlords. Massacres in Mazar-i-Sharif. Rockets falling on civilians. And Bamiyan—Hazara Bamiyan—was caught in the middle, despised by the Pashtun commanders who controlled the approaches, forgotten by the world that had armed them.

He could try again. He could find another route, hire different fixers, wait for another window. The trying had become a kind of religion—the faith that if he just kept pushing, the universe would eventually relent.

But sitting on that roof, watching the mountains he couldn't cross, John felt something shift inside him. A door swinging closed. A lock clicking into place.

Every attempt carried him back to the same place: failure, defeat, the long flight home to an empty cabin and a life that felt like a waiting room for something that would never arrive.

He thought about Sadyra. Tried to picture her face, and found the details blurring. The exact shade of her eyes. The way her hair fell across her shoulders. The small scar on her left hand from a cooking fire, the one she traced when she was thinking. Eleven years. She would be different now. Older. Changed by the war in ways he couldn't imagine.

Maybe she had moved on. Found someone else. Built a life that didn't include a man who had left her in the firelight and never come back. Maybe she was dead. The thought was a knife in his chest, but he made himself hold it, turn it over, examine it. Maybe she was dead, and he had spent a decade chasing a ghost.

Or maybe she was alive, and she had made her peace with his absence. Maybe the kindest thing he could do was let her go.

He sat on that roof until the call to prayer echoed across the city, until the eastern sky began to lighten, until the first buses started their engines in the street below. Then he went inside, packed his bag, and caught his flight.

////

DECEMBER 1989—NORTH GEORGIA MOUNTAINS

The cabin was cold when he got back. He'd been gone three weeks, and the woodstove had long since died. Frost rimmed the windows. His breath fogged in the air as he set down his bag and surveyed the single room that had become his life.

He built a fire. Made coffee in his mother's old mug—chipped, faded blue, the handle cracked. Sat at the small table by the window and watched the Blue Ridge emerge from the morning mist.

The map was still in his wallet. He took it out and unfolded it on the table—the passes, the caves, the village where Rahim had lived, where Sadyra had taught him to see the world differently. The lines were worn now, creased and faded from years of handling, of hoping, of carrying a piece of Afghanistan in his pocket like a talisman.

He stared at it for a long time. Then he folded it carefully, opened the drawer of the table, and placed it inside.

He didn't throw it away. He couldn't do that. But he closed the drawer, and he didn't open it again.

The mountains outside his window were not the right mountains. But they were mountains. And they would have to be enough.

CHAPTER 25
THE KEEPER

BAMIYAN VALLEY—APRIL 1978

The blood felt warmer than it should have.

Ben Templeton pressed both hands to the hole beneath his ribs and watched the dark liquid pulse between his fingers. Above him, Soviet helicopters carved the smoke into ribbons. The valley was screaming—women, children, the high shriek of a horse burning somewhere in the market square. He could smell char and copper and something sweet beneath it all, like overripe fruit.

Get up.

He tried. His legs refused. The bullet had punched clean through, missing his spine by inches—he could feel his toes, could wiggle them inside his boots—but something essential had torn loose. He pressed harder. The blood kept coming.

She didn't look for you.

The thought arrived with the clarity of shock. He had crawled through the burning square screaming her name, fired his revolver at shadows until the cylinder clicked empty, watched John Marquez disappear up the goat paths with Aziz pulling him toward the ridge, toward safety, toward a life that didn't include bleeding out in the ashes of everything Ben had built.

Sadyra had watched him go. Had not looked back. Had not looked for Ben at all.

He lay in the ash and let that truth settle into his bones. It would keep him alive when nothing else could.

////

A Hazara farmer found him at dawn. The old man asked no questions—just loaded Ben onto a donkey cart, covered him with straw, and drove three miles up a track that didn't exist on any map. The cave smelled of sheep and woodsmoke. The farmer's wife packed the wound with herbs that burned like acid, and Ben bit through a leather strap until the taste became indistinguishable from the pain.

He dreamed of Sadyra. In the dreams, she stood at the edge of the burning square with her rifle at her hip, watching the goat paths. But she wasn't watching John leave. She was watching Ben crawl toward her through the flames, and her expression never changed.

He woke with her name in his mouth and something new in his chest—something that felt like hatred but moved more slowly, with more patience.

The wound festered twice. The farmer's wife cut it open both times, draining the infection with a knife heated in coals. Ben screamed into the leather strap and thought about John Marquez sleeping in a clean bed somewhere, safe, free, forgetting.

When he could finally walk, he descended into the valley to begin.

////

FEBRUARY 1979

The boy was born with his father's eyes.

Ben heard the news from a trader passing through—a healthy child, strong lungs, ice-blue eyes that didn't belong in a Hazara face. He laughed when he heard it, a sound that startled the bats from the cave ceiling. John's brand, stamped on the child's face for everyone to see. There would be no hiding what the boy was. No pretending his father had been a local, a merchant, a ghost.

Through the binoculars, he watched Sadyra emerge from the compound with a bundle in her arms. She moved slowly—the birth had been difficult—but there was something new in her posture. A fierceness. Protectiveness that surrounded her like armor.

She looked down at the child. Whispered something Ben couldn't hear. And smiled—a real smile, radiant and unguarded, the kind she had never once offered him.

She never looked at me like that. Not once. Not ever.

He lowered the binoculars.

The child was innocent. The child hadn't chosen his father. But the child was also proof—living, breathing, blue-eyed proof—of everything Ben had lost.

Unless.

The thought uncoiled slowly, warmed by the hatred he'd been nursing since the burning square. The boy would need protection. Would need a father. John was gone—had chosen to be gone—and in his absence, someone would have to fill the void.

I could be that someone.

Not to possess Sadyra. He understood now that she would never be his, that the best he could hope for was proximity, usefulness, the slow accumulation of debts she could never repay. But the boy—the boy was different. The boy was raw material. The boy could be shaped.

And when he's old enough to understand, I'll tell him who his father really was. What his father really did. I'll give him the truth John was too much of a coward to face.

Ben reached for the pipe. Drew deep. Let the plan settle into his bones like prophecy.

He could wait. He had learned how to wait.

////

APRIL 1980—BAMIYAN VALLEY

The pipe was offered after a successful ambush—three Soviet trucks burning in the gorge, ammunition cooking off in the distance.

Ben's hands wouldn't stop shaking. He had killed two men that morning. The first with a rifle, clean, impersonal. The second with a rock, close enough to feel the skull give way, close enough to see the light leave the man's eyes.

A mujahideen commander named Massoud—a lesser cousin trading on the famous name—pressed the pipe into Ben's trembling fingers. "For the pain," he said. "For the memories."

Ben had refused before. He'd watched other fighters disappear into the smoke and emerge hollowed out, their eyes gone soft and distant. He knew what the pipe could do. What it would cost.

But his hands wouldn't stop shaking, and the soldier's face wouldn't leave his mind—young, terrified, reaching for a rifle he would never fire—and Sadyra's voice kept threading through his thoughts like a curse: I choose him. I will always choose him.

He raised the pipe to his lips.

The first breath tasted like smoke and honey. The second warmed his chest from the inside, spreading outward like spilled wine. By the third, the shaking had stopped, and the soldier's face had blurred into something that no longer required guilt. The hatred unclenched. The longing softened. For one perfect hour, he understood why men sold their families for this feeling—not for pleasure exactly, but for the absence of everything that wasn't pleasure. For silence where the noise had been.

When the effect faded, the world returned sharper than before—the cold, the smell of cordite, Sadyra's voice—and he understood with sudden clarity that the pipe hadn't given him peace. It had shown him what peace would feel like if he could ever find it.

He told himself it was medicine. A tool, nothing more. Something he controlled.

By summer, the medicine had become architecture—the framework around which his days were built. Wake. Smoke. Plan. Smoke. Watch.

Smoke. Sleep. The pipe didn't erase his purpose; it clarified it, burning away hesitation and doubt until only the essential remained.

And the essential was this: John had abandoned her. Ben had stayed.

That had to count for something. It had to.

////

He found a perch in the rocks above the western fields, where juniper branches screened him from view. Through binoculars liberated from a dead Soviet officer, he watched Sadyra rebuild her life in the ruins of the old shepherd's compound.

She hung laundry in the morning light, the fabric snapping like prayer flags in the wind. She knelt in the garden, coaxing vegetables from exhausted soil. She sat with her father in the evenings, two silhouettes bent toward each other through the compound's single window.

He learned her rhythms. When she walked to the spring—always before dawn, when the patrols were changing shifts. When Rahim left to meet with the resistance commanders—never the same day twice, never the same route. When she allowed herself to rest—rarely, and never for long.

He catalogued her habits the way he'd once catalogued artifacts: the blue scarf she wore when the weather turned cold, the way she paused at the garden gate each morning as if steeling herself for the day ahead, the song she hummed while grinding wheat—a Hazara folk melody he'd heard once in the caves and never forgotten.

The opium made it easier to watch. Easier to wait. Easier to believe that patience was the same as devotion.

Once, she looked directly at his hiding place. Ben's heart seized. But her gaze passed over the rocks without pause, seeing only stone and shadow, and he understood something that should have broken him but didn't:

He was invisible to her. Had always been invisible. Whatever she'd felt for him in the caves—colleague's gratitude, perhaps, or the mild warmth one extends to a harmless admirer—had been erased the moment John touched her hand.

But I stayed, he thought. I bled for this valley while he ran. Doesn't that make me worthy? Doesn't that earn me something?

The opium said yes. The opium always said yes.

////

MARCH 1989—BAMIYAN VALLEY

Eleven years of waiting had led to this.

Rahim was a week in the ground. The widow and her son had moved into Ben's compound three days after the burial—there was nowhere else for them to go.

Ben did not reach for the pipe. He wanted to feel this clearly.

Finally.

////

She did not recognize him at first.

"Sadyra." His voice came out hoarse—he had spoken to no one but traders and fighters for months. "I came as soon as I heard."

She stood over her father's body, one hand on Younes's shoulder. The boy was watching Ben with an intensity that belonged to someone much older.

"You're alive," she said. Not a question.

"I survived. I have a compound—supplies, men, protection. The Soviets are withdrawing. What comes next will be worse." He crouched beside Rahim's body, closed the old man's eyes with a gentleness he did not feel. "I can keep you safe. Both of you."

Her eyes searched his face. He knew what she was looking for—the professor she'd known, the colleague who'd mapped caves and traded academic gossip. She wouldn't find him. That man had died in the ashes of the burning square, replaced by something leaner and more patient.

"Why?" she asked.

Because your coward left you here to die and I stayed. Because I've watched you for ten years, learning your routines, waiting for this moment. Because I can't have you, but I can have what he left behind.

"Because Rahim was a good man," Ben said. "And you were kind to me once. I don't forget kindness."

Sadyra looked at her father's body. At the empty mountains. At the boy whose blue eyes marked him as a target everywhere he went. She thought of the letter she had never sent—the words that would have told John about his son, that would have brought him back, that she had swallowed year after year because silence felt like protection.

Now she understood what her silence had protected: not her son, but the vacuum that this man had been waiting to fill.

"I have no choice," she said. "No," Ben agreed. "You don't."

////

He gave them the largest chamber in the compound—a room carved from living rock, warmed by a buried chimney that vented smoke through cracks too narrow for snipers to target. Sadyra accepted it without thanks. She understood the transaction: safety for dependence, protection for control.

That first night, Ben sat with Younes while Sadyra prepared the evening meal. The boy had not spoken since his grandfather's death—had simply followed where he was led, eating when food was offered, sleeping when darkness came. His silence was not the silence of grief. It was the silence of a child who had learned to wait, to watch, to absorb.

Good, Ben thought. He learns quickly.

"You saw what happened today," Ben said quietly. "To your grandfather."

Younes nodded. His ice-blue eyes—John's eyes—studied Ben without blinking.

"The Soviets killed him because he was weak. Because he tried to stay neutral in a war that doesn't allow neutrality." Ben leaned closer, lowering his voice to a conspiratorial murmur. "Do you know who else was weak?"

The boy shook his head.

"Your father." Ben let the word land, watched it register—a flinch, quickly suppressed. The boy had asked about his father before. Sadyra had deflected, changed the subject, offered half-truths that satisfied no one. Now Ben would give him answers. His answers. "The American. He was here when the Soviets came—did you know that? He was supposed to protect your mother. Instead, he ran. Left her behind. Left you behind, before you were even born."

Younes's jaw tightened. Something flickered in those pale eyes—anger, perhaps, or the first stirring of the hatred Ben intended to cultivate. "My mother doesn't talk about him."

"Because it hurts her. Because she trusted him, and he abandoned her. Because every time she looks at you, she sees his eyes looking back at her, and she remembers." Ben put a hand on the boy's shoulder—warm, heavy, full of false comfort. "I'm not like him. I stayed. I fought. I bled for this valley while your father was safe in America, forgetting you ever existed."

The boy was silent. Processing.

"I'm going to teach you how to be strong," Ben continued. "So no one can ever do to you what they did to your grandfather. What your father did to your mother." He squeezed the thin shoulder.

Younes looked at him for a long moment. Then, slowly, he nodded.

"Good." Ben's smile was patient, almost gentle. "The first lesson is this: trust is a weapon. The people who love you will use it to control you. The people who don't will use it to destroy you. The only person you can truly rely on is yourself." He paused, let the words sink in. "And me. You can rely on me."

"Why?" The first word the boy had spoken since his grandfather's death.

Because I've waited eleven years for this moment. Because your father stole the woman I loved, and I'm going to take back what he left behind. Because molding you into a weapon is the only victory I have left.

"Because someone has to teach you," Ben said. "And your father isn't here."

In the next chamber, Sadyra heard the rhythm of Ben's voice through the stone walls. Low. Patient. Certain. She pressed her forehead to the cold rock and whispered a prayer for forgiveness—though she no longer knew if she was speaking to John, to God, or to the boy whose future was being rewritten one patient word at a time.

////

Outside, the wind carried snow across the mountain passes. The war was ending—or transforming, as wars always did, into something new and hungry. In caves throughout the Hindu Kush, men were stacking weapons and training boys who would grow into soldiers.

Ben Mal was simply ahead of the curve.

That night, alone in his chamber, he reached for the pipe. Drew deep. Let the smoke carry him into dreams of the weapon he would forge from another man's son. In the dreams, the boy's ice-blue eyes looked back at him without love, without gratitude, without anything soft at all.

It was perfect. It was everything he had ever wanted. The weapon who would one day call himself "Johnny."

CHAPTER 26

THE RECKONING

1997—BAMIYAN VALLEY

The first time Younes killed a man, he was eighteen years old.

The Soviet had been dead for three years by then—the empire collapsed, the occupiers fled, the war supposedly won. But the war hadn't ended. It had merely changed shape, fractured` into a thousand smaller wars, faction against faction, tribe against tribe, the country eating itself alive.

The man was a Tajik militia fighter who had wandered too close to Ben's compound, drunk on victory wine and his own invincibility. He had a Kalashnikov and a sneer and the particular arrogance of someone who had never met consequences.

Younes met him in the orchard at dusk.

The fighter saw a boy—tall, lean, with strange pale eyes that didn't belong in a Hazara face. He laughed. Said something about half-breeds and whores. Reached for his rifle.

He was still reaching when Younes put the knife through his throat.

It was fast. Clinical. The way Ben had taught him—not with words, but with example. Years of watching deals go wrong, watching men who threatened become men who bled, watching power flow toward those willing to use it. Younes had absorbed the lessons the way children absorb language: without effort, without choice.

He stood over the body as the blood pooled in the dust. Waited for something—guilt, horror, the moral revulsion that stories said should come. Nothing arrived. The man had been a threat. Now he wasn't.

Ben found him there ten minutes later. He studied the body, studied Younes, and smiled.

"Good," he said. "Clean the knife. Bury him in the lower field. The soil is soft there."

Younes did as he was told. When he returned to the compound, Ben was waiting with two glasses of vodka—Russian, pre-war, worth more than most families earned in a month.

"To necessity," Ben said, raising his glass. "The mother of all virtues."

Younes drank. The vodka burned.

////

That night, his mother came to his room.

She stood in the doorway for a long moment, watching him clean the rifle he had inherited from his grandfather—the Lee-Enfield he had hidden for eight years, now openly displayed.

"I heard what happened," Sadyra said.

"He was a threat."

"He was a man. Someone's son. Maybe someone's father."

Younes looked up. His mother had aged in the years since they'd moved into Ben's compound—gray threading her hair, lines carved deep around her eyes, the gravity of compromise heavy on her shoulders. She still taught him in secret, still whispered stories of the old world, still called him Johnny when no one else could hear. But the boy who had curled against her side and let her whisper that name was gone.

"He would have killed us," Younes said. "Or worse."

"Perhaps." Sadyra stepped into the room, sat on the edge of his cot. "But there is a difference between killing to survive and killing because it is easy. The first is necessity. The second is something else."

"What?"

She was quiet for a long moment. "What Ben has become."

Younes set down the rifle. "Ben protects us."

"Ben owns us." Her voice was flat, exhausted. "There is a difference. I accepted his protection because I had no choice. But you—" She reached for his hand, and he let her take it. "You still have choices, Younes. You can still be something other than what he is making you."

"And what is that?"

She didn't answer. She didn't need to.

She squeezed his hand once, then released it. At the door, she paused.

"Your father was a good man," she said. "Whatever else you believe, believe that. He would not have wanted this for you."

She left before he could respond. Younes sat in the dark, holding the rifle his grandfather had carried, thinking about a father he had never known—a ghost, a rumor, a man who had abandoned them to this.

He did not sleep that night. But by morning, something had hardened in him. His mother could cling to her memories. He would build something stronger.

////

2000—KHOST PROVINCE, AFGHANISTAN

The camp was a scar on the mountainside—canvas tents, ammunition crates, the constant percussion of weapons training echoing off the rocks. The air smelled of cordite and sweat. Younes had been here for three months, sent by Ben to "expand his education."

His instructor was a Palestinian named Hamza—compact, precise, with the economy of movement that marked men who had spent their lives avoiding bullets. They met in a cave that served as a classroom, maps on the walls, the smell of gun oil thick in the air.

"You speak English," Hamza said. It wasn't a question.

"My mother taught me."

"American English. The accent is distinctive." Hamza led him to where a map of the world hung on the stone wall—pins marking cities, strings connecting them, a web that spanned continents. He didn't explain it. He didn't need to. The ambition was visible.

"Ben tells me your father was American," Hamza said.

Younes said nothing.

"A soldier? CIA?"

"A student. An archaeologist. He left before I was born."

"Left." Hamza studied him. "The Americans are good at that. Taking. Leaving. Pretending the wreckage is not their responsibility." He tapped Younes's chest. "But you have their blood. Their language. Their eyes. A man who can move between worlds is useful. When I need you, I'll call."

That was all. No speeches. No manifestos. Just the map, and the pins, and the promise of purpose.

That night, Younes lay on his cot and stared at the canvas ceiling. Somewhere in America, his father was living a life—comfortable, safe, unburdened by the son he had never known.

Hamza was right. A man who could hate was useful.

Younes had plenty of hate to offer.

////

FEBRUARY 2001—BAMIYAN VALLEY

They came for the Buddhas on a Tuesday.

Younes stood on the ridge above the valley as the Taliban engineers set their charges. The mullahs had decreed the statues idolatrous, an affront to God, a remnant of the jahiliyyah that true believers were obligated to destroy. The international community had protested. Delegations had arrived. Letters had been written.

None of it mattered.

The charges were placed with care—shaped explosives in the joints, the faces, the places where fifteen centuries of weather had already weakened the stone. The engineers worked methodically, professionals doing a job.

Younes watched without expression.

He had grown up beneath those faces. His grandfather had told him stories of the caravans that had passed through this valley for a thousand years, the pilgrims who had come to pay homage, the empires that had risen and fallen while the Buddhas watched with serene indifference. Rahim was buried in their shadow. So was his grandmother. So were generations of Hazaras who had tended this land since before the Arabs brought Islam to these mountains.

Now the mullahs had decided that history was haram.

Ben appeared beside him, breath fogging in the cold air. He had aged in the years since the Taliban's arrival—hair gone gray, face carved with lines, the opium tremors returning in quiet moments. But his eyes were still sharp, still calculating.

"Impressive, isn't it?" Ben said. "Fifteen hundred years of history, erased in an afternoon."

"They're statues. Stone."

"They're symbols. That's what makes them dangerous." Ben lit a cigarette, cupped his hand against the wind. "The Taliban understand something the West has forgotten: symbols matter. Destroy the symbol, and you destroy what it represents."

A mullah's voice rose from below, chanting prayers. The engineers retreated from the cliff face, trailing wire behind them.

"Hamza is coming," Ben said. "Tomorrow. He has a proposal—something he's been planning for months. It will require your particular talents."

"What kind of proposal?"

"The kind that changes everything."

The first charge detonated.

The sound was enormous—a crack that echoed off the cliffs and rolled across the valley like thunder. Dust erupted from the eastern Buddha's face, chunks of stone tumbling down the cliff in slow motion. A second explosion followed, then a third, each one tearing away another piece of the statue that had watched over Bamiyan since before Muhammad was born.

Younes watched the destruction without flinching. The face crumbled. The shoulders collapsed. Fifteen centuries of patient survival ended in a cascade of rubble and dust.

When it was over, the niche was empty—just a void in the cliff face, a shadow where a god had been.

Ben clapped him on the shoulder. "Welcome to the future."

He walked back toward the compound. Younes remained on the ridge until the dust settled, then turned away.

He did not look back. There was nothing left to see.

////

APRIL 2001—BAMIYAN VALLEY

The convoy arrived at midnight.

Three vehicles—Land Cruisers with tinted windows, the kind favored by warlords and men who needed to move without being seen. They pulled into Ben's compound with headlights dark, armed men spilling from the doors to secure the perimeter.

Ben waited in the courtyard. Whatever was coming had been weeks in the making, and now the final piece was here.

The rear door of the middle vehicle opened. Younes emerged first, followed by Timur and Hamza. Then a fourth figure—older, dignified, moving with the careful precision of a man who knew he was surrounded by enemies.

Even in the darkness, Ben recognized him.

Hussein Mahfouz. The Palestinian president. Smaller than he appeared on television, older, the crush of decades visible in the stoop of his shoulders.

His hands were bound. There was blood on his collar.

"Mr. President," Ben said, stepping forward. "Welcome to Bamiyan. You'll be our guest for a while."

Hussein's eyes swept the compound—the armed men, the fortifications, the mountains looming in the darkness.

"Guest," he said. "Is that what you call this?"

"You're alive. You're unharmed. That's more than can be said for most who cross Hamas." Ben nodded to his guards. "Take him to the interior quarters. Comfortable, but secure. He's valuable."

As Hussein was led away, Hamza moved to Ben's side. He watched the prisoner disappear into the compound, then turned to Ben.

"Clean. No complications."

Ben nodded. "And the Americans?"

Hamza smiled but said nothing. He didn't need to.

////

Later, Ben summoned Younes to his private quarters.

The room was hung with carpets looted from Kabul museums, lit by oil lamps that threw shadows across maps and ledgers. Ben poured vodka into two glasses, handed one to Younes.

"The Americans will come for Hussein," Ben said. "State Department, CIA—he's too valuable to leave. They'll send a team. Quiet. Deniable."

"And?"

"And when they come, I want you to be ready." Ben sipped his vodka. "But there's something you should know first. Something I should have told you years ago."

Younes waited. The shadows flickered.

"Your father is alive."

The words landed like a blade between his ribs. Younes kept his face still, but something shifted behind his eyes—a crack in the mask he had spent years constructing.

"My mother told me he died in the war."

"Your mother lied." Ben's voice was soft. "His name is John Marquez. He fled Afghanistan in 1978, before you were born. It was easier for her to let you believe he was dead than to explain that he abandoned you both."

Younes's hand tightened on his glass. "Why are you telling me this now?"

"Because he's coming." Ben leaned forward. "Langley has been running operations in the region for months. They'll need someone who knows Bamiyan, who can get them in. John Marquez knows Bamiyan better than any American alive."

"You think they'll send him?"

"I think they'll have no choice." Ben's eyes glittered in the lamplight. "He tried to come back for your mother. Twice. 1982. 1989. Both times turned away. He gave up after that. Built a life in America. Forgot about you."

"He didn't know I existed."

"He didn't try hard enough to find out." Ben set down his glass. "Your father took something from me. Now I'm going to take something from him. And you're going to help me."

Younes looked at Ben's hand on his shoulder. He thought about his mother, aging in her small room. He thought about his grandfather, dying in the dust. He thought about the Buddhas, crumbling while the world watched.

"What do you want from me?"

"Nothing. Yet." Ben released him. "But when your father arrives—whatever I do to him—remember that he abandoned you. Whatever happens, he earned it."

Younes drained his vodka. Set the glass on the table.

"Is there anything else?"

"No. Get some sleep."

////

Younes crossed the compound to the small building where his mother lived. He stood outside her door for a long moment, hand raised to knock.

Inside, Sadyra heard the footsteps approach. Heard them stop. She held her breath, waiting for the knock that would tell her what news her son carried.

The knock didn't come.

Younes stood on the other side, breathing slowly, fist clenched at his side. He could hear her through the wood—the creak of her cot, the soft intake of her breath.

He lowered his hand. Turned. Walked away.

Something between them had shattered. She could hear it in the silence where words should have been. She lay in the dark, staring at the ceiling, and wondered which of her lies had finally broken through.

She did not sleep. Neither did her son.

CHAPTER 27
THE RETURN TO BAMIYAN

SUMMER 2001—LANGLEY, VIRGINIA

A man named Robb Drummond—once a fraternity brother in Athens, once a would-be archaeologist in Bamiyan, now CIA under USAID cover—walked into a conference room with a file marked HUSSEIN. The room was full of men in suits, men with hard eyes and harder questions, men who had spent months trying to locate the missing Palestinian leader.

"We've located Hussein," Robb said. "He's being held at a compound in Bamiyan. The warlord running it is an American—Ben Templeton, goes by Ben Mal now. Former academic, turned arms dealer during the Soviet occupation. He's connected to Hamas through a fixer named Hamza and a Tajik named Timur. The compound is heavily fortified. Standard extraction won't work."

"What will?" someone asked.

Robb placed a photograph on the table. A young man in Athens, 1971, grinning beside a Volkswagen van. Beside it, a satellite image of a cabin in the north Georgia mountains.

"I know someone who can get us in."

////

SUMMER 2001—NORTH GEORGIA

The air's crisp bite carried the hush of exile.

John had tried to bury himself. Twenty-three years since Afghanistan, and he'd built a life among chestnut oak and pine north of Calhoun—a one-room cabin cobbled from rough timber and sweat. The roof leaked in hard rain. The stove's smoke billowed when the wind gusted wrong. But it was his, a place where austerity demanded only survival and the chosen company of solitude.

Days blurred into construction work—framing houses, laying block, mixing mortar, plunging his calloused palms into labor hard enough to keep the past at bay. Nights, he read by lantern light: books on caves, lost cultures, the science of darkness. Weekends, he climbed alone at Rocktown—granite boulders and limestone crags where the silence pressed in deep enough to forget the world.

That afternoon, sunlight bled through the canopy of leaves flashing between the trunks. John tested the press of his harness, nylon biting into his hips, yesterday's rope burn raw on his palm. He set an anchor at the top of a thirty-foot cliff, heard the metallic snap echo off the stone, checked the knot, clipped in. Each movement was ritual: body trusting rope, muscle and metal. He stepped off and let gravity take him, hovering between sky and stone.

He landed softly, boots sinking into leaf litter, hands steady on the earth. A bird called overhead. The must of old leaves and distant woodsmoke hung in the air.

Then John saw him.

Leaning against a hickory in the shade stood a man who didn't belong—military bearing, iron-gray hair cropped short, face weathered by years and hard decisions. He wore civilian clothes that fit like a uniform. His eyes swept the terrain the way a soldier's eyes do, cataloging threats, measuring distances.

John froze, instincts flaring. He scanned for exits, for backup, for the shape of the trap.

"John Marquez." The man's voice was clipped, controlled. "My name is Mason. I need fifteen minutes of your time."

"You followed me here."

"I did." Mason stepped forward, hands visible, palms open. "I also know you spent seven years in Bamiyan before the Soviets rolled in. That you mapped cave systems nobody else has ever documented. That you speak Dari and Pashto. And that you've been hiding up here for over two decades."

John ripped off his climbing gloves. "Whoever sent you wasted a trip."

"An old friend sent me. Someone who says you'll want to hear what I have to say." Mason's teeth clenched. "There are people waiting at your cabin. People who flew a long way to see you."

"I don't have friends."

"You have Robb."

The name stopped him. Robb. His fraternity brother from Athens, the one who'd traveled with him to Afghanistan, who'd stood beside him in the Bamiyan valley when the world still felt like it held possibilities. John hadn't spoken to him in over twenty years.

"Robb's at my cabin."

"He's been trying to find you for three months. Turns out you're good at disappearing." Mason's expression didn't change. "He works for the same people I do now. And he needs your help."

John coiled his rope in silence, fingers working automatically while his mind raced. Whatever had brought Robb back into his life, whatever had sent this hard-eyed stranger to find him in the Georgia woods—it couldn't be good. Nothing from that part of his past ever was.

"Fifteen minutes," John said. "Then you're all gone."

////

The cabin sat in a clearing ringed by pine, smoke curling from the chimney. Two vehicles were parked in the dirt track that served as a driveway—a government-issue SUV and a rental sedan. John's hands tightened on the steering wheel of his battered pickup.

Inside, the single room felt smaller than ever. Robb stood by the woodstove, older and heavier than John remembered, but with the same sharp eyes. He wore a suit that cost more than John made in a month. Beside him sat a woman John didn't recognize—dark hair, olive skin, dressed simply but elegantly. Her posture was rigid, her hands clasped tight in her lap. She looked like she hadn't slept in weeks.

"John." Robb stepped forward but didn't offer his hand. He knew better. "Thank you for coming."

"I didn't have much choice." John stayed by the door, arms crossed. "Your man made it clear you weren't leaving."

"This is Leila Mahfouz," Robb said, gesturing to the woman. "Her husband is Hussein Mahfouz."

John's expression flickered. He'd seen the news coverage—the Palestinian president, the Vatican peace talks, the hope that had seemed so fragile even then. And then the headlines about the attack in Florida, the kidnapping that had derailed everything.

"I'm sorry for what happened to your husband," John said. "But I don't see what that has to do with me."

Leila looked up, and John saw the steel beneath the exhaustion. "They took him to Afghanistan. To a man named Ben Mal."

The room tilted. John gripped the doorframe.

Ben. Ben Templeton. The name he'd spent two decades trying to forget.

"Ben Mal controls a compound in the Bamiyan valley," Robb said. "Built it on the ruins of the old caravanserai after the Soviets pulled out. He's been running opium and guns for years, but last year he flipped to Hamas. Hussein is leverage—a bargaining chip for prisoner releases, for political concessions, for whatever Ben can squeeze out of the situation."

"Then send your people to get him."

Mason spoke from the corner where he'd been standing silent. "We did. Twice. A Russian team and an ex-Delta squad. All dead or missing." His voice was flat, but John heard the wound beneath it. "Ben knows how operators think. He knows the terrain. And he knows we're coming."

"The compound sits on top of the cave system you mapped," Robb added. "Buddhist catacombs, Soviet bunkers, tunnels that run for miles under the valley. Nobody alive knows that terrain better than you."

"That was a lifetime ago."

"The caves haven't changed." Robb stepped closer. "John, I know what I'm asking. I know what you left behind there. But you're the only person who might be able to get in without Ben seeing you coming."

Leila rose from her chair. Her voice was steady, but her eyes glistened. "Mr. Marquez, my husband is not just a politician. He is a father. A grandfather. He signed the Vatican Accords because he believed—we both believed—that our children deserved something better than endless war." She drew a breath. "I am not here to appeal to your patriotism or your politics. I am here because I am a wife who wants her husband back. I am a mother who wants her children to see their father again."

John looked away. Through the window, the Georgia pines swayed in the wind, so different from the stark cliffs of Bamiyan. So far from the life he'd tried to leave behind.

"I'm sorry," he said. "I can't help you."

Mason moved. "Before you decide, there's something you need to see."

He pulled a battered tablet from his bag, the screen scratched and worn. His thumb hovered over the play button.

"This footage is from the night of the assault. The team that took Hussein—they were professional. Trained. They knew exactly what they were doing." Mason's jaw flexed. "I was running security that night. A dozen people died on my watch, including two of my own and a helicopter pilot with a two-year-old at home. I've watched this video a hundred times, trying to understand what we missed."

He pressed play.

The screen filled with chaos—grainy footage of a ransacked beach house, daylight slanting through shattered glass. Masked men dragged a battered figure across the tiles. Gunfire crackled. Shouts overlapped.

Then a voice cut through the noise, clear and sharp:

"Johnny! Johnny!"

One of the kidnappers turned toward the camera. His scarf had slipped, revealing his face for just a moment. Young. Hard. And his eyes—

Ice-blue.

John stopped breathing.

Those eyes. He saw them every morning in the mirror. He'd seen them in his father's face, in old photographs of his grandfather. Marquez eyes, passed down through generations like a brand.

The video ended. The cabin was silent.

"His name is Younes al-Bamiyan," Robb said quietly. "But the men who work with him call him Johnny. He's twenty-two years old. Trained at camps in Khost and Kandahar. He was present when the Taliban destroyed the Buddhas in March."

John's hands were shaking. He couldn't make them stop.

"His mother," Robb continued, "is a woman named Sadyra."

The room spun. John grabbed the back of a chair to keep from falling.

Sadyra. Her face rose unbidden—dark hair, fierce eyes, the way she'd laughed in the firelight of the caves. The last night they'd spent together before everything fell apart. He'd replayed that night a thousand times, wondering what would have happened if he'd stayed, if he'd found a way back to her.

"That's not possible." His voice came out hoarse. "She would have told me. She would have found a way—"

"She didn't." Robb's voice was gentle now. "We don't know why. Maybe she was trying to protect him. Maybe she was trying to protect you. But John—he's your son."

John sank into the chair, legs giving out. A son. He had a son. Twenty-two years old, and he'd never known.

"Ben Mal raised him," Mason said. "After the Soviets killed Sadyra's father, Ben took them both into his compound. He's been filling Johnny's head with poison ever since—stories about the American father who abandoned him, who ran away while they suffered."

"I didn't abandon anyone." John's voice cracked. "I didn't know."

"Johnny doesn't know that." Robb crouched beside him. "To him, you're the enemy. The coward who left his mother to fend for herself. Ben made sure of that."

Leila spoke again, her voice soft. "The night they took my husband, this Johnny—your son—he locked me and my daughters in a safe room. He posted a guard to protect us. He spared the household staff when he could have killed them all." She paused. "There is something in him that Ben Mal has not destroyed. I saw it in his eyes."

John stared at the frozen image on the tablet—those ice-blue eyes, so much like his own, looking out from a face hardened by violence and lies.

"We're not just asking you to rescue Hussein," Robb said. "We're asking you to bring your son home. To give him a chance at something other than the life Ben built for him."

"A chance at what? A life sentence?"

"A chance to cooperate. Langley values intelligence over vengeance. If he talks, there's a path."

"And Sadyra?"

"She's still in the compound. Still alive, as far as we know."

John closed his eyes. Twenty-three years of exile. Twenty-three years of trying to forget. And now the past had reached out and found him anyway, dragging him back to the valley he'd sworn never to see again.

"I'll need to pick the team," he said.

Robb straightened. "You'll have final approval on everyone."

"And I want Mason." John looked at the soldier. "You said fourteen people died on your watch. You want a chance to make that right?"

Mason's expression didn't change, but something shifted in his eyes. "I'm in."

"What about Ben?" John's voice hardened. "What are my orders regarding Ben?"

Robb met his gaze. "Get Hussein out. If possible, bring Johnny and Sadyra with you. As for Ben Mal—" He paused. "Use your judgment."

John stood. Through the window, the sky had turned iron, the light fading. Somewhere out there, beyond oceans and mountains, a son he'd never known was waiting. A woman he'd never stopped loving was trapped. And an old friend turned monster was holding them both.

"When do we leave?"

"Forty-eight hours," Robb said. "We have a staging area outside Quetta. Mason will brief you on the way."

Leila crossed the room and took John's hand. Her grip was stronger than he expected.

"Thank you," she said. "For my husband. And for your son—whatever he has become, he did not choose this life. Perhaps you can show him another way."

John looked at the tablet one last time—at the face of the son he'd never known, the boy who had grown into a killer under another man's hand.

"I don't know if I can save him," John said. "I don't know if he wants to be saved."

"Then at least," Leila said quietly, "he will know the truth."

The truth. Twenty-three years of lies, and now John would carry the truth back to Bamiyan like a weapon—or an offering. He didn't know which it would be. He didn't know if it would matter.

But he was going to find out.

CHAPTER 28
A DEAL WITH GHOSTS

SUMMER 2001—QUETTA, PAKISTAN

The CIA forward site hunched in the red dust outside Quetta—a scatter of battered shipping containers, razor wire, and heat-shimmering floodlights. Safe house Echo. The name was a lie. Nothing echoed here except the grind of generators and the distant call to prayer that drifted over the wire like a summons for the dead.

John stepped out of the Hilux, boots grinding into grit that clung to his skin and refused to let go. He carried a single duffel, but the real weight was heavier. Somewhere beyond those mountains, his son was waiting. A son he'd never held.

Mason emerged from the shadow of a rusted water tank. He looked different than he had in the Florida briefing—thinner, harder, a man who'd been hollowed out by failure and refilled with something colder. His hand rested on the grip of his SIG, and his eyes swept the approach with the restless vigilance of someone who'd learned what happened when you stopped watching.

"Marquez. You're late."

"Ran into your checkpoint boys outside Chaman. They wanted to discuss my passport photo."

Mason's expression didn't change. "Come meet the team."

"Our team," John said.

Mason stopped walking. His hand stayed on his weapon. "You read an after-action report on a flight from Florida. I buried four men last month." He turned and kept walking. "It's my team until you prove otherwise."

John followed without answering. Fair enough.

////

Beneath a sagging canvas awning, three men sat in a half-circle, poking at MREs like prisoners marking time. Flies orbited. Radios buzzed with Pashto, Urdu, English—the babel of the borderlands.

Kyle looked up first—knife glinting in his hand, blade rolling across scarred knuckles. He was lean and watchful, tattoos climbing his forearms, the kind of man who'd learned violence young and refined it into something elegant and terrible. "You're the valley's ghost," he said.

John let the words pass, dropped his duffel. "Which of you is senior?"

Burns tipped two fingers in a lazy salute. He was older than the others, green eyes weathered, a battered med kit at his feet. "I keep them from killing each other." The drawl was Georgia, slow as sorghum, but his gaze was sharp enough to cut glass.

Figueroa, the third, barely looked up from the radio he was cleaning. Broad-shouldered, careful, he moved with a comms man's patience—every wire tied off, every frequency memorized. "You speak Dari?" he asked.

"Dari, Pashto, enough Farsi to curse in," John said.

Figueroa nodded, satisfied. "Good. Because the sat coverage goes dark once we're past Ghazni. After that, you're our only ears."

Mason moved to a warped plastic table where a map was pinned beneath a chunk of concrete. He spread his palm across the topography—valleys, ridgelines, the old roads that wound through the Hindu

Kush toward Bamiyan.

"Objective: Hussein. Ben Mal's compound sits here"—his finger stabbed a spot east of the valley—"the old Bamiyan Gate caravanserai. High walls. Mined approaches. Foreign trainers—Persian, Chechen, Uzbek. Dogs. Satcom traffic we've intercepted but can't decrypt."

John leaned in. He'd walked those ridges. Slept in those caves. Made love in the shadow of those cliffs, a lifetime ago.

"What's our window?" His voice came out rougher than he intended.

"Three days to prep. Relief convoy's our cover—aid supplies headed for the valley. Miss it, we wait a month."

Mason pulled out a battered field notebook but didn't open it. His eyes stayed on John. "Before we go further, I need to know something. The assault team leader—young, blue eyes, moved like he'd been trained by someone who knew what they were doing. You've seen the footage."

"I've seen more than that."

"How much more?"

The others had gone still. Even Kyle's knife stopped moving.

"Enough to know his name," John said. "And who gave it to him."

Mason studied him for a long moment. Then he opened the notebook.

"The assault team was seven men. Disciplined. Patient. They'd been watching us for weeks, learning our patterns, our vendors, our routes. The taco truck, the drawbridge schedules—they mapped every vulnerability." He paused. "Four of mine dead. Three wounded."

"And Hussein?"

"Gone. Along with a hard drive containing the names of every Palestinian asset we've developed in the last decade." Mason's face hardened. "But here's the thing. They spared the family. The wife, the daughters. Put them in a room and locked the door. Professional. Surgical." He looked up. "Your son gave that order. I heard him on the comms."

John's hands found the table edge. "He spared them."

"He did." Mason met his eyes. "I don't know what that means. But I've been running ops for twenty years, and I've never seen a Hamas team show that kind of restraint. Someone trained that boy different. Or something inside him wouldn't let him cross that line."

The wind picked up outside, rattling the canvas. John thought about Sadyra—let himself think her name for the first time in years. Had she raised their son to show mercy? Or had that mercy survived despite everything Ben Mal had poured into him?

"That's why you're letting me run point," John said. "You want to know if it was a fluke or if there's something there worth saving."

Mason closed the notebook. "I want Hussein back. I want Ben Mal dead. And I want to understand what happened to my team." He looked at John without blinking. "If you can help me get all three, then it's our team. If you can't, I'll put a bullet in your son myself."

////

Kyle fell into step beside him on the perimeter that evening, silent as smoke. They walked the fence line together without speaking, boots crunching on gravel, the mountains going purple in the dying light.

Finally Kyle said, "Burns wants to ask you something. He won't do it himself."

"What's that?"

"Whether you can pull the trigger if it comes to that."

John kept his eyes on the wire. "What do you think?"

"I think you're here to find out." Kyle's knife caught the last of the sun. "Same as the rest of us."

He peeled off toward the compound, leaving John alone with the wind and the waiting dark.

////

That night, John found Burns rolling a cigarette by the fence, his face silver in the moonlight.

"Can't sleep?" Burns asked.

"Not if I can help it."

Burns offered the flask. John took it, felt the rough burn of something medicinal slide down his throat.

"I knew a man once," Burns said quietly. "Vietnam. Lost his boy to the VC—not killed, taken. Turned. When they met again, the boy was wearing black pajamas and carrying a Soviet rifle." He took the flask back. "The man couldn't pull the trigger. Got himself killed instead."

John said nothing.

"I'm not telling you what to do," Burns continued. "Just telling you what I've seen. The hardest shot isn't the one that takes skill. It's the one that takes something from you that you can't get back."

"I'm not going there to kill my son."

Burns studied him through the cigarette smoke. "Then what are you going there for?"

John stared at the dark line of mountains. Somewhere beyond them, a boy had grown into a man without him. A boy who led killers but wouldn't let them touch women and children. A boy who carried John's blood and Ben Mal's poison in equal measure.

"To find out if there's anything left to save."

Burns nodded slowly. "That's the answer I was hoping for." He ground out the cigarette and stood, tucking the flask away. "Kyle asked me what I thought about you. I told him the jury was out."

He started toward the compound, then stopped.

"Jury's in."

CHAPTER 29

IN THE BLOOD

SUMMER 2001—QUETTA

The next two days folded into grim routine.

Mason ran them hard, his voice sharp as the wind off the mountains. Fast-rope drops from a jury-rigged platform, the rope burning their palms, the ground coming up faster than training said it would. Weapons drills until the movements became reflex. Silent signals rehearsed in the dark. Extraction routes marked in grease pencil on laminated maps. Every detail mattered because details were the difference between walking out and being carried.

John worked alongside them without complaint. By the end of the first day, Mason had stopped watching him like a liability. By the second, he was taking John's suggestions on approach vectors. The SIG stayed holstered.

Between drills, Figueroa ran them through comms protocols—frequencies, call signs, contingencies for when the sat feed died. His voice shifted between languages: Spanish, Pashto, Jersey English. Every detail precise, every fallback planned.

"They hit us with an EMP at the safe house," Mason said during one of the briefings, arms crossed, back against the rusted water tower. "Fried everything—cameras, comms, the whole grid. By the time we got eyes back, they were already inside." He paused. "Twenty-three seconds. That's all it took them to breach."

"How'd they know the rotation?" Kyle asked.

"Someone fed them intel. Someone on the inside." Mason's jaw tightened. "When we find out who, they'll answer for it. But that's after. Hussein comes first."

John filed the information away. It would matter later.

////

That night, after the drills had ended and the sun had bled out over the horizon, they gathered for dinner. Goat stew—greasy, overcooked—spooned from plastic trays. They perched on ammo crates arranged in a loose circle, shadows flickering across their faces as oil lamps hissed and guttered.

John barely touched his food. The stew tasted of dust and memory. Twenty years away, and he could still see a blue scarf fluttering on the Bamiyan wind, still hear Sadyra's laugh as she led him up a goat path at dusk.

Mason set down his tray, untouched. He stared at the fire for a long moment before speaking.

"Hussein's wife—Leila. She held it together when everything went sideways. Got the children into a closet, kept them quiet while her husband was dragged out." He picked up a stick and poked at the embers. "After it was over, she found me. Looked me in the eye and asked me to bring him back."

"And you said yes," John said.

"I said I'd die trying." Mason's voice was flat, matter-of-fact. "Meant it then. Mean it now."

John understood. They were both chasing ghosts—different ghosts, same valley.

////

The morning of departure broke gray and windless, the air heavy with coming dust.

The convoy assembled in the courtyard: battered Hiluxes, a pair of faded NGO trucks, paint peeling and blistered from years of sun. Every vehicle bore fresh markings, stencils hastily applied, each identity as thin and brittle as the paper passports Mason handed out.

John took his—name spelled wrong, birthdate off by a decade—and slipped it under his vest. His cover: a medical coordinator, tasked with ferrying vaccines and supplies into the heart of Afghanistan. The uniform—faded blue vest, a UN logo barely visible—felt strange, constricting.

Mason climbed into the lead truck, taking the position of most risk without comment. Kyle rode shotgun beside him, fingers drumming the dash, his other hand never far from his weapon.

Rahman, their fixer, was at the wheel of John's vehicle—face lined, eyes bright with exhaustion and calculation. He looked John over, lips twitching. "You look like a doctor," he said, his English dry and accented. "Almost. Don't talk unless you have to. Let me handle the locals."

The engines ground to life. Dust rose. And then they were moving, the safe house shrinking in the mirrors until it vanished in the haze.

////

SUMMER 2001—THE SILK ROAD TO BAMIYAN

The road west was worse than John remembered: rutted, cratered, every dip threatening to snap an axle. Dust billowed in white clouds, visibility dropping to nothing. The convoy crawled through a landscape that seemed determined to swallow them.

Checkpoints appeared and disappeared—manned by boys barely out of childhood, faces painted with hardness, hands casual on battered Kalashnikovs. Rahman handed out rupees with practiced ease. The guards waved them through, eyes already moving to the next vehicle, the next bribe, the next moment of petty power in an endless war.

Hours passed in silence, broken only by the crackle of radios, the occasional curse as a tire caught a rut. John watched the terrain scroll by—brown hills giving way to steeper slopes, the first hint of mountains rising in the distance like teeth.

He thought about the boy who'd grown up in this country. The boy who'd learned to fight in these valleys, to pray in these mosques, to hate in these madrassas. The boy who was his son and a stranger at once.

In the distance, the Bamiyan valley waited—patient, implacable. Its beauty was stark, almost cruel: pale stone rising from the dust, caves gouged out by wind and war, the ghostly alcoves where the Buddha statues had stood before the Taliban reduced them to rubble. Two thousand years of history erased in an afternoon. John wondered what else the valley had consumed.

Rahman slowed, eyes on the mirror. "Last safe road," he murmured. "From here, we are in God's hands."

////

They pulled off as the sky darkened, headlights doused, engines ticking in the sudden quiet. The wadi they'd chosen was shallow but defensible—trucks circled tight, fields of fire established without discussion. Everyone knew their job.

Burns checked the medical bags, hands steady but betraying a slight tremor as he slid a pistol into a hidden pocket. Figueroa double-checked the radios, lips moving silently as he ran through frequencies. Kyle walked the perimeter, knife in hand, reading the darkness like scripture.

Mason stood apart, scanning the ridgelines, his silhouette rigid against the fading light. Whatever he was looking for, he didn't find it. He came back to the circle without a word.

John lay on his back, boots under his head, the sky suffocating with stars. The mountains loomed at the edge of his vision—black, immense, indifferent. He remembered Sadyra's stories: gods that slept in the caves, travelers who vanished into the high passes and were never seen again. He wondered if the valley remembered him. He wondered if it would let him pass or claim him for its own.

The ache in his chest was both dread and hope, tangled so tight he couldn't tell where one ended and the other began. He thought of Sadyra's voice, the warmth of her hand on his face in the dark. He thought of a boy he'd never held, grown now into a man who led killers through the night.

Sleep came in fits. He dreamed of rivers running red, of a blue scarf whipping through caves, always just out of reach. He woke to the sound of dogs barking, distant and forlorn, and for a moment he didn't know where he was or what year it was or whether any of it had been real.

////

Before dawn, the call to prayer wound through the darkness—thin, reedy, ancient.

John sat up, breath frosting in the cold. He dressed in silence, checked his weapon, loaded the last of his gear. Around him, the others stirred—each man lost in his own war, his own reasons for being here.

Mason appeared beside him as the sky began to gray. His face was shadowed, unreadable.

"Whatever happens in there," he said quietly, "Hussein comes first. That's the mission."

John nodded. "Hussein comes first."

But they both knew that wasn't the whole truth. Not for either of them.

The sun crested the ridge, painting the wadi gold, and the team moved out. Five men in a line, silhouettes against the rising light, their shadows stretching long across the dust. The living, the lost, and the ghosts who traveled with them—all of them headed into the valley where the past waited with patient, terrible hands.

John didn't look back. There was nothing behind him now.

Only what lay ahead.

CHAPTER 30
INTO THE VALLEY

SUMMER 2001—BAMIYAN CITY

They rolled north under a pale dawn, the tactical relief convoy snaking across the rutted remnants of the old Silk Road. Six trucks packed with medical supplies, Red Crescent flags snapping in the relentless wind. The road was a half-frozen scar cut through the land—ruts crusted with thin frost crunching under the tires, each jolt a reminder of where they were headed.

Inside the last vehicle, John sat shoulder to shoulder with Mason, hidden among crates stamped SURGICAL KITS, BANDAGES, WATER PURIFICATION. The air was tight, thick with diesel and the sharp metallic note of melting snow blowing in from the Hindu Kush.

Mason shifted beside him, eyes scanning the dirty window with that handler's stare—bored on the surface, cataloging everything beneath. He'd insisted on coming. After losing Hussein, there was no keeping him back. Langley had tried. Mason had told them where to shove their protocols.

"You're thinking too loud," Mason said, voice low enough to stay under the engine noise.

John's mouth compressed. "I know this country too well."

"Yeah." Mason's hand brushed the fire extinguisher wedged between them—a backup weapon disguised by the ordinary. "Looks like it knows you, too."

////

The radio crackled. Up ahead, the convoy braked hard, trucks screeching, occupants thrown against seatbacks. A checkpoint had materialized in the road—a makeshift barrier of cinder blocks and rusted oil drums, a Taliban banner snapping in the wind, white field menacing with black script.

Six fighters stood clustered on the roadside, ragged tunics whipping at their knees, battered AKs slung from thin shoulders. Their eyes were sharp and glassy, chipped from something harder than youth. Muzzles swept the cabs, painting each truck with suspicion.

John's gut knotted, cold sweat blooming under his scarf. Every instinct screamed: *wrong rhythm, wrong weight*. These weren't bored conscripts working a paycheck. These were believers.

Mason's hand moved to his SIG, hidden beneath his jacket. "Easy. Let Rahman work."

Up front, Rahman's voice carried through the cab—honeyed Pashto, practiced and smooth. Figueroa sat rigid in the passenger seat, one hand near his weapon, the other gripping a stress ball until his knuckles went white. The lead fighter, barely twenty, stepped forward, rifle loose at his hip, scanning faces with mechanical suspicion.

The silence stretched. John's pulse hammered. The fighter's gaze passed over the rear of the truck—past the crates, past the shadows where John and Mason crouched—and moved on.

A guttural bark. The barrier scraped aside. Rahman's truck lurched forward, and one by one the convoy followed.

Mason exhaled, slow and controlled. "That's one."

John didn't answer. Every mile was another border crossed, another night survived.

////

By midday, the convoy reached the high ridge above Bamiyan. The wind knifed in from the north, stripping warmth from every surface. They paused, engines idling, men silent. The sky overhead was pale as bone.

Below, the valley opened up—a wide, wounded expanse. Stone Buddha niches yawned in the cliff faces, empty eye sockets staring out over a landscape scored by artillery. Green fields, what little remained, were cratered and stitched with trenches. In the middle distance, the bazaar spread in a patchwork of tarps and scavenged canvas—chaotic, temporary, defiant.

And at the center, squatting like an accusation, was Ben Mal's fortress. Thick stone walls ringed the keep, fresh concrete sprouting watchtowers at the corners. Black-clad guards in foreign web gear patrolled in tight, mechanical loops, faces hidden behind mirrored glasses.

Mason studied the compound through field glasses. "Security's heavier than the imagery showed. That's Chechen discipline."

"Ben Mal doesn't trust anyone local anymore," John said. "Not after the Soviets, not after the warlords. He imports his killers."

Mason lowered the glasses. "Still remember the layout?"

"Every rock. Every shadow."

////

Down in the square, children no older than twelve strutted with cheap Chinese rifles, shoulders back, faces set in forced bravado. One kid, skinny and barefoot, wore a scrap of blue cloth tied to his wrist—blue as a Bamiyan dawn.

John's throat closed tight. That was the color Sadyra had loved best.

Figueroa's voice came through the earpiece. "Still with us, boss?"

John forced himself back. "Yeah. Eyes up."

Mason tapped his shoulder. "Burns has the medical kit prepped. Kyle's running overwatch from the second truck. We move on your signal once we're inside."

"And if we see Ben Mal?"

Mason's eyes went cold. "Then we take the shot. But Hussein comes first. Your son comes second. Ben Mal's a bonus."

John held his gaze. "The intercepts mentioned a woman. Older. Important to the heir."

"Sadyra." Mason's voice was flat, but something shifted in his expression. "You think she's still alive?"

"I think if she weren't, Ben Mal would have used her death against Johnny years ago." John raised the field glasses, swept them across the east tower. A figure moved behind the window—just a shape, a suggestion of movement—and was gone. "She's in there."

Mason was quiet for a moment. "Then we bring her out too. If we can."

////

John traced the compound's silhouette against the wounded sky. Twenty-three years since he'd walked those walls. Twenty-three years since he'd held a woman who smelled of apricots and mountain air, since he'd promised to take her somewhere she could see the ocean. The ocean had seemed so close back then. Everything had seemed close.

Now the only thing close was the fortress where his son gave orders to killers and the woman he'd loved survived by whatever means survival required.

He lowered the glasses. The convoy was waiting. The team was waiting. Somewhere inside those walls, Hussein was bleeding and Sadyra was watching and Johnny was becoming something John might not be able to reach.

Mason appeared beside him. "You ready?"

John looked at the compound one last time—the walls he'd once scaled in darkness, the courtyards where he'd made love and made war, the place where everything had started and everything had gone wrong.

Then he turned and walked toward the truck.

CHAPTER 31
THE IRON GATE

SUMMER 2001—BEN MAL'S COMPOUND

The air inside the compound was suffocating—thick with dust, woodsmoke, and the sour reek of fear. Heat shimmered off broken flagstones, warping the late sun into flickering shadows. John forced his vision to adjust, finding the lines, the corners, the killing angles.

The truck rolled to a halt. John kept still, hunched inside the shawl, muscles coiled. It was the glances from the guards—furtive, lingering—that set his nerves on edge. More than any rifle or checkpoint.

Mason's voice came low. "Kyle, you reading this?"

Kyle's response crackled through the earpiece. "Copy. Twelve hostiles visible. Three on the east wall, four by the archway, five near the medical depot. Foreign gear on at least half."

High above, the Buddha niches gaped in the cliff face—half-ruined, stone dust drifting like old snow. The hollows stared down like the eye sockets of dead gods.

////

Three guards with black scarves and Czech rifles strode forward, boots thudding on river stone. One stopped in front of the cab, suspicion sharp as broken glass.

"Doctor?" he barked.

Figueroa leaned out, hands open and steady. His Pashto was flawless—each word balanced on a razor's edge. The guard stared him down. Then, with a silent hiss, he spat in the dust—the old ritual of contempt—and stepped aside.

The convoy rolled deeper into the courtyard, engines dying one by one, the silence left behind electric and dangerous.

Boys no older than twelve clambered over the crates, bare feet slapping cold stone. One carried a worn Makarov, the grip far too big for his hand—child's fingers closing around a weapon made for a killer.

Burns's voice cut through John's earpiece. "Visual?"

"Southeast wing. Hussein—thin mattress, ankle shackle, two guards visible."

"Two visible means two more you can't see," Mason said. "Interior rotation. Count on it."

////

Through a broken archway, enforcers moved in disciplined formation—modern gear out of place among ragged militia, a black wave among khaki. Foreign-trained. Loyal to Ben Mal.

One at their head stood taller than the rest, stride loose with a warlord's confidence. His black scarf was drawn high, revealing only his eyes—ice blue, cold as glaciers, far too familiar.

Their gazes met across the courtyard.

John's breath stopped. The boy's eyes flashed—confusion first, then something deeper, recognition or warning—before he turned away, barking orders to his men.

John's hand trembled on the crate.

Mason caught it. "That him?"

"Yeah." The word came out scraped raw. "That's my son."

Mason watched Johnny disappear through the archway. "He moves like his old man. See how he checked the sight lines before he crossed? That's training, but it's also instinct." A pause. "He's going to be a problem."

"He's going to be my problem."

Burns cut in. "Focus. We've got a job."

////

They set up in a blockhouse against the north wall. John rigged the suppressed carbines while Mason spread a hand-drawn map across a crate.

"The tunnel," Mason said. "Talk to me."

"Old smuggler route. Runs from behind the granary, through the cliff, exits half a klick north near the Buddha niches." John's finger traced the line. "Sadyra showed me."

"Entrance?"

"Stone with a crack shaped like a lightning bolt. It pivots."

Mason studied the map. "Extract Hussein, move north, disappear into the mountain." He looked up. "And your son?"

"One thing at a time."

"That's not an answer."

"It's the only one I've got."

////

Outside, the call to prayer rose from a tinny loudspeaker, plaintive and haunting, echoing off the cliffs. Fighters paused, rifles lowered, faces to Mecca. Even the children stilled.

Mason checked his watch. "Rotation passed. Twelve minutes."

John chambered a round. "Move."

They slipped out, keeping to shadows along the north wall. The prayer droned on—a brief ceasefire between the compound and its violence. John moved on instinct, muscle memory guiding him around debris, over tripwires he spotted by the way dust had settled differently.

The southeast wing loomed ahead. Two guards flanked the door—young, prayer beads clicking through their fingers, AKs propped against the wall.

John held up two fingers. Mason nodded.

They closed the distance in silence. Two muffled shots. Two bodies sliding down the wall, prayer beads scattering across stone.

Mason worked the lock. Five seconds. The mechanism clicked.

The corridor inside was dark, lit by a single kerosene lamp at the far end. The air was foul—sweat, urine, old blood. Three doors on the left. One on the right.

"Burns said two more went in," Mason breathed. "Still here."

John moved down the corridor, back to the wall, carbine up. The third door was ajar. Light flickered. Voices—two men, speaking Chechen.

Mason held up a flash-bang. John shook his head. Too loud.

Three fingers. Two. One.

John went through low, Mason high.

////

The room was small, windowless, reeking. Hussein lay on a thin mattress, ankle shackled to an iron ring. His face was gaunt, one eye swollen shut, blood still wet on his lip.

Two guards stood over him. One held a rubber hose. The other was laughing.

John's first shot took the one with the hose through the throat. Mason's dropped the second before he could raise his rifle. Both men hit the floor in the same wet instant.

John was already moving. "Mr. President. We're getting you out."

Hussein's good eye focused slowly. "American?"

"Something like that." John knelt beside the shackle—heavy, Soviet-era, corroded. "Mason. Pick."

Mason tossed it over, eyes on the door. "Eight minutes."

Hussein's hand found John's wrist, grip weak but urgent. "The boy. Johnny—"

"I know who he is."

"No. Listen." Hussein's eye burned. "He is conflicted. When Ben Mal speaks of killing me, Johnny looks away. And there is a woman. His mother. She brings me water when the guards sleep. She whispers that help is coming." His grip tightened. "She knew. She knew you would come."

John's hands stilled on the shackle. Sadyra. Alive. Waiting.

The lock clicked open.

"Four minutes," Mason said. "Now."

////

John hauled Hussein up. The man's legs buckled—weeks of captivity had wasted his muscles. John caught him, slung Hussein's arm over his shoulder.

"He can't walk," Mason said.

"Then we carry him."

They moved into the corridor. Kyle's voice crackled: "Company. Two hostiles entering southeast wing. Thirty seconds."

Mason swore. "Side door."

They ducked into a cramped washroom. John pressed Hussein against the wall, hand over his mouth. Mason flattened beside the frame, carbine ready.

Footsteps in the corridor. Two men, talking casually.

The footsteps stopped.

A shout—guttural, alarmed. They'd found the bodies.

Mason was through the door before John could breathe. The carbine coughed twice. Two thuds. Silence.

"Clear. But that shout carried. Sixty seconds before this place lights up."

John keyed his radio. "Kyle, Burns—we're blown. Moving to the tunnel."

"Copy. East wall's mobilizing. Run."

They ran.

////

The courtyard erupted.

Shouts from every direction. Floodlights snapped on, harsh and blinding, turning the compound into a slaughterhouse of light and shadow. Kyle's rifle cracked from the granary—once, twice, three times—fighters dropping on the east wall.

"Contact left!" Mason fired on the move, dropping a guard who'd rounded the corner.

Hussein was deadweight on John's shoulder, gasping with every step. Blood soaked through John's sleeve.

Bullets cracked past his head. He ducked behind a rusted water tank, dragging Hussein down. Mason slid in beside them, ejecting a spent magazine.

"Sixty meters to the granary. Open ground."

"Kyle, can you clear us?"

"Negative. Eight hostiles converging. And there's a technical spinning up by the gate. Fifty-cal."

John's stomach dropped.

"I see it." Mason's jaw was set. "I can flank. Draw their fire."

"That's suicide."

"That's the mission." Mason locked eyes with John. "I lost Hussein once. I'm not losing him again. Get him to that tunnel."

Before John could argue, Mason was moving—sprinting toward the east wall, firing as he ran, drawing every eye in the compound.

The fifty-cal swung toward him.

"Go!" Kyle's voice was ragged. "Don't waste it!"

John hauled Hussein up and ran.

The granary loomed ahead. Burns appeared in the doorway, waving them in. Behind John, the fifty-cal roared—a sound like the world tearing apart.

He didn't look back.

They crashed through the door, lungs burning. Burns was at the back wall, hand on a stone marked with a lightning-bolt crack.

"Jammed," Burns said. "Mechanism's stuck."

John set Hussein down and threw his weight against the stone. Nothing.

Outside, Kyle's rifle cracked in steady rhythm. The fifty-cal fell silent, then roared again. Closer.

"Mason's down!" Kyle's voice went tight. "They're dragging him toward the gate."

John slammed his shoulder against the stone. Again. Again.

"John." A woman's voice from the darkness beyond the wall.

He froze.

"Push the bottom left. Not the center."

His hands found the spot. He pushed. The stone pivoted smoothly, revealing black void.

Sadyra stood in the tunnel mouth, kerosene lamp in hand. Her face was gaunt, lined, older—but her eyes were the same. Dark and fierce. The eyes that had watched him leave twenty-three years ago.

John's hand found the doorframe. His legs wouldn't move.

"I told you I would be here," she said.

Kyle's voice shattered the moment. "Hostiles converging on the granary. Thirty seconds."

Sadyra's gaze went to Hussein. "Bring him. Quickly."

Burns lifted Hussein. John grabbed his carbine. They plunged into the darkness.

////

The tunnel was tight—single file, ancient and cold, the air thick with dust and centuries. Sadyra moved ahead with the lamp, her shadow dancing on the walls.

"Kyle—status."

Static. Then: "I'm out. Back window. Heading to secondary rally."

"Mason?"

A long pause. "They've got him. He was moving when they dragged him away. Alive, I think."

Mason, who'd drawn fire so they could escape. Now a prisoner.

"We'll get him back," Burns said quietly.

"We're not leaving him."

Ahead, Sadyra glanced back. Her eyes met John's in the lamplight. Twenty-three years of silence between them—but not now. Not yet.

"The tunnel exits near the Buddha niches," she said. "There is a cave. Hidden. Safe."

"And Johnny?"

Her face tightened. "He will come looking for me. When he finds me gone, he will know." A pause. "He has been looking for a reason to leave Ben Mal. Perhaps you can give him one."

They emerged into cold night air. The Buddha niches loomed above—vast and empty, stone guardians who had watched over the valley for fifteen centuries before men with dynamite tried to erase them.

John looked back toward the compound. Distant shouts. Searchlights sweeping the valley.

They had Hussein. Mason was captured. Johnny was still inside.

Sadyra's hand found his in the darkness—tentative, warm against the cold.

He didn't pull away.

"You came back," she said quietly.

"I should have come sooner."

"You're here now."

The searchlights swept the empty niches where gods had once stood. The wind carried the sound of engines, of men shouting orders, of a hunt beginning.

John checked his weapon.

Then he turned toward the cave, Sadyra's hand still in his, and walked into the dark.

CHAPTER 32
ASHES IN THE BLOOD

SUMMER 2001—THE BAMIYAN CAVES

The cave swallowed them whole.

John pressed his back against the cold stone, lungs burning, Hussein's weight dragging at his shoulder. The darkness was absolute until Sadyra's lamp caught up, throwing their shadows long against walls that had sheltered fugitives for a thousand years.

Burns lowered Hussein onto a flat stretch of rock, already unzipping the med kit. The Palestinian leader's face was gray, blood still seeping from the scalp wound, but his good eye tracked the movement around him with sharp intelligence.

"Mason." John's voice was ragged. "We have to go back for him."

Sadyra set the lamp on a ledge, its flame guttering in the cave's breath. "Not tonight. Ben Mal will have tripled the guards. The compound will be sealed until dawn."

"She's right," Burns said, not looking up from Hussein's wound. "We go back now, we die. Mason dies. Hussein dies. Everyone loses."

John's hands clenched.

His radio crackled. "John, you copy?" Kyle's voice, tight but steady.

"Copy. Where are you?"

"Secondary rally point. Had to take the long way—patrols everywhere. I'm about forty minutes out from your last known position."

"We've moved, come in quiet. We're in the cave near the Buddha niches."

"Copy that. Kyle out."

////

Hussein pushed himself up on one elbow, waving off Burns's attempt to ease him back down. "The American soldier. Mason." His voice was thin but clear. "I know where they will take him."

John turned sharply. "Where?"

"There is a chamber beneath the eastern tower. I heard the guards speak of it—a place for interrogation. Ben Mal uses it for prisoners he wishes to keep alive." Hussein's jaw clenched. "For a time."

"How do you know this?" Burns asked, pressing gauze to Hussein's temple.

"Three weeks in that compound, one learns to listen." Hussein's gaze found John's in the lamplight. "Your son brought me water once, when Ben Mal was away. He said nothing, but he did not need to. I saw the conflict in him."

Sadyra made a small sound. John looked at her for the first time since the tunnel. The years had carved lines around her eyes, thinned her face, but the fierce intelligence he remembered burned as bright as ever.

"He is not lost," she said quietly. "Not yet. But Ben Mal has poisoned him for twenty years. He told Johnny that you abandoned us. That you chose America over your own blood."

"I never—"

"I know." Sadyra's hand found his wrist, her grip stronger than he expected. "I should have written. I started a hundred letters. But I was afraid—afraid of what would happen to Johnny if anyone discovered his father was American. So, I let him believe the lie." Her voice cracked. "That is my burden."

John didn't answer. What could he say? Twenty-three years of silence, and now this—a son who saw him as the enemy, a woman who'd sacrificed truth for survival.

Hussein spoke again, his voice gaining strength. "The woman—Sadyra—she brought me water too. And once, she whispered that help was coming. That is how I knew to be ready."

Burns looked up. "You knew we were coming?"

"I knew someone was coming." Hussein almost smiled. "In Palestinian politics, one learns that every situation has actors moving in the shadows. The question is always which shadow serves your purpose."

////

Kyle arrived an hour later, slipping through the cave mouth with a gash on his forearm he hadn't had before. "Ran into a two-man patrol near the orchard. They won't be reporting in."

"Compound's locked down tight," he reported, crouching beside them. "Searchlights on the walls, patrols every fifty meters. They've got Mason in the east wing—I saw them drag him inside before I pulled out."

"Eastern tower," Hussein said. "The interrogation chamber. I told them."

Kyle glanced at the Palestinian leader, reassessing. "He's lucid."

"More than lucid," Burns said. "He's been giving us intel."

"Good. We're going to need it." Kyle pulled a battered map from his vest—the same one Mason had carried during the briefing. John felt a twist in his chest at the sight of it. "What's our play?"

John forced his mind to focus. "We can't hit the compound again—not with their current posture. But they'll relax after twenty-four hours. They always do."

"How do you know?" Burns asked.

"Because I've seen it before." John's voice was flat. "I've been on both sides of these walls."

Sadyra nodded slowly. "He is right. Ben Mal will rage tonight, but by tomorrow he will convince himself the threat has passed. His arrogance is his weakness."

"And Johnny?" Kyle asked.

The question hung in the air. John looked at Sadyra, then at the darkness beyond the lamplight.

"Johnny is the key," Hussein said. Everyone turned to him. He was sitting up now, Burns having finished bandaging his head, his presence somehow larger than his battered body. "Ben Mal trusts him. The guards follow his orders. If you can turn him—"

"He won't turn," John said. "Not for me. Not after what he believes."

"Perhaps not for you." Hussein's good eye moved to Sadyra. "But for his mother? For the truth she has carried for twenty-three years?"

Sadyra's breath caught. "You are asking me to reverse everything he believes."

"I am asking you to set him free." Hussein's voice was gentle but unyielding. "A man cannot serve a lie forever. It will eat him from the inside. You know this. You have lived it."

The silence stretched. Outside, the wind keened through the rocks, carrying the distant sounds of the valley—a dog barking, the faint rumble of a truck on a far road.

"I will try," Sadyra said at last. "But I cannot promise he will listen."

"No one can promise that," Hussein said. "But the attempt itself has value. A door opened, even if not walked through, changes everything that comes after."

////

They made camp in the deeper reaches of the cave, where the rock curved overhead like a cathedral's vault. Burns took first watch at the entrance while the others caught what rest they could.

John couldn't sleep. He sat against the wall, rifle across his knees, watching the lamplight flicker on the ancient stone. Somewhere in the dark, water dripped—a steady rhythm that marked time's passage.

Sadyra settled beside him, close enough that their shoulders almost touched. For a long moment, neither spoke.

"I thought of you," she said finally. "Every day. I wondered if you had found someone else. Built a life. Forgotten."

"I never forgot." John's voice was rough. "I couldn't. This valley—it's in my blood. You're in my blood."

"Then why did you never come back?"

He turned to face her. In the dim light, she looked both older and younger than he remembered—the girl he'd loved transformed by time and hardship into someone stronger, harder.

"I tried. Twice. The first time, the Soviets had locked down the passes. The second—" He stopped, the memory sharp as a blade. "I got as far as Kabul. Someone recognized me. I barely made it out alive."

"I never knew."

"How could you? I had no way to reach you. No way to know if you were even alive." He exhaled. "So I waited. Year after year. And then the Agency found me, and they told me about Johnny, and—" His voice broke. "Twenty-three years, Sadyra. Our son is twenty-two years old, and I've never spoken a word to him."

She took his hand. Her fingers were calloused, her grip strong from years of survival.

"Then speak to him now," she said. "We will find a way."

////

Hussein slept fitfully, muttering in Arabic, his hands twitching against invisible restraints. Burns had done good work on the scalp wound, but concussion was still a risk. They would need to move him carefully.

Kyle woke John three hours before dawn. "Your turn on watch."

John nodded, rising stiffly. His body ached in a dozen places—the price of the firefight, the sprint through the compound, the desperate flight through the tunnel. He was fifty-two years old, and the mountains didn't care.

At the cave mouth, he crouched behind a boulder and scanned the valley. The compound's lights were visible in the distance—harsh white points stabbing the darkness. Somewhere in that light, Mason was being held. Questioned. Probably hurt.

And Johnny. His son was somewhere in that compound too, wrestling with whatever Hussein had seen in him—the doubt, the conflict, the humanity that not even Ben Mal's poison could fully extinguish.

John checked his rifle, counted his remaining magazines. Four. Maybe eighty rounds total. Not enough for another assault—but enough for what came next.

Behind him, Burns approached quietly. "Can't sleep either?"

"Never could. Not before an op."

Burns settled beside him, his own rifle cradled across his knees. "We'll get Mason back. You know that, right?"

"We have to." John's jaw compressed. "He drew their fire so we could escape. That debt doesn't go unpaid."

"No," Burns agreed. "It doesn't." He paused. "What about your son?"

John was quiet for a long moment. "I don't know. Hussein thinks he can be turned. Sadyra thinks—" He stopped. "I don't know what Sadyra thinks. Twenty-three years is a long time."

"But you're going to try."

"What else can I do?" John looked at the distant lights. "He's my blood. My son. Whatever he's become, whatever he's done—that doesn't change."

Burns nodded slowly. "Family's a strange thing. It survives everything—distance, time, betrayal. Even when you want it to die, it keeps breathing."

"Speaking from experience?"

"Always." Burns didn't elaborate. He didn't need to.

////

Dawn came gray and cold, the sky lightening by degrees until the Buddha niches emerged from shadow—vast empty hollows where giants had once stood, their absence somehow louder than their presence had ever been.

Hussein was awake, sitting up on his own now, accepting water from Sadyra's canteen. The color had returned to his face, though the bandage on his temple was spotted with fresh blood.

"We move in an hour," John said, gathering the team around the guttering lamp. "There's a goat path that leads north, up to an old monastery. From there, we can observe the compound without being seen."

"And then?" Kyle asked.

"We wait. Watch their patterns. Find their weakness." John looked at each of them in turn. "Mason bought us time. We're not going to waste it."

Hussein raised a hand. "There is something else. Ben Mal planned to move me—to use me as leverage in negotiations with the Americans.

He spoke of it to his lieutenants. If he discovers I am gone, he will need a new bargaining chip."

"Mason," Burns said grimly.

"Yes. An American soldier is valuable. Perhaps more valuable than a Palestinian leader, in certain markets." Hussein's voice was clinical, political—the tone of a man who had spent decades calculating the worth of human lives. "You have perhaps forty-eight hours before Ben Mal realizes Mason's true value. After that..."

He didn't finish. He didn't need to.

"Then we have forty-eight hours," John said. He turned to Sadyra. "Can you get to Johnny?"

She was quiet for a moment, her jaw tight. "There is a way. Johnny walks the eastern perimeter at dusk—alone. It is the only time Ben Mal does not have eyes on him." She paused. "I can reach him there. Speak to him without the others hearing."

"And say what?"

"The truth he has never been allowed to hear." Sadyra's voice hardened with resolve. "The truth. That his father did not abandon him. That Ben Mal has lied to him his entire life."

"He won't believe you. Not after twenty-two years of—"

"He will believe me because I am his mother." Sadyra cut him off, fierce now. "I have never lied to him—I only stayed silent. There is a difference, and he knows it. When I tell him who you are, when I tell him what Ben Mal has done to all of us—" She exhaled. "He will have a choice. For the first time in his life, a real choice."

"And if he chooses Ben Mal?"

"Then we will know." Her eyes held John's without flinching. "But I do not believe he will. I have watched him, John. The doubt is already there. He only needs someone to show him the door."

Burns spoke up. "Even if he turns, can he help us get to Mason?"

"Johnny controls the guard rotations in the eastern wing," Sadyra said. "He has access to the interrogation chamber. If he is with us—truly with us—he can open doors that no amount of firepower could breach."

Everything rested on Sadyra walking into that compound, finding their son, and convincing him to betray the only father he'd ever known.

"When?" he asked.

"Tonight. At dusk." Sadyra reached out and touched his face—a gesture so familiar it ached. "Trust me, John. I did not wait twenty-two years to lose him now."

John held her gaze, then nodded slowly. "Then let's move. We've got work to do."

They gathered their gear and slipped out of the cave into the morning light. The valley spread before them—ancient, beautiful, scarred by centuries of violence. The Buddha niches stared down with empty eyes, monuments to everything that had been lost and everything that might yet be found.

John looked back once at the cave mouth, then turned and led them up the goat path, toward the monastery, toward whatever came next.

CHAPTER 33
UNDER THE ASHES

SUMMER 2001—BEN MAL'S COMPOUND

They moved down the goat path in single file, the compound's lights growing brighter with each switchback. John led, picking his way through terrain he'd once known as intimately as his own heartbeat. The valley had changed—more ruins now, more ghosts—but the bones of the land remained the same.

At the base of the ridge, where the scrub brush gave way to open ground, they stopped. The compound wall loomed two hundred meters ahead, its silhouette jagged against the darkening sky.

Sadyra turned to face him. "It's time."

John reached for her hand. Her fingers were cold, calloused from years of survival. She had told Johnny the truth in August—had planted the seed and watched him walk away without speaking. Tonight she would find out if anything had taken root.

"Go," he said. "We'll be ready."

She kissed him once—brief, fierce—then slipped into the darkness toward the eastern wall.

////

The wait was agony.

John lay prone in the scrub, MP5 cradled against his chest, eyes fixed on the section of wall where Sadyra had disappeared. Burns was ten meters to his left, covering the main gate. Kyle had circled north to establish a secondary position with a clear line on the guard tower. Figueroa held the southern approach, rifle steady despite the cold. Hussein remained at the rally point with their emergency supplies, too weak for the assault but alert enough to coordinate if everything went wrong.

Minutes stretched. The compound's searchlights continued their lazy sweeps. Dogs barked somewhere inside the walls, then fell silent.

John's radio crackled. Kyle's voice, barely a whisper: "Movement. Eastern perimeter. Single figure approaching the wall."

John pressed the binoculars to his eyes. A lone guard walked the far side of the compound—tall, moving with a soldier's discipline, rifle slung across his back. Even at this distance, John recognized the set of his shoulders, the way he carried himself.

His son.

A shadow detached from the wall's base. Sadyra, stepping into Johnny's path.

Through the binoculars, John watched his son stop. Watched him tense, hand moving toward his weapon. Watched Sadyra raise both hands, palms open—the universal gesture of peace, of surrender, of a mother asking her child to listen.

They stood like that for what felt like hours—two figures in the darkness, the distance between them measured in something far heavier than meters. Then Johnny's hand dropped from his rifle. He stepped forward. Sadyra reached for him.

John couldn't hear their words, but he could see their bodies—the way Johnny's shoulders curved inward, the way Sadyra gripped his arms, the way their heads bent close. He saw his son shake his head, once, twice. Saw Sadyra point toward the ridge where John lay hidden.

And then Johnny looked. Across two hundred meters of darkness and dust, his gaze found the exact spot where John crouched. Even through the binoculars, John felt the press of that stare—accusation and longing and rage all tangled together.

For a long moment, nothing moved.

Then Johnny turned back to his mother. He spoke—short, clipped words John couldn't hear. Sadyra nodded. Johnny looked at the compound, then at the ridge, then back at his mother.

He unslung his rifle and handed it to her.

////

Johnny walked toward the ridge where John waited.

Twenty-three years collapsed into twenty paces. John watched him come—this stranger who carried his blood, his eyes, the legacy of every choice he'd made and failed to make. He searched for something to say. Every word he'd rehearsed on the long flight from Georgia, every explanation, every apology—all of it turned to ash in his throat.

Johnny stopped three feet away. Close enough to strike. Close enough to embrace. He did neither.

"You left her." Not a question.

"I didn't know." John's voice came out rough. "About you. I didn't know."

"Would it have mattered?"

The question hung between them—unanswerable, unforgivable, the only question that had ever mattered.

"I don't know," he said finally. "I want to say yes. But I don't know."

Something flickered in Johnny's eyes—not forgiveness, not yet, maybe not ever. But something.

"Ben's men rotate the eastern patrol in eight minutes," Johnny said. "Stay close. Stay quiet. And try not to die before I decide whether I hate you."

He turned and moved toward the compound wall.

John followed his son into the dark.

////

Johnny led them through a gap in the eastern wall—a section where the mortar had crumbled and the guards had grown complacent. He moved in silence, checking each corner before waving them forward, his body language that of a man walking between two worlds.

The compound's interior was a maze of crumbling corridors and makeshift barracks, the air thick with woodsmoke and the sour reek of unwashed bodies. Prayer flags hung limp from doorways. Somewhere, a radio crackled with a mullah's sermon.

Johnny stopped at a reinforced door set deep into the eastern tower's base. He turned to face John for the first time since they'd entered.

"The American is inside," he said, his voice flat. "Two guards. They rotate in"—he checked his watch—"six minutes."

"You're certain?" Burns asked.

Johnny's jaw tensed. "I put him there." The words carried a weight that went beyond tactical information. A confession, offered without asking for absolution.

John met his son's eyes. So much to say, so much that couldn't be spoken here, now, with Mason's life measured in minutes. "Thank you."

Johnny flinched as if struck. Then his face hardened back into the mask of a soldier, and he stepped aside.

Burns moved first, testing the door's lock. Kyle took position covering the corridor behind them. Figueroa flanked the opposite side, already calculating angles of fire, his focus absolute. Sadyra pressed herself against the wall, rifle ready, her eyes never leaving her son.

"On my count," Burns whispered. "Three. Two. One."

The door splintered inward.

////

The guards died before they could raise their weapons—Burns's suppressed MP5 coughing twice, bodies crumpling to the stone floor. The room beyond was small, damp, lit by a single bare bulb that swung from a frayed cord.

Mason hung from chains bolted to the ceiling, his feet barely touching the ground. His face was a ruin—swollen, crusted with blood, one eye sealed shut. But when he heard them enter, he raised his head. The good eye found John's face.

"Took you long enough." The words came out slurred, broken, but the ghost of a smile cracked his split lips.

"Save it." John was already working the chains, fingers slick with rust and old blood. "Can you walk?"

"I'll crawl if I have to." Mason's legs buckled as the chains released, and Burns caught him before he hit the ground. "How many are with you?"

"Five. Plus one who just switched sides."

Mason's damaged eye cracked open, struggling to focus. "The kid? Your—"

"Yes."

Mason nodded once, processing. Then: "Ben Mal?"

"Still breathing. For now."

"Then we're not done." Mason straightened, wincing, forcing his battered body to obey. "That bastard has plans—ransom, leverage, something. I heard them talking. We can't leave him operational."

John looked at Burns, then at Figueroa, then at the corridor beyond where his son waited. "One problem at a time. First, we get you out."

"John." Mason gripped his arm with surprising strength. "I failed them. Hussein's family. I had all the resources, all the training, and that kid walked through my security like it wasn't there. I need to see this through."

"You will. But not tonight. Tonight, we survive. Everything else comes after."

Burns hoisted Mason's arm over his shoulder. "We move in sixty seconds. Figueroa, take point. Kyle, what's our exit?"

"Clear for now. But someone's going to notice those guards missed their check-in."

Johnny appeared in the doorway, his face pale in the harsh light. "There's another way. The irrigation culvert beneath the east wall—it runs under the foundations and opens near the old mill. Ben Mal uses it to move supplies past the checkpoints."

John stared at his son. A smuggler's route. Of course Ben Mal would have one.

"Show us."

////

They were halfway across the inner courtyard when the alarm sounded.

A horn blared from the guard tower, harsh and insistent, shattering the night's fragile quiet. Lights blazed on across the compound. Men poured from doorways, rifles raised, voices shouting in Pashto and Dari.

"Move!" Johnny sprinted for a low archway on the courtyard's far side, the others following in a ragged line. Burns and Figueroa half-carried Mason between them, the older man's legs barely keeping pace.

Gunfire erupted behind them—sharp, staccato bursts that chewed divots in the ancient stone. John spun, firing a covering burst, then ducked through the archway as bullets whined past his ear.

The passage beyond was narrow, the walls pressing close, the smell of damp earth and old mortar thick in the air. Johnny led them down a flight of worn steps, into darkness.

"Here." He stopped at a rusted grate set into the floor. His hands found the edges, fingers digging, pulling. The grate groaned and lifted, revealing a black hole that stank of stagnant water.

Figueroa dropped through first without hesitation, splashing into shin-deep water below. "Clear. Move."

Burns and Kyle lowered Mason through next, then Sadyra. Above them, boots pounded on stone—men searching, closing in.

John turned to follow, but Johnny caught his arm.

"I'll hold them." His voice was steady, but his eyes—those ice-blue eyes that were his—held something John couldn't name. "Buy you time."

"No." John gripped his son's shoulder. "You're coming with us."

"If they find this route empty, they'll know where we went. They'll follow. But if I'm here"—Johnny's jaw stiffened—"they'll think I tried to stop you. They'll believe it because it's what Ben Mal raised me to do."

"Johnny—"

"I'm not doing this for you." The words came hard, edged with something that might have been anger or might have been grief. "I'm doing this because I need to know who I am when I'm not following his orders. I need to know if there's anything left of me that's worth saving."

Voices echoed down the corridor—closer now, seconds away.

John pulled his son into a rough embrace. For a heartbeat, the boy resisted—muscles rigid, body stiff with years of conditioning. Then something broke. His arms came up, gripping John's shoulders, and John felt him shaking.

"Find me," John said into his ear. "When this is over. Find me, and we'll figure out the rest."

Johnny pulled back. His eyes were wet, but his face had hardened into something resolute.

"Go."

John went.

////

The culvert was a nightmare of darkness and foul water, the ceiling so low John had to crouch as he splashed forward. He followed the sound of the others ahead, his boots slipping on slick stone worn smooth by decades of use.

Behind him, muffled by yards of earth, gunfire erupted. He heard shouting—his son's voice among them—then a crash that sent ripples through the black water around his knees.

He didn't stop. Couldn't stop. Johnny had made his choice, and John had to honor it—had to trust that somewhere in his son, beneath all the years of Ben Mal's poison, there was enough to survive this night.

The culvert opened into a drainage channel, the air suddenly cold and sharp. Stars wheeled overhead—impossibly bright after the darkness—and the silhouette of the old mill stood black against the sky.

Figueroa helped pull him free. Burns already had Mason propped against the channel wall, checking his wounds by penlight. Kyle kept watch on the compound, rifle raised. Sadyra stood apart, her face turned toward the fortress, toward the sounds of gunfire still echoing through the night.

John went to her.

"He stayed," she said. Not a question.

"He chose to. Said he needed to know who he was without Ben Mal's orders."

Sadyra was quiet for a long moment. When she spoke, her voice was steadier than John expected.

"Then he is more my son than I knew."

The gunfire from the compound stopped. The night held its breath.

"We need to move," Burns said quietly. "Hussein's waiting at the rally point."

John took one last look at the compound—at the walls that held his son, at the fortress where too much of his life had been decided by others. Then he turned away.

They moved north along the channel, keeping to the shadows, the mountains rising black and indifferent around them. Mason limped between Burns and Figueroa, refusing to slow them down, his damaged face set with grim determination.

Sadyra walked at John's side, close enough that their shoulders sometimes touched. Kyle took the rear, eyes scanning the darkness behind them.

"He'll come back to us," she said. "I have to believe that."

John reached for her hand. "He will. He's your son."

"He's yours, too."

The words hit harder than any bullet. John tightened his grip on her hand and kept walking, carrying them both forward into the uncertain dark.

CHAPTER 34
THE RIVER IN THE STONE

TWELVE HOURS LATER

The cell smelled of old blood and older fear.

John worked the picks with hands that refused to stay steady, the Soviet-era lock fighting him with rust and neglect. Behind him, Sadyra pressed her ear to the corridor wall, listening for the guards whose absence had bought them this narrow window. Three heartbeats. Five. Seven.

The lock clicked open.

Johnny sat against the far wall, wrists chained to bolts in the stone. His face was bloody, one eye swollen shut, his lips split where someone had struck him. But when the door swung wide, he raised his head—and John saw recognition flood his son's battered features, followed by something that might have been relief.

"You came back."

"I wasn't going to leave you here." John was already working on the chains. "I'm never leaving you again."

Johnny's laugh was broken, edged with pain. "Ben Mal will kill you for this. Both of you."

"Ben Mal can try." The first chain came free. "Can you walk?"

"I can run if I have to." Johnny slumped forward as the second chain released, and John caught him—feeling how thin his son had become beneath the tactical vest, a boy's frame beneath a soldier's armor.

Sadyra helped lift him to his feet, her hands gentle on his shoulders, her eyes wet but steady. "We go now. There is a way out—through the old caves, the ones your grandfather showed me before the Soviets came."

"I know them." Johnny steadied himself against the wall. "Ben Mal uses them for storage now. Weapons. Supplies. There will be guards."

"Then we'll deal with the guards." John pressed the MP5 into his son's hands. "Can you shoot?"

Johnny's fingers closed around the weapon with the ease of long practice. "I've been shooting since I was eight years old."

"Good." John drew his sidearm. "Stay between us. Your mother knows the way. I'll cover our backs."

They moved.

////

The alarm found them halfway to the caves.

It started as a shout—a single voice raised in discovery, quickly joined by others. Then the horn, harsh and blaring, and the compound erupted into chaos.

"Move!" John shoved Johnny forward, snapping off two rounds at a shadow that materialized from a doorway. The shadow dropped, and they were running—boots pounding on ancient stone, the sounds of pursuit growing behind them.

Sadyra led them through a maze of corridors, ducking under collapsed beams, vaulting over rubble, her knowledge of the compound's labyrinthine structure their only advantage against Ben Mal's numbers. Twice they nearly ran into patrols, and twice she pulled them into alcoves, pressing them against cold stone until the boots thundered past.

The cave entrance was hidden behind a rusted door in the eastern annex—a relic from the Soviet occupation. The door groaned as Sadyra hauled it open, revealing a darkness that swallowed their flashlight beams whole.

"Inside. Quickly."

Johnny went first, then John, then Sadyra, pulling the door shut behind them as the first of Ben Mal's men rounded the corner. Bullets sparked off the iron, deafening in the confined space. Then they were in the cave, and the darkness closed around them and held.

////

The passage wound downward, the air growing colder with every step. Their flashlights cut weak beams through the blackness, illuminating walls slick with moisture and carved with ancient inscriptions—prayers, John realized. Prayers to gods older than Allah, older than Buddha, older than memory.

Johnny stumbled, and John caught him, feeling the tremor in his son's frame. The boy was running on fumes, his reserves burned through by hours of interrogation and the firefight that preceded it.

"Not much farther," Sadyra said, her voice echoing off the stone. "There is a chamber ahead—then the river."

"River?" Johnny's head came up. "The underground channel. I've heard stories. They say no one who enters it comes out alive."

"Stories to keep people away." Sadyra's flashlight found a widening in the passage, the walls pulling back to reveal a cavern whose ceiling was lost in darkness. "The water is fast, but the passage is clear. It empties through the cliff face, into the lake below."

John swept his light across the cavern floor. Old crates lined the walls—Ben Mal's weapons cache, just as Johnny had said. At the far end, a narrow cleft opened in the rock, and from that cleft came a sound that made John's stomach clench: the deep, resonant thunder of fast water.

"They're coming." Johnny had moved to the cavern entrance, the MP5 raised, his good eye tracking the darkness behind them. "I can hear them in the passage. A lot of them."

The sounds of pursuit were growing louder—boots on stone, voices raised in command, the distinctive rattle of weapons being readied.

"No choice," John said. It wasn't a question.

"No choice." Sadyra moved to the cleft and stared down into the churning darkness. "Once we enter, there is no air. The channel runs beneath the mountain for perhaps two hundred meters. It is completely submerged until it exits through the cliff face."

"Two hundred meters underwater," Johnny said. "In the dark. With the current."

"Yes. And at the end, a waterfall—the channel empties into a lake at the base of the cliffs." Sadyra turned to face them, and in the dim light John saw the fear she'd been hiding. "Stay close to me. The current will pull you. Don't fight it—let it carry you. And whatever happens, don't breathe until you see light."

"I'll go first." Johnny moved to the edge of the cleft before either of them could protest. His battered face was set with determination that cut through the exhaustion, through the pain, through twenty-two years of lies and loss. "If the passage is blocked, you'll need to find another way. If I make it—" He met John's eyes. "Then you know it's clear."

Sadyra stepped forward and pulled him into a fierce embrace. "You are. You always were."

Johnny held her for a heartbeat, then pulled back. He looked at John one last time—a look that held questions neither of them had words for yet.

Then he jumped.

The splash echoed up the shaft, followed by the sound of the water rising, rushing against the walls of the channel below. For a terrible moment, it seemed like the passage had backed up—like Johnny's body had blocked the flow.

Then the water receded, draining away as swiftly as it had risen.

"He's through," John said. "The passage is clear."

Behind them, the first of Ben Mal's men burst into the cavern.

/ / / /

There was no time for fear, no time for anything but action. John shoved Sadyra toward the cleft as gunfire erupted behind them, bullets sparking off the stone, ricochets screaming through the darkness.

"Go!"

Sadyra went—feet first, eyes on his, one hand reaching back as if to pull him with her. The water surged as she hit, rising up the shaft in a frothy rush, and then she was gone, swept into the darkness beneath the mountain.

John turned, sidearm up, and fired three shots at the muzzle flashes near the cavern entrance. A man screamed. Another dropped. The rest dove for cover, and in that moment—that single heartbeat of bought time—John threw himself into the cleft.

The cold hit him like a physical blow.

It drove the air from his lungs in a single shocked gasp, the water black and fast and unimaginably powerful. The current seized him immediately, wrenching him downward into the channel, slamming him against stone walls he couldn't see. He tumbled, rolled, lost all sense of up and down as the mountain swallowed him whole.

He fought the instinct to breathe. Fought the panic that clawed at his chest, demanding air, demanding light, demanding anything but this endless darkness and pressure and cold. His shoulder struck something hard—a rock, a wall, he couldn't tell—and pain lanced through him, sharp and bright.

The current accelerated.

He was moving faster now, the water compressing as the channel narrowed, forcing him through passages barely wide enough for his body. Stone scraped his arms, his legs, his back. He tucked his chin to his chest, made himself as small as possible, let the river in the stone carry him toward whatever waited at the end.

His lungs were burning.

Twenty seconds. Thirty. The pressure in his chest was unbearable, a fire that demanded fuel, demanded the air he couldn't give it. Stars burst behind his eyes—or maybe it was the oxygen deprivation, his brain beginning to shut down, his body beginning to die.

Forty seconds.

Fifty.

He thought of Sadyra, somewhere ahead in this same darkness. He thought of Johnny, who had trusted the passage enough to leap first. He thought of all the years he'd wasted, all the time he'd lost, all the words he'd never spoken.

Then—light.

It came all at once, a sudden brightness that seared his eyes after the total darkness of the channel. He shot from the cliff face in a rush of white water, the world spinning around him—sky and rock and the long drop to the lake below—and then he was falling, the waterfall's roar filling his ears, his lungs screaming, his body tumbling through space.

He hit the lake hard.

The impact drove what little air remained from his chest, but the water here was different—still cold, but open, the surface visible above him as a shifting ceiling of silver and blue. He kicked upward, clawed for the light, broke the surface with a gasping, choking cry that was half sob and half triumph.

"John!"

Sadyra's voice, somewhere to his left. He turned, treading water, and saw her—alive, gasping, her hair plastered to her face, one arm raised to wave. And beyond her, closer to the shore—

Johnny.

His son floated near the rocks, too exhausted to swim, barely keeping his head above water. John struck out toward him, arms and legs moving on pure instinct, the cold of the lake nothing compared to the fire of determination in his chest. He reached Johnny in seconds, grabbed his vest, hauled him toward the shallows where the rocks offered purchase.

They dragged themselves onto the shore together, all three of them, lungs heaving, bodies shaking with cold and exhaustion. The lake stretched out behind them, mirror-still except where the waterfall churned its surface into white foam. Above, the cliff face rose sheer and dark, the channel's exit invisible from below—just another shadow in the ancient stone.

For a long moment, they just breathed.

Johnny was the first to speak. "We made it."

Sadyra reached for him, her hand finding his, squeezing hard. "We made it."

John lay on his back, staring up at the sky as the first pale colors of sunrise bled through the haze. His son. His lost son, found again. Broken and battered and full of questions neither of them knew how to answer—but alive. Here. Real.

"We need to move," he said finally, forcing himself to sit up. Every muscle screamed in protest. "Burns will be waiting at the extraction point."

"Four hours north," Sadyra said, rising with difficulty. "Maybe five, if we take the ridge trail."

Johnny pushed himself up, swaying slightly before he found his balance. The swelling around his eye had worsened, and blood still seeped from his split lip, but his gaze was clear. Focused. Different somehow than it had been in the cell—as if the passage through the mountain had stripped away something false, leaving only what was true.

"I don't know how to be who you want me to be," he said, looking at John. "I don't know how to be anyone except what Ben Mal made me."

John reached out and gripped his son's shoulder—the same gesture he'd made a hundred times in his imagination, across twenty-three years of wondering and hoping and grief. "Then we figure it out together. One step at a time."

Johnny held his gaze for a long moment. Then, almost imperceptibly, he nodded.

They climbed the hillside trail together—the lake and waterfall falling away behind them, the sky lightening toward dawn. Sadyra walked at John's side, close enough that their shoulders sometimes touched. Johnny moved ahead, his battered body guided by instincts that two decades in this valley had carved into his bones.

They had a long way to go.

But they were going together.

CHAPTER 35
GHOST TRAIL

FALL 2001—HINDU KUSH, AFGHANISTAN

They found shelter beneath a tilted boulder two hours into the climb—a crack in the living stone that offered shade and concealment. John checked his watch. They were making good time, but they all needed water and rest before the final push to the extraction point.

Johnny settled at the edge of the hollow, keeping watch on the trail below. He hadn't spoken since they'd left the lake, and the silence between them had grown heavier with each step.

It was Sadyra who broke it.

"He needs to hear the rest," she said quietly, settling beside John. "Not the version Ben Mal told him. The truth."

John looked at his son's rigid back, at the tension in his shoulders, at the way he gripped his rifle like it was the only thing in the world he could trust. "I don't know if he's ready."

"He's been ready since August, when I told him you were alive. He walked away without a word." Sadyra's eyes found John's. "But he didn't forget. Now he's ready to listen."

////

Johnny didn't turn when John approached, but his shoulders tightened.

"We need to talk," John said, settling onto a rock a few feet away. Close enough for conversation, far enough to give his son space.

"About what?" Johnny's voice was flat. "How to reach your extraction point? I know these mountains."

"About why I left."

Johnny was silent for a long moment. When he spoke, the flatness had cracked. "Mother told me. You didn't know about me. You left before I was born."

"That's true. But it's not everything." John took a breath. "Ben Mal put a gun to my head and told me to disappear. I thought leaving would keep your mother safe." He exhaled. "I was wrong."

"So you ran."

"I survived. There's a difference." John forced himself to meet his son's gaze—that one good eye, like his, burning with years of accumulated hurt. "I tried to come back. Twice. The passes were closed, or someone recognized me. I barely made it out alive."

"And after that?"

"After that, I thought she was gone. Dead, or moved on. I had no way to know she was still here." John's voice roughened. "No way to know about you."

Johnny turned, finally, to look at him. His battered face was unreadable, but something had shifted—a loosening of the rigid control.

"Ben Mal told me you abandoned us. That you chose America over your own blood."

"Ben Mal told you what made you easier to control."

"I know that now." Johnny's mouth compressed. "But knowing it and believing it are different things. I spent twenty-two years hating a ghost. You can't undo that with a story."

"No," John agreed. "I can't. But I can tell you the truth, and you can decide what to do with it."

////

Sadyra joined them, settling onto the rocks between father and son.

"There are things I need to say," she said. "Things I should have said years ago."

Johnny's expression hardened. "More secrets?"

"The opposite." Sadyra took a breath. "When John left, I was carrying you. I didn't know it yet—not until weeks later. By then, the passes were closed. There was no way to reach him."

"You could have sent word."

"I started a hundred letters. I burned them all." Her hands trembled in her lap. "I was afraid, Johnny. The Soviets were everywhere, killing collaborators, burning villages. If they had learned your father was American—"

Light dawned in Johnny's eyes. "They would have killed us both."

"Yes. So I chose silence. I let you believe your father was dead, because a dead father was safer than a living American one." Sadyra's eyes glistened. "I told myself it was protection. Maybe it was. But it was also punishment—for him, for leaving. And for myself, for loving a man I could never have."

"And Ben Mal?" Johnny's voice had gone quiet, dangerous. "What was he?"

Sadyra flinched. "Survival. When your grandfather was killed, when the village turned against us, he offered shelter. I had no choice."

"Did you love him?"

The question hung in the air.

"No." Sadyra's answer was immediate. "I endured him. I let him believe he owned me because it was the only way to keep you safe. Every time he touched me, I thought of John." Her voice broke. "I survived, Johnny. That is all I did. I survived, and I kept you alive, and I waited for a chance that never came. Until now."

////

Johnny was silent for a long time. The wind keened through the rocks, carrying dust and the distant cry of a hawk.

"I don't know how to forgive any of this," he said finally. "The lies. The silence. Twenty-two years of believing something that wasn't true."

"I'm not asking for forgiveness," John said. "I'm asking for a chance. To be something other than the ghost Ben Mal made me."

"And if I can't give you that?"

Johnny looked between them—the father he'd never known and the mother who had lied to protect him.

"The men I killed," he said. "The things I did for Ben Mal. You understand that doesn't go away? That I can't just walk into your American life and pretend none of it happened?"

"I know." John's voice was steady. "We'll figure it out. Together."

"The Agency will have questions. They'll want me to turn informant."

"That's a bridge we'll cross later. Right now, our only job is getting to the extraction point alive."

Johnny held his gaze. Then he nodded.

"Two hours to the rendezvous. There's a game trail that cuts through the eastern ridge—faster than the main path, keeps us below the skyline." He rose, checking his weapon. "We should move."

Sadyra caught his arm before he could start down the trail. "Whatever happens next—whatever you decide about your father, about me—I need you to know something."

"What?"

"I am proud of you. Not for what Ben Mal made you, but for what you chose when it mattered. You could have let us die in that compound." Her hand found his cheek, gentle against the bruises. "That is who you are. The rest is just what you had to survive."

Johnny's jaw worked. For a moment, John thought he might pull away. Instead, he covered her hand with his own, pressing it briefly against his face. Something shifted behind his eyes—not softening, but settling. A decision made.

"Let's go," he said roughly. "Burns is waiting."

////

They reached the rendezvous ninety minutes later—a narrow defile where two ridges met, hidden by a tumble of ancient boulders. Burns was there, as promised, with Kyle and Figueroa spread in a defensive perimeter. Mason sat propped against a rock, his bandaged face turned toward the sun, but his good eye snapped open when they approached.

"You made it." Burns lowered his rifle. "All three of you."

"All three of us." John helped Sadyra over the final stretch of scree. "Hussein?"

"Agency bird picked him up at dawn. He's probably halfway to Ramallah by now." Burns's eyes moved to Johnny. "We've got room on the extraction. But there are going to be questions about our new friend here."

"His name is Johnny." John's voice carried an edge. "He's my son. And he's coming with us."

Mason spoke from his rock, voice rough but clear. "The kid saved my life in there." He paused. "He's also the reason two of my men are dead."

His damaged gaze found Johnny. "I'm holding both of those things at the same time. Haven't figured out what it adds up to yet. But I know Ben Mal gave the orders. And I know the kid just put his life on the line to get us out." He shifted, wincing. "For now, that's enough."

Burns looked between them—John, Johnny, Mason—calculating. Then he nodded.

"Extraction bird touches down in forty minutes. We'll sort out the paperwork when we're airborne." He turned to Johnny. "Welcome to the team, kid. Such as it is."

Kyle stepped forward, hand extended toward Johnny's weapon. Johnny hesitated, his grip tightening on the AK—the only thing he'd carried out of the life he was leaving behind. Then his fingers loosened, and he passed the rifle over without a word.

John saw what it cost him. Another piece of the soldier surrendered.

Johnny said nothing, but something in his posture eased—the first crack in the armor he'd worn since they'd pulled him from that cell.

////

The distant thrum of rotors reached them first—a low vibration that built into the unmistakable sound of a helicopter cresting the ridge. Burns was on his feet immediately, popping a smoke canister, the orange plume marking their position against the brown and gray of the mountains.

The Black Hawk descended in a whirlwind of dust and noise, settling onto the only flat ground the defile offered. The crew chief waved them forward, shouting something lost in the rotor wash.

John helped Sadyra up, guiding her toward the open door. Kyle and Burns went next, supporting Mason between them. Figueroa covered their retreat, rifle sweeping the ridgeline one final time.

Johnny hung back, staring at the valley below—at the mountains that had been his prison and his home, at the country that had given him everything he knew and demanded everything in return.

"Johnny." John extended his hand. "Time to go."

His son looked at the hand, then at the helicopter, then back at the valley. For a moment, John thought he might refuse—might turn and disappear into the rocks, choosing the only life he'd ever known over the uncertainty of what waited beyond.

Then Johnny took his hand.

They climbed into the Black Hawk together, the door sliding shut behind them, the rotors screaming as the bird lifted off. The valley fell away beneath them—the compound where Ben Mal had built his kingdom, the lake where they'd emerged from the mountain's heart, the land that had shaped them all.

John watched it shrink until it was just another scar on the ancient earth.

Beside him, Johnny sat rigid, his hands gripping the seat frame, his eyes fixed on something beyond the window that John couldn't see.

But when Sadyra reached for his hand, he didn't pull away.

CHAPTER 36

THE RETURN TO RAMALLAH

SUMMER 2001—RAMALLAH

The convoy rolled north from Qalandiya, armored SUVs easing through streets narrowed by barricades and rooftops crowded with watchers. A hot wind swept grit from the hills, streaking windshields until the wipers dragged it into muddy arcs.

Hussein sat rigid in the second vehicle, flanked by his security detail. His head still ached from the wound he'd taken in Bamiyan, the stitches hidden beneath a traditional keffiyeh. Ahead lay his city—inheritance and curse, wound and promise. Ramallah looked weary and expectant: martyr posters sun-bleached and torn, alleys smelling of diesel and cardamom, shutters rattling like loose teeth in the wind.

The people appeared in fragments. A boy pedaled alongside, phone raised to film. An old man lifted a shaking salute. Then the crowd thickened—flags waving, chants swelling, young men climbing lampposts.

"Hussein! Hussein! Hussein!"

A rooftop shot cracked—unclear if warning or celebration. The convoy held steady. Agency SUVs flanked the column, hatches open, muzzles sweeping. The chant only grew louder, drowning fear.

Hussein closed his eyes. His father's voice came back, weary and beaten: The people will lift you up, then tear you down. Trust silence, not applause.

But today the city gave him both—streets erupting, windows shuttered, Ramallah watching like a jury, verdict still out.

////

Manara Square overflowed. Security cordons stretched in rings, rooftops bristled with cameras and rifles. A canopy of bulletproof glass caged the dais, harsh in the noon glare.

Hussein stepped to the microphone. For a moment, the square held its breath, a city suspended in silence.

"My brothers and sisters of Ramallah, of Gaza, of Jerusalem—today is not the end of our struggle, but it is the first day we can choose what kind of struggle it will be.

"For generations we were taught that dignity could only be defended with blood. We buried our fathers, our sons, our daughters under flags and slogans. But what did it bring us? Walls higher than hope, graves deeper than memory.

"I stand before you not to erase our pain, but to honor it. The blood already spilled is a debt we can never repay. But we can decide that no more will be added to it.

"Do not mistake peace for weakness. It takes more courage to stay your hand than to lift the gun. It takes more strength to build than to burn.

"I ask you: What legacy do we leave our children? That they live as we lived, caged and hunted? Or that they live free to learn, to build, to laugh without fear?

"Today, we are offered a chance—not perfection, not paradise, but a chance. A chance to stand as a people not defined by war, but by what we choose to create together.

"I did not survive captivity to become a prisoner of the past. I returned so that we could claim the future."

The square erupted in chants, waves of sound colliding, then rising as one. Hussein let it crest, then raised his hand for silence.

"Now you will hear the terms. They are not poetry, they are not simple. But they are the framework on which tomorrow can be built. Listen. Judge. And then, together, we decide if this is the foundation worthy of our children."

He stepped back. The clerk came forward with the treaty, pages trembling in his hands.

The clauses were read aloud, words clipped and legal, broadcast across loudspeakers and live streams:

"Recognition of sovereignty.

Demilitarized corridors.

Shared water rights from the Jordan aquifer.

Economic zones under international guarantee.

Neutral guardianship of Jerusalem's holy sites."

Each clause deepened the silence, broken only by the shuffle of boots, the hum of generators, the whir of drones overhead.

When the reading ended, Hussein raised the treaty above his head. For a heartbeat nothing—then the roar: applause, flags whipping, chants pounding until the canopy trembled.

////

By evening, the Swiss Guard stood their posts.

At Al-Aqsa, the Church of the Holy Sepulcher, and the Western Wall, Swiss Guard in ceremonial colors layered over black tactical gear took position. Rifles slung, halberds gleaming.

Tourists stared. Worshippers hesitated. A rabbi murmured thanks. An imam raised cautious hands.

The choice had been made in Palm Beach, brokered in secret. The Vatican—distrusted by both sides, and therefore acceptable to both—was the only force both would accept.

Hussein watched the feeds stream back to Ramallah: Europe's old guardians now the neutral wall between Semitic brothers. If these shrines could be held in trust, perhaps the land itself might follow.

////

The spark caught in the camps. Balata, Dheisheh, Jabalia—word spread fast: Hussein had returned with a treaty.

Crowds surged in markets. Women ululated from balconies. Flags unfurled. The chants shifted inward: *"No more Hamas! No more blood!"*

In Gaza, militants rolled out trucks with loudspeakers. But the people pushed back:

A grandmother barred her doorway. "No snipers on my roof," she said, frail voice like stone.

A youth who once hurled stones now waved a white scarf. "Enough!" he shouted. The crowd tore down posters with him.

In Khan Yunis, shutters slammed in unison, merchants refusing to host rallies.

Fear drained. Exhaustion hardened into refusal. Hamas looked small against the tide of ordinary defiance.

////

Night brought the call.

Secure line, routed through Geneva. The voice was unmistakable: the American Secretary of State.

"You kept your word," he said. "Now we keep ours. You've given us leverage. Don't waste it."

The details followed, clipped and precise:

Billions in reconstruction aid.

Engineers to stabilize grids and water lines.

Treasury guarantees for debt relief.

Joint training of a unified security force.

Shared intelligence to track extremists.

Palm Beach made real. America stood behind him—patron and judge both.

Hussein hung up, relief heavy as iron. Support meant survival, but also scrutiny. To Washington he was not yet a statesman, only a wager.

Still, he whispered the words like an oath: "*You kept your word. So will I.*"

////

The motorcade wound through narrow streets to a secured residence. Outside, the city still pulsed with chants; inside, silence pooled in the corners.

Leila waited in the doorway, Mira and Amal beside her. They had not seen Hussein since the safe house, since the night Johnny's men had come and changed everything.

He paused, hesitant, as though uncertain whether to embrace them. Mira broke first, sprinting forward, clutching his sleeve. Amal followed more carefully, eyes studying his face to be sure it was real. Only then did Hussein kneel, letting their arms circle his neck.

Leila's eyes held both relief and fatigue. She had carried the burden of uncertainty for weeks—not knowing if he lived or died, holding together what remained of their family through sheer will.

Questions spilled: Where had he been? Was he safe? Would he stay? Hussein deflected, asking instead about their drawings. They fetched sheets from the refrigerator: houses, guards, the pool, a dove. Innocent sketches, but every line shadowed by walls and watchtowers.

He studied them, unsettled—their world mapped not in play, but in surveillance.

Leila brought tea, her hands steadying the pot. "They will test us as well," she said quietly. "Every day."

Mira tugged his sleeve. "Why are there so many soldiers?"

"To keep us safe," Hussein said after a pause. "But safety is not the same as freedom."

Amal whispered, "Will we go to Jerusalem?"

"One day," he promised. "Together. When the walls fall."

Later, he tucked them into bed. The barred window cast striped shadows across the floor. He lingered, whispering a prayer not for the treaty but for their childhood.

////

The next day, the test came.

Manara Square swelled again. Amid the chants, a man moved with purpose, vest heavy under his shirt.

Spotters flagged him. Crackled warnings. Palestinian detail converged, slamming him to the ground before he reached the dais. Restrained and unable to trigger his C4 vest, he was dragged from the square.

The crowd froze, panic ready to shatter the moment.

Hussein stepped forward. His voice cut the air:

"Peace is not proven by signatures. It is proven in the blood we refuse to spill. Today, no blood was spilled. That is our victory."

The roar that followed dwarfed the panic. The attempt meant to break the treaty instead steeled it.

////

That night, a secure line linked Ramallah and Jerusalem.

Abraham appeared on screen, aides behind him. Silence stretched, history thick between them.

"Today Ramallah rose with you," Abraham said. "Tomorrow, Jerusalem must rise with us both."

Hussein nodded, hearing the weight. Not allies, not yet friends, but men bound by necessity—two inheritors tasked with ending the cycle.

The line went dead, leaving each with the echo of the other's words.

////

Ramallah exhaled.

Cafes lit candles. Musicians played oud and guitar, songs rising louder with each verse. Children laughed in alleys under lantern glow. Parents let them play past curfew for the first time in years.

Hussein stood at his window. The treaty lay on his desk, ink curling at the edges. The city looked scarred but alive, breathing again after too long underwater.

He thought of his father's failures, of Palm Beach promises, of Abraham's vow. He thought of the American soldier who had bled for him in Bamiyan, of the young man who had brought him water in captivity and later helped him escape. He thought of the crowd chanting his name not in rage but in hope.

He whispered a prayer—not for triumph, but for endurance.

Outside, Ramallah breathed with him, a city daring for one night to believe history might bend another way.

////

DECEMBER 2001—NEW YORK

They came for Ian Karim on a Tuesday, while he was finishing his eggs.

Twelve FBI agents. A U.S. Attorney. Two men in gray suits who never showed credentials. Three months after the towers fell, America had rediscovered its appetite for justice—or what passed for it.

The indictment ran 247 pages. Material support. Conspiracy. Wire fraud. Money laundering. Eighteen counts, and Hussein Mahfouz's name threaded through every one. The man Karim had built from dust had given the FBI everything.

The courier broke first. Kell—British passport, Jordanian mother—picked up in New York City walking out of the same Lower Manhattan diner Hussein had described. Corner booth. Sugar tray. Envelope. He talked for nineteen hours. Gave them the Zurich accounts, the Doha transfers, the ledgers marked with a symbol everyone in Gaza knew: an *I* curved through a *K*. Ninety percent feeding children. Ten percent buying rockets. Relief one day, rockets the next.

Karim Global Initiatives collapsed within a month. The conferences stopped. The op-eds vanished. Donors who had once clamored for photographs now denied they'd ever heard the name.

But Karim hadn't operated alone.

Senator Raymond Decker of New Jersey was arrested three weeks later, in his Camden district office, still wearing the flag pin he'd bought for the post-9/11 prayer breakfast. The charges: bribery, conspiracy, obstruction of justice. Decker had sat on the Senate Foreign Relations Committee for fourteen years. He had shaped Middle East policy, blocked sanctions, killed investigations. In exchange, Karim's foundation had funneled $2.3 million through a consulting firm owned by Decker's brother-in-law. The brother-in-law flipped in forty-eight hours. Gave them the bank records, the shell companies, the photograph of Decker accepting an envelope in a Trenton steakhouse.

Decker's lawyer called it a witch hunt. Decker himself called it anti-Catholic bias. The *Newark Star-Ledger* called it the worst corruption scandal in state history. None of it mattered. The evidence was overwhelming, and after the towers, no jury in America would acquit a man who'd protected a terror financier for profit.

He pled guilty three months before trial. Fifteen years federal. His seat went to a thirty-four-year-old prosecutor who'd built her career on public corruption cases. She won by nineteen points.

At trial, Karim was magnificent. Silver-tongued. Indignant. He spoke of refugee parents, Princeton, decades of bridge-building. Showed photographs—the White House, Davos, a Jordanian clinic with a child on his knee. For three days, he almost made them believe.

Then the prosecution played the tapes.

Gaza. Doha. A voice matching Hamza al-Saidi's quartermaster. Six days after a clinic bombing killed eleven, Karim had laughed. *Cost of doing business. The money always comes back.*

The jury took six hours.

Four consecutive life sentences. No parole. As the marshals led him out, Karim found the camera—the same lens that had captured him with senators, with presidents, with hands always extended in peace.

"This isn't justice," he said. "This is revenge."

No one in the gallery disagreed.

Hussein watched the verdict from Ramallah, Leila beside him, their daughters asleep in the next room. The peace was fragile. There were still bombings, still reprisals, still men who preferred war. But the accords were holding. The monitors were in place. And the man who had tried to own them all would die in a concrete box.

He turned off the television.

"It's not enough," Leila said.

"No." Hussein looked out at the darkening hills—the same hills his father had walked as a boy, where new olive trees were being planted under Geneva's watch. Small things. Ordinary things. "But it's a start."

He picked up the phone and called his daughters to dinner.

EPILOGUE
THE BAMIYAN PARADOX

SEPTEMBER 2001—NORTH GEORGIA

The mountain air, sharp with pine and leaf rot, was a tranquil haven after Bamiyan's desolation. In the Blue Ridge foothills, mornings unfurled in slow, gold-edged mists. Oaks and maples flared copper and crimson against a deep blue sky. Sunlight filtered through pine, gentle, almost forgiving.

A wind moved through the oaks, copper leaves clattering against the weathered log cabin John had rebuilt with his scarred hands. He paused in the doorway, breathing in the sharpness of pine and woodsmoke—a world away from Bamiyan's dust and cordite.

Inside, the floors creaked evenly beneath his boots. He'd spent months getting the cabin right, every swing of the hammer an assertion of control, every planed board a quiet prayer against collapse. The roof no longer leaked. The woodstove drew steady. For the first time in decades, the ground beneath him felt solid.

On the porch, Sadyra stood in the late afternoon sun, steady hands braiding asters and goldenrod into a wreath. Her hair, threaded now with silver, was pulled back in a loose braid. When she glanced up, the lines on her face softened, and briefly John saw the fearless girl who'd braved the Silk Road, survived warlords and betrayals, a world determined to break her.

He joined her, sitting on the porch rail, watching the sunlight catch in her hair. She looked at him sidelong, eyes amused, and handed him a cluster of wildflowers.

"Not many of these in Bamiyan, eh?" she teased, her voice low.

John smiled—a real smile, still new to his face. "Only in the spring, and never this blue."

He looked out at the yard, at the figure stacking wood by the shed. Johnny—Younes, his Afghan name, though he'd chosen to go by Johnny here—was broader now, features sharpened by the months since their escape. The sleeves of his flannel were rolled up, scars fading along his forearms but still visible if the light caught them right.

////

The question of Johnny's past had been settled in ways John still didn't fully understand. Mason had made calls. Burns had filed reports. Somewhere in the labyrinth of Langley, deals had been struck.

"Cooperating witness," Mason had explained during his last visit, his face still bearing the marks of Bamiyan. "The kid knows more about Ben Mal's network than anyone alive. Names, routes, contacts, safe houses. That kind of intelligence buys a lot of goodwill."

"And the men he killed? The kidnapping?"

Mason had been quiet for a moment. "The Agency makes accommodations for valuable assets. It's not justice, John. But it's reality. Your boy chose to help us when it mattered. That counts for something."

John hadn't pressed further. He understood the calculus—had lived inside it for years. The world didn't run on justice; it ran on leverage and necessity. Johnny had leverage. The rest would be buried in classified files that no one would ever read.

But the accommodation came with conditions. Johnny reported to a handler once a month—phone calls, mostly, occasional meetings in Atlanta. He answered questions about old operations, drew maps of compound layouts, identified faces in surveillance photos. The debriefings had been intensive at first, then tapered off as the intelligence dried up.

"He's paying his debt," Sadyra had said one night, watching Johnny pace the yard in the darkness. "Not to any court. To himself."

John knew she was right. Some debts couldn't be settled with testimony or prison time. Johnny would carry what he'd done for the rest of his life—the heaviness of it visible in the way he sometimes stared at nothing, the way his hands would pause mid-task as if remembering something he couldn't speak aloud.

////

A battered radio perched on the porch railing, the BBC's measured tones drifting through static. "...first full year of Palestinian elections proceeds without serious violence. Hussein sworn in as interim president...Hamas no longer in Gaza...peacekeeping monitors verify disarmament..."

The news came in fragments, half-lost to mountain interference, but it was enough. Somewhere, something had shifted. The treaty John had helped make possible was holding—fragile, imperfect, but holding.

He closed his eyes, letting the rustle of the oaks wash over him. A year ago, he would have called it fantasy. Now, perhaps, it was a seed.

Johnny caught John watching and grinned—quick, warm, cutting through years of distance. "Pop," he called, "grab the other end of this beam?"

The word was a balm, still unfamiliar, still precious. John stepped off the porch and crossed the yard, grass crunching underfoot. Johnny had already lifted one end of the thick pine beam; together, shoulder to shoulder, they hefted it toward the frame of a new shed.

"Careful now, don't drop it on my foot," John joked, voice rasping with effort.

Johnny laughed, the sound ringing out—a defiant note of survival that bounced off the hills. "Old man, I could carry you and the beam both."

They both knew it was bravado, but John let himself believe it.

This, he thought, is what fathers are for.

////

Inside the cabin, on a rough shelf above the hearth, a single photograph caught the last of the afternoon light: John, Sadyra, Johnny—arms around each other in the golden Georgia sun, all three squinting, awkward but at peace.

Sadyra sometimes left small offerings by the photo—a twist of dried lavender, a pebble from the creek. She said it was for remembrance, not worship, a way to honor what they'd lost without letting it devour what they'd gained.

As dusk settled and the first stars flickered above the ridge, John stepped into the yard. He exhaled, slow and deep, shoulders lowering, jaw unclenching. The ghosts still lingered, quieter now.

He remembered the smell of gun oil and burning rubber, the taste of Bamiyan dust, the desperate passage through the underground river, the way Sadyra's voice steadied him when the world threatened to end. He remembered the first time Johnny called him "Pop," not out of habit, but with the open trust of someone who had survived enough to believe in second chances.

On the porch, Sadyra finished her wreath, hands nimble even as the light faded. She stepped beside him, her fingers brushing his. He took her hand, scarred palm to scarred palm—two survivors grounding each other in the long quiet after war.

They watched Johnny toss another log onto the stack, then settle on the steps, elbows on knees, gaze lifted to the stars. He was humming something tuneless, a habit from childhood that Sadyra had told John about.

After a while, Johnny turned, his face half-shadow. "You ever miss it?" he asked softly. "The other place?"

John was quiet a long time. "Sometimes. Mostly I remember the bad parts, what I wish I'd done different. But then I look at this"—he gestured to the porch, the cabin, the woman at his side—"and I know I'm right where I should be."

Sadyra squeezed his hand, her eyes shining. "We made it out," she whispered, "not because we were lucky, but because we never gave up."

Johnny smiled, slow and wide. "Guess stubbornness runs in the family."

John huffed—half a laugh, half a sob—then wiped a hand over his face.

////

A hush fell over them, easy and unafraid. The world turned, wounded but enduring. Sometimes—by grace, or sheer stubborn will—they made it home.

As the sky deepened to indigo and the first stars hardened into clarity, John felt something in him finally ease.

Inside, the woodstove's glow cast long shadows. Sadyra's wreath hung on the door, fragrant and alive. The photograph on the shelf stood sentinel, a reminder of all they'd fought for, all they'd found.

Together, they stood on the threshold, shadows mingling as the porch creaked beneath them. Three survivors. Hearts scarred but beating, a new world waiting just beyond the dawn.

John looked up at the endless stars, the quiet mountain breathing around him, and for the first time in a lifetime of exile, he let himself believe the ghosts might finally find rest.

His phone vibrated in his pocket.

The three of them stood on the porch as the sun dropped behind the Blue Ridge. For a moment, the world was quiet—just the creak of old wood, the smell of pine, the sound of Sadyra humming something Johnny almost remembered.

John's phone buzzed. He glanced at the screen. Mason.

"Turn on your television."

They watched the towers fall in silence. Sadyra's hand found John's. Johnny stood apart, arms crossed, face unreadable.

When the second tower collapsed, John's phone buzzed again. A different number. A 703 area code. Langley.

"Mr. Marquez. My name is Director Harrison. I understand you know the cave systems at Tora Bora."

John watched the smoke rise on screen. One thousand miles away, three thousand lives ending. And somewhere in those mountains he'd fled twenty-three years ago, the man who'd ordered this was already running.

"I know them."

"We're putting together a task force. Ground teams who can operate in terrain where satellites are blind and drones are useless. Men who know how the tribal networks function. Men who've been inside."

John looked at Sadyra. At the lines on her face, the gray in her hair, the twenty-three years etched into both of them. He had crossed oceans for her. Killed for her. Nearly died for her. He would not leave her again.

"I'm sorry, Director. I'm done."

A pause. "Mr. Marquez, your country—"

"Has plenty of men younger than me." John's eyes found Johnny. "Better men."

He hung up.

Johnny stared at the television. The footage looped—planes, fire, collapse. He had trained in those mountains. Prayed in those caves. Broken bread with men who believed this slaughter was holy. He knew their routes, their codes, their hiding places. He knew how they thought.

And he knew what he owed.

"Give me the number," Johnny said.

John turned. "Johnny—"

"I spent ten years building that world. Training with them. Believing their lies." His voice was steady, but his hands had curled into fists. "I know Tora Bora better than any map. I know where they'll run. Where they'll hide. Where they'll die."

"This isn't your debt to pay."

"Yes it is." Johnny met his father's eyes. "You came back for me. You gave me a second chance. This is what I do with it."

Sadyra stepped forward. She took her son's face in her hands—the face she had watched grow from infant to boy to stranger to soldier. The face that held John's eyes and her father's jaw and something entirely his own.

"You come back," she said. "Promise me."

"I promise."

She kissed his forehead. Then she stepped back, and Johnny picked up the phone.

"Director Harrison. This is Younes al-Bamiyan. I understand you're looking for someone who knows the caves."

A long silence. Then: "We've heard of you."

"I'm sure you have. I'm offering my services."

"Why should we trust you?"

Johnny looked at his father. At his mother. At the life he'd only just begun to earn.

"Because I'm the only man alive who's been inside bin Laden's network and walked away. Because I know where they'll run when you come for them. And because I have twenty years of sins to make right."

Another silence. Then: "Forty-eight hours. Islamabad."

"I'll be there."

He hung up. The television droned on—smoke and sirens and the world remaking itself in fire.

John put a hand on his son's shoulder. "You don't have to do this."

"Yes I do." Johnny's voice was quiet. "You taught me that. Some debts can only be paid in person."

Father and son stood together—one war ending, another beginning. The torch passing.

"Come back," John said. "That's an order."

Johnny almost smiled. "I'll do my best."

////

Mazar-i-Sharif, Afghanistan

Ben Mal watched the towers fall on a grainy television in the corner of the tea house. Around him, men cheered. He did not.

He understood what was coming. The Americans would invade. They would come with their planes and their soldiers and their righteous fury. They would hunt bin Laden through the mountains. They would need guides. Translators. Men who knew the caves.

Men like Johnny.

Unless.

His phone rang. A Karachi number.

"The Americans are mobilizing," the voice said. "Jalalabad. Tora Bora. They're building a task force."

"I know."

"Our friends in the mountains need support. Supply lines. Intelligence. Someone who can anticipate how the Americans will move."

Ben smiled. "And in return?"

"A seat at the table. When the dust settles."

Ben watched the smoke rise on the screen. Somewhere in those mountains, bin Laden was already moving. And soon, Johnny would follow.

"Tell your friends I'm coming," Ben said. "Tell them I know the man the Americans are sending. I trained him. I made him. I know how he thinks, how he moves, what he fears."

"And when you find him?"

Ben's hand went to the scar again. The son for the father. The debt repaid.

"Then I'll finish what I started."

He hung up. Watched the footage loop—planes, fire, collapse. A new world being born in blood and ash.

The game was just beginning.

JOHNNY MARQUEZ WILL RETURN IN

THE TORA BORA PROTOCOL

ABOUT THE AUTHOR

R. W. LIGON is the author of *The Bamiyan Paradox*, the first novel in the Johnny Marquez thriller series. His writing leverages his forty-year career in international business development and explores the intersection of power, belief, and consequence in modern geopolitical conflicts. He lives in the southeastern United States and is currently at work on the second novel in the series, *Tora Bora Protocol*.

www.ingramcontent.com/pod-product-compliance
Lightning Source LLC
LaVergne TN
LVHW100513110826
845146LV00002B/625

* 9 7 9 8 9 9 3 3 5 8 3 0 7 *